Meet Me at Midnight

max monroe

New York Times & *USA Today* Bestselling Author

Meet Me at Midnight
Published by Max Monroe LLC © 2024, Max Monroe

ISBN: 979-8-9918435-0-8

Editing by Silently Correcting Your Grammar
Formatting by Champagne Book Design
Cover Design by Peter Alderweireld

Author's Note

Dear Reader,

We feel it is our duty to provide the following warnings prior to reading.

#1: This book may cause uncontrollable laughter. Do not read while in public or next to a sleeping spouse, child, or pet.

#2: This book may cause a serious amount of distraction. Do not read while operating heavy machinery, while you're on a first date, during the birth of your child, or on your wedding day.

#3: This book may cause sleeplessness. You might think you'll be able to fit in a quick chapter before bed, but multiple* research groups have proven otherwise.

#4: This book may cause antisocial behavior. Once you start reading, you won't be able to put it down. This is not the book to take with you to social events, family dinners, nightclubs, bars, and Christmas with your in-laws—*that is, unless you don't like your in-laws.*

#5: This book may cause incessant smiling, swooning, and giggling. The moment you start reading, you will be at an increased risk of developing feelings for a fictional character. You may start calling your significant other Beau Banks.

XOXO,
Max & Monroe

Research groups may be fictional. Official, final results pending.

Dedication

To anyone who has ever had a secret crush.
We hope you get your Midnight soon.

PART 1

Juniper

Chapter 1

I'VE DREAMED ABOUT THE DAY BEAU BANKS WOULD NOTICE MY pussy.

I've had years—a decade, even—of fantasizing about my best friend's older brother perceiving me as more than an extra appendage of his younger sister, Avery. Years of wondering what it'd be like to have him put me and sex in the same stratosphere, and instead, I have no choice but to settle for *this*.

His dad—my boss, Neil Banks—asking about the cat filter that's covering his face during a very important virtual meeting. But instead of just saying cat, he keeps saying *pussy*cat over and over and *over*, while Beau and a dozen other important people from my new place of employment, Banks & McKenzie Marketing, look on.

And no, as much as I wish I were, I'm not dreaming and I'm not high.

This is happening, live and in color—*beet fucking red, specifically.*

"I'm a pussycat, Juniper. Do you see I'm a pussycat?" Neil asks, confused why his face isn't his face.

"I see, Mr. Banks," I answer, fighting like hell to keep myself from falling into the black hole his son sucks me into whenever he's around. Right now isn't the time to focus on Beau's warm brown eyes or sexy dark hair or the way his expensive gray suit hugs his most perfect shoulders and biceps. It isn't the time to wonder if his hands would feel just as good on my skin as they look sticking out of the cuffs of the sleeves of his expensive white shirt.

I have a cat-filter emergency to worry about, and as the seconds tick by without my doing something about it, it gets more and more out of control.

Every time Mr. Banks speaks, a cat's mouth moves on the screen while the Hughes International execs watch on via Zoom. A Zoom *I* am responsible for setting up.

Just moments ago, my focus went to shit when Beau strode into the conference room and found an empty seat at the massive table, and my gaze is *still* trying to keep track of his every move. But Neil is getting more and more unhinged as he tries to figure out how to remove the whiskers and fur and pointy cat ears from his face.

"Why do I look like a pussycat, Juniper?" Mr. Banks asks from his fancy leather chair at the head of the table where I stand directly beside him.

Inadvertently putting a funny filter on your boss for an important meeting is bad enough, but his calling the kitten a "pussycat" is making it irrefutably worse. I didn't know anyone still used the word without being facetious, but I guess that's what you get for assuming.

Ass, meet me, Juniper Perry, brand-new marketing intern extraordinaire and the next resident of whatever the nearest spot to the earth's crust is.

"I'm trying to fix it," I assure Mr. Banks, silently cursing myself when my eyes wander from the screen of the laptop in front of us to Beau for a flash of a second. Clearly, when it comes to him, I have no control. It's a wonder I'm not actively fantasizing about how his mouth would feel on me right now.

Annnd now I am…

Great, Juniper, just great.

"Why am I a pussycat?" Mr. Banks asks yet *again,* seeing as I've yet to master his daughter—*and my best friend*—Avery's computer settings enough to get it turned off.

I swear, I'm going to absolutely throttle her for sticking me with this Zoom responsibility with no warning this morning. She all but shoved her laptop into my hands as we were heading out the door and told me she'd meet me at work.

She's still not here, by the way.

"Your pussycat is cute, Juniper, but it's not ideal for this meeting," Mr. Banks comments, and I can actually feel my face heating up beneath my skin.

"What? *No.* It's just a funny filter, Mr. Banks. Avery must have been messing around with it," I explain in a panic as I hit the escape button. Surely ending this Zoom and having to start over is no longer the worst-case scenario when my boss keeps talking about *my pussycat* in front of a room full of people.

But nothing happens. The screen is frozen up.

"A filter?" he questions. "Of your pussycat?"

Someone save me.

"It's not my cat," I say through a tight throat, my face hotter than the surface of the sun. I don't dare look up at anyone in the room as my fingers gently tap the touch pad of the laptop in an endeavor to move the still-frozen cursor. "It's just a funny filter of a random cat."

Mr. Banks edges in, pounding his meaty Boomer clubs on the keyboard like that's somehow going to fix it. In reality, even with his grayish-white hair, he's more of a Gen X-er than a Boomer, but his lack of technological savvy is wildly Boomer behavior.

"Neil? You there?" the CEO of Hughes International, the literal biggest social media holding company on the planet, asks on his end of the screen. I know for a fact that he wasn't expecting to take this meeting with a cat, and I can't imagine he'll have the patience to watch us fumble with it much longer.

"Hold on, Marcus," Mr. Banks comments from behind me, allowing me back to the keyboard again. "We're having some issues." His face is still a cat, and mine is now too. For me, at least, it covers my skin, which is officially the color of a tomato.

"Mr. Banks," I whisper toward him. My heart is pounding so

hard, it might beat itself straight out of my throat. Likely, of course, to be followed by vomit. "Let me see if I—"

"Oh man. Now, I'm all wet," he mutters, dejected, and proceeds to move his fingers back to the keyboard to tap whatever keys he can reach. "A wet pussycat."

The filter has changed from "cat" to "cat in bathtub," and is it just me, or has Mr. Banks said the word pussy no fewer than one hundred times already? It should be illegal to hear your best friend's father say the word pussy this much, and the fine should be doubled at eight in the morning.

I know he's technically saying pussy*cat*, but it's the way he says it. *Pussy*, far too long pause, *cat*.

My gaze flicks to Beau again—*of course*—but he's not looking at me. He's actively gesturing toward two of his coworkers to do something, anything that'll be more productive than sitting here watching his dad and me wrestle with a laptop.

"I think I got the pussycat off," Mr. Banks says then, clicking the remote to the projector to turn the Zoom off the main screen and then clicking it back on. "Uh-oh. It's back. Your pussycat is back, Juniper."

I want to die a slow death as the entire room suddenly comes down with a cold to cover their laughs. Beau's is the most distinct, but the rest of our coworkers are at an unfair disadvantage—I've been studying the man's every move, sound, and smile since I was a scrawny eleven-year-old girl with braces and he was a studly six-teen-year-old high schooler who spent his summers shirtless and surfing. Take in the fact that I'm now twenty-three, I've got a de-cade-long track record of observing Beau Banks, and I'd swear I know him better than I know myself.

I'm sweating now, pits and tits and everything in between, and things are getting serious. My boss has been a cat for a full three minutes, and I'm starting to wonder if the Zoom app will ever be pussy-free again. The screen, no matter what I press, isn't budging. "Mr. Banks. Please. Let me shut down the computer and restart."

Officially out of skills, Mr. Banks turns operations completely over to me.

"Then what?" he asks.

The truth is, I don't know. If I knew why Avery's computer was frozen on cat filters, I would have turned them off a long time ago.

"Let's go old-school and switch to a conference call," Beau suggests, jumping up from his seat and peering out into the hall to get his assistant Natalie's attention.

"Marcus, we're having a system malfunction, so we're going to reconnect on the conference line," Mr. Banks says then, his kitty mouth moving ever so cutely for all to see. "Please accept my apology for the delay."

I scoot all the way into the frame, doing a force quit on the meeting and all the running apps, and when that doesn't work, I hold down the power button with brute force. My pink silk bra-covered boobs are the only thing on-screen for a flash of a moment as I lean over and they peek out of my white blouse, and then thankfully, *blissfully*, the laptop shuts down and everything goes black.

I close my eyes to will away an impending cry and restart Avery's computer. Beau and Natalie are making quick work of setting up the conference call, and before I know it, the meeting is back in progress without the unfortunate addition of *pussy*.

My first day at work as a fresh-out-of-college intern is set to qualify as a national disaster—*seriously, I wouldn't be surprised if FEMA bursts into the room with aid*—and I only have my best friend to thank for it. Starbucks, in her mind, was way more important than this meeting, and when your dad owns the company and you have a conscientious friend like me, you can get away with reprioritizing the official schedule to align with that.

Neil assigned this task to her when we had orientation with him last week and Avery was pretending to be all serious about the new job so she could get an additional allowance for new "work attire." The thousands she spent at Hermès and Saks have yet to even see the fluorescent light of the office, and because we all know her so well, none of us are even surprised.

From the moment we became friends in kindergarten, Avery has always loved her rich-kid-of-Miami lifestyle. She doesn't have a dream job because she'd never waste her dreams on labor. She's got a flighty attitude and a quick wit but, most importantly, a heart the size of Texas—the reason she gets away with the rest of it.

She and her family are the backbone of everything significant in my life, and I love them more than words can express, even when Avery is a royal pain in the ass and Beau is witnessing Neil repeatedly ask me about my pussycat.

"Sorry about that, Marcus," Mr. Banks apologizes to *the* Marcus Hughes as soon as Natalie and Beau get the conference call connected. Every relevant social media app you can think of these days is owned by him, and the revenue that landing one of his accounts could bring Banks & McKenzie is overwhelming. Sickening, really, if you're the one potentially screwing it all up.

Oh God. Three deep breaths through my nose do nothing to ease the rage of my nerves, and I have to put a hand to my stomach to stave off a potential upchuck.

"This is a firm full of thinkers," Beau chimes in, his voice a charming balm of confident charisma. "You can't tell me any other firm has had the forethought to break the ice on some serious negotiations with kittens."

"No," Marcus responds on a laugh, his voice full of a levity I'm not expecting. "I can't say that they have. Let's just hope some of that ingenuity rubs off in our favor."

"Oh, I can assure you it will," Neil hedges. "Chris's flight from New York was delayed this morning, but he should be here shortly, and I've got a boardroom full of young creatives, ready to hear about your latest development."

Almost thirty years ago, Neil Banks and Chris McKenzie founded this Miami-based marketing firm that now has hundreds of employees on its payroll. Brick by brick, they built it into one of the topmost-performing ad agencies in the country. Beau joined on when he graduated college several years ago, worked his way to the top of the totem pole, and now spearheads numerous campaigns as one of the principal ad execs in the company.

The road could have been easy for him, but I know it wasn't. He's worked for everything he's gotten despite the obvious nepotism, and I aspire to do the same. I could've worked for my father's real estate empire—the world-renowned Perry Enterprises—with little to no effort and astronomically high pay, but I'd rather flip burgers at a fast-food joint than do that.

"Midnight is our latest social media app that we'll be releasing early next year," Marcus Hughes explains, and I quickly pull my phone out of my pocket and start taking diligent notes. I've got a major redemption arc to write for myself if I want to prove I'm anything other than Avery's ditsy friend who can't figure out fucking Zoom filters. "Think of it as an app meant for dating and conversation, but you can stay anonymous while you do it."

"Anonymous?" Neil questions, tilting his head to the side. "You think that's what people want these days?"

"It reminds me of that reality show, *Love is Blind*," Beau chimes in, and I hate how fixated my gaze becomes on his mouth as it moves. The plush lips, the white teeth, the hard jaw—he's just so perfect.

"That's a great comparison," Marcus agrees. "Social media these days is all about showing everything, about allowing viewers into your private life and private spaces. We follow people in their homes and their jobs and to their Brazilian waxes, for shit's sake. But Midnight is the opposite of that. It's discreet. It allows users to maintain a sense of privacy and anonymity while still experiencing a depth of conversation that gets to the heart of things."

"Mm-hm," Beau hums, pulling my wanton slut of an attention span right back to him. A few strands of his wavy, dark hair edge toward his eyes as he leans into his own laptop to check his prep notes, and his long fingers reach up to swipe them away. I sink my teeth into my bottom lip, willing myself not to stare at his broad shoulders beneath his suit jacket or linger as his biceps flex when he lifts his elbows to the table. "And what interface are we dealing with here? Gusta or Veronix?"

As I add a few more notes into my phone, a text message flashes across the screen. I discreetly open it, but no one is looking at me anyway. Now that I'm not intimately entrenched in causing massive stress, I've faded quite nicely into the background. The far corner of the room, to be exact. Honestly, if I could've buried myself into the soil of the big potted plant beside me without my new coworkers thinking I'm off my rocker, I would've done it.

Avery: Do you want anything from Starbies?

If I could sum up my best friend in one text message, this would be it. She's considerate and completely out of touch, all at the same time. Asking me if I want a drink now, when she was supposed to be here an hour and a half ago, is like the dentist asking me if I'd like some Novocain when the root canal is over.

Me: You're just going to Starbucks NOW?

Avery: I had to run back to the condo because I wasn't liking what my hair was doing today. You know how sometimes it does that annoying frizzy thing with the whoosh and the poof?

Having attended kindergarten, elementary, middle, high school, and college together—and sharing a condo now—I know the whoosh and poof she's talking about well. So well, in fact, I know it's not even really a thing, and missing your first day of work because of it is truly unbothered behavior.

In all reality, it's how I *should* behave too. My parents are wealthier than the Bankses, and for as little love as they've given me over the years, they've still managed to drown me in privilege. If it exists, and I want it, I can have it.

Which makes it painfully ironic, of course, that the only thing I've ever wanted is the one thing I can't have—a whole, happy, loving family with parents who didn't divorce when I was a kid and spend the rest of my life losing their minds.

That's probably why I clung to the Banks family during my parents' split. They were everything I didn't have and had always wanted, and Avery was generous enough to share them with me. I spent nearly every waking moment at their house when I wasn't at school and, after a couple years, even started staying with them to celebrate all the major holidays.

Neil and Diane are like second parents, and Avery is a sister in every way but genetically.

Beau, though…he spurs a different kind of reaction. His handsome good looks and charming smile and alluring personality make my brain go control-alt-delete.

I can't even talk about some of the things I've fantasized about related to him without risking spontaneous combustion, and I sure as hell can't talk about them in front of his family. *Especially* with my best friend. Avery would think I'm completely nuts if I told her the truth about my years-long crush on her only sibling.

To them, to him…he's my pseudo-older brother.

To me, he's my wildest fantasy.

Put the two of them together, and I'm at the center of an altogether taboo romance. And now, I'm going to be working with him every day.

What in the hell was I thinking? Yeah. Great question.

Chapter 2

AN HOUR INTO THE CONFERENCE CALL WITH MARCUS Hughes and the important execs from his company, and my best friend is still nowhere to be found.

Though, she hasn't stopped texting me random shit as the minutes have ticked by.

> Me: At this rate, I'm not even sure if you're going to show up at all.
>
> Avery: Chill out, June. I'm walking into Starbs now.
>
> Me: Great. I'm still trying to recover from hearing your dad talk about pussies for the first five agonizing minutes of this meeting you were SUPPOSED TO SHOW UP FOR, and you're "walking into Starbs now."

I start to close out of our ongoing text chat, but just before I can head back to my Notes app and, you know, try to do my job and listen to whatever Marcus Hughes is currently saying about the Midnight app his company has developed, another message from my best friend grabs my attention.

> Avery: Neil talking about pussies? Sorry, but that doesn't track. And it's a little gross, tbh.

Me: The cat filter, AVERY, on your laptop. We couldn't get it off, and your dad is evidently a time traveler from the fifties or something because he can't say the word cat without putting pussy in front of it. PUSSYCAT PUSSYCAT PUSSYCAT

Avery: Omg, the filter! I almost forgot about that. Isn't it great?

I quickly send three rapid texts, each one popping on the screen right after the other.

Me: "Is this your PUSSYcat, Juniper?" -Neil Banks

Me: "Oh man. Now, I'm all wet. A wet PUSSYcat." -Neil Banks

Me: "I think I just got the PUSSYcat off." -Neil Banks

Avery: HAHAHA

Me: It's not funny, dude. We were already connected to the Hughes International people while this was going on. I flashed my tits trying to get it off the screen. I was so panicked!

Avery: Did you record any of it? I wanna see some footage before my mani/pedi at noon.

Me: Are you serious? You're not even here, and you're already talking about leaving again? This is our first official day.

Avery: Yeah, so?

Me: Not sure if you realize, but we're supposed to actually work.

Avery: Oh my God, June. You're too funny. Like my dad would actually fire us or something. Plus, they shouldn't have expected us to work a full freaking day after Labor Day weekend. Like, I

partied hard, you know? We should've at least
had Monday off to recover.

Me: Avery, we did have Monday off. It's Tuesday.

I roll my eyes and start to slide my phone back into my
pocket to concentrate on the meeting—*okay, on Beau*—but when
it vibrates again in my hand, I glance at the screen.

Avery: Well, then they definitely should've given
us today off too. I barely had enough time to fit
in my hydration IV this morning.

Me: Hydration IV this morning? Wait… I thought
you said you went back to the condo to fix your
hair?

Avery: I did. While Carlton was giving me my IV.
Anyway, you want a mani/pedi too? I can add
you to the schedule. Oh! Maybe you need a
massage? You do seem really stressed…

Me: I'm stressed because it's the first day of
our intern job at YOUR DAD'S company, and
even though we both left the condo at the
same time, you're still not here because you're
doing hydration IVs and Starbucks and shit.

Avery: You sure you don't want a Starbucks?

Me: OH MY GOD. NO.

Avery: I'm definitely scheduling you a massage.
Be at the office in like 10 min. Love you!

Clearly, I'm not leaving work at noon to go get a freaking
massage, but it's not even worth explaining that to Avery. Instead,
I go back to focusing on the meeting and taking notes—and how
Beau's eyes look like dark honey beneath the conference room's
lights.

I scan my bullet point list about all things Midnight as one of Marcus Hughes's many minions continues to explain logistical details about profile settings and sign-up options.

- **Users create a profile and pick a profile name to stay anonymous within the app.**
  - ○ **They can search for users to chat with by interests, location, and sexual orientation.**
- **Once a user decides they want to chat with another user, they'll obtain a Dream Code that will create a private chat room for both users.**
  - ○ **That chat room stays active unless one of the users decides to leave it.**
  - ○ **Once a user exits the chat, all records of the chat are deleted.**
  - ○ **Users can send pictures, videos, and voice memos in the chat room. They can even choose to do a video call, if they desire.**
- **The app keeps all users' information anonymous. Only the profile name is available.**
- **The app has advanced safety and security that keeps all email addresses and other info associated with a profile private. The app also prevents users from taking screenshots or saving the private chats.**
- **Official launch date is spring of next year.**

They want Banks & McKenzie to spend the next four months using the app personally and coming up with a campaign idea to pitch at the end of the year, and for as much as Beau seems excited about the possibility, Neil isn't so certain.

"So, you don't want to give us the contract, but you want us to show you a marketing plan?" Neil questions with a business-worthy smirk. "That's a big ask, Marcus. Almost feels a little one-sided."

"Yeah, Marcus," Chris McKenzie, my other new boss, adds, having arrived about thirty minutes ago with his son Seth, another ad executive at the company, following behind him. "Feels like we're doing a hell of a lot of legwork without any reward."

Marcus grins like a guy who's squeezed a few nuts over the years. Which makes sense, I guess—you don't build a billion-dollar social media empire without twisting a few testicles. "Yeah, well, if you guys create a marketing plan we love for Midnight, we'll be moving everything under the Hughes International umbrella over to you as well."

"How many apps does that include?" Neil questions, but Beau answers before Marcus can.

"Thirty-five and counting."

Marcus nods, impressed. "That's correct."

My pussycat contracts with a purr, captivated too. *Gah, I am in so much trouble if I can't find a way to rein myself in and soon.*

Neil nods and taps his chin thoughtfully. "All right, then. I guess your Yale education did a decent job of teaching you risk and reward system management."

"Yeah, well. Not everyone can spend their formative years chasing tail in the sun of the University of Miami, Neil," Marcus retorts, his playful take on snobbery hitting above the belt quite nicely. The whole room smiles, despite just about all of us being graduates of U of M. "You're on board?"

"We're on board," Chris McKenzie agrees. "And come January 1st, Banks & McKenzie will have all of Hughes International under our umbrella."

Marcus chuckles. "Love the confidence, Chris."

"Oh, it's not confidence, Marcus. It's fact."

The conference call ends shortly after that, and as Neil and Chris open the room up for questions, Avery slides in like a water moccasin—head held high above the water and completely devoid of shame. She's wearing the nude Louboutins she bought at Saks, carrying her latest Birkin bag, and showcasing a matching cream Chanel tweed jacket and skirt that would make most people want to puke over the price tag.

Neil's brow furrows as he watches his daughter walk around the boardroom table with a Starbucks cup in her hand, taking a seat damn near at the head of the table while I sink farther into the wall. "Running a little behind?" he questions.

"Feels like I'm right on time, Daddy," Avery says with a shrug, gently tossing strands of her long, dark hair over her shoulder.

Beau shakes his head silently, meeting my eyes in a conspiratorial moment. I try not to melt on the spot, but it's hard, given the level of heat building between my legs every time I freaking look at him.

"Please proceed," my best friend adds with a nonchalant wave of her hand.

Neil shakes his head on a laugh. He knows Avery doesn't give a fuck, and even if he tried to get her to find one, she'd outsource the job and go for margaritas instead. She is what she is, and for the sake of ease, Neil has chosen to accept it. He moves his attention back to the room. "This campaign is big shit, guys. We want Hughes International as a client, and Midnight is the way we're going to do it."

Avery jumps out of her seat, noticing me against the wall for the first time, and comes to stand beside me. "What'd I miss?" she whispers, officially sending my ability to listen to Neil, Chris, Beau, and Chris's son Seth as they start discussing the particulars into orbit.

What'd she miss? *Ha.* "Everything."

She shrugs. "You're never going to believe who I saw at Starbucks."

I don't respond, trying like hell to listen to whatever Chris McKenzie is currently saying, but Avery doesn't get the message.

"Remember that guy we met at Luna, like, three weeks ago?" she asks, her entire body turned toward me like we're in the middle of a gabfest and not in the middle of an important work meeting. At this point, it doesn't matter what I say or do; she wants to tell me this story, and I'm going to hear it. Her father's company's success and our jobs be damned. "David. The one with those incredible blue eyes. He bought our table service in VIP, and I ended up back at his place. Remember him?"

I nod. I do, in fact, remember David. But I also remember that Beau was at Luna that night, dancing with some brunette chick with long legs. It was *painful.*

"Well, he was ordering a caramel macchiato this morning two people in front of me," Avery comments, her eyes alight with a future hookup. "He still looks good as hell, and he wants us to meet him at Neon tonight."

I don't say anything to that, but I already know there is no way in hell I'm going to Neon. I'm not in college anymore. I have a job. A job I'm trying to be good at, mind you, so that I can further my career in marketing and make use of the degree I spent four years earning at the University of Miami.

"I'd like to head the team for this campaign," Beau declares, yanking my attention away from coming up with a cover story of excuses to get out of Avery's late-night plans and back to the important work shit going down in front of us. And, you know, back to *Beau.*

"Actually, I think I should be the one doing that," Seth McKenzie fires back, a cocky smile on his face. "We both know I always win, Beau."

It's a statement so cataclysmic, even Avery pipes down to listen. A little over a year ago, Beau's longtime girlfriend Bethany left him for Seth, who was his best friend at the time, and they got engaged within two months of her big breakup with Beau. It sounds like a plot from *General Hospital,* I know, but for Beau, it's reality.

Internally, I still haven't figured out how to reconcile how angry I am on Beau's behalf with the unexpected, hope-building status of his singledom. I practically had my all-black, funeral-inspired outfit picked out for Beau and Bethany's future wedding, and then *boom,* the dirty hussy dropped a bomb. I cannot fathom having Beau and fumbling him for Seth. Don't get me wrong, Seth McKenzie is attractive with his light-brown hair and ocean-blue eyes, but he's no Beau Banks. *No one is.*

Beau narrows his astute gaze. "That's cute, Seth, but you'd be in way over your head on this, and we both know it."

"In over my head? I don't think so, man," Seth responds, his voice rising with irritation. "I just finished the campaign for Clover Athletics, and, not sure if you remember, but I knocked it out of the fucking park."

The tension is growing by the second, stretching tight between Beau and Seth like a rubber band as they stare each other down, and all I can do is watch, completely riveted and on edge at the same time.

"You didn't even come close to what my campaign for Dalencia Fashion did," Beau refutes, his voice deep with sarcasm. "We're lucky Clover even wants to work with us again after the pathetic numbers you generated."

Both Avery's and my heads bounce back and forth like volleyballs being smashed across a net. This spat may be work-related, but the inherent tension is nearly enough to set the whole damn building on fire.

"Pathetic numbers?" Seth nearly shouts, and strands of his silky hair fall toward his eyes. "They doubled their sales!"

"Is this, like, some kind of lovers' quarrel?" Avery asks, her voice managing to rise above both Seth and Beau. She's unserious about everything, but the people who really know her know this is her way of trying to defuse a situation. "Or do I need to go find a tape measure so you can compare your dicks?"

"Avery," Neil chides, though the grin stretching across his handsome face belies his whole intent.

"What?" she insists. "Tell them to put Peter and Paul Pogostick away, and we'll move on."

Neil's face pinches in consideration. "You know, maybe what we need is a little friendly competition. If you're both so ready to take this on, you both should. Right, Chris?"

Chris crosses his arms below his round, barrel chest. He's a big guy, a few inches taller than Neil, but not nearly as good-looking.

18

Honestly, if he'd stop doing the weird, slicked-back hair look on his curly gray hair, he'd increase his appeal tenfold. "Getting Hughes International as a client is important. Hell, it's the most important thing right now. And the more ideas we have, the better."

"You don't need more than one idea when you're confident you have the best one," Seth challenges, and the tone of his voice does the tango with annoyance.

"What's the matter?" Beau asks, his mouth kicking up at the corners and settling the tiniest of dimples in his cheek. It's the size of a pinpoint, really—an insignificant feature to anyone else. But I, on the other hand, spent nearly a month of my life during eighth grade studying the characteristic every chance I got. "Scared no one will hear your voice if it's not the only one in the room, Seth?"

"No," Seth counters through a hard jaw. "But you should be, with your track record."

"Enough," Chris commands. "I want full pitches with all the bells and whistles from both of you by New Year's Eve. You'll run through the pitches with us, and then you'll present directly to Marcus Hughes, and he'll decide. Sound good, Neil?"

Neil purses his lips in thought, his eyes briefly flitting over to Beau. As a father, this has to be about the shittiest situation he's ever created for his son, and knowing Neil, he's feeling conflicted. But to my surprise, he nods. "Yeah. I think that sounds perfect."

Avery nudges me with her elbow, but I don't dare look away. I need to know everything that Beau is feeling and thinking right now, and I need to know the cheat codes for how to fix it.

"So, we're competing against each other?" Seth asks for confirmation, a sneaky smile flashing across his lips.

"Yeah." Chris nods. "Friendly competition, of course. Banks & McKenzie is the only thing we truly need to win."

"Of course," Beau agrees, his jaw a firm mask over his normal good nature.

Is it just me, or has someone sucked all the air out of the room?

"Oh boy," Avery mutters toward me. "This sounds like a disaster waiting to happen. Maybe I should AirDrop my therapist's number to Beau when we leave here."

Chris smiles big, and a giant cloud of anticipation and bad juju fills the air. I war with myself, wondering if watching Beau go through this is going to help my crush or fan the flames.

Either way, I guess we're about to find out.

Let the games begin.

Chapter 3

NEON IS PACKED LIKE A DAMN CAN OF SARDINES. MUSIC vibrates from the massive speakers that sit throughout the warehouse-style nightclub, and the dance floor is filled with writhing bodies.

And I, Juniper Perry, am right in the middle of it, even though I said I wouldn't be. But it's not that big of a surprise. When it comes to Avery, I have a painfully low streak of resistance.

"Aren't you so happy you decided to come out tonight?" Avery questions, a vodka cranberry in one hand as she wraps her arm around my shoulder.

"Do you want me to tell you the real answer or the answer you want to hear?"

"The answer I want to hear," she responds unabashedly, her red lips curving up into a smile.

"I'm having the time of my life," I say, voice monotone but eyes dancing with sarcasm.

Avery laughs at that and spins me around to face the dancing crowd that sits below our feet.

Six bartenders work the big glass bar in the center for the commonfolk, but we sit tight as waitresses deliver us bottle service. Avery's hookup buddy David reserved the VIP section in the hope of landing a quick bang, and Avery has been full-on flirtatious with him in return. She doesn't need men to pay for her drinks—her trust fund and obscene monthly allowance ensure that—but she loves the thrill of the chase as men fight to keep her attention.

And trust me, she's a master at the game. A twenty-three-year-old certified man-eater who has no plans of settling down anytime soon. Oddly enough, I admire her audacity. Admire her confidence and ability to put herself first in all situations. Admire her ability to go after what she wants, no matter what other people think of it.

If I were more like Avery, I probably wouldn't give a shit about how absent my parents have been for most of my life or the fact that my father would rather buy my affection with expensive gifts and cash than show up. I probably wouldn't be scared to show Beau how I truly feel about him.

The wealthy lifestyle is a privilege I don't take lightly, but for a few simple things, I'd trade it all in a heartbeat.

"I think we need to dance," Avery announces, and her boy toy David might as well be a puppy on a leash. His tail is practically wagging as he sidles up beside my best friend, raring to go.

"Then let's go dance," he says and wraps his arm around her waist, tugging her closer to his side and removing her arm from my shoulder in the process. It's only then that I sort of get why Avery thinks he's hot. His blue eyes have something alluring about them, and his willingness to jump at her every whim is unmatched.

"You want to dance with me?" Avery questions, fluttering her eyelashes.

"You haven't ever seen moves like mine, baby," David says, and I cringe. He's hot, but he should say a lot less—maybe even nothing. He should just smile more, you know? Like people love to tell women.

"Hold that thought for, like, fifteen minutes, 'kay?" Avery says and kisses the tip of her index finger before pressing it to the corner of David's mouth. "I need a little best-friend time with June. Be back."

"Don't keep me waiting too long, baby. My dick's already a fucking bat," David says, and I fight the urge to vomit in my mouth.

All the *baby* usage and dirty talk is unsettling my stomach. I don't know if I'm broken or something, but to me, all men but Beau Banks are creepy as fuck.

Avery responds by blowing him a kiss before grabbing my hand and dragging me out of the VIP section. She offers a flirty smile to one of the security guards working the VIP entrance stairs before guiding us into the crowd of dancing bodies.

Of the two of us, Avery has always been the lead partier. I followed her because I'd be flogged if I didn't—even got pretty good at downing shots in college—but the more I go out, the more I end up in some weird internal crisis about what life has to offer other than *this*. Realistically, are parties and booze and money and fancy yachts and big mansions with the best ocean view going to be it for me?

Or is there more? Something better? Something *real*?

And how shitty of a person do I have to be to complain about how rich I am? I don't want to be ungrateful, I swear. I know I've been afforded a million things that so many people do nothing but dream about. But I just...I don't know. It all feels fucking shallow. Like there's no substance or purpose at all.

It's so complicated.

I sigh. *See? Crisis.*

Avery drags us to the middle of the dance floor, having no qualms about pushing people out of our way as she does, and doesn't let go of my hand until she finds an open spot in the middle of the floor she deems worthy of our dance moves.

When we're in the zone, we take up a lot of space, especially when Avery does her personal modification of a twerk. She calls it the "booty rizz," and I don't think we've been to a party or a club in the last five years where she hasn't used it.

She shakes her ass, smiling over at me as she does, and I force myself to let go and vibe with the beat of the music. It's not long before I'm fully immersed in the song, raising my hands in the air, and circling my hips. I lean my head back and can feel the swish of my long red locks on the bare area of my lower back.

Despite my reservations, it actually starts to feel good. I guess all that bullshit they tell you about moving your body being beneficial for your mind has some truth to it.

But Avery's moves are a Miami mating call, and it's not long before the vultures are circling. A big, muscular guy with a buzz cut and a toothy smile slides in beside me, and a tall guy with blond hair is now on the receiving end of Avery's signature ass-grind. *So much for David, I guess?*

"You wanna dance, sweet thing?" Buzz Cut asks me, his meaty hands already grabbing my hips, and my blood pressure skyrockets.

I make a snap decision to slip out of the dancing crowd and head toward the bar, using the ASL alphabet I learned in third grade to pretend I'm deaf when Buzz Cut calls after me. I know it's shitty to appropriate a disability like that, but men are scary. Sometimes, moral compromise is the lesser evil.

I get a water from the bartender and slide into an empty barstool as soon as it's vacated. I chug half the bottle before turning back to keep tabs on Avery—who is now making out with the blond.

"Great," I mutter, a sardonic laugh that probably makes me seem mentally unstable to the people around me. But if they had any idea how many times I've been on crime-scene cleanup due to Avery's fickle affection, they'd be talking to themselves too.

I try to distract myself from the likelihood of David's impending breakdown when he sees Avery on the dance floor sucking face with some random dude by people-watching the crowd, but it gets me into even more trouble.

There's a dark, wavy, familiar head of hair in one of the VIP sections above the dance floor, and my heart kicks up into a sprint on its chest treadmill.

Beau Banks is here, and suddenly, nothing else matters.

He doesn't frequent clubs or bars like his sister, but it's not out of the ordinary to see him out either. Especially on a day like today—with the way work ended in a Celebrity Deathmatch with

Seth—it makes sense that he's blowing off steam. He's the definition of an Extroverted Introvert personality.

He's with a few guys I recognize, friends of his I've met over the years because I spent more time with the Bankses than I did my own family, and his smile is showstopping, even from here.

He laughs at something his buddy Henry says, and a flock of butterflies escapes their cage inside my belly. I hang on Beau's every silent word, trying like hell to read his lips as a blond stunner in a red bodycon dress sidles up beside him.

She's the kind of gorgeous and sexy that's obvious. You know the ones—big boobs and a thick ass paired with a small waist and one of those collarbones that looks ethereal or carved out of stone or something. And she's standing so close to him that every time she laughs at whatever Beau says, her pushed-up breasts brush his arm.

In a head-to-head matchup, my gangly, long legs and overly freckled skin would get KO'ed in the first round, and yet, I find myself fantasizing wildly about him brushing her off to come talk to me instead.

I'm delusional at this point. Truly.

Sometimes, I think my life would be so much easier if I could get over my crush on Beau. But after a decade of trying to move on and failing miserably, I'm starting to think it's going to take an exorcism or, I don't know…death…to actually do it.

I wallow in my misery for a few minutes longer, watching the way she reaches up to brush some of Beau's perfect hair out of his eyes, but when I feel like he's getting a little too smiley with her, and I get that stabby, can't-breathe level of jealousy in my chest I used to get when I watched him with his ex Bethany, I avert my attention.

"What are you drinking?"

The question feels like it comes out of nowhere, but I'm pretty sure that's the heartbroken disassociation talking. When I look to my right, I see a man standing beside me. He's pretty tall, has light-brown hair, gray eyes, and a nice smile that isn't threatening or over the top. His appeal is more boy-next-door than dark and dangerous, and for once, I consider the possibility that maybe I shouldn't immediately scare him away like I usually do with most random men who approach me in nightclubs.

Avery is always saying the best way to get over someone is to get under someone else, and while I normally think she's insane, seeing Beau smiling at big-boobed blonde bombshells is enough to shake my reality.

"Uh…water," I answer, shrugging one shoulder as I glance down at my now half-empty bottle.

"Water?" he questions, a smirk on his mouth.

"I know," I respond with a grin, trying on something flirty rather than my usual scowl. "Kind of lame, huh?"

"Well, that depends."

"On what?"

"If you're on probation or a recovering alcoholic, then it wouldn't be lame at all. It'd be pretty smart."

"And if I were either of those, would you still be standing here?" I test. "Or would you already be searching for your exit strategy?"

"I'd never shame someone for trying to get healthy from an addiction. But it'd definitely depend on what you're on probation for…"

I quirk a brow. "Murder."

"You managed to get probation with murder?" he challenges back, amusement in his eyes.

"I had a really good lawyer."

"Well, then, no." He laughs. "But I would be focused on getting your lawyer's info because that's pretty good."

"Why? You planning on murdering someone?" I tilt my head to the side, challenging him again. "Because I don't fuck with guys like that."

"Man," he says through another laugh, running a hand through his brown hair. "You're something. Was that trap preplanned or organic?"

I take a long sip of my water, holding eye contact as I swallow. "That information is classified."

He smiles at me, his gray eyes dancing with entertainment. "I'm Miller, by the way." He holds out his hand, and I take it.

"June." I never give my full name in a situation like this. Juniper is too easy to find in an internet search should Miller turn out to be of the stalker variety and, quite frankly, too distracting. Once they hear it, they can never leave it alone.

"Well, June, can I buy you a drink?"

"I appreciate the offer, Miller, but I'm staying sober tonight, and the water's free."

"And what about tomorrow night?" he questions, his body leaning closer to mine. "Even if you don't want to drink, I could offer dinner at an earlier hour."

"You trying to ask me out?"

He shrugs. "If I say yes, will you give me your number?"

I dig my teeth into my bottom lip, hesitation heavy in my mind. On the one hand, Miller seems like a perfectly nice guy, but on the other, meeting strangers in clubs or bars has never really ended in anything great. Out of the two times I've tried it in the past, I got an excited texter who only used capital letters and exclamation points for every single word he exchanged and a guy with a horror-film-style apartment, complete with mold and actual fecal matter, that ruined the term bachelor pad for me for eternity.

In fact, besides Kai, a guy I met at a house party at the University of Miami and dated on and off for a year, no one I've tried dating at all has lasted more than an outing or two.

Which I guess makes sense on an intrinsic level—usually, when you fall in love, that's your cue to stop looking. From personal experience, it's a little trickier when they don't love you back.

"C'mon," Miller cajoles. "You can't tell me a free meal is *that* bad of an idea."

"I don't know… I'm not big on meeting strangers in clubs."

"What about parks?"

"Parks?" I question, puzzled over whatever angle he's trying to take, but intrigued all the same. I have to admit that he's determined, at least, and getting this level of attention feels nice.

"I have a little bulldog named Sadie. I walk her every Wednesday afternoon—"

"Everything okay here?"

I glance over my shoulder to find Beau standing there, his brown eyes flitting between me and Miller in concern. I furrow my brow as I look behind him to the VIP section he left behind, where his buddy Henry is the one talking to the blonde in red now.

"Yeah, man," Miller says. "Everything's great."

"You sure, June?" Beau's eyes are on me now. "This guy isn't causing you any trouble, is he?"

A wave of excitement rushes over me as I consider the possibility that my wildest dreams are coming true. *Did Beau actually leave behind the woman in red to notice me? To care about me? To love me?*

"You know this guy?" Miller asks, a double question to cancel out my need for an answer to the first.

They're swinging dicks of protection, and a little trill of glee makes me sit up straighter. In my mind's eye, Beau's next move will be to throw fists now and ask questions later. I am his damsel, in need of assistance and care, and he's going to do it in gallant—

"Yeah, she knows me," Beau answers for me. "We grew up together. I'm basically her brother."

Every cell inside me withers and dies a slow, free fall of a death from my imaginary princess tower. My fairy tale is over, my bubble burst.

I'm basically her brother? Someone shoot me now and put me out of my fucking misery.

"June!" Avery shouts, her chest dewy with sweat and her eyes desperate as the blond dude she was making out trails behind her on their way toward me. "Get your ass back out here! We have more dancing to do!"

Five minutes ago, I never would have dreamed of walking away from a situation where Beau Banks was paying attention to my existence, but my corpse has other rules. She only allows for one emotional murder per night, and the brother line definitely finished the job.

"Coming!" I say, scooting out from my spot on the stool in between Miller and Beau and leaving my nearly empty water bottle on the bar.

I wave goodbye to both of them, and I don't look back. My dignity won't allow it.

Knowing I'll wake up tomorrow morning still in love with the guy who sees himself as my brother is more than bad enough.

Chapter 4

AVERY PULLS HER BLACK MERCEDES G WAGON THROUGH the entrance of Altos Del Mar, the exclusive community in Miami we both grew up in, and I scroll my phone to distract myself.

There are a lot of wonderful memories here, but a number of bad ones all the same, and the more I look out the window, the more they come rushing back to me.

Sitting on the front steps of my house, hoping one of my parents would come home and surprise me on the night of my twelfth birthday and ending up opening gifts sent by mail while my newest nanny looked on.

Hearing my parents fight like cats and dogs while I hid my head under my pillow and cried when my dad told my mom he wanted a divorce the year before.

Hoping for a family vacation but getting a guided solo tour of Europe with my nanny the year before that.

My dad still owns the house I grew up in—he kept it after the divorce—and I go to it on very rare occasions, but eleven bedrooms and their corresponding baths can't fill the empty space being alone in ten-thousand square feet creates in your heart. Even though it's still filled with staff who keep it maintained, it feels emptier than a morgue.

I don't even have to text my dad to know he's not home today.

He's never home. Between running his real estate empire and his wife, my twenty-seven-year-old stepmom, Lola, Richard Perry's life is one of jet-setting and expensive hotels on endless repeat.

And my mom isn't any better. After my parents divorced when I was eleven, she turned herself into Julia Roberts and *Eat Pray Love-d* with reckless abandon. She never stays in one place and is always going on unconventional spiritual retreats in places like Fiji and Bali to find herself. After twelve years of doing that, you'd think Jackie Perry would have a handle on who she is, but it's a never-ending quest. Maybe it's all just a guise to spend her days relaxing on exotic beaches while living off all the money she got in the divorce settlement, or maybe she really is lost. I don't know.

All I know is she isn't here. Ever. And the only way I know her whereabouts is from the sporadic texts she sends me. The last one came in two days ago and consisted of **Hi, my darling. Sending you love from Milos, Greece.**

That message was followed up with a picture of my bikini-clad mother standing on the beach with some tanned, muscled-up, shirtless guy I've never seen before.

Ironically, not even twenty-four hours before that, Lola sent me a picture of herself and my father standing on some fancy yacht in the South of France and a text message that only made me roll my eyes.

> **Lola: Your father and I miss you, Avery! When we're back in town, let's have a family dinner together, okay? I have a killer steamed mussels recipe that you need to try! Kisses from France, sweetheart!**

I don't have anything against my father's wife, but her trying to act like she's a mother figure in my life when I'm a grown adult and she's only four years older than me is the world's biggest joke. Plus, she doesn't cook—my father's staff does that—and the last time I had a family dinner with my actual family was years and years ago, before Lola was even in the picture.

Needless to say, everything about my family life is nonconventional at best. Completely dysfunctional and devoid of true love and affection at worst.

Avery pulls up to the gate blocking the entrance of her parents' home and types the code into the security keypad. Once the gates slide open, she pulls inside and parks in the circular driveway of the Bankses' eight-thousand-square-foot mansion and shuts off the engine.

I click out of my dad's message telling me to "Have a good first day of work next week" from this morning and figure his assistant Shirlene must have gotten the calendar entry wrong by a week. I also laugh to myself—*because crying is useless*—over the fact that my twenty-seven-year-old stepmother makes a bigger effort than my own father. At least her messages come from her.

Avery is the first out of the car, and her mom Diane has the door to the house open shortly after.

Diane Banks is the definition of a woman who ages gracefully. She's fairly tall, with shiny dark hair, and her face showcases just the right amount of wrinkles to make her look sophisticated and wise but still ten years younger than her actual age. She's also one of the kindest human beings I've ever known. A true mother, that's Diane.

Her smile is warm and excited as I jog to catch up with Avery, and the two of us get to the door at the same time. "Aw, my girls!" Diane exclaims and pulls us both in for a tight hug. "Dinner's almost ready. Are you hungry?"

Eating dinner at the Bankses' house at least once a week—and sometimes way more than that, depending on how lazy we are—is a routine Avery and I have been doing ever since we graduated high school and started living on our own.

"Starved," Avery comments and drops her purse in the foyer before traipsing across the Italian marble floors and heading straight for the kitchen. Linda, the Bankses' housekeeper, picks up the YSL bag, and I smile apologetically as I hand her mine more politely.

Avery isn't as rude as she seems. She's just self-involved. Linda, thankfully, knows that better than almost anyone. She's been around pretty much as long as I have.

"How was the first week of the new job?" Diane asks, wrapping an arm around my shoulders as we follow Avery into the kitchen.

"Good. But my boss is a real hard-ass," I tease, knowing Neil can probably hear me, and she laughs.

"Dad got mad at me for leaving work early today for hot yoga, Mom!" Avery calls over her shoulder, milking the opportunity I've given her for all it's worth. "You know I can't miss those sessions. Callie is impossible to rebook!"

"Neil!" Diane exclaims, her lips curving up into a smile as we enter the kitchen. "Are you being hard on our girls?"

Mr. Banks sits at the massive marble counter in the center of the kitchen, a newspaper in his hands. He barely lifts his eyes above the pages. "Hard on Avery?" He chuckles. "There's no time to be hard on her. She barely shows up for work as it is."

"That's not true," Avery counters defensively. "I was at work today."

"You showed up an hour late, took a two-hour lunch, and then only stayed for an hour because," he changes his voice to a high-pitched, girly one, *"I have hot yoga, Daddy. I can't miss it."*

Diane grins at Avery, unfazed. Her daughter's behavior may not be a reflection of her own work ethic, but she accepts it for what it is. "Where'd you go for lunch?"

"I didn't even have time to eat, Mom!" Avery complains. "I had to get my nails done."

It's been less than a week since Avery's nail appointment last Tuesday—you know, the one she scheduled in the middle of our first day of work. Frankly, I'm not surprised that's where she went today. She's been complaining about the color of her polish for almost every waking moment since she got it.

"Neil, your daughter didn't even get to eat lunch," Diane comments, tsking her lips with an amused smile. "Sounds like the work conditions are not ideal."

"Oh yeah." Neil snorts and adjusts his reading glasses on his nose. "Horrible work conditions when the boss lets you just come and go as you damn well please."

"You knew she was going to be like this," a deep, oh-so-intoxicating voice adds, making my heart kick into a gallop. I don't dare look over my shoulder as Beau joins us, hugging Diane right behind me before chucking me on the shoulder with a buddy-ol'-pal fist. First, the brother comment, and now this. It just gets worse and worse for my delusions around here.

"Shut up, Beau," Avery announces with a roll of her eyes. "Just because I'm not a workaholic like you doesn't mean I'm not an asset to the company."

"An asset?" Beau questions, a bright but sarcastic grin covering his perfect mouth as he leans into the kitchen island across from me. I try not to stare at the strain of his biceps against the sleeves of his T-shirt. "And what exactly do you bring to the table?"

"Wouldn't you love to know," Avery goads.

"Actually, yeah," Beau agrees. "I honestly would. What exactly are you bringing to the marketing firm, Ave?"

"That's for me to know and you to find out," Avery says, sticking out her tongue at him.

"Remind me not to hold my breath while I wait." Beau shakes his head and runs a hand through his hair, and I immediately miss his previous posture. If I stare at any of the obvious bulges now, I'm going to get myself in a lot more trouble than I can handle.

But damn, he looks good in jeans. So good.

"Yeah," Neil adds with a smirk. "Me either."

"Daddy!" Avery cries with a little pout on her lips.

"I'm just messing with you, princess," he coddles, and she walks over to him to give him a big hug. "I'm happy I get to see you at the office now. Even if it's only for an extra ten minutes each day."

"I was at work longer than ten minutes today!" she retorts on a laugh, and for the first time, I have both the urge and the ammunition to join in on the fun.

"Avery's right, guys. She was at the office for at least forty-five minutes. Honestly, it might've been a full hour."

Avery flips me the bird, but the smile on her face is evidence of the truth. She doesn't give a single shit about any of it, and I admit, it's freaking impressive. She's so secure in her personality, nothing can bring her down. Not her brother telling her she's lazy or people thinking she's shallow—she owns it.

"Oh!" Avery exclaims as she grabs an olive from the charcuterie board on the kitchen island and pops it into her mouth. "Beau! Tell June the good news!"

I look between Avery and Beau, confusion in my eyes and the dumbest intrusive thoughts about what the news could be jumping around my mind like ping-pong balls. *That he also has a crush on me? That he's in love with me and wants to marry me? That the sooner we get started making and having a million of his dark-haired, brown-eyed babies, the better?*

Clearly, I have a problem.

"W-what's the good news?" I say, clearing my throat as I do.

"My big brother is moving in to our building," she says and walks over to wrap her arm affectionately around Beau's shoulders. "He just can't stand being away from his baby sister so much that he decided he needed to move closer to her."

"Half of that's true, Juni," he says through a laugh.

"Uh…which half?"

"Seriously, June? I might miss you, but it's a little hard to miss Avery," he says, the words sending a zap of electricity from my cooch to my toes. The rational part of me knows he doesn't actually miss me, but she's currently being smothered by the irrational, mooning, far-too-hopeful girl with stars in her eyes. "But the part about me moving in to your building is true."

"You…" I pause and clear my throat again to stop myself from asking about him missing me. It's one thing to harbor delusion internally, but spewing it all over the Bankses' countertops would be embarrassing. "You're moving in to our building?"

"Yep," he answers with a nod. "Since my house isn't going to be ready in time for my lease expiration date, I made a few calls to your dad. He was kind enough to let me rent out one of the condos while I wait for the contractors to get their shit together."

About six months ago, Beau purchased a fancy-schmancy mansion that overlooks the water on Biscayne Bay. It has a pool and a private dock, and I think about the comment he made about the hot tub the day he gave Avery and me the dime tour to this day.

"I'm excited about the hot tub, but I am definitely getting it cleaned. It's one of the topmost-used locations for fucking, according to Google."

I'd definitely fuck Beau in a hot tub. I'd fuck him in a paper bag if we could fit in it.

But yeah…the house. Right.

It requires a hell of a lot of reno, which is probably why it's taking so long for him to be able to move in, but it's gorgeous all the same. I know he's proud of saving up and paying for it himself, and he should be. He's one of the hardest workers I know.

"And," Avery adds with a big smile. "not only is he in the same building—he's our neighbor."

"Our neighbor?" I question, my mind still buffering somewhere between Beau's brown eyes and the thoughts of Beau fucking me in a hot tub.

"Yes! He rented the condo right next to ours," she says. "Like, if we go out on our balconies at the same time, we'll see each other. Stalk much, bro?" she teases with a roll of her eyes. "It's like you're obsessed with me or something."

Beau chuckles. "It was the only unit available."

The only unit available. Right next to ours. My first thought is one of elation.

My second is one of outright dismay as I watch Beau pull his phone out of his pocket to take a call.

"Hey," Beau says, his voice sultry in just the way my mental spiral needs to nose-dive straight toward the ground.

As much as I wish he were, Beau is not my boyfriend. He's not anyone's boyfriend at the moment, but he's also not lacking for female attention, as proven by what I *know* is a woman on the other end of his current call.

If Beau lives right next to us...so will a never-ending train of his hookups and their loud moans, potentially separated from my ears by nothing more than a wall.

Dear Judy Blume, it's me, Juniper. Could you have Margaret get a line to God for me and do it pronto?

I know I'm twenty-three, but I think the thirteen-year-old girl inside me is about to have a coming-of-age tale she'll never forget.

And her hero Beau won't be around to dry her tears anymore either. He'll be too busy banging bimbos while she listens.

Chapter 5

The Past
Ten years ago

AVERY IS ALL SMILES AS HER DAD DRIVES US HOME FROM Melanie Mendez's party, the nearly midnight traffic of the city making me feel twice my age. There's something dangerous and exciting and forbidden about it I can't explain.

We're teenagers now, officially thirteen, and after spending tonight at an actual boy-girl party, I just know our whole worlds are about to change. We're not little girls anymore, and what lies ahead is a mystery I can't wait to explore.

"What?" I mouth toward her.

She shakes her head, but her mouth crests up into the biggest grin. She doesn't want to talk in front of her dad, and I don't blame her. I heard a rumor when I was using the bathroom before we left that Vic Lorren touched her boob, and I'm *dying* to know if it's true.

I eye her intently, a silent, *"You better freaking tell me what happened as soon as your dad's not around!"* passing meaningfully between us.

Avery is my best friend. Basically, my sister. We don't keep secrets from each other. *Ever.*

Her eyes avert to Mr. Banks again as he messes with the radio, and when it seems like he's sufficiently distracted by finding the perfect song, she leans over in the back seat to whisper directly in my ear. "He kissed me."

My eyes widen in excitement, and I turn to whisper back. "Who? Vic?"

She shakes her head, scooting back into her seat and biting her lip with her teeth. She scrolls through her phone for a minute before holding it out for me to see. On the screen is a picture of Brandon Worley.

Instantly, my heart drops to the Chanel flats my father gave me as some kind of let-me-buy-your-love-with-gifts thing he's been doing ever since he and my mom split, and I turn to look out the window to cover up the immediate sting of tears as they hit my eyes.

My heart pounds and my ears ring as I try to make sense of what I'm feeling. Avery didn't know, but I decided last week that Brandon was the boy *I* was going to go for. Now that I'm turning into a woman and all, I need to give boys my own age a shot instead of spending all my time mooning over her brother Beau.

Brandon Worley was at the very *center* of that plan.

Avery's hazel eyes are wide with excitement when I turn back to look at her, but when I don't give any reaction, she leans over to whisper into my ear again. "Brandon kissed me."

My best friend just had her first kiss…with my crush.

"Like, on the actual lips. With tongue," she adds quietly, and her giddy giggle vibrates my ear.

My best friend French-kissed my crush, and I feel like I'm going to vomit all over Mr. B's black leather seats.

Avery's gaze is locked on mine again as her dad pulls through the gated entrance of their massive beachfront home, her excitement untethered. I'm a mess of emotion as I try to sort out being happy with her and mourning my whole scheme to get over the one and only Beau Banks at once, but I try to smile.

She's just happy enough not to notice that it's brittle.

Mr. Banks pulls into the garage, and Avery all but drags me out of the car and into the house. By the time we get upstairs to her room and she slams the door, she tackles me to her bed with a giant hug.

"Brandon Worley kissed me, Juniper!" she whisper-yells. "He freaking tongue-kissed me!"

"I can't believe you guys frenched." I feign a smile and laughter and all of the things I should be feeling for my best friend. I do everything I can to hide my truth because Avery deserves all the best things in the world even more than I do.

When my dad screwed his secretary Tiffany and told my mom he wanted a divorce, Avery saved me. She gave me an escape. She gave me a family. She gave me support.

The least I can do is give her Brandon Worley.

"I know, right?" she squeals. "It came out of nowhere, June. Like, one minute we were just standing there talking, and the next, he was grabbing my hand, pulling me toward Melanie's dock, and *kissing* me."

"Is he…is he a good kisser?" I ask, my voice hesitant as I push myself through discomfort. When Brandon transferred to our school last month, something about his brown hair and brown eyes made me feel like he'd be a good stand-in for Beau. I always wondered, though, if Brandon's kisses would be anywhere near the ones I'd fantasized having with Avery's older brother, and now that Avery has the information, I can't help but analyze it.

"Oh my God. He's, like—" she starts to say, but she instantly pauses when her phone starts ringing from her purse. Her eyes go wide with a thrill, and when she snags her phone into her hands, a giant smile consumes her face, along with two shades' worth of blush. "It's him." Her eyes flit from the screen of her phone to me. "Brandon is calling me, June!"

She doesn't even wait for me to respond before she's tapping on the screen to answer. "Hey," she says, her voice sounding nothing like it did mere seconds ago when she was about to wax poetic about his magical tongue.

I don't know what Brandon says on the end, but Avery laughs

like whatever he says is the funniest freaking thing she's ever heard in her life and sits down in her favorite loungey chair by the window, one index finger twirling a strand of her long dark-brown hair.

"Oh my God, Brandon. You're so crazy," she says, and more flirty giggles fall from her lips.

Suddenly, I feel like I'm intruding. Leaving isn't an option, though, because my mother is busy moving in to her new penthouse condo in South Beach and my dad is busy with Tiffany, so I settle on a middle ground and tell Avery I'm going to go grab a snack from downstairs.

She barely even hears me, her mind one hundred percent fixated on whatever Brandon Worley is saying to her.

I don't want to be jealous of my best friend, but I am. I want someone to want me like that. I want to feel pretty. So much so, I could cry.

I roll my eyes at myself as I head down the steps and into the kitchen. Avery's parents are already in bed, but I've been spending so much time at my best friend's house over the past year, I have no qualms about making myself at home.

Ever since my mom found out about my dad's affair with bimbo Tiffany, my home life exploded. The fights and arguments between my parents grew nasty and vile, and spending the night at Avery's was way better than having to hear the ugly details of my parents' failing marriage through the walls. The Bankses have been welcoming, and I've gotten good at going with it. Heck, last year, *for Take Your Daughter to Work Day*, both Avery and I went with Mr. Banks to his marketing firm and sat through a conference call where a Chinese translator was needed for the client. It was probably the coolest thing I've ever been a part of.

When nothing sounds good, I grab a bottle of water and head into the living room and through the sliding glass doors that lead to the outside.

The soft sounds of the ocean are soothing as I traipse across the large patio area, past the infinity-edge pool, and out toward the deck steps that lead to the sand. It's not long before I make it all the way to the beach and plop my ass down just mere feet from the water.

I wiggle my toes into the sand and run my fingers through it too, trying to make sense of how jealous I'm feeling while watching the light from the moon bounce off the gentle lap of the water.

My best friend had her first kiss tonight, and I haven't kissed anyone. Probably never even will.

Melanie Mendez kissed Anthony Lazarus when she was eleven. And since then, she's also kissed Greg Bolger, Evan Meyers, Lucas Wilson, and Marty King. That's five freaking people she's kissed, and I'm still at a big fat zero.

Tara Reynolds has already kissed three boys from our grade, and Jenny Steward has kissed four.

And now, Avery has joined their group, and I'm the lone wolf. Just sitting out here on my lonely rock of I-haven't-kissed-anyone-yet.

Or maybe, it's the fact that no one wants to kiss me.

A stupid tear escapes my eye and runs down my cheek as pity for myself starts to rage.

I'm the only girl in my class with copper-red hair, freckles, and blue eyes. Everyone else is either blond or brunette, and their boobs did some serious growing over the summer.

I'm the flat-chested, skinny redhead with—

"You okay?"

My gaze jerks up on a startle, and my chest locks instantly. Holy shitoly, Beau Banks looks good from this close up. I shift my eyes to his feet in the sand to get myself together as I nod.

"Fine." It's a lie, and he, I, and the ocean all freaking know it. Not five seconds ago, I was sniffling like a crybaby.

He sits down beside me, leaning back into his tanned hands and making his white T-shirt ride up on his perfect abs. He's eighteen—five years older than Ave and me—and he's, hands down, the most gorgeous human being I've ever seen in my whole freaking life.

When I don't say anything else, he nudges me with his knee to

get my attention, and my stomach flips over on itself. "How about
you tell me what's going on. Maybe I can help?"

I shake my head. "It's nothing."

"Oh, c'mon, Juniper June, I promise I won't tell a soul."

Juniper June. Beau Banks is the only one who can make my
name sound good to my own ears. His calling me "Juniper June" or
"Juni" are my two favorite sounds in the world. Well…maybe second and third after his laugh.

"You're going to think it's lame," I say, fighting my embarrassment by fiddling with a few grains of sand at my side. Beau is practically *grown*. He's a man. He's going off to college in the fall. Me
worrying about my first kiss eclipsing sometime before the end of
the world is *so* not going to be important to him.

"I swear, I won't."

I eye him knowingly. "You will."

Beau holds both hands up in the air, his face as serious as I've
ever seen it. "You have my word, Juni."

Here's the thing with Beau, when he gives you his word, he
freaking gives you his word. He's always been that way. Even being
significantly older than Avery and me, he's never not kept a promise. Not once.

He's…the best.

I turn to him quickly, crossing my legs like applesauce and holding out a pinkie. "You can't tell anyone."

He nods, linking his finger with mine and promising purely. I
take a deep breath and then, shakily, let it all hang out. "Avery had
her first kiss tonight. Which is awesome for her. I'm happy for her,
really. But… I don't know… It just feels like it's never going to happen for me. It feels like every other girl in my class has had their first
kiss besides me." I sigh. "I know it probably sounds dumb to you…"

"No," Beau refutes immediately. "It's not dumb."

I tilt my head to the side and let myself meet his gaze for the
briefest of moments. His chocolate-brown eyes are soft and warm.
Basically, the opposite of judgy. "You don't think it's stupid?"

"Of course not," Beau comments and nudges my knee with his. "But can I give you a little piece of advice that I wish someone would've given me when I was your age, worried about the exact same thing?"

Beau Banks worried about getting his first kiss? *Puhlease.* Every girl in school—and a lot who didn't even go to the same school—has been in love with him at one time or another. His girlfriend is *the* Bethany Williams, known by everyone as the B Triple Threat—blond hair, blue eyes, and big boobs.

Beau and Bethany have probably been tongue-kissing each other for years now, and they probably even have *sex.*

My stomach pitches at the thought. I don't know much about anything, but looking at Beau right now, I'm pretty sure sex with him must be the ultimate freaking experience. Bethany is so lucky it's not even funny.

"You want the advice?" he repeats, his voice teasing, and I realize how long I've just been sitting here. I try not to blush, but I fail. I'm beet red; I can feel it.

I nod instead of replying, and he smirks at me.

"Don't rush your first kiss," he says. "Don't worry how long it takes to come. Don't worry about being the only girl in your class who hasn't had it. Don't worry about any of it. Focus on making sure you find the right boy to give that first kiss to. Because, Juniper, it's an honor. Any boy who gets your first kiss should consider himself lucky, not the other way around."

"Yeah?"

"Yeah." He winks. "You're not waiting to get it. You're waiting to *give* it. Don't settle for anyone who doesn't deserve the gift."

Goodness, how does he always make everything sound so good?

"Thanks, Beau."

"Anytime, Juniper." His smile is brighter than the moon. "You going to be okay?"

"Yeah." I nod. "I will."

He leans toward me and wipes the remnants of my tears away

from my face, and the feeling of his touch sends me into overdrive. He leans in to kiss me on the cheek, and I turn my head at the last minute, just barely catching his mouth with the corner of mine.

It's subtle, so much so, I'm not even sure he notices. But to me, it's *everything*.

"Night, Juni," he says before climbing to his feet and heading back for the house.

My chest pounds and my ears ring, but now, it's for an entirely different reason. I can still feel the sensation of his lips, right on the corner of my mouth.

It's not the traditional first kiss any of the other girls in my grade got, nor anything like the one Avery got tonight from Brandon, but I think it might be better.

Beau Banks dried my tears and gave me my first kiss all in one night.

I'm a goner. Hook, line, and sinker. *And I'm going to marry that man someday.*

Chapter 6

I RUB AT THE CARTIER RING MY FATHER'S ASSISTANT SENT ME in the mail on his behalf for my high school graduation and yawn while my second cup of coffee gurgles in the fifteenth floor's break room Keurig.

Sleep for the last week has been…tricky. Between Avery coming home at all hours of the night and the intense awareness of Beau being nothing more than a wall away now that he's moved in next door to us, my circadian rhythm has been bouncing off the walls. I can't be sure, but I think it's gone from circadian to straight-up cicada. *The noisy little bastards.*

"Hey, Juni," Beau's smooth voice greets, startling me so hard I bang my knee against the cabinet in front of me, trying to stand up.

"Ow," I groan, grabbing at the joint and biting my lip so hard it almost pops. A million trashy words run through my mind as I try to subdue the blinding pain and embarrassment, but Beau does me the favor of saying one aloud.

"Fuck, June, are you okay?"

I nod manically to shake it off. "Oh yeah. Yeah, yeah. Totally fine."

"Are you sure? Let me see it," Beau insists, hunching over toward my black pencil skirt to take a look.

Hah. No. One touch from Beau on my bare leg and the only work I'll be doing today will be done remotely, from the clouds.

"I'm fine. Really." I tap his shoulder to stand him up again and smile through the burn. "Clumsy, but fine. I just didn't get as much sleep as I should have last night."

His barely there dimple sinks into his cheek as he leans his ass against the kitchenette counter and crosses his arms over his broad chest. "Avery have you out at the club again?"

"Nope." I shake my head, take my now coffee-filled mug from the Keurig, and try to concentrate on adding some sugar and cream to it. You'd think it'd be an easy task, but nothing is easy for me when Beau Banks is around. Not to mention, my knee still stings like a son of a bitch. "I was in bed early, just couldn't seem to fall asleep."

His brows draw together, forming a tiny wrinkle at the top of his straight nose. "Oh, man. I didn't hear anyone over there at all. I guess the walls are pretty soundproof."

He chuckles and I swallow hard. *It's hard to hear someone you don't even know exists half the time.* Funnily enough, I heard every freaking move he made. I swear, if I'd let myself listen any closer, I'd probably know his bladder's schedule.

I take a sip of my freshly made coffee and recoil immediately. *Good grief. How many freaking sugars did I put in this thing?*

"Still not a huge fan of coffee, huh?" Beau asks as I rub at my now-watering eyes.

"What?"

"During the Summer No-Sleepathon," he explains with the kind of handsome smile that has the power to make me lose brain cells. "Avery made you do it that time my parents were out of town when you were, what...fifteen?"

"Fourteen," I correct, the memory catapulting over me like an avalanche.

The summer after Avery's and my freshman year of high school, Neil and Diane went out of town. For the first time ever, instead of getting an official sitter, Beau was in charge of watching us since he was home from college. He had Bethany and Henry and Seth and some of his other friends over to surf and hang out, and Avery and I clung to the lot of them like a couple of groupies. For some reason, she got it in her head that we shouldn't sleep at all, so we wouldn't miss even a minute of our newfound independence. When things got really dire, she started force-feeding me coffee at a criminal pace.

Adult Juniper likes coffee just fine—enjoys it, actually—but letting Beau think I'm still coffee averse is way less embarrassing than admitting I'm so distracted by every freaking facet of his being that I can't even fix it right.

Instead of correcting him, I smile. "I had no idea adulthood would feel so similar to a no-sleep challenge from childhood."

"Yeah." Beau snorts. "Just wait a few years. I was up until almost one a.m. trying to figure out the inner workings of the Midnight app."

Sadly, I already knew this information. *I can literally hear him through my bedroom wall.* I'd say it's borderline stalker behavior, but it's hard to be a stalker from your own bedroom, you know? Like, I'm not actually trying to listen to him. At least, not *that* closely.

A small laugh escapes my lips—half embarrassed that I know too much and the fact that I think Beau's hilarious. *And smart. And sexy. And funny. And perfect.* Even though it's always a danger-ous move, I let myself meet the soft, warm, ooey, gooey choco-late-chip-cookie depths of his eyes. "I guess the older you get, the harder technology—"

"Beau," a voice calls from the door of the break room, robbing me of the opportunity to linger in his beautiful gaze and handsome smile *or* finish my sentence. His assistant Natalie is leaning around the doorjamb, urgency in her smile. "Golfate Capital is waiting on a call for you."

"Right," Beau says, shoving away from the counter and dis-missing himself with a wave. I watch as he leaves, long enough to study his firm ass until it's fully out the door, and then dump the truly offensive cup of coffee down the drain. I load the mug in the break room dishwasher, scoop up the file Neil gave me fifteen min-utes ago, and walk into the hallway. I have a million copies to make, and stopping for a cup of coffee wasn't supposed to take more than a minute or two.

I wasn't counting on getting caught in Beau's vortex of perfection, of course, but I can't say that I regret the time. Even when I'm a bumbling idiot in his presence, it's better than not being in his presence at all.

And yes, I'm fully aware of how pathetic I am.

I power past my cubicle, rubbing at my cheeks aggressively to rid them of the scorching-fire feeling that's settled beneath my skin. The adrenaline dump of five whole minutes alone with Beau has me wide awake, but my rosy face tells the tale of its price. *Maybe it's Maybelline? More like, maybe it's Beau.*

"Whoa, whoa, whoa!" Avery calls toward me, jogging to catch up with me as I move toward the hallway that leads to the copy room. "Where's the fire?" she says through a laugh. "There's no way in hell you're just going to walk past my desk and not say hello, friend."

"Ave, I live with you." A sigh escapes my lungs, but I keep walking. "I see you every day. Hell, we rode to work together this morning."

She falls into step beside me, our high heels making a muffled clip-clop on the carpeted hall. "Yeah, but it's been, like, three hours since then, and mama's got a hankering for some chips and queso. Let's go get lunch."

"No." I shake my head on a laugh as she shimmies her shoulders and shakes her long, dark hair excitedly.

"Please, June!" She holds both of her hands together as if she's going to start praying to Jesus right here in the middle of the office. "You know how all-consuming my food cravings get. I'll be thinking about chips and queso all freaking day! I won't be able to work."

"You won't be able to work if we're at lunch either," I retort. "And I'm too busy. I have to get your dad these copies, and then Seth wants me to be available as a runner for his team meeting in thirty minutes."

She snorts and rolls her eyes. "You act like that stuff is more important than chips and queso, and I know my best friend wouldn't *dare* be so blasphemous about our favorite snack."

I laugh. "Of course not. You know I'd drown myself in cheese dip if given a good opportunity, but Ave, I actually care about this job."

She wrinkles up her nose. "Are you serious?"

"Yes," I say, stopping slightly to shake her shoulder with my one free hand. "I know it's a foreign concept, but if I wanted an easy road, I would have just worked for my father."

"Ohhhh!" she exclaims with eyes dancing. "Maybe that's what we should do! We should quit this job and go work for your dad. He'd let us get away with anything, and we could swim in queso every day!"

"Avery, honey," I say, voice cajoling. "I'm going to go make these copies for your dad, okay?"

"Ugh. You're so boring." She blows out a breath. "What am I supposed to do now?"

I shrug. "Work?"

"Yuck! No thanks," she scoffs. "Oh! I know. I'll go get a spray tan. Want to come?"

"Nope," I call over my shoulder, purposely heading back on my path, down the hallway and toward the copy room. She flashes me the finger and then blows me a kiss before retreating back down the hall toward our cubicles, destination God knows where.

I scan my badge to get in the copy room door, sidle around Chris McKenzie's assistant Carla as she hole-punches and binds several pitch booklets, and get to work. I have twenty pages, front and back, that Neil needs several sets of for files. It's a little archaic, making copies of contracts when we're in the digital age of everything being online, but both Mr. Banks and Mr. McKenzie are old-school sticklers for keeping backup hard copies on file.

After power went down for the whole city last week and our internet was on the fritz for two hours while everyone panicked, I can see why. I mean, Florida isn't exactly known for consistently perfect weather. Hurricane season always brings uncertainty.

The machine whirs to life, and I scan the first page, setting the screen to spit out double-sided pages in sets of twenty.

"Sorry," I apologize to Carla, laughing when the rumble of the machine damn near vibrates the floor.

She rolls her eyes with a laugh. "No worries. That dinosaur might as well be friends with Chris Pratt, it's so old." She stacks her booklets and scoops them up, gesturing to me with their bulk. "I'm done anyway. The room is all yours."

"See ya," I say politely as she leaves the room. Everyone here has been truly friendly, and for that, I'm grateful. It's always scary starting something new, and this job, in particular, is something akin to jumping in open water with a bunch of sharks. Everyone is rabid, everyone is focused, and more than anything, everyone wants to win.

On the one hand, it's exhilarating. On the other, I spend half my time wondering if I'm truly cut out for it. I've never in my life been cutthroat or bold or pushy. Things I desperately need to learn to be if I'm going to succeed in the world of advertising.

The copier comes to a rest, and I ready the next sheet, placing it facedown on the glass top and closing the lid. I'm about to push the button and fire it up when a muffled voice on the other side of the wall pulls me up short.

"Oh, c'mon, Laura," a male voice croons, the edges of the sound blurry but the context clear. It's like something over a radio—if I strain hard enough, I can make out exactly what they're saying. "Just tell me what the plan is."

"You know I can't do that, Seth," she responds, and a few soft giggles follow. "I'm not on your team."

"You should've been on my team," Seth says, a flirtatious lilt that makes the hair at the back of my neck stand on end. I lean closer to the wall, my heartbeat freaking *thundering* in my chest. If I can't get it to calm down, I'm not going to be able to hear anything but the sound of blood whooshing around my body like it's on a racetrack.

Seth McKenzie and Laura Keller, a very important member of Beau's Midnight team, are talking in the conference room next door, and a very sinking feeling inside me says they shouldn't be. I mean, a little flirting is hardly international espionage—*though, Seth is engaged to Beau's ex-freaking-girlfriend, let's remember*—but it feels like it is. In fact, with everything that's on the line with the "friendly competition," it feels like the biggest freaking deal of my life.

"You wanted me on your team?" Laura asks, and when I can't hear Seth's response, I press my whole dang ear to the wall.

The words are still muffled, and I feel like I'm tiptoeing through a highly guarded museum in the middle of a heist. My breathing is shaky, and my stomach flips over with nerves. I glance over my shoulder, looking toward the still-closed door in the copy room and then press my ear back to the wall, forgoing any more intake of oxygen in an effort to hear.

"I'm on Beau's team, Seth," Laura says. "Not yours." I don't know her very well yet, but I'm starting to like her a little more. I know the pressure of having someone in Seth's position push you for information must be immense, but so far, she seems to be holding up. She is mighty. She is powerful. She is woman. *Or fucking something, I don't know. I'm freaking out.*

"We've already established that," he comments. "But what we haven't established is what the benefits would be if you gave me a little insight into where he's guiding his big campaign…"

"Are you trying to bribe me, Seth?"

Ohhh, shit. Body, mind, and soul, I am an actual piece of this stupid wall now. Tape and spackle and paint me over, I'm here to stay.

"Of course not." He chuckles. "Just trying to find something that's mutually beneficial for both of us."

"Sure." Laura laughs. "Find someone else to hound."

"What? So, that's how it's going to be?" Seth asks playfully, though I can perfectly imagine his crooked smile as he tries to save face. Just like with Bethany and Henry and all of Beau's other friends, because of my proximity to the Banks family, I've had more than enough occasion to be in his company over the years to learn some of the things that make him tick. He has a quick wit and a flashy smile, but if he's not getting his way, he's scheming to figure out a way around it.

Honestly, I don't know if even Beau noticed the narcissistic qualities of Seth's personality as soon as I did, but I understand. It's not exactly normal behavior to study people's words and expressions and moods as closely as I do. It's a by-product of trauma and missed connection and, in part, I'm sure, of feeling like my only option for emotional satisfaction was to watch Beau from a distance. *Very* intently.

"That's exactly how it is," Laura comments with finality. There's a muffled sound of shuffling and then the small creak of the conference room door opening and shutting. I quickly shove myself away from the wall and trip gracefully over my own foot.

"Ow, shit!" I whisper-yell, catching myself on the copy machine with an offensively loud bang. My heart gallops like a fence-breaking horse, and I snatch up the next paper in my stack as quickly as I can to get back to copying. *Bing, bing, bing,* my eyes flit to the door over and over, just waiting for Seth to come in and throttle me for listening in.

But when I finish the stack of work without Seth—let alone anyone—coming in and sniffing me out, I finally start to relax.

I'm fine. It's fine. Everything is fineeee. Laura turned Seth's treasonous offers down, and I don't have to worry about the next big fiasco in my undying love and devotion to Beau Banks.

It's all good, and I can and *should* go back to doing my job.

Emotionally settled, I take my neat little stack of copies and head for Neil's office. It's at the end of the hall, on the easternmost corner of the building with the best ocean view, of course, and as a matter of geography, I have to pass nearly everyone else's office on the way there.

Seth's blondish-brown hair and evil smile are unavoidably noticeable through Jay's glass wall, and my hackles start to rise again with great immediacy. Jay is on Beau's campaign team too, and while Seth pretends to practice his golf swing in front of Jay's desk, Jay laughs uproariously.

I slow my walk to a shuffle and crane my neck in a way I hope isn't too obvious, but I can't hear either of them well enough to make any headway before I'm well past the door.

I can't stop or linger—it'd be way too obvious.

But regardless of whether Jay caves or not, I've got the ominous, unshakable feeling that Seth won't stop until *someone* does. I've now witnessed him sidling up to two of Beau's team members with my own eyes and ears, and I can't be in more than one part of the office at a time. The building is big, fifteen floors in total, and I'm generally relegated to the top floor where Mr. Banks's and Mr. McKenzie's offices are located. Both Beau and Seth's offices are on this floor too, but the people on their teams are scattered throughout the various floors of the building.

What has he already done that I haven't managed to see?

What a freaking sneaky snake!

Heat licks my ears and my heart throbs as I drop the copies on Neil's empty desk and consider what in the hell to do next.

I'm not Sherlock Holmes. I'm not even Nancy fucking Drew! I don't know how to sleuth or investigate or keep tabs on someone's shady behavior at all. But I can't let this go unchecked.

Seth has the potential to ruin Beau's whole freaking campaign without him even knowing!

Gah. I cannot let that happen.

I sneak back to my cubicle and quickly use the Midnight app I just downloaded last night to get a code and scratch out a quick note to go with it. It's a long shot, I'm sure, but not even twenty minutes ago, Beau told me with his own luscious lips that he's been using the app to get acquainted with it.

And because of Midnight's anonymous features, I figure it's the safest way to go. I have to let Beau know, but the thought of trying to deliver the news in person makes my whole chest seize up tight. This app is the only way I can follow through.

As nonchalantly as I can manage, I sneak back down the hall and into Beau's currently empty office to leave a Post-it note on his computer.

Meet me at Midnight.
9 p.m.
Dream Code: 62814

The sooner he knows about Seth's conniving, the better.

Chapter 7

MY BEDROOM DOOR SLAMS OPEN WITH A BANG, THE sound ricocheting off my vaulted ceiling like a gunshot. A purple throw pillow from my bed and my worn copy of *Pride and Prejudice* hit the floor with soft thuds thanks to a frightened elbow spasm upon the violent entry, and I clutch my chest to slow my breathing as Avery barges straight toward me, her six-inch, pointy-toed black heels clacking on the white marble of our flooring.

"Holy hell, Avery!" I gasp. "You scared the shit out of me."

My phone sits beside me on the bed, Dream Code typed in and ready. *Thank everything, it wasn't the thing I sent plummeting toward the floor.* I think I'd actually expire if I got to nine o'clock and wasn't able to log on to see if Beau shows up because I broke my damn phone.

"Is that... Are you wearing *sweatpants*? And...a shawl?" Her face, covered by a full beat of beautiful makeup, twists in disgust. "By God, June, it's not even ten."

In contrast to my gremlin attire, she looks stunning in a body-hugging, cut-out-sporting black-and-gold dress that barely covers her nipples. It's designer, I'm sure, but to be totally honest, I don't know which one. I don't keep up with the trending items nearly as closely as she does.

"I know." A hearty sigh escapes my lungs. "But I didn't sleep well last night. Actually, I don't feel like I've slept well in a week or two. I'm exhausted."

It's not a lie per se. But it's not really the truth either. I could fly to China with just the flap of my arms with the adrenaline I have running through my body right now, despite not getting good shut-eye in ages.

I guess the possibility of clandestine meetings with the motherfreaking man of your dreams will do that to you.

Avery pouts. "Why didn't you tell me sooner? I have that Tradelopan the hot doctor who works at the sleep clinic gave me."

"Ha," I chuff. "Thanks, but no thanks. Taking rando medications from even more rando men isn't really my jive."

"Yeah, but if you would, then you wouldn't be tired, and I wouldn't have to deal with a lame-o friend bailing on TauTau with me."

TauTau is one of the newest nightclubs to hit the Miami party scene. And it's one of those exclusive clubs that you need to know someone to get in—aka, exactly Avery Banks's jam.

"You know…" I eye her knowingly and wrap the Prada wool-and-cashmere shawl my dad sent me three years ago for a birthday present—*he was too busy entertaining Lola on one of his yachts in Monaco to give it in person*—tighter around my shoulders. "Something tells me you'll recover by finding twenty other friends to fill my void."

"Well, duh." She rolls her eyes and puts a hand to her slim hip. "Like I'd wallow by myself? Puh-lease."

I laugh at her dramatics and brutal honesty. "I'm sorry. Truly. But you know the comfort of my bed is my true habitat anyway. Let me be content in my warm little nest."

"Whatever, loser. Don't wait up for me."

I snort. "Oh, trust me, honey. I won't."

"Ta-ta!" she says with a final blown kiss, walking out my door and slamming it behind her. I listen intently for reactionary movement on the other side of the wall—a wall I just figured out two nights ago butts up to Beau's bedroom. Not just his apartment—his freaking headboard, people!

Now that the coast is clear, I slide farther under my covers, grab my phone, and find the one and only chat I started in Midnight— *Dream code 62814*.

ElizaBeth has entered the chat appears on the screen when I open it up, announcing my arrival to…no one because I'm the only one in here. The name is cheesy—I know it is—but it's the absolute best I could come up with while I was sitting here earlier, paging through *Pride and Prejudice*. It's, hands down, my favorite book in the world and one I've read a hundred times. The biggest draw that always brings me back to its pages is *Elizabeth Bennet*. She's fearless and outspoken in ways I could only wish to be.

Mind you, the other username options were *DownComforterForLife* and *KillMeNow*, so really, I think we can all agree I settled on the best one.

When no one enters the chat a minute later, I start to self-combust. I thrash out of my shawl to reveal my plain white tank top as sweat drips down my back, and I throw my hair into a sloppy ponytail. Frantically, I swipe down on the upper right-hand corner of my phone to look at the time and see it's 8:59 p.m. Clearly, I'm a little early.

Freaking relax, Juniperrr.

I take a deep breath, settle into my green velvet headboard, and chew on the skin of my knuckle. I do okay for a little bit, but when the clock strikes 9:01 p.m., and then 9:05 p.m., I silently wonder if I turned myself into a ball of nerves for no reason at all.

What if he didn't even see the freaking note before he left the office? Or even worse, saw it and very sagely chose to ignore it?

I don't know why I thought this whole cloak-and-dagger thing was a good idea. I mean, I could have—

ThunderStruck has entered the chat, the notification pings, rolling a vibration through my thighs. My heart jumps into my throat at the sight, and I scoop up my phone so quickly it bobbles in my hands before I finally snag it steady. *Holy shit.*

I can't believe he picked that freaking AC/DC song he spent the entire summer before his senior year of high school playing on his electric guitar. It's a dropkick to my past obsession with that cute little rocker phase he went through, and my vagina convulses.

ThunderStruck: Hello?

Shaking fingers to the screen, I type out a response.

ElizaBeth: Hi.

My God, could I be any more blandly lacking in character? So ho-hum? So boring?

I am so nervous that nausea triggers a tingle in my throat. I don't know why I thought this was a good idea or why I thought I'd be able to handle it.

I finally have Beau, the boy I've loved for what feels like fifty lifetimes, all to myself in an anonymous chat, and words have tunneled through the freaking wall like Andy Dufresne to escape me.

ThunderStruck: Who is this?

I ponder all the facetious answers I could give if I weren't so cowardly. *The woman of your dreams. Your future wife. Your wildest fantasy. The future mother of your brown-eyed babies.*

Ha. Ha. Ha. My chest feels tight in a way I don't think it's supposed to at twenty-three. And I have no family history of heart disease or defects, so I'm guessing I need to calm down.

Just breathe, June. Keep it simple.

ElizaBeth: I can't tell you that.

The sounds of footsteps come from the other side of my wall—from Beau's condo—and my ears confirm that he's literally in his bedroom. Right now. While he's talking to me.

More footsteps move around his room, and instinct makes

me hold my breath. *Boom, boom, boom.* My heart pounds in my ears, but when a new message pops onto the screen, all the air leaves my lungs in a shaky whoosh as I read it.

ThunderStruck: Why not?

Why? Right. *Whyyyy can't I tell him who I am, other than that being the literal scariest thing I've ever heard of?* I shake my hands in the air and turn from side to side as though a reason is going to pop up on a magical holographic screen in the middle of my bedroom.

Maybe I should ask my dad for one of those for his next emotional buy-off gift? I mean, maybe we can work together to make my complete lack of familial fulfillment worthwhile for once.

ThunderStruck: Hello?

Right. Shit. There's a very real, very sexy human on the other side of my freaking bedroom wall waiting for answers. I've got to get myself together here.

Just type the first thing you think of and send it, I coach before silently laughing sardonically to myself. *Oh yeah. That's bound to go well.*

But as the seconds tick by along with the painful realization that he might disappear if I don't answer him, I quickly type out the most realistic answer I can think of.

ElizaBeth: Because I need to stay anonymous.

ThunderStruck: And why do you need to stay anonymous?

ElizaBeth: I overheard something at the office that I think you should know about.

ThunderStruck: ?

ElizaBeth: There's a cock sniffing around your henhouse.

> *ThunderStruck: Excuse me?*

My face flames with embarrassment when I realize how ridiculous what I sent sounds. *Cock in the henhouse? Really, June?* I *knew* being spontaneous was going to get out of control at some point. I need to just be blunt.

> *ElizaBeth: Someone is sniffing around your Midnight campaign.*
>
> *ThunderStruck: Oh, really? Let me guess…that someone's name starts with an S and rhymes with Beth.*
>
> *ElizaBeth: Bingo.*
>
> *ThunderStruck: He make any progress with the sniffing around?*
>
> *ElizaBeth: Not from what I overheard, but he's trying. Hard.*
>
> *ThunderStruck: And what did you overhear?*
>
> *ElizaBeth: I don't think I should get into that.*
>
> *ThunderStruck: Sounds exactly like what someone who just wants to stir up drama would say. In fact, maybe you are Beth with an S trying to set me up for self-sabotage by not trusting my team when I should. If this were really happening, why wouldn't they be telling me about it?*

Okay, that's…insane but plausible. Maybe I'm going to have to give a little more information than I thought.

> *ElizaBeth: Seth cornered Laura in the conference room and tried to flirt his way into a coalition. Her force field is strong. She refused. Later, I saw him in Jay's office, shooting the shit and pretending to practice his golf swing. Or maybe he was practicing since he absolutely flubbed*

*the company tournament last year, I don't know.
But he was swinging and they were laughing and
he looked particularly smarmy the whole time.*

A minute passes by before he responds. And I hold my breath the entire time. I even note footsteps moving farther away on the other side of the wall. They retreat so far that eventually, I don't hear them at all.

Shit. Is he going to leave the chat? Is he going to tell me fuck off? Is he—

*ThunderStruck: All right, I believe you're legit
now, based on your knowledge of how shitty
Seth golfs. And I believe you're not him, because
there's no way he'd ever admit that himself, even
if it was to take me down.*

Phew.

ElizaBeth: See? I know things.

ThunderStruck: What else do you know?

*ElizaBeth: Well...nothing, actually. But I'll keep
an eye out.*

*ThunderStruck: And who did you say you were
again?*

ElizaBeth: I didn't.

ThunderStruck: Maybe you should change that...

*ElizaBeth: Uh-uh. I've never heard a story of a
whistleblower who didn't disappear. Mysterious
car accident. Building explosion. High-speed
boat chase during a hurricane. I'm not risking it.*

*ThunderStruck: Haha. You're not dealing with
nuclear codes. You're dealing with ad marketing
campaigns. Surely there's no risk to your life
with this.*

> *ElizaBeth: You never know. Money and power are involved. Some people get desperate.*

> *ThunderStruck: But if you told me who you were, then I could protect you…*

Beau Banks protecting me? I picture him in a cute, regal uniform with a sword at his side and a cartoonishly big smile. Other people would look ridiculous, but he still looks good. *Too good.*

So good I consider stringing him along a little longer just so I can pretend.

"Snap out of it," I mutter to myself. "Now isn't the time to think with your tits. This is his career."

I shake my head and type out another message—one I can be morally proud of.

> *ElizaBeth: I'm good. Thanks.*

> *ThunderStruck: So, that's it?*

> *ElizaBeth: That's it. Goodnight, Beau.*

> *ThunderStruck: Goodnight, Mystery Whistleblower. Stay away from cars, buildings, and boats, okay?*

Is he…is he flirting? I swipe out of Midnight and burrow myself under my covers, my whole body shaking.

Maybe thinking with my tits isn't such a bad thing?

Chapter 8

"**W**HERE IN THE HELL HAVE YOU BEEN?" AVERY ASKS, peeking around the corner of the wall between our cubicles and startling me into a jolt.

Not only was she not at her desk when I walked by it a minute ago, she hasn't been in the office all morning. I've been running around like a headless Chicken Little to cover both our asses, so I would know. Her questioning my whereabouts is the height of irony. The Mount Everest of irony, really.

"Oh, I don't know," I say, my voice playfully jeering. "Taking notes for Mr. McKenzie in his call with Big Energy in London, running to Starbucks for the whole exec wing, toting spreadsheets for Tom in Accounting, running to the fourth floor for Carla with changes for Digital Marketing for the commercial that goes live next month for Langley, and sorting through *our* email box to see what needs to be done next." I've been hustling my little ass all morning, but the real travesty is that I've been so busy, I haven't had time to check in on Beau or ascertain if our messages last night are on his mind at all.

Avery just stands there, her work-averse mind refusing to digest the words that just left my lips.

"Where in the hell have *you* been for the last two hours?" I ask, and a secretive smile crests her lips.

"You know Luke from Copywriting?"

I shake my head, but my eyes are focused on the screen of my laptop, organizing emails into folders and assigning myself tasks in Asana, our company's work management platform. If I stopped what I was doing every time Avery showed up with a story, I'd end up getting the same amount of work accomplished as she does.

I'm not self-centered enough to think I'm vastly important to the operation of Banks & McKenzie as an intern, but I definitely take a chunk of busywork off everyone else's plates that would lower production at least a little.

"What?" Avery questions, rounding the thin wall and jumping up to sit on my desk. It's just *Pretty Woman*-toned enough to make me worry she's going to unzip her over-the-knee black Prada boot and start pulling out condoms. "You must be living under a rock if you don't know who the hottest guy in the company is!"

I snort. She would be horrified if she knew who I think the hottest guy in the company is.

"Anyway," she continues, immersed in her own story enough to carry the conversation herself. "I saw him in the elevator, after I ran to Starbucks to get a coffee, and let's just say, he's a really good kisser."

"Avery!" I chastise, dropping my voice to a whisper. "You do realize this is your father's company, right? You can't just run around kissing employees in the elevator."

"Oh, relax. I didn't kiss him in the elevator," she retorts. "I kissed him in his office on the eighth floor."

"So, let me get this straight," I say, leaning back in my chair to stare at her. "You stayed out late, woke up late, went to Starbucks, and then kissed Luke whatshisface in his office on the eighth floor, and I got Chris McKenzie's *Men in Black* face."

Avery covers her mouth and giggles. Because of Beau's friendship with Seth in college, I've known his father Chris much longer than any other intern would. I know the quirks of his attitude and what drives him nuts, and I know, when he's really angry, he looks like Vincent D'Onofrio in *Men in Black*. This morning, on the call with London, he was full-on alien.

Beau does a great impression when he's off the clock and you get a few beers in him, but the real thing is much scarier.

"I keep inviting you to join me. There are a lot of certified foxes on the eighth floor. We could have found one for you," she counters.

I roll my eyes. "Remind me again why you wanted this job."

"Because I love working with my best friend." She nudges me with her knee.

"It's funny when you say working... Is it a code word for something? A secret message? Please, help me understand."

"Okay, fine," she replies. "I love *hanging out* and *watching* my best friend work."

I laugh at that. "If I didn't love you so much, I'd probably hate you."

"It's part of my charm, you know? I'm irresistible." She winks. "Just ask Luke Harrington."

"You do realize that if your dad knew you were hooking up with his staff during office hours, he'd lose his shit, right?"

She shrugs. "He'd get over it."

"But would he?" I question, but her response is interrupted when the phone on my desk starts ringing. I shove Avery's hip out of the way so I can answer it, and she jumps down and waves goodbye with wiggly fingers. "Hello?" I say into the receiver as Avery heads off to do anything but actual work. Hell, I wouldn't be surprised if she comes back to my cubicle in an hour to tell me she let some hot dude in HR touch her tits.

"Juniper, it's Steve down at reception. You have a delivery."

My eyebrows knit together. "A delivery?"

"Yes. Do you want to come down and get it?"

"Uh...sure. Be down in a sec." I hang up the phone and stand up, and a quick crane of my neck shows Avery has Houdinied completely.

I'm not expecting a package. Butterflies dance in my stomach as I beat feet from my cubicle to the front of the floor, past the reception desk, and over to the elevator to call the cart.

The most pathetic part of me wonders if Beau figured out who I am from our chat last night and has decided to start a mystery romance. *It's not likely per se, but fairy tales are built on exceptions to the rule, aren't they?*

The elevator ride to reception is a balloon of wild thoughts. Somehow, I even manage to squeeze it through the doors without popping it when I get down to the lobby. Right in front of Steve sits a giant bouquet of pink roses, and my heart races, daydreams of a Beau and June love story sending it into overdrive.

"Are those for me?" I question tentatively, bringing Steve's head up from the desk at the sound of my voice.

He looks down at his notes and then back up at me. "Are you Juniper Perry?"

I nod and flash him my badge.

"Well, then, yes, these are for you," he says and leans down to pick up a white box wrapped with a Tiffany-blue bow from where it sits beside his computer screen. "And this too."

My hands pluck the note from the roses, my fingers shaking with anticipation. I open the tiny envelope and pull out the card, and instantly, my giant balloon of hope and daydreams and delusional Beau-filled fantasies deflates until it's a pathetic, shriveled-up piece of latex.

I recognize the handwriting painfully well—my father's assistant, Shirlene.

Juniper,
I still think you should come work for me.
Then I'd get to see you more.
Love and miss you so much, my darling girl,
Daddy

Ugh. Same old words, same old actions. Even if I worked for my dad, I'd still see him as much as I see him now—a big fat never. His and Lola's feet practically never touch the ground.

I don't even bother opening the box, already knowing it's probably some expensive bracelet or necklace from Tiffany's. From the outside, the stuff seems nice—that at least the thought counts. But that's only if the thought comes from the right person, and I know for a fact that this one came from Shirlene.

Almost all of them do. Well, except the ones that come from Carmen, my father's backup assistant when Shirlene is too busy with all of his day-to-day shit.

"Do you have a girlfriend, Steve?" I ask, my voice audibly scratchy. Swallowing tears always makes my throat raw.

"I'm married, actually."

"Perfect," I comment and slide the pink roses and Tiffany box back toward him. "I think you should take these gorgeous flowers and this box and give them to her when you get home tonight. Or, if you can, sneak away and surprise her with them."

His eyes go wide. "I don't... That's way too much. I can't take—"

"Please?" I plead. "You'd actually be doing me a favor."

"I'd be doing you a favor by taking these flowers and gift?"

"A huge one."

I don't want to see any more reminders of my father's make-believe. I don't want to face how naïve I was to hope it was anything else.

He searches my eyes for a long moment and then smiles, giving in with a nod. "She's gonna lose her mind."

I grin. "Good."

I leave before he has a chance to protest, staring down at the marble floor as I make the loneliest walk I've ever done back to the elevator. I rub at my forearms furiously, their position crossed over my stomach, and try valiantly not to cry. I don't know if anything will ever be the way I want it to be—with my father or Beau—and freaking hell, does reality sting.

The elevator dings its arrival, and I step on. But just as I do, Beau comes jogging toward me, one arm held high. "Hold the elevator!"

Nerves prick at my belly, and I almost let the doors slide closed, trying to avoid him entirely, but when he adds, "June!" I can't ignore him.

Beau strides on, and I slip into the far corner, trying to hide my somewhat obvious feelings from one of the most observant men on the planet.

"How's the day, Juniper June?" he asks, and I clear my throat before answering.

"Good. Busy, but good." I'm surprised but proud of how normal I actually sound.

"Good," he says, his eyes looking up to a small elevator screen that shows each floor as we pass. He turns to smile at me, and my knees wobble. "I stayed up way too late last night. I've been behind all damn day."

I suck my lips into my mouth, nod, and pray like hell he can't see that my whole body is vibrating with nerves.

The elevator dings.

"Have a good day, June," Beau says, striding off the cart without another word, and I follow after him, looking painfully like a dutiful puppy, thanks to our matching routes.

Beau stops at an office just across from my cubicle, catching Mary from Public Relations on her way out. I sit down and wake up my computer, but my ears have their own agenda.

"Have a good night last night, Mary?" Beau asks, making me smile. Even being as busy as he is, he always makes time to be personable with all the employees. I know he has at least two campaigns coming to a head this week, plus the Midnight prep and planning, and still, he's taking the time to stop and chitchat with Mary.

"I did," she replies, a sweet smile in her voice. "How about you, Beau?"

I open an email from Neil with a contract he needs copied and start to type out a reply. Still, my ears...they listen.

"It was good. Interesting, actually." He chuckles. "Unexpected, if you will." As he pauses, so do my fingers on the keyboard. "Did you do anything fun?"

"Just made Bill and me some dinner and watched a little TV."

"So, you didn't do any *Midnight* chatting?"

Oh my God. I pause mid-type, and my fingers hover over the keys. *Is he…trying to find out who the whistleblower is?*

Clicking print on Neil's contract as quickly as I can, I stand and make my way to the printer between Avery's and my cubicles. Hers is a little closer to their conversation, and along with the ears, the eyes are now involved.

"Oh no, honey," Mary says, patting him on the shoulder. "Bill and I are in bed by ten at the latest."

Beau smiles and dismisses himself, and I stretch my neck to watch as he walks down the hall toward his office. His head swings back and forth, peering in on coworkers as he goes, and my stomach does a backflip on itself.

Holy hell. I wonder if he's going to be questioning everyone all day about his Midnight Mystery Chatter.

I also wonder if I should be hurt that we already had alone time in the elevator and he showed absolutely no signs of suspecting it to be me.

No way. This is good. This is exciting. In fact, this is an opportunity.

What might I not be afraid to say if I were truly anonymous? What would it be like to be more *than me?*

Chapter 9

WITH BELLIES FULL OF MEXICAN FOOD FROM OUR favorite restaurant up the street from our condo, Avery and I walk through the lobby of our building and step onto the elevator.

She's busy texting with I-don't-even-know who, and I'm dreaming about crawling into my bed. It's not easy being a secret whistleblower—discreetly spying on Seth McKenzie's every move—and anonymously conversing with my lifelong crush, who just so happens to be my best friend's older brother, who also happens to be a man I now work with on a daily basis.

Trust me, *I know*. When I lay it all out there, it sounds batshit crazy.

"Once we get upstairs, you have exactly ten minutes to get your ass in gear," Avery says, taking a selfie of herself in the floor-to-ceiling mirror wall of the elevator.

"My ass in gear for what?" I scrunch up my nose. "Because if it's for anything but crawling into my big, cozy bed, I'm not doing it."

"Oh, get serious," she says through an amused snort, as if what I'm saying is the epitome of ridiculous. "You're not going to bed, Grandma June. You're coming to Allure with me. We already established this at dinner."

If I'm being honest, I didn't hear half the shit Avery said during dinner. Once she started telling me about some college football player she thinks I need to bang, I started tuning her out and just focused on keeping my exhausted eyes open long enough to eat my enchiladas.

The cart beeps as it rises and passes the floors below ours, and Avery slides her phone back into her purse and turns her attention back to me. "Come on, June. You can't freaking miss this," she says, a proverbial knife to my throat. "It's DJ Johnny! I'm begging you. Go in your room, put on something that shows your cooch, and come with me to Allure."

"Avery, I'm exhausted. I have cheese dip in my hair from falling asleep at dinner. I'm going to take a shower and go to bed early. Maybe, if you're lucky, I'll be rejuvenated for the weekend."

"But DJ Johnny won't be at Allure this weekend, and Bo Daniels will be back in Alabama to play football against other teams or something. You have to come tonight!"

Somehow, earlier today, after the kiss with Luke from Copywriting, she left work to check out some sale at Saks and ended up meeting part of the University of Alabama football team. Evidently, they played against the University of Miami this past weekend and then got stuck here when all the flights were grounded due to weather. She's convinced herself I need a boning from Bo Daniels to keep as a souvenir of his visit. I've got a different Beau on my mind, though, and as confusing as the names might sound, there's no confusion in the old hoochie-coochie whatsoever.

"Ave, I'm going to hold your hand while I say this, but no," I say just as the elevator dings its arrival on our floor.

"I swear, it's like you're trying to avoid men or something. You need to open your eyes, girl. The Miami dating pool is smokin', and there're plenty of fish in our hot-as-fuck sea." She sighs and steps forward to tap me on the vagina, and I crumple forward as she spins on her heels and heads out the now-open elevator doors. "Seriously. Is your beaver broken?"

"Avery!" I shout, following her into the hall, intent on cold-cocking her right back. But the hall isn't empty.

"Hey," Beau says, a giant smile on his face. "What's going on?"

His best friend Henry stands beside him, his eyes unabashedly scanning Avery. I don't know if he's actually interested or not, but her outfit is hard not to look at. I had to pull the gold mesh back over her nipples at least three times during dinner.

"June's being boring," Avery says matter-of-factly, smashing the elevator call button no fewer than fifteen times. Apparently, she's given up on talking me into going out—*thank everything*—and fully focused on getting her ass in the club.

"June? Boring?" Beau questions with a smile I want to kiss right off his lips as he runs a hand through his slightly sweaty hair before slipping a baseball cap over it.

Damn, he looks good in a hat. I'm talking, downright delectable.

I shrug and cross my arms over my chest to cover my suddenly excited nips. This tank top is a lot more sheer than I remember. "Guilty."

"Beau's boring too," Henry teases with a big grin. Out of all of Beau's closest friends, Henry is the biggest player and the wildest of the bunch. He's an adrenaline junkie from way back—which is probably why his company is called exactly that. And truth be told, I don't think I've ever seen him leave a club or bar without a random girl on his arm. Which makes sense. He has a James Dean kind of bad-boy dangerous vibe to him. Women flock his way almost as much as they flock to Beau.

"We just ran six miles. I'm fucking tired," Beau retorts. "There's a difference."

Henry ignores him and smiles at my best friend. "The bastard said he'd rather *shower and lie low* than go out because he *has to get to the office early tomorrow.*" His voice is mocking, and Avery's face is delighted.

"Beau and June, sitting in a tree," she sings, "L-A-M-E-O-L-D!"

Beau guffaws. "Lame old?"

Avery nods, high-fiving Henry as he holds up a hand for her

to smack. "Yep. She's lame. You're old." The elevator dings. "And I'm outta here."

Henry blocks the doors from closing. "Where you heading, Avery?"

"Allure."

"Funnily enough, that's exactly where I'm heading too." He flashes a wink over his shoulder as he steps onto the elevator with her. "Later," he says to both Beau and me.

"Henry, are you flirting with me?" Avery questions with a hand to her hip, and he just laughs.

"Avery, honey, you're not really my style."

"Excuse me?" A scoff escapes her lungs. "I'm everyone's style."

Beau and I stand there together as the doors close in front of them, blocking out their flirty but harmless banter that I've witnessed a hundred times, and an awkward silence envelops us as soon as they're on their way.

He shakes his black T-shirt away from his body. "Well...I'm gonna head in to shower. Six miles is a lot harder than it used to be."

I snort. "Yeah, well, it's about five point nine miles more than I can do, so good for you."

Beau's smile settles into his almost-dimple, and I settle myself deep inside it in turn. He really is the sexiest man alive. Hot, sweaty, casual, dressy, or anything in between—he's freaking perfect.

"Night, neighbor."

I push into our door and meet his eyes one final time. I feel the brown all the way to the bottom of my soul. "Night."

Padding softly, I grab a bottle of water from the refrigerator and head for my room, turning the lights off as I go. I climb into my bed and get under the covers, leaning back into my headboard and pervishly waiting for the sound of Beau's shower to start. It may not be Avery's wild time with an Alabama football player, but my little hoochie-coochie will get double the enjoyment out of fantasizing about the man next door with the auditory evidence of his nakedness as a soundtrack.

I close my eyes, ready to wait, but a ping notification from my phone goes off in the silence instead, scaring the living crap out of me. I snag my phone from its spot on the bed and claw my way to sitting straight.

New Message from ThunderStruck sits front and center on the screen.

Beau is messaging me? Holy shit!

When my phone chimes again with the same little chirpy sound and **New Message from ThunderStruck** pops up on the screen for a second time, I almost jump all the way to my ceiling.

Beau is messaging me!

With shaky fingers, I fight to slip my phone over and switch off the ringer on the off chance that he pays attention to my side of the wall and gets suspicious, and I ready myself to read what he has to say.

Two deep breaths, in and out, in and out. *Fuck, I'm nervous.*

My heart threatens to burrow into my throat at the thought of Beau sitting just on the other side of my wall, but I swallow hard against it and force myself to open Midnight.

ThunderStruck: I need to know. Who are you?

ThunderStruck: Seriously. It's driving me crazy.

I let out a deep exhale of air, thankful that he hasn't suddenly figured out who I am. Clearly, his interrogation of half the staff this morning didn't give him any leads, and as much as the naïve part of me wishes it were obvious it's me, the realistic part knows this is way better. I'm not...forward. I'm not bold. I don't take what I want and ask questions later like Avery does, and I don't even know how to start.

Beau sees me like he does for many reasons—way more than being his five-years-younger-sister's best friend. I've never in my life pushed the envelope when it comes to him, despite feeling like I should nearly every damn day.

Maybe this…maybe being anonymous is my shot to try it. Maybe tonight, I shouldn't cut the messaging off at the knees before it has a chance to get interesting.

I mean, this is my shot. A chance to lay it all out there and see if we'd actually be a good match. If we're not, maybe then I'll be able to put this lifelong crush behind me.

Determined to see where this goes, I type out a response.

> **ElizaBeth: Driving you crazy? That doesn't sound good.**
>
> **ThunderStruck: Exactly. It's not good. Dangerous, even.**
>
> **ElizaBeth: Dangerous? Should I call Crime Stoppers?**
>
> **ThunderStruck: C'mon, just tell me.**
>
> **ElizaBeth: I can't.**
>
> **ThunderStruck: How about you just tell me your first name?**
>
> **ElizaBeth: Nope.**
>
> **ThunderStruck: Your initials.**
>
> **ElizaBeth: Come on. You know that would make it too easy to figure out who I am.**
>
> **ThunderStruck: The company has hundreds of employees. It wouldn't be THAT easy.**
>
> **ElizaBeth: We both know it'd only take a quick search through the Human Resources database to narrow down the options. And we also both know that since you're Neil Banks's son, you could easily get Cheryl to help you.**
>
> **ThunderStruck: Are you Cheryl?**

ElizaBeth: I don't know. Does this seem like something Cheryl would do?

ThunderStruck: No. I guess not. Not likely for anyone in Human Resources at all to be messaging secretly.

ThunderStruck: Or maybe it IS LIKELY? And that's why you're trying to keep this all hush-hush?

ElizaBeth: If I WERE in human resources, would I have to be a resource for humans? Because I'm not sure that's me.

ThunderStruck: Fucking hell.

ElizaBeth: LOL.

ThunderStruck: If you were on your way into work and you had the option to stop for Starbucks and be late or skip the Starbucks and be on time, which would you do?

I snort to myself, knowing full well he's currently wondering if his own sister is fucking with him. It's an option I'm quick to dispel since flirting is my end goal. His thinking it's Avery would really get things weird fast.

ElizaBeth: I'd be on time.

ThunderStruck: Okay. Are you the type of person who goes to church every Sunday but listens to death metal music while you're working on spreadsheets?

ElizaBeth: Excel isn't a strength. I Google shortcuts every time I have to use it, but death metal has its moments.

ThunderStruck: When's the last time you shared a recipe on Facebook, and what crockpot meal was it for?

ElizaBeth: LOL. Not a single time in my life, and I don't own a crockpot. I should probably get one, tho. I hear they're nice. Also, are these actual things our coworkers have done? Or are you pulling shit out of thin air?

ThunderStruck: I'm not at liberty to say.

ElizaBeth: Oh my God. Now I'm scared.

ThunderStruck: Have you ever left a one-star review on Amazon for a pair of toenail clippers because you didn't feel like they cut smooth enough?

ElizaBeth: Oh, sweet Jesus. I do not want to know who this is about.

ThunderStruck: Dean Marks from Accounting.

ElizaBeth: I said I didn't want to know!

ThunderStruck: And I said I wanted to know who you are. Maybe if you tell me now, I won't have to tell you about Donny Lewis in Public Relations.

ElizaBeth: What if I am Donny Lewis?

ThunderStruck: Then you're a bit of a closet freak with a balloon fetish.

ElizaBeth: BALLOON FETISH? WHAT DOES THAT EVEN MEAN?

ThunderStruck: Haha, I guess we can cross Donny off the list.

ElizaBeth: You're cruel.

ThunderStruck: So are you.

ElizaBeth: Does it help if I confirm that I'm a woman?

ThunderStruck: It definitely helps me feel a little better about spending my late nights talking to you, at least.

ElizaBeth: Late nightS? As in, you're planning on more?

ThunderStruck: I guess I'll have to if you really won't tell me who you are.

My stomach dances. The excited crush-holder inside me wants to keep this conversation going forever, but the emboldened woman behind the keyboard knows better. Anticipation makes the heart grow fonder, and if I want Beau fond of me, I need to drag this out as long as possible.

ElizaBeth: Goodnight, Beau. Thanks for the nightmares.

ThunderStruck: Goodnight, Mystery Woman.

Despite my better judgment, I sent him one final message.

ElizaBeth: Goodnight but not goodbye?

ThunderStruck: There'll be more Midnight chats. I'll make sure of it.

His words probably shouldn't make me feel so damn happy, but they do. *Sigh.*

Chapter 10

TWO NIGHTS AGO, BEAU MESSAGED ME ON MIDNIGHT, AND I haven't stopped thinking about what our babies will look like since.

For the last forty-eight hours, I've checked the chat every hour on the hour, hoping for another message from him, and so far, nada.

There'll be more Midnight chats. I'll make sure of it, I mock in my head, chastising the pathetic girl who clung to those words like gospel.

"Earth to Juniper," Denise, Mr. Banks's assistant, says teasingly, her bright blond head shining in the fluorescent light coming from above my cubicle. I shove back from my computer, where I've been pretending to look at emails for the last hour and a half, and smile.

"Sorry, Denise. I'm a little zoned out today."

She waves her hand. "Forget it. We're all in the clouds today. It's Thursday, which is almost Friday, and all the horses can smell the weekend barn."

I laugh. "What did you need?"

"Neil is going to need twenty copies of these packets for his three o'clock meeting with the Public Relations team. I have to run over to the lawyer's office and pick up lunch on the way back, so would you mind?"

I blink myself out of my Beau-induced stupor and take the

packet from her outstretched hand. "Uh, yeah. Of course. Sure thing."

"Thanks, honey," she says and offers a little tap to the top of the cubicle wall before heading back toward her desk.

As she retreats, I stand, smoothing the wrinkles from my black pencil skirt as I do, and force my legs to un-numb. I've been sitting here daydreaming so long, I can almost feel myself morphing into Avery.

As I'm on my way to the copy room, my phone vibrates with a message, and my traitorous little bitch of a heart puts her whole savings account into its stock.

The thrill and rush I get from the possibility of chatting more with Beau should send me running straight to a therapist, but all it's done is make me want *more*. Every message, every Asana ping, every Teams meeting chime, every email—I'm a woman deranged.

I want all I can get, even if it's crumbs. After you've crushed on a man for most of your life, you find yourself happy with whatever hangs out at the bottom of a ten-year-old toaster.

But it's not Beau. It's a text from Avery.

> Avery: Want to get sushi for lunch?
>
> Me: I already ate lunch.
>
> Avery: You bitch! You didn't even offer to bring me anything back!
>
> Me: I ate at my desk.
>
> Avery: Ate at your desk? What the hell did you eat? A stapler?
>
> Me: I told you this morning I was going to pack a lunch.
>
> Avery: I thought you were joking, Juni!
>
> Me: Why would I joke about something like that?

> Avery: Because it makes you sound like you live in, like, a third-world country.

> Me: Do you even know what a third-world country is?

> Avery: Of course I do. Remember when my dad made us go to the ranch in Montana?

> Me: Avery, Montana isn't a country. It's a state in OUR country.

When she doesn't answer, fear that I just made her brain explode urges me to send another text.

> Me: You okay?

> Avery: Yeah. I just get bored when you start talking about geometry.

> Me: Geography, sweetie. GEOGRAPHY.

> Avery: Whatevs.

> Me: Where are you?

> Avery: In the supply closet.

The supply closet on our floor is Avery's go-to place whenever she's nice enough to grace us with her presence at the office. Two days ago, I caught the sneaky bitch napping in it.

> Me: Okay, well, you have fun in there. I'm going to keep working.

> Avery: You think I can get DoorDash delivered in here?

I ignore her message completely and swipe my badge to enter the copy room door, my gaze lingering on Seth McKenzie's slimy smile as he walks down the hall with his fiancée Bethany attached to his arm.

I was so sure she was pregnant when she and Seth got engaged so quickly after she ended things with Beau, but I've yet to see her trim waist expand enough to fit a piece of bread, much less a baby.

But she *is* currently planning a wedding to Beau's now ex-best friend—whom I now know she was sleeping with behind Beau's back—and shows up at the office more than Avery does at this point.

If I hadn't already hated her for being with the man I love for so long, I'd hate her by proxy. Beau got the freaking shaft from those two, and still, he never takes anything but the high road.

I let the copy room door fall closed behind me and imagine it smashing Bethany's head as it disappears in an optical illusion.

It isn't nice, but it does make me smile, and by the time I finish all twenty copies, organize them, and slide them into the little folders Mr. Banks prefers, I'm in a pretty good mood.

In my head, Bethany's corpse lies beyond the copy room door, mangled and bloody, her two fake boobs popped and deflated.

Unfortunately, upon exit, I find her kissing Seth instead of KO'ed, her departure to the elevators following shortly after. Seth heads in the direction of his office but stops at Madeline Till's door instead, and my hackles rise immediately.

Madeline Till is on Beau's Midnight team.

Is there more intel to be had? If there is, I'd have a reason to message Beau instead of having to wait for him.

Yes. I know. I'm pathetic.

Pointedly ignoring all the reasons I shouldn't even consider spying, I discreetly walk toward Madeline's office—where Seth is currently sitting down and chatting with her—and peek inside as I move by. Through her glass door, I see Seth's mouth moving as a cocky smile crests his lips and Madeline looking down at her desk, her cheeks aflame and her eyelashes batting like a hummingbird's wing.

Be cool, June. Act busy, but do it in eavesdropping vicinity.

As luck would have it, the water cooler is directly outside her door, so I stop at it and bend down gently, filling a cup for my very thirty thirstiness. I drink slowly but realistically, which unfortunately means I'm an entire cup in by the time Seth actually says anything of interest. Madeline's Italian summer getaway plans? Fun but insignificant. Seth's last trip to Naples? Vapid and unimportant. But this…this is big stuff.

"Maybe some people will find themselves on Italian adventures, thanks to the Midnight app," Seth segues like the sneaky snake he is. "How's it coming along for you, by the way? Getting the hang of it?"

I pour a second cup of water and start chugging, despite the bloat in my stomach.

"Oh yeah. It's pretty straightforward. And Beau's been doing a great job of debriefing with us every day if we have any questions."

"You know, I was pissed when you weren't on my team. I thought we would have worked really well together."

"You were?" she asks, her voice not even close to hiding her satisfaction over the complete lie of a compliment. It's the same fucking line he used on Laura, but she doesn't know that. I wish there were a way to tell her—a smoke signal, a carrier pigeon, freaking something. As it is, even standing here pounding water at this point is at tenuous risk of breaking the fourth wall.

"Madeline," he says, and I flit my eyes up and into the office like scanning laser beams. "You're one of the most talented ad execs here. Of course I wanted you on my team."

The woman actually blushes. It's a shame he's so freaking handsome. It gives way too much credibility to his bullshit.

"Did you eat lunch yet?" he asks. "I haven't had a chance, and I was thinking about heading to that sushi restaurant up the street. You want to go?"

"I don't know, Seth," she says, her voice hesitant. "I don't know if…"

"C'mon, Madeline," he cajoles. "I'd love to pick your brain over how you came up with that brilliant ad campaign for Carmen Love's perfume line. I obsessed over it for weeks."

Damn, he's good. Slimy, but good.

"Um… You doing okay, Juniper?" someone asks from directly behind me, startling the paper cup of water out of my hand. The damn thing plummets to the floor and sprays liquid all over Mr. Banks's shoes and pants from the ankle down.

"I'm so sorry. You scared me," I say in a rush, bending down to pick up the water, but dropping half the packets in my hands to the floor as I do.

Mr. Banks bends down to help me, but I try to shoo him away with shaking hands. "I've got it, Mr. Banks."

He ignores me completely, though, managing to grab five of the packets and hand them to me as we both stand back up.

"Thanks."

"No problem, June," he says, concern creasing his normally plump cheeks. "Are you feeling sick today?"

"No." I shake my head. "Why?"

"You've been standing here drinking water for a while. Normally, you're on the move."

"Oh!" My laugh is loud and awkward and completely weird. I pretend it isn't. "I managed a quick workout at lunch."

His chin jerks. I've never, in all the years the man has known me, done an actual workout that wasn't for the greater purpose of an activity. Paddleboarding? Yes. Swimming? Yes. Gym-ratting on my lunch hour? Not a freaking chance.

"Not an actual *workout* workout," I hedge, swallowing hard around the bulge of lies. "But I ran up and down the stairs shuffling files back and forth, and in heels like these, it's, like, an extra challenge, you know? Really gets those calf muscles burning."

He eyes me curiously, so I give his shoulder an awkward pat.

"All good in the marketing hood, Mr. Banks," I say as I adjust the packets in my arms, bulldozing right over his open-jawed preparation to talk by chattering on. "You need me to do anything else for you before your meeting at three?"

He shakes his head, but it's slow and his eyes are still searching my face like he's trying to figure out if I'm in the middle of a psychotic break. And I kind of am, so good for him for being so on the nose.

Immediately, I spin on my heel, just as Seth and Madeline are walking out of her office and heading for the elevators, and I offer a little wave to Mr. Banks as I do. "See you later, boss! I'll leave these in your office." I gesture with the folders of copies and smile. I know I must look scary, but I don't acknowledge it.

Instead, I head directly for Mr. Banks's office, drop off the packets on Denise's desk, and then make a detour to Beau's office next door. He's not inside, thank God, so I snag a Post-it from his drawer and scribble out a note as fast as I can.

My message is simple.

Meet me at Midnight. 9 p.m.
-Mystery Woman
PS: Don't bring any balloons.

Chapter 11

THE TIME ON MY PHONE SWITCHES FROM 8:59 TO 9:00 P.M., and I pull open Midnight. My heart races with excitement as I put in the Dream Code and open the chat, **ElizaBeth has reentered the chat** appearing in the little box.

My knee bounces against the surface of my bed, ruffling my comforter and making my headboard shake just slightly. For literally every other venture in life, Beau is early, but for our chats, he's always late.

Which is a universal joke meant to torture me, I assume.

"What are you doing?" Avery asks, entering my room so dramatically the door slams into the wall and makes my teeth chatter.

I bobble my phone in my hands, dropping it onto my comforter before snatching it right back up to keep it safe. "My God, Avery. Knock much?"

Avery's brows draw together. "Like I've ever knocked on your door in my life." She chuffs. "Anyway, I just came in to see what time you want to leave."

It's then that I realize she is dressed to the nines in a sparkly silver top I'm almost positive is Chanel Couture, leather Givenchy pants, and yet another pair of Louboutin heels she runs through like water.

She's the rich Miami girl personified, and unlike me, she lives for it.

"Leave for what?"

She rolls her eyes. "For Oceanview, duh. You promised we could go tonight."

Oceanview is Avery's favorite club in downtown Miami and one we've frequented on more than a hundred occasions. Back in college, I was a lot easier to drag along, and Avery talked her way to a C in every class enough to keep her dad off her back, so we were considered regulars in every way you can imagine.

We did have a conversation earlier today in which I promised to go to Oceanview on Saturday, but seeing as today is still Thursday, this is Avery's version of trying to pull a fast one.

"I promised we would go Saturday night. Today is Thursday."

"Are you sure today isn't Saturday?"

I roll my eyes. "Pretty sure, considering we had work today and the calendar says Thursday."

"Okay, but, like, I'm ready now, so why don't we just go?"

I shake my head and laugh. "No way, José. I'm already ready for bed."

"For *bed*? Please, June, you're just making my argument stronger. I mean, really, this is a cry for help."

"I'm not going out tonight." My phone vibrates in my hand, and **ThunderStruck has reentered the chat** populates on the screen.

Holy shit. He's back.

Immediately, I can feel my pulse thrumming at the base of my neck. It takes everything I have not to stare at the phone while Avery is still in the room, and I'm nowhere near strong enough to resist a glance or two.

When he still hasn't said anything fifteen seconds later, I start to wonder if I should be the one to break the ice since I *am* the one who left the note to meet me here.

"Are you listening to anything I'm saying?" Avery asks frustratedly, yanking my attention back to my door.

"Yeah."

"Then what did I just say?" Her stance is defiant and challenging, and I search my mind for any remnant of her words. When I can't find any, guilt niggles. I'm completely ignoring my best friend in favor of my secret boner for her brother—*if this isn't the whole reason for every tête-à-tête for this particular trope, I don't know what is.*

Still, I don't want to go out, and I really need her to leave. I try to nudge her in that direction as gently as possible.

"I'm really sorry I wasn't listening, Ave. Really. I'm just tired and distracted and *seriously* not in the mood to go out. But we'll catch up soon. A whole convo, margs, club crawl, and pajamas and takeout at five a.m. kind of night, I promise. Okay?"

"God, June," she huffs, even stomping her stiletto-covered foot. "We're young. We're supposed to be going out, living life, getting guys to cover our tabs, and dancing our assess off. What we shouldn't be doing is sitting home on a Thursday night like some kind of single mom who works two jobs."

"Does she love her kids? Does she never stop?"

"What?"

"Nothing." *Just Reba.*

Avery narrows her eyes and charges toward me, plopping down onto my bed and making my heart rate soar right past fat-burning mode and straight to max capacity. At the same time, my phone vibrates in my hands, and I clutch it as tight to my lap as I can manage without drawing her attention.

I don't know what the message says, but now, thanks to my bedmate, I'm going to have to wait.

"C'mon, June." She reaches out to pat my sweatpants-covered thigh. "Just get up, get dressed, and come out with me."

"Sorry, Avery, but I'm staying in tonight."

She flashes her famous sad eyes at me, the same desperate eyes she gives her dad whenever she wants him to add an increase to her already-large monthly allowance. "Please?"

I shake my head.

"June!" she cries again, snatching my phone from my claws and waving it in the air. My lungs seize and my heart drops, my wide eyes bouncing back and forth as she waves my phone dramatically. "What are you even doing, by the way? Spending all night on your phone?" She shakes her head. "You know, I read a study about how bad it is to be addicted to technology. You should really do something about it."

"A study?" I question harshly, reaching for my phone and jerking it out of her grasp.

She rolls her eyes. "Fine. A TikTok. Same difference. I mean, look at you. You're practically salivating."

The phone vibrates in my hand again, and I clench my jaw. I cannot look. Will not look. Not until she's gone.

"I'm just…" I search for an explanation quickly, worry building over how long Beau will stay in the chat if I don't respond soon. The first thing that comes to mind is work, and I run with it. Thanks to her hands-off office disposition, she won't know what I'm talking about anyway. "I'm just looking through some spreadsheets your dad's assistant wanted me to double-check."

"Spreadsheets for what?"

Of all the fucking times for Avery to give a single shit about the work we both should be doing but I always end up doing alone… You've got to be kidding me!

"Spreadsheets for…" I rack my brain for a fruit salad of words that will give her a headache. "Quantum physics campaigns that showcase how the age of digital marketing has shown significant advancements over the course of the past decade and how the steady—"

"Oh my God, shut up," she cuts me off and hops off my bed. "Whatever you just said sounds contagious, and I don't have time to come down with the nerd gene."

"Have fun," I tell her, my fingers already hovering over the screen of my phone, ready to respond to Beau the instant she steps out of my room.

"I'd tell you the same, but I think we both know that's impossible with your plans," she calls over her shoulder at my door. "Text me if you shape-shift into someone fun!" A minute later, I hear her grab her keys and purse, and the door closes on a click.

Thank everything! My sigh of relief is audible as I unclutch the phone from my chest and finally read the messages that are waiting for me.

> **ThunderStruck: Hello, Mystery Woman.**
>
> **ThunderStruck: You there?**

I put my fingers to the screen and respond as fast as I can.

> **ElizaBeth: I'm here.**

His response comes ten seconds later.

> **ThunderStruck: I thought maybe you weren't going to show.**
>
> **ElizaBeth: Sorry about that. I was a little preoccupied, but yeah…I'm here.**
>
> **ThunderStruck: Anything interesting doing the preoccupying?**
>
> **ElizaBeth: If I told you, I'd no longer be the Mystery Woman.**
>
> **ThunderStruck: Then who would you be?**
>
> **ElizaBeth: I see what you did there. Nice try.**
>
> **ThunderStruck: I don't know if you know this about me, but I'm a pretty determined kind of guy. When I want something, I usually don't stop until I get it.**

I don't think his words are meant to be sexual, but man, do they spur some fantasies inside my head. What would it be like if Beau Banks wanted *me*?

> **ElizaBeth: I'm fully aware of what kind of guy you are, Beau.**

ThunderStruck: Oh yeah?

ElizaBeth: Yeah.

ThunderStruck: How?

ElizaBeth: I have my ways.

Ways. I nearly snort. I've been watching Beau Banks like a creeper for more than half my life. I know everything there is to know about him that doesn't happen behind closed doors or inside the zipper of his pants.

I am, of course, eager to fill in the gaps in my education posthaste.

ThunderStruck: Are you trying to tease me, ElizaBeth?

ElizaBeth: Is it making you mad?

ThunderStruck: Honestly? I'm not sure what it's making me other than hard.

I sit up so quickly, I choke on saliva. It's a Herculean effort, but somehow, I manage to almost die silently.

ThunderStruck: Sorry. That was unbelievably inappropriate. But this is the third time you've convinced me to come into this chat, and if that's not a sign that I'm thinking with my dick, I don't know what is.

ElizaBeth: Technically, I've only convinced you twice. One of those times, you convinced me.

ThunderStruck: I guess you got me there.

Through the wall, I hear footsteps. They move closer and closer before ending right at the wall. Best guess? Beau is now in bed.

Good grief, this is all so insane. And so wrong for a million different reasons.

But I can't stop. Don't want to stop.

> **ThunderStruck: How old are you, Mystery Woman?**

I don't know why, but having Beau Banks call me Mystery Woman instead of Mystery Girl makes me feel some kind of way. It's the dream, really. Being seen as grown-ass June instead of Avery's little best friend Juniper.

> **ElizaBeth: How old do you think I am?**

> **ThunderStruck: Does it matter what I say if I know you're not going to confirm it?**

> **ElizaBeth: How can I be a Mystery Woman if I confirm things? That wouldn't be very demure or cutesy of me.**

> **ThunderStruck: Well, sure. Being secretive is very demure AND cutesy. But it's also incredibly difficult to read.**

> **ElizaBeth: Ah, the beauty of Midnight...**

> **ThunderStruck: Marcus Hughes would certainly love the plug.**

> **ElizaBeth: Well, we are in his app after all.**

> **ThunderStruck: Is there a reason you wanted me to come on here tonight?**

> **ElizaBeth: I have some new intel.**

Not to mention how disappointing it was to go two whole days without hearing from him. I have a feeling I'd have come up with a reason to make this happen tonight whether I'd overheard Seth and Madeline or not.

> **ThunderStruck: About Beth with an S?**

> **ElizaBeth: Uh-huh.**

ThunderStruck: I'll be honest, I'm not even sure if I want to hear it.

ElizaBeth: Oh. Really? Because I think you do.

ThunderStruck: I just don't know that it's gaining me more than it's costing me.

ElizaBeth: What's it costing you exactly?

ThunderStruck: My morals, I guess.

ElizaBeth: You could give me something in return if that's your concern.

Your lips on mine. Your hands on my skin. Your body on mine. You inside me. Over and over again. My cheeks heat with embarrassment when I realize how rogue my thoughts have just gone. I have no shame. I have no control. I am an animal.

ThunderStruck: I was thinking more in terms of the behind-the-back thing, but I guess I should give you something too, to make it a fair exchange. What do you want?

ElizaBeth: I'm not sure... What are my options?

ThunderStruck: You want multiple choice?

ElizaBeth: It's always the easiest part of the test.

ThunderStruck: All right. A. I take you out to dinner. B. I take you out to dinner. C. I take you out to dinner.

ElizaBeth: D. None of the above.

ThunderStruck: A nice dinner.

ElizaBeth: You and I both know I need to keep my spy status on the DL. Dinner would mean showing my face.

ThunderStruck: But what if I want to see your face?

ElizaBeth: Sorry, Beau, but that's not an option.

ThunderStruck: I think it should be. I want to meet my Midnight Mystery Woman.

His Midnight Mystery Woman. Sigh.

If only he knew who I was and this were real.

It's a sad thought and one that spurs me to tell him what I know instead of prolonging this conversation that's twisting my heart up into a hundred tiny knots.

It's making me feel hopeful this could be more than an exchange of work intel, and I'm not so sure that's a good thing.

ElizaBeth: Seth convinced Madeline to have a late lunch with him this afternoon after a lot of sweet talking. It was the same ol' song and dance routine he used with Laura, but this time, it worked. I don't know if he got anywhere at lunch, as they did not invite me to attend a meal, as you so graciously just did.

ThunderStruck: The gracious offer is still there.

ElizaBeth: And I wish I could take it. But I can't. Goodnight, Beau.

ThunderStruck: Wait... That's it?

ElizaBeth: Yep. That's it. I need to get to bed. You know, to work in the morning.

ThunderStruck: You think we should accidentally meet in the break room? Say around 9:30 a.m.?

ElizaBeth: LOL. No, I do not.

ThunderStruck: Still worried about your whistleblower status?

More like, worried about you realizing that your Mystery Woman isn't a mystery at all. And downright terrified over what your reaction would be if you found out.

ElizaBeth: Something like that. Night, Beau.

ThunderStruck: Sleep well, Mystery Woman.

In my dreams, Mystery Woman is replaced by June, and Beau doesn't just tell me to sleep well tonight, but *every* night.

Too bad my dreams have never been much of a glimpse into the future. If they had, Beau and I would have been together a long time ago.

PART 2

Beau

Chapter 12

EVERY WEEK, I HAVE A CHECK-IN MEETING WITH MY TEAM to discuss the various accounts we're running. But as of a few weeks ago when the Midnight campaign was added to our already overfilled plate, all things Hughes International have become our biggest priority.

And today's meeting showcases that tenfold. It's all we've been discussing since we stepped through the conference room door.

"How are the mock slides coming along, Jay?" I ask, directing my attention to him.

"Good." He nods, looking down at the screen of his laptop as his fingers quickly scroll through whatever is on the screen. "I got confirmation from Ned in Content, and he anticipates rough first drafts will be ready by end of week."

"Did you manage to get him the font changes we decided on yesterday?"

Jay frowns and fidgets with his pen. That's a no if I've ever seen one, but I get it. We're fucking swamped right now. My team alone is responsible for nearly thirty campaigns, not including Midnight, and that means burning the wick at both ends.

I can hardly fault Jay for a mistake I could have made myself just as easily.

"Get those to him by today, okay?" I request. "Otherwise, the mocks are useless. If we can't see the vision completely, we might as well be blind."

"And if he says that will delay us?" Jay questions. Uncertainty sits in his eyes, and I smile to break some of the tension.

"I think we need to go ahead and anticipate a delay. But push him to get it to us by early next week."

The last thing I'm going to do is ream his ass. Now, if he doesn't manage to get the mock slides updated at all, that's a different story. But Jay is reliable, and I've never found it conducive to productivity—or, most importantly, creativity—if the members on my team have chests full of anxiety because they're afraid of me.

Leadership is a delicate balance of encouragement and accountability. And an iron-fisted ego isn't the way to achieve that. I have my father to thank for that knowledge. He's a great leader because he doesn't inspire his employees to have confidence in him. He inspires them to have confidence in themselves.

Now, Chris McKenzie is another story. He's harsh most of the time, and if it weren't for my father's true understanding of leadership, I honestly don't think Banks & McKenzie Marketing would be where it is today. They're the definition of a good cop-bad cop dynamic.

"Will do," Jay agrees, typing out an email as he talks. "Sorry about that, Beau. I can't believe I forgot."

"No worries," I answer, clasping him on the shoulder. "We're all ten feet under right now, Jay. Setbacks and mistakes are going to happen, and we'd rather them now than at the charge to the finish line."

Jay nods, and I move my attention to Laura, who sits directly across from me at the conference table. "How many versions of copy do we have?"

"At least fifty so far," she answers. "Though, most of our focus has been for the digital space, so character limit is prohibitive. Should I get something else going for print and editorial?"

"Yes. I'd like to see at least twenty long-form. I'm pretty confident we'll get placement in *Cosmo, Elle, Men's Daily, Fitness,* and

Good Housekeeping from our past connections, but I want to have this in every major magazine on shelves. When Susie Somebody picks up her airplane read in Hudson News, I want Midnight to be unavoidable."

She nods. "I'll get with Luke this afternoon."

I roll through the rest of my team, asking for updates from Harry, Eddie, and Madeline as I go, each member assigned to different tasks related to our Midnight campaign.

When I ask Madeline about the progress she's made with our Public Relations team in the viability of getting specific influencers and celebrities to join our campaign, I can't stop myself from silently wondering how her lunch with Seth McKenzie went the other day.

Did she talk a little too much about our campaign? Spill the beans on the direction we've chosen to go? And, if yes, will that affect our pitch, come end of December?

As much as I've enjoyed the messages with my Mystery Woman, I could do without the mental unrest. I don't want to have doubts influence my decisions with my team. It's a weak take as a commander and not at all how my father taught me to do business.

I need to be able to be confident and decisive, and looking over my shoulder for the next double agent would affect my ability to do that positively.

"Oh, Beau," Eddie chimes in. "Alice just sent me a rough cut for the commercial."

All right, Beau. Time to tune out the noise.

"Let's see it."

He turns the screen of his laptop to show everyone at the table, and with one click of his finger, the screen comes to life.

A dark night sky with moon and stars is the only thing in frame until an attractive woman with long, dark hair and smoky eye makeup steps onto the screen. "There's no curfew at Midnight," she whispers, a little smile on her lips.

The screen flashes to a handsome man in a suit as he fixes his cuff links and then looks directly into the camera. "There are no rules," he says before the woman is back in the frame next to him.

She lifts her finger to her lips and smirks. "Shh… Don't tell anyone." The Midnight logo appears on the screen behind them and pulls forward, fading them out into the background as they embrace each other.

It's alluring and intriguing and exudes a tangible scale of wealth—all things that sell.

"What do you think?" I ask, looking around the room while I try to gauge everyone's reaction.

"I think I love it," Eddie comments with a big smile.

"Me too," Laura agrees. "But I can't decide if we need to give the viewer a little more of an idea of what Midnight is about, or if the ambiguity is the point."

"We're on the same page, Laura." I nod. "Let's consider showing this to a few selective focus groups after we get the final cut. I'd love to get some objective feedback on it. Open feedback, of course, but let's also lob a specific follow-up question about the ambiguity after we get their initial thoughts."

"I'll work on getting that set up," Madeline offers, and I give her a thumbs-up.

"Perfect. Let's also add a question that weighs the favorability of how exclusive it feels. Is that selling, or do we need it to feel more relatable?"

"Will do." Madeline jots notes on her pad and nods.

I glance down at the Rolex on my wrist and see I have about forty minutes until my next meeting—a teleconference with the CEO of Dalencia Fashion. It's not much time, but it's going to have to be enough to grab a bite to eat and go through all of the unanswered emails my assistant Natalie has already forwarded to my inbox.

"All right, I think we can close up shop for the day." I shut my laptop, grabbing it and my files from the table. "Thanks for all your hard work on this. Any questions before we regroup next week?"

"I think you covered everything," Harry remarks cheekily as Eddie pretends to bow.

"Our fearless leader has it all covered," Laura adds, and I actually laugh.

"I wish it were as glamorous as it sounds."

"Oh, we know it's not glamorous." Madeline snorts. "That's why we let you do it."

I nod, chuckling. The five of them file out to their offices, and I follow, a running list of questions I have for Natalie swirling through my mind.

Wednesday meeting with Voltare timing? Are we still golfing with the Walman's execs next week? Has she heard from Accounting on the budget numbers for the rest of the quarter with Wellness Pro?

It's a fucking mess of shit, and I'd be lying if I said my brain didn't feel like a ping-pong tournament at all times.

As I pass by Hillary Smith's office, I offer a smile and she waves, and my mind immediately bounces in yet another direction.

ElizaBeth, my Midnight Mystery Messenger.

With the nature of my job, I spend a large part of my day outside the walls of my office, talking to staff. I jump between floors and offices and get on the phone more times than I can count. But ever since I started chatting with my Mystery Woman, every single bit of it has become dual purpose. I do my job, and I do PI work at the same time.

It's only been a week, and we've only had a few conversations, but I can't get her out of my mind.

Everyone I come into contact with is suspect—or, at the very least, a new lead in my search for her identity. This morning alone, I questioned Steve, who works at the front desk downstairs, and Cal, the night janitor, who was just trying to finish cleaning up as I arrived. I don't really suspect that they're the ones messaging me anymore—I'm fairly confident it's really a woman now that we've been actively flirting—but anyone could have knowledge that could help find out who she is, and I *need* to know.

There's just something about her. Something…irresistible.

There'd have to be, I guess, for me to keep going back over and over, despite knowing full well how stupid and fucking reckless it is.

I'm a top executive in the company, for shit's sake, and I'm teetering on the cliff of some very inappropriate behavior with an employee whose identity I haven't a damn clue about.

If I'm being honest with myself, I shouldn't be doing it at all.

Hell, yesterday, I questioned Luke from Copywriting, who spent the majority of his time asking me about my fucking sister—the reason for which, I absolutely don't want to know—and I tried to talk Ella, a twentysomething girl in Web Development, into sharing some of her personal details while we rode in the elevator together.

She either thinks I'm insane or is filing a harassment suit against me as we speak, I would assume. Though, she did smile when she was getting off the elevator, and it wasn't shaky or scared. Hell, for all I know, she *is* the Mystery Woman. None of my questions were direct enough to know for sure.

I take my time walking toward my office, looking around the massive space, taking in the faces and making a mental checklist of the names of the people on my floor.

There are at least twenty women up here who are in the right age range, have been around long enough to know the details of the office that my Mystery Woman does, and would've had every opportunity to be in Seth's vicinity to overhear the things she did.

Clara Lay's office, for example, is across the hall from mine and right beside Seth's. If anyone is within hearing distance of that bastard every day, it's her. And I'm pretty sure she's only a few years older than me, early thirties, and the last I heard, she just got out of a long-term relationship.

Maybe I could just go over and say hello?

A hand on my bicep squeezes, and I startle, and Bethany's always red-painted lips curl into a smile. "Aren't you going to say hi?" she greets, intrinsically thrilled to have gotten me with the element of surprise. She spends so much time here, I'm starting to wonder if we're cutting her a check.

"Hi," I say, any other words I might have had for her in the past lost somewhere between her open legs and Seth's dick. It's a sloppy, messy, dirty place, and I've got absolutely no desire to wade in there for the sake of fucking small talk.

She squeezes my bicep again. "I feel like it's been forever since we talked, Beau."

"Probably because it has," I answer, looking over her shoulder and into Seth's office to see why she's wasting her time with me instead of powwowing with her fiancé.

Fiancé. What a joke.

Not even two months after we broke up, she and Seth were engaged. She's never admitted the reality that she had an affair with him behind my back while we were still together, but she doesn't have to. The proof is in the pussy—Seth's, I mean, not hers. There's no way he would have pulled a *Desperate Housewives* on me if she weren't putting out well before the announcement of their future plans.

"I hate that it's like this between us, you know?" she says, and her mouth turns down at the corners. "We used to be so close, Beau."

Yeah. We did. But then you fucked my best friend, so...

A very small part of me wants to say those words to her, but the larger part of me, the part that's more than over this woman, chooses to be the bigger man here. Seth might be a fucking lying prick, but I refuse to stoop to his level of bullshit. I also refuse to waste my time on her.

"This is just how it has to be, Beth," I answer, shrugging her hold off my arm with the motion of my shoulders and taking a step back.

"I disagree," she refutes. "I think there's too much history between us to just act like complete strangers whenever we're around each other."

"The history between us is very much what keeps us apart."

"Come on," she replies, her eyes narrowed. "You don't miss being friends?"

"No," I say simply, satisfaction buoying my chest when her ears turn red. She may not be mine anymore, but we were together so long, she couldn't hide that kind of tell if she tried. My casual refusal is killing her.

She wants control over me in both mind and emotion, and I refuse to give it to her.

"Why not?"

"Because friends treat each other with respect."

"Beau, I'm showing respect right now. I'm showing you that we can be friends," she whispers, a wave of emotion making her face crumple. I don't know if it's bullshit or real, but I'll never be the best judge of that—I thought our relationship was real for a long time, when, obviously, it wasn't. I don't say anything. Not because I can't, but because I don't want to. I put this shit behind me six months ago, and all I'm interested in doing is moving forward.

She glances between me and Seth's office, and when he starts to stand up from his chair and head toward her, her entire demeanor changes. Puppy-dog eyes and pouty lips morph into a straight back, her head held high, and her very best smile plastered across her face.

She's putting on a show, that's for sure. I just can't decide if it's for him or for me.

"Hi, honey," she says, welcoming him with a chummy smile and far-too-graphic kiss. Internally, I sigh. I should have walked away and left her here minutes ago.

"Hey, baby." Seth pulls her in for a hug, making a pathetic show of squeezing her ass as he does. "Little reunion?" he questions, holding eye contact with me.

"Just saying hi," Bethany says, but I don't say anything at all.

Instead, I just smile at him. Just smile like a man without a single fucking care in the world.

I may be over the betrayal, but I'll take every opportunity to make this asshole doubt and wonder until I'm buried in my grave. You don't go behind your best friend's back and steal his girl without consequences. And if he is going behind my back and trying to steal my Midnight campaign, fuck him for that too.

As far as I'm concerned, Seth McKenzie can blow a fucking goat, and from the way he acts, he feels the same way about me too. It's Bethany who's the tougher nut to crack, and the more I think about her attitude, the more my Spidey-senses start tingling.

I'm showing you we can be friends, Beau. Her words repeat in my mind, and they most certainly don't sit well in my gut.

I swear to fuck, I'll break something if I find out Bethany is the Mystery Woman and started all this just to screw with me.

"You ready to go to lunch?" Bethany asks him, trying to move his attention back to her, and turning him away.

I smile at Seth again, my exterior iron-clad while my mind races with Midnight messages as I try to remember them all. But I no longer have the urge to chat with Clara Lay—or anyone else in the office, for that matter.

I'm on edge now. My mood ruined. And I won't feel better until I know who Mystery Woman is.

Chapter 13

THE SCREEN OF MY PHONE IS BRIGHT AGAINST MY EYES AS I stare at it, moonlight pouring through the skylight window on the far side of my bedroom.

My hair is still wet from my shower, and a chill coats my bare skin as the air conditioning kicks back on. Thanks to the growing, glowing pile of embers in my stomach, I didn't make it past a pair of plain black boxer briefs in my quest to get dressed.

I opened the Midnight app five minutes ago, but thanks to Henry and my other buddies, I haven't had a chance to send a message yet. Our ongoing group chat is miles long, and their recent chatter is downright insane. Seriously. My fucking phone won't stop buzzing. Quickly, I scroll toward the end, ignoring a shit-ton of nonsense, and read the last few messages they've sent.

> Henry: What time are you meeting us here, Beau?
>
> Mav: Allure is poppin', bro.
>
> Ronnie: Yesssir.
>
> Henry: Stop treating us like a Tinder fuck, Beau-nana dick. Ghosting goes against our bro-code.

I've known Henry, Ronnie, and Maverick for most of my life. We went to grammar school together, high school together, and attended college together at the University of Miami, with Seth as the fifth member of our group. If he hadn't ruined shit by fucking my girlfriend behind my back, I'd probably be able to find shit from eighth fucking grade in this thread still.

Fingers to the screen, I type out a response.

> Me: We don't have a bro-code. If we did, making sure Ronnie stays away from whiskey would be rule number one.

> Mav: I second this. Ron turns into a psycho when he's on the whiskey-sauce.

He's not lying. The last time we went out and Ron imbibed in some Jack, he ended up getting kicked out of Neon for dragging a fucking sofa onto the dance floor and jumping around on it.

> Ronnie: But I likes it.

> Mav: Shut up, Ron.

> Ronnie: K.

> Henry: How you feeling, Beau? You take a good shit and get all that toxic energy out of your system after I left your condo?

After work this evening, Henry and I weight-trained in my condo's gym before heading out on a six-mile run. He bitched about being tired the whole damn time.

> Me: Don't blame the fact that you couldn't keep up with me today on anything other than yourself. Maybe you need to train a little harder.

> Henry: You were running on pure rage, dude. A fucking cheetah couldn't have kept up with you.

> Me: Rage? I'm nothing but kumbaya, son.

> Henry: HA. That's bullshit. You want me to send you the Fitness app data? We set an all-time

personal record. Or maybe, you know, you should
tell me what the fuck is going on with you lately?

Clearly, there's a lot going on with me. A whole bunch of shit,
in fact, but getting any sort of feedback or advice from these fuckers
is like going to a psychic when you're in debt in hopes they'll give
you the winning lottery numbers.

Me: I'm peachy keen, baby.

Henry: Fucking fantastic. Then you can come
have a few drinks with us at Allure.

I flip back over to my Midnight chat and look for a sign that
Mystery Woman has any intention of showing up.

The chatbox is filled with all of our prior conversations—that
I've read and reread a hundred times this evening—and the last
notification inside of it showcases **ThunderStruck has reentered
the chat**.

Anxiety gnaws at my chest, and I war with myself over whether
I should even keep engaging with whoever is the real face behind
ElizaBeth. Even thinking about the username sends me into a
tizzy now. Like, has it been *that* painfully obvious the whole time?
ElizaBETH. BETHany. I can only imagine how tickled she would
be with herself if it was true.

Fuck.

A text notification pops up on the screen yet again, and I switch
back over to Henry's badgering.

Henry: Hello? Is this thing on? Get your old ass
off your couch and come to Allure.

When I don't respond, a few more messages from my group
of buddies populate on the screen.

Mav: Remember Alyssa? The chick in the red
dress? She's here, and she's asking for you.

> Henry: Let's be real…she was asking for me first, but I gallantly deferred her attention to you.
>
> Me: Let's actually be real…I've never needed you to defer attention to me.
>
> Ronnie: Fucking sizxzle and burnnn. SHeeet that's a dig, henro

Clearly, Ronnie's more than a few drinks deep. But that's Ronnie. The guy has two speeds—sleeping or full throttle. There's never any in-between.

> Me: Have a few more drinks for me, Ron. I'm gonna skip this one.
>
> Mav: Hate to miss ya, but…more pussy for me!

I don't bother with a response, knowing full well it'll just be more of the same. Explaining anything about what I'm doing tonight to the three drunk amigos would make me even stupider than I already am.

And fuck me, I am *stupid*.

Back to the Midnight app, I type out a message, my whole body tensed over the niggling notion that Bethany Williams could be fucking with me all over again. I swear I'll lose my mind.

Still, coming out with guns blazing isn't going to get me any real answers, so I've got to play it cool.

ElizaBeth isn't in the chat yet, but I fire off a message anyway. Maybe when she gets the notification that I sent it, it'll force her to join.

> *ThunderStruck: I have a question for you. But I want a real answer this time.*

I wait and wait and wait. My skin crawls with anticipation, so much so, I start to feel like I need another shower. I'm about ten seconds away from giving up entirely when *ElizaBeth has reentered the chat* appears below my message.

ElizaBeth: A real answer, huh? That sounds dangerously vulnerable, tbh, but I'll give it my best shot.

ThunderStruck: I'm serious. I get being vague, but at some point, it goes too far. I want a direct answer to this one question, and I want your promise that it'll be truthful.

ElizaBeth: DANG. Okay. We mean business. I get it. I promise a truthful, concise answer to this one question (as long as it's not "What's your name?" because that'd be very cheat-ish to the whole anonymous thing).

Clearly, I want to know her fucking name. But baby steps.

ThunderStruck: I don't need your name. Not yet. For now, all I need to know is if I've dated you before.

I don't like how long it takes to get a response, but eventually, I do.

ElizaBeth: Have you dated me before? Is that the question? Because if so, the answer is no.

ThunderStruck: Why'd it take so long to answer? And are you trying to be funny? Because from where I sit, shit is starting to feel a little fucking shady.

ElizaBeth: I'm not trying to be shady or funny. When I try to be funny, people laugh. What happened? Seriously? What's going on? Because I thought we had something going here. Sure, it started as intel because I wanted to make sure you didn't get screwed over, but I don't know. I thought...I thought we were enjoying each other.

ThunderStruck: Do you actually work at Banks & McKenzie?

ElizaBeth: Yes.

ThunderStruck: And you fucking swear we've never dated before?

ElizaBeth: Yes. I swear. We've never dated.

I stare at her message for a long moment before I decide to stop beating around the bush.

ThunderStruck: And your name isn't Bethany?

Her response is instant.

ElizaBeth: HA. No. My name is NOT Bethany, but now I understand why you're so worked up. That would definitely be some real shady shit. But hey, I guess she's already done some shady stuff in the past, so why not this? I get why you'd be on edge.

I breathe a sigh of relief. And more than that, I actually believe her.

ThunderStruck: Well, thank fuck for that. I'm driving myself crazy. I didn't think you could be her, but once the intrusive thought struck, I couldn't get rid of it.

ElizaBeth: But doesn't that make this kind of fun, though? The not knowing?

ThunderStruck: Is it fun that I'm messaging with a mystery woman who works at my dad's company? I mean, I guess it is if I ignore the fact that it's pretty fucking reckless on my part.

ElizaBeth: LOL. I know it seems risky, but I promise you that whatever is said in this chat stays between us. For both of our sakes.

ThunderStruck: It also helps that you can't take screenshots in it.

ElizaBeth: Very true. Five stars and a unicorn sticker for that idea on Hughes International's design team.

ThunderStruck: A unicorn sticker?

ElizaBeth: The ultimate prize, obviously. And, I guess you could also consider these little chats of ours as, like, research, you know? You are spearheading a campaign for it after all...

ThunderStruck: Haha.

ElizaBeth: What? Why's that funny?

ThunderStruck: It's like you're giving me a free pass, even though we both know this isn't exactly a good idea for me.

ElizaBeth: Well, I know I'm anonymous, but I CAN share that I'm not a domestic terrorist, an active deployment in corporate espionage, or a member of any of the alphabet agencies...at this time. Can't predict the future, of course.

Man, she's funny. I came into this conversation like a Grade A asshole, and still, she's managed to turn the whole thing around in the blink of an eye.

ThunderStruck: And your age?

ElizaBeth: Somewhere between 23-34. I'm out of school, but I'm not your grandma either. Though, wouldn't that make for a fun little diddy at Christmastime?

ThunderStruck: Anything else I should know about you?

ElizaBeth: Well…this one is actually hard for me to say…

ThunderStruck: What is it?

ElizaBeth: I got way too curious about Donny's balloon fetish. The things I found on Google were DISTURBING. I should probably hate you for putting that into my head.

ThunderStruck: Technically, I didn't tell you to research it. If anything, I spared you from all the freaky details.

ElizaBeth: Wait…so…you're not even going to offer an apology?

ThunderStruck: It's not my fault your curiosity got the best of you.

ElizaBeth: You're evil. I'm totally pouting right now.

ThunderStruck: And I'm sitting here thinking about how your pouting is really fucking adorable right now. If only I could see it in person…

ElizaBeth: Nice try. LOL.

ThunderStruck: How about you tell me some more things I should know about you?

ElizaBeth: More things about me? Well…I like the sound of the rain, but I hate thunderstorms. And I'm not a Disney adult, but sometimes I get scared that I could be a closeted one.

ThunderStruck: What the fuck are Disney adults?

ElizaBeth: You know, the people who love going to Disney World, to the point of wearing Mickey ears and Minnie Mouse sweatshirts even though they have no kids.

ThunderStruck: Why do you think you could be a closeted one?

ElizaBeth: This is so cheesy, but...I really want to believe in happily ever afters.

ThunderStruck: What's holding you back from believing now?

ElizaBeth: Everything.

ThunderStruck: I think you need to let that go. You need to let yourself believe.

ElizaBeth: That's easier said than done, you know? My childhood didn't inspire hope for Prince Charming.

ThunderStruck: Is that what you want? Prince Charming?

ElizaBeth: That would be a big fat no. He's too... predictable. Too...boring.

ThunderStruck: I think Cinderella would disagree.

ElizaBeth: Yeah, but I'm not her biggest fan either.

ThunderStruck: And what exactly do you have against her? The poor girl was mistreated by that evil stepmother of hers and worked for everything she got.

ElizaBeth: And her stepsisters. Don't forget about them.

ThunderStruck: My thoughts exactly. Why the beef with Cinderella?

> *ElizaBeth: I don't have beef with her. LOL. I just think she deserves better than some man who has to go around putting her shoe on people's feet to find her. He should've known who she was the moment he looked into her eyes. It just feels like their connection wasn't soul-deep, you know? And that's what she deserved.*
>
> *ThunderStruck: Is that what you want? Soul-deep?*
>
> *ElizaBeth: Isn't that what every woman wants?*

I snort to myself. My answer to that question is an obvious one.

> *ThunderStruck: I don't know. I'm a man.*
>
> *ElizaBeth: Oh boy, macho macho. I man. I strong. I beat chest.*

A soft laugh jumps from my throat.

> *ThunderStruck: I didn't say that. lmao. I'm just saying I don't know how the female mind works. If I did, I wouldn't be single and starting fights with nice women on the internet, thinking they're my ex.*
>
> *ElizaBeth: Well, I can't speak for femalekind, but I'd like to think everyone wants the soul connection, wouldn't you? What are we here for if not?*
>
> *ThunderStruck: I don't know. All I know is that I've never had it.*
>
> *ElizaBeth: Me either.*

Silence hangs heavy around me as I consider the thing we're both not saying.

What if this thing between us *is that?*

> *ElizaBeth: Well, I hate to cut this chat short, but I have to get up for work in the morning. Not sure if you know this, but I work at this marketing firm called Banks & McKenzie.*
>
> *ThunderStruck: Oh yeah? You like it over there?*
>
> *ElizaBeth: I do, actually. I mean, there's this guy named Beau Banks who's kind of demanding, but he's at least handsome enough to make it tolerable to deal with him.*
>
> *ThunderStruck: He kind of sounds like a prick.*
>
> *ElizaBeth: I didn't describe him well, then. He's pretty perfect.*
>
> *ThunderStruck: Ha. You must not know him that well.*
>
> *ElizaBeth: I guess we'll just have to keep meeting at Midnight until we find out.*

Fuck me. I've got a big feeling I'm not going to be able to give this up anytime soon.

> *ElizaBeth: Goodnight, Beau Banks.*
>
> *ThunderStruck: Goodnight, Mystery Woman.*

Until we meet again.

Chapter 14

ElizaBeth: I can't believe you actually left me a box of cookies in the seventh-floor break room fridge.

ThunderStruck: Yeah, well, I would have left them in YOUR floor's break room fridge if you'd tell me what floor you work on, but I did my best to pick a neutral location almost halfway up the building. I can't believe you've lived in Miami your whole life and never had Cindy Lou's Cookies.

For the past week, every night around nine, I log in to Midnight, enter the chat with **ElizaBeth,** and talk with her for an ungodly amount of time. Last night, I finally went to bed around two in the morning and was dragging ass on my way into work. Though, I didn't forget to make good on my promise to bring her Miami's best cookies.

ElizaBeth: I guess I've been deprived. Tell me, Mr. Grinch, when did you first discover Cindy Lou?

ThunderStruck: In college, actually. My mom isn't an almond mom, but she's not the type to bake either. By the time I got to UofM, I was desperate for sugar.

ElizaBeth: Wow. Talk about a wild college rebellion. LOL

ThunderStruck: What can I say? Cookies are safer than hookers and blow. So...how many floors did you have to go in the elevator to get to that break room? Or did you not even have to take the elevator?

ElizaBeth: Like I'd tell you that.

ThunderStruck: I had to try. It's not easy being the only one in the dark about identities.

ElizaBeth: You're right. I guess it is a little unfair that I know who you are but you don't know who I am.

ThunderStruck: So...you're finally going to bring me into the light?

ElizaBeth: Nope. LOL.

ThunderStruck: You're a cruel woman.

ElizaBeth: Not cruel. Cautious.

ThunderStruck: Cautious of what?

ElizaBeth: Of what all the things coming out of the dark would mean.

ThunderStruck: I have to assume an ominous tone with that last bit, but have you considered all the positive things that might happen in the light?

ElizaBeth: Like what?

ThunderStruck: Kissing. Touching. Dating. I'm a really good dater. Very good at the wine and dine.

ElizaBeth: All that sounds incredible. Really. But

I don't think we can move forward without doing something else first.

ThunderStruck: What?

ElizaBeth: Rating cookies.

ThunderStruck: If there were a blue balls form of message, that would be it.

ElizaBeth: LOL Sorry. But this is important. Because you think these cookies are the best. I'm not so sure. Chocolate Chip... 8.2/10

ThunderStruck: What??? Only an 8 out of 10?

ElizaBeth: Lemon Cloud... 7.5/10

ElizaBeth: Rocky Road... 8/10

ThunderStruck: Did you give a single cookie a 10???

ElizaBeth: Red Velvet... 7.8/10.

ThunderStruck: Oh my God. Are you sure you were eating the right cookies?

ElizaBeth: The box with the "For Mystery Woman" note on the top and Cindy Lou emblazoned on its every surface? Pretty sure.

ThunderStruck: I think you're a cookie snob, ElizaBeth.

ElizaBeth: Or maybe my palate is just more discerning than yours.

ThunderStruck: Wow, insulting my cookies and my palate? What's next?

ElizaBeth: I don't have any other complaints. But with the way you raved about these cookies, I honestly thought it would feel like heaven was touching my tongue the moment I took a bite.

ThunderStruck: BECAUSE IT IS LIKE THAT.

ElizaBeth: It's okay, Beau. You don't have to be good at everything, you know? Everyone has at least one flaw for the sake of the rest of us.

I laugh. Out loud. In my bedroom. All by my fucking self. I don't know what it is about this woman, but I like her. And the more we chat on Midnight, the more I want to chat with her. She clearly still hasn't told me who she is, but I've learned so much about her in other ways.

I know she's incredibly smart. Hilariously sarcastic. And gets me to talk about the most unexpected shit. She's a breath of fresh air that has come at a time in my life when everything was starting to feel stale.

I feel invigorated, which is insane, because I don't even know this woman. She could be catfishing me for all I know, but I just... *can't stop talking to her.* Can't stop thinking about her. Can't stop hoping that one day soon, she'll tell me who she is.

ThunderStruck: Do you think you'll ever tell me who you really are?

ElizaBeth: I don't know.

ThunderStruck: If you don't...where do you see this going? I mean...it'll have to end at some point, won't it?

My pulse thrums at the thought of never talking to her again, but at this point, I have to push the envelope. I understand taking it slow, but I'm going to want more to hold a year from now than my fucking phone.

ElizaBeth: I don't want it to end. Truly. I just... don't know how to give more than this. It's terrifying.

ThunderStruck: Why don't we take it one step at a time, then?

ElizaBeth: One step at a time?

ThunderStruck: Sure. Any progress is progress, right?

ElizaBeth: Okay. What's step one?

ThunderStruck: Maybe you can give me a tiny hint. Some kind of something to let me know that you're actually real.

ElizaBeth: You afraid I'm just some AI bot?

ThunderStruck: Fuck me. That'd certainly be an unexpected twist, but it is the world's fastest-growing technology.

ElizaBeth: Hold, please...

A minute or two goes by before a picture message appears inside the chatbox.

It's grainy and dark but showcases the length of her bare arm. A few small freckles form a zigzag path from her wrist to her elbow.

I'm real, she says.

She's real. And even from her arm, I know that she's beautiful. But I can't decide if I know that because of the picture or because of the words we've shared inside Midnight.

For the past year, I've basically drowned myself in work. The initial two months after Bethany and I broke up and she got engaged to Seth were a mindfuck. It wasn't easy losing a best friend and a girlfriend in one fell swoop. It was downright misery, if I'm honest.

And the few months after that, I tried to date. Went out and partied with the guys way too often. Even had a handful of one-night stands.

But nothing ever felt fulfilling.

Sure, work gave me purpose, but I know a cushy office with no one at home isn't the fucking finish line. I want a life with someone.

I thought I had that life with Bethany, but now, looking back on it all with eyes that aren't clouded by love, I know our relationship had truly run its course.

We'd grown into two different people with different priorities and different visions of the future. Bethany wants glitz and glamour. I want *real*.

A wife and kids I'm actively engaged with, dirty diapers I changed in the trash, and a home-cooked dinner I made on the stove. To have that, I need a woman who prioritizes time with our future kids over jet-setting across the damn world just because we have the money to do it.

ElizaBeth feels like she could be all those things and more.

> *ElizaBeth: Step two tomorrow?*
>
> *ThunderStruck: I can't wait.*
>
> *ElizaBeth: Goodnight, Beau.*
>
> *ThunderStruck: Goodnight, Mystery Woman.*

Fuck me, she's *addictive.*

I know I don't know her. And I know this shit is completely reckless on my part, considering the implications for myself, my father, and the company if this would go wrong. But I can't bring myself to stop.

I can't bring myself to do anything but keep going until I win… or shit explodes.

Whichever comes first.

Chapter 15

"HOW ARE THINGS GOING WITH DALENCIA AND SONAR?" my dad asks from behind his massive desk, one ankle crossed at the knee and his elbows resting on the arms of his vintage black leather Egg chair my mother spent twenty grand on for part of his Christmas present five years ago.

He's put together as always, his more salt than pepper hair combed neatly from his part and wearing a crisp gray suit.

I'm slightly less vibrant this morning, the lack of sleep starting to catch up with me, and I fake a cough to cover a yawn.

"Dalencia just launched their winter campaign," I explain, leaning back in the leather chair across from his desk and interlacing my fingers. "It's too early to pull any data, but their runway show in Paris did well."

"Did well?" He quirks a brow, and I smile, knowing full well that, to him, "did well" means nothing. Neil is a fan of hard data, not supposition.

"They just released their first run into stores. Thirty of the forty-two Saks Fifth Avenue locations are already requesting more inventory. Nordstrom is doing much the same. And their couture inventory at Bergdorf Goodman and Bloomingdale's is no longer available."

Neil smiles, enjoying the shop talk just as much as I do. While his relationship with Avery is one of coddling and comfort, he and

I share a very different bond. In this building, we're not father and son—he's my boss, and he demands a level of excellence.

I don't resent the difference, but rather, I thrive on it. Nepotism got me in the door, but I've been fighting for every success since then, just like everyone else.

My first campaign was for dog biscuits. Kibble Treats was a small, family-owned company that grossed just under one million a year. I realize that sounds like a lot of money to most people, but in terms of business, especially the kind of major corporations that Banks & McKenzie works with, Kibble Treats's revenue was peanuts.

And now, because of my hard work and the achievements of my first campaign and the campaigns that followed, my father and Chris promoted me to an executive position and let me run campaigns with some of the biggest corporations in the world.

I'm at the top of a ladder *I* built, which is something I'm incredibly proud of.

My father nods in approval, a small grin curving his lips upward. "That's more like it."

"Gotta keep you on your toes *sometimes*, sir."

My dad laughs. "That's a great perspective in life, but not in business. We should be ten steps ahead all the time."

"Last I counted, we were twelve steps ahead."

He shakes his head, amused. "You'd better be if you're going to beat out Seth on the Midnight venture."

Ironically, I'm way more aware of the need to be ahead of Seth than my father knows. He's still sniffing around my people on a regular basis, and a feeling in my gut tells me he's already gotten plenty of information. To get ahead of him now, I'm probably going to have to go back to the drawing board completely, but I'm not dejected. Two years ago, a marketing executive named Doug Stamper held my job. He had a lot of Seth's personality traits, and, as is obvious by the fact that he's no longer with the company, karma caught up with him. I just have to stay my own course.

"We're well equipped to handle everything Seth McKenzie throws at us and then some."

"That's good." He fiddles with a glass paperweight from his desk, passing it back and forth in his hands. "You know, sometimes hindsight is twenty-twenty."

"Meaning?"

"I'm just wondering if I was a little overzealous in my agreement to pit the two of you against each other for this so-called friendly competition."

"Why?"

He eyes me knowingly. "Come on, Beau. You and I both know why."

Everyone in the office knows why. Within thirty days, Bethany went from stopping at my office for lunch to stopping at Seth's. Even if you're not the type to dive into the office gossip, it was kind of hard to ignore.

"I appreciate the concern, Neil, but there's no need for it."

My dad's eyes are warm with affection. "I don't know if I tell you this enough, but I'm proud of you, Beau. Really proud of you."

"Is this my dad or my boss telling me this?"

He smiles. "Both."

"Thanks," I say. "It's appreciated."

The sound of the door swinging open behind me pulls my attention to over my shoulder, and June strides in with a stack of files in her hands.

"Hey, June," I greet, making her head jerk up and her eyes jump to mine.

"Oh!" she says in a rush. "I'm sorry if I'm interrupting. Denise wasn't at her desk, and I just assumed you were free, Mr. Banks."

"You're not interrupting anything, Juni," my dad says with a gentle wave of his hand. "It appears you have quite the stack there. Please tell me it's for Beau," he teases, and the sweetest-sounding laugh escapes her lungs.

"Well, sir, Beau didn't ask me to get every paper contract we've ever signed with Clover Athletics. You did." She pauses and shrugs. "Though, I guess I could pretend he requested it if you let me go back outside and start over."

"First of all, Juni," my dad interjects with a big smile, "how about we drop the 'sir' stuff? It makes me feel a hundred years old."

She rolls her eyes. "You're my boss."

"True. But you're also my Junebug, and if you're old enough to be calling me sir, I must be getting close to retirement."

"Hi, June," I say again, pulling her eyes to me once more. She blushes a little and waves, adorably annoyed with my cries for attention.

"Hi, Beau."

"Just call him Neil," I add. "That's what I do."

My dad laughs, and June's cheeks turn even rosier. A lock of red hair falls in front of her face, and she tucks it behind her ear.

"Well, *Neil*," she says, overemphasizing his name for good measure. "Where should I put these files so I can get out of your hair?"

"Put them on Denise's desk." He offers her a little wink. "They'll be a nice surprise when she gets back from lunch."

I guffaw, and June's eyes jump to mine again, bemused. I hold them for longer than necessary, watching with fascination as her embarrassed grin turns into a gorgeous smile. All the pretty, girl-like features of Avery's best friend I used to know are gone, a full-fledged, beautiful woman in her place.

I don't know when it happened, but the transformation is definitely complete.

"No offense, Neil, but I'm glad I won't be here to see that," she remarks, and I bite my lip and look down at my lap to smother a smile.

My dad laughs.

"Need anything else?"

"No, Juni. I'm all set. Beau?"

I shake my head and meet her eyes. "I'm good, June. Thanks."

Her long red hair swishes along her back as she turns on her heel to exit, and I allow myself a small peek at how long her legs look beneath her black skirt. Her skin is creamy and freckled, and a bolt of something runs through me I can't quite place.

It's like searching for the right word in a sentence while your brain whirs around it.

There's a crunch and a groan as she makes it to the doorjamb, my sister's voice echoing around us as the two of them run into each other head on.

June stumbles back, dropping several of the files in her arms to the floor in a chaotic flurry.

"What the hell?" Avery asks, walking right around June and settling her hand on her hip. I jump up from my seat to help collect the files for June.

"Sorry, June," Avery finally apologizes, noticing the scene a bit better, now that I'm helping. "But color me a little shocked that there's a family reunion going on here and no one invited moi."

"We didn't even know you were at work today, princess," our dad comments with a tickled smile. It doesn't matter that she's twenty-three, shit at being an intern, and basically milking his fucking payroll—he's never, ever angry with her.

"Daddy!" Avery protests with a roll of her eyes. "Of course I'm at work today."

"Sorry, love. I hadn't seen you. What time did you get here?"

"Does it matter?" she tosses back, lifting her fresh cup of Starbucks to her lips. "I'm here, and I'm ready to roll!"

"Oh, great," my dad comments. "Then you won't mind running a few errands for me?"

"Actually, Daddy." She frowns. "I already have, like, two other things I need to do today. Maybe tomorrow, okay?"

My dad laughs. I give June the last folder and stand, offering her a hand when she struggles to get up in her heels. She looks up at me from under her lashes, her blue eyes shining with gratitude.

Her hand slips out of mine, and she waves, heading out the door once again.

"June, where are you going?" Avery questions then, just realizing her sidekick is leaving her behind.

"To do work," June calls over her shoulder, setting the files on Denise's desk and disappearing down the hall. I follow her out with a wave to my father, and Avery stays behind to give him a little more hell before her next spa appointment or whatever.

I stop briefly at Madeline's office to get a quick influencer list update, and then I head straight for my office. I need an energy drink—or five—and then I need to churn and burn on storyboard approvals for five different campaigns.

A small container sits on my desk as I round my way to the back of it, along with an attached note that I see on closer inspection.

I pull the note off the top and lift the lid, revealing three fist-sized chocolate chip cookies.

Now these are 10/10 chocolate chip cookies.
-Mystery Woman

My smile is practically too big for my face—seriously, I should be ashamed of it—as I feverishly snatch up a cookie and take a taste.

Moist, chocolatey, and just a tiny pinch of salt—they're fucking incredible.

God, that's good. And just what I needed to get me through the next several hours.

I pick my phone up off my desk and swipe into our chatbox, the blinking cursor waiting on my words. Taking this chat from after hours to during work is not the smartest idea.

It's risky. It's questionable. It's all the you-shouldn't-be-doing-this things.

But I do it anyway. I can't wait for tonight. I have to thank her now.

ThunderStruck: Where'd you get these cookies from? Heaven?

Not even a minute later, **ElizaBeth has reentered the chat** appears on the screen.

> **ElizaBeth: LOL I didn't get them anywhere. I made them. Good, huh?**
>
> **ThunderStruck: 10/10.**
>
> **ElizaBeth: Yeah?**

She's messaging me during office hours. Which means she's somewhere in this building watching the screen of her phone like I'm watching the screen of my phone. My eyes flit out of my door, scanning the other offices along the edges and the giant cubicle area in the center.

I don't know what I think I'll find, but with ninety-five percent of the workforce on their phones, I come up with nothing. *Damn, I wish I could just figure out who she is.*

> **ThunderStruck: I can only think of one single thing that would make them better.**
>
> **ElizaBeth: What?**
>
> **ThunderStruck: Having them hand-delivered.**
>
> **ElizaBeth: By, like, a courier?**
>
> **ThunderStruck: Don't be cute.**
>
> **ElizaBeth: Sorry. Cute's all I know how to be.**

Oh, ElizaBeth, I know.

Her cuteness is like quicksand. And I'm in so deep, I don't know if I'll ever get out.

Chapter 16

MY EYES ARE HEAVY, AND I'M DOING EVERYTHING I CAN to pay attention during my Midnight team's weekly meeting.

Eddie is in the process of getting a final cut of the commercial, the edits he wanted to put into action already approved by me last week, and Madeline's current list of influencers and celebrities interested in joining our campaign if our team does end up getting the green light from Hughes International is impressive. Laura and Jay have made significant progress on copy for the digital space and slide mock-ups for the presentation we will be giving in front of the Hughes International executives in a couple of months, and Harry has secured fifteen additional magazine spots.

The test groups have given unbelievably good feedback, and everything is running full steam ahead.

Everything, that is, but me.

Two more weeks of my late-night chats with *ElizaBeth* have flown by, the exhilaration of each of them keeping me up well into the night. But during the day, the lack of sleep is starting to get grating, and I'm kind of wondering how long I'll be able to go on without anyone noticing.

As it is right now, I'm supposed to meet Henry for lunch, but I think I'm going to have to cancel and take a power nap instead.

"Great work, everyone. I know this has been a marathon already, but we're finally getting somewhere. By next week's meeting, we'll almost be halfway there. Keep positive. Keep innovative. Keep pushing. I'll see you back here next week for our meeting, but you know where to find me in the meantime. You know what I always say about fires?"

"Time only fans the flames," the five of them recite in unison, making me laugh.

"Right." I laugh. "Get out of here. And all of you promise me you're going to get some rest whenever you can."

Laura and Jay are the first to scoot out, and she doesn't hesitate to tell me, "You'd better get some rest too."

I smile and nod. There's no denying I look like hell.

Harry, Eddie, and Madeline follow shortly after, and I bring up the rear, flipping off the lights on my way out the door. We don't normally convene in the conference room on the fourth floor, and the cardinal rule of using spaces that aren't yours is to leave them how you found them.

I'm not going to extreme measures at this point, but I figure meeting where I know Seth and his team won't be is a necessary and basic precaution.

I look through the unfamiliar offices and cubicles as I follow my team to the bank of elevators at the front of the building, willing my Mystery Woman to stand out in the crowd.

I'm ready to know who she is—ready to see what could happen if we take things outside of the chat—and finding her organically would expedite the process.

When I step on the elevator, my mind is at odds. *How can I simultaneously want what we have to go on forever and know that if it goes on for much longer, it's liable to kill me?*

When a Post-it note is the first thing I see on my desk, a rush of excitement consumes my chest. Ready or not, I have to risk kicking this up a notch.

"Adrenaline is nature's way of telling you 'don't fuck up.'"
-M.W.
PS: You better not cheat with Google on me.

I smile at the ongoing movie quote challenge we've been playing for the past two nights. The two nights before that, the name of
the game was song lyrics. She never chooses easy stuff to test me
with and surprises me constantly. Today, she's raw and obscure.
Tomorrow, she may very well be something else.

The not knowing puts me in knots. I can't imagine what it'll be
like when I actually get to see her. Touch her? Kiss her? *Be* with her?

Fuck.

I have to know. Soon.

My phone is back in my hands and Midnight is back on the
screen before I can stop myself. It's time to lay it all out on the table.

> *ThunderStruck: When I figure out what movie
> this is from, I want one thing and one thing only
> in return.*

> *ElizaBeth: And what's that?*

> *ThunderStruck: To meet you. And this time, I
> can't take no for an answer.*

PART 3

Juniper

Chapter 17

"THERE'S NOT MUCH TO EAT HERE, UNLESS YOU COUNT ME and June," Avery teases, looking between Beau and Henry before smacking Henry in the chest, her eyes aflutter with flirtation.

Beau leans against our kitchen counter while Henry raids our cabinets, and I stand to the side, my heart racing like freaking Seabiscuit.

They were just getting back from their five-mile run when Avery was on her way into the building, and somehow, that led to a pow-wow in the middle of our kitchen.

"Ah-ah," Beau chides, wiping some excess sweat from his forehead before placing his baseball cap back on his head. "No, no, Henry. Don't listen to her. There's nothing to eat. Period."

"What?" Avery feigns confusion. "I was just saying!"

"Sure, you were," Beau mutters through a laugh. "Just like you *said* things to Mav last summer."

"That was one time!" Avery disagrees.

"And Grady at Mom and Dad's Fourth of July party."

"Obsessed with me much?" she retorts, smacking Beau in the stomach before lifting herself up and onto the counter to sit. "How about you focus on your own life and stop cockblocking mine, Beau? I offered up June too, by the way, so it's not like Henry doesn't have options."

"Whoa," I break in, a single finger in the air. "I don't remember putting myself on the menu. No offense, Henry."

Henry laughs, bemused by Avery's antics as she dances around in front of him, shaking her braless tits from her spot on the counter.

"You know you love me, Henry," she says, and he just smirks at her.

"Always the instigator, huh?"

"I'm not instigating anything." Avery stops dancing to put a hand to her hip. "But maybe that's your subconscious talking."

"And what exactly is my subconscious saying?" Henry questions, and Avery leans closer to him, basically brushing one of her boobs against his arm.

"That I'm totally your style." She blows him a kiss, and a heavy sigh escapes Beau's lungs.

"You know, Ave," Beau says, "if you put as much effort into your job as you do into flirting with my friends, Dad would probably be planning on letting you take his place when he retires."

Avery cackles. "Like I'd ever want to work a nine-to-five. Get real, Beau."

"News flash, Ave," I chime in. "You *do* work a nine-to-five."

"Yeah, but, like, I don't actually work those hours, you know?" She winks. "They're flexible."

All three of us laugh at her absurdity and gives-zero-fucks attitude, and when Beau's brown eyes meet mine, I hate how a rush of satisfaction zips from my head all the way down to my toes. "Juniper June, it's one of the mysteries of the world how a nice girl like you can put up with my sister."

"Because she loves me, Beau!" Avery insists. "And you love me too, even if you're resistant to show it. Actually, you and Henry should shower off all your sweat and come out to Beluga with us in a little bit."

"I'm not going out," Beau and I both say in unison, making Henry laugh and Avery shriek.

"Gah, you guys are so weird! What is with the two of you lately?

I don't even know if I can associate with you much longer if you keep this up."

"I'll go to Beluga," Henry offers, to which Avery cheers and Beau groans.

My best friend's MIA status for the evening should be a good thing. And three days ago, I would've been chomping at the bit to see her leave so I could log in to Midnight and chat with Beau.

But that was before he sent me the "**To meet you. And this time, I can't take no for an answer**" message midday and without provocation. Ever since then, I've been a cowardly chicken, unable to bring myself to say anything back.

It's the last message that's occurred inside our chatbox, besides the **reentered the chat** notifications that pop up anytime either of us logs on.

We've both reentered the chat so much, it's starting to become a thread of its own, but he hasn't added anything and I haven't answered either. We're at an impasse—a true shit-or-get-off-the-pot moment—and neither of us is backing down.

Beau thinks he wants to meet me, which, in theory, is invigorating. But realistically, Beau already knows me…as his little sister's best friend.

I can't imagine that the buildup of everything he's picturing doesn't crash and burn as soon as he finds out, and I'm not ready. I want to stay in our Midnight chat bubble forever and ever. *Amen.*

A silent but deep sigh escapes my lungs as Henry and Avery finish making their plans to meet up, and Beau and he leave with nothing more than a chin tip and a wave. And nausea sits like a rock in my gut, reminding me that I'm at a crossroads I wish I would've never reached.

Avery shuts the door behind them and charges toward me, her eyes like lasers. "I'm not even going to beg you to come out tonight, June."

"You're not?"

"Nope." She shakes her head and pokes her index finger into the center of my chest. "I'm done chasing your sleepy little tail."

I laugh. I can't help it. "I get the feeling you're expecting that to be bad news, Ave."

"Oh, come on!" she cries, stomping her foot in time with each word. "The reverse psychology was supposed to work!"

I shake my head and sit down on one of our kitchen stools as she twerks up against me. "I'm sorry. Really." I shove her away on a laugh. "But tonight isn't the night. I think I'm coming down with something."

Beau fever, to be specific.

"Well, whatever. Henry's meeting me in two hours, and Hilly and Bella are already at SoPo House. If you're really not going, I'll leave now."

I smile. "Have fun."

She glares at me but grabs her stuff from the counter and heads for the door anyway. "You'll regret it!" she taunts, opening the door and standing in the opening for a beat. "Call me if you change your mind."

"Love ya, Ave. Be safe."

"Yeah, yeah, you too." She rolls her eyes and spins on her heels, calling over her shoulder as she actually exits the door this time, "Don't stick any dildos anywhere I wouldn't, okay!"

"That won't be a problem, you weirdo," I respond, and just like that, the door slams behind her and she's gone.

I look down at my cell phone on the counter, mocking me, reminding me that **ElizaBeth** is going to have to respond to **ThunderStruck** soon—or all of it will have been for nothing.

I ignore it, choosing to head into my bedroom and grab some underwear and pajamas for a quick shower. Usually, I prefer to take my showers in the morning, but I'm hoping all the heat and steam will scrub the uncertainty and fear and confusion from my brain.

When I'm done and rummaging through some of the clean

laundry that sits on my dresser, all of it folded but not put away, I hear the soft sounds of footsteps coming from the wall behind me.

Beau.

He's in his bedroom.

It feels like a cruel trick from the universe that his bedroom is adjacent to mine.

I sit there, only a pair of underwear on, and my sleep shorts and tank top clutched in my hands. My ears are far too focused on whatever noise they can latch on to to finish getting dressed. I'm listening so intently that the beats of my heart and the breaths from my lungs are damn near deafening.

*What is he doing? Is he thinking of how **ElizaBeth** hasn't responded? Is he getting ready to shower from his run, or was he showering at the same time I was?*

Ha. Now, that's a thought. *A thought that you need to stop thinking because you need to freaking message him back!*

I blow out a harsh breath from my lungs, making my lips vibrate with each wave of air, and get the lady balls to pick my phone up off the bed and open our chat once again.

I need to answer him.

Even though it's the very last thing I want to do, even though I love having Beau all to myself inside our little Midnight chat, I need to cut the cord before this leads me somewhere dangerous.

Pretty sure we can all agree the risks I'm taking aren't calculated at all. They're straight-up thoughtless and careless and impulsive and everything in between.

My fingers hover over the screen, ready to type out a goodbye message when a new message appears in the chatbox.

ThunderStruck: What are you afraid of?

My heart jumps to a gallop, and I clutch my pajamas even tighter against my naked chest. What am I afraid of? *Finding out that my feelings for you will never be anything more than one-sided.*

It's what I wish I could tell him most, but the one thing I can't find the courage to say at all. Instead, I greedily grip the tiny strings of opportunity, hoping to suck him back into my land of make-believe.

> *ElizaBeth: Strange noises in the middle of the night. The moments when I have to keep my eyes closed when I'm washing my hair in the shower. Other people's saliva blowing into the air at, like, 90 miles per hour when they sneeze. Tofu.*

I hit send and keep typing more as I plop down onto my bed.

> *ElizaBeth: The possibility of ankle-grabbing monsters being under my bed. Thunderstorms. Loneliness. Believing in happily ever afters but getting my heart broken. Kombucha. Worst-case scenarios. Getting stuck while driving through a tunnel. The Seven Mile Bridge.*

I hold my breath and wait for him to respond, and I just about fall off my mattress when his next message humors me rather than calling me out on avoidance.

> *ThunderStruck: Tofu?*

> *ElizaBeth: Is it cheese? Is it milk? Is it a weird blob of white stuff that comes from an animal's genitals? I don't know what it is, and that's scary.*

> *ThunderStruck: It's milk. Soya milk. That's been curdled.*

> *ElizaBeth: Curdled milk? Ew. See? Scary! Thanks a lot, Beau.*

> *ThunderStruck: Ha. Sorry to be the bearer of bad news. I guess I shouldn't ask about the kombucha then, huh?*

> *ElizaBeth: NO.*

> *ThunderStruck: And what about the ankle-grabbing monsters?*

ElizaBeth: Look, I can't prove they're real, but I CAN feel their presence. It's an intuition thing.

ThunderStruck: Savages.

I know instantly he's referring to the last note I left on his desk three days ago.

ElizaBeth: You figured out the movie.

ThunderStruck: Without Google.

ElizaBeth: I'm impressed.

And terrified. I let things go for so long that he actually got it, and now, he's going to be relentless in going after his reward. Meeting me. In person.

ThunderStruck: I was hoping you would be.

ElizaBeth: You want to impress me, Beau Banks?

ThunderStruck: I want to do a lot of things with you.

My cheeks heat with the arousal that sits heavy within his words. Knowing he wants me, knowing he's right next door…it makes me *feel* things.

And the June who always holds back is telling me to leave the chat, throw my phone across my bedroom, and hide under my comforter. But she's not the one running the ship tonight. We're too far out to sea for that.

ElizaBeth: Like what?

ThunderStruck: Meet you, for one.

ElizaBeth: And when you meet me?

ThunderStruck: Look into your eyes. I need to know what color they are.

ElizaBeth: And when you look into my eyes?

ThunderStruck: I imagine I won't be able to stop myself from looking at your mouth. I want to see it move when you speak. Want to know if your lips are soft and plush. Want to know what they taste like.

Without even thinking, my fingers move to my lips, just barely skimming across the warm flesh.

ThunderStruck: I wouldn't be able to resist kissing you.

Beau kissing me. It's something I've dreamed and fantasized about a million and one times.

ElizaBeth: I think I'd kiss you back.

ThunderStruck: You think, or you know?

Who am I kidding?

ElizaBeth: I know.

ThunderStruck: I'd kiss you soft at first. Just a little brush of my lips against yours. But when that's not enough, I'd kiss you deeper, slide my tongue past your lips and find out what you taste like. I'd kiss you long. Long enough to breathe in your moans.

ElizaBeth: The mere idea of that is...

ThunderStruck: Is...?

ElizaBeth: It's a little embarrassing to admit...

ThunderStruck: Tell me.

ElizaBeth: It's intoxicating. I have goose bumps. My nipples are hard. And I feel...a delicious throb... deep inside me...

ThunderStruck: I need you to slide your hand over your breasts and tell me if you can feel your nipples beneath your clothes.

I pause, reading his words while my face flames with fire again. But it doesn't take long before I'm doing what he asks. Hesitantly, I lift my left hand and brush it over my breasts, feeling my soft curves.

ElizaBeth: I can feel my nipples, but there aren't any clothes. I'm still naked from my shower. All but my panties.

ThunderStruck: Fuck.

ThunderStruck: Move your hand down your belly now and just barely slip your fingers under your panties.

I follow his command.

ThunderStruck: How do you feel now?

I don't know what comes over me, but I take a picture, just like that, with my hand just barely inside my panties. And I send it to him. I hardly even recognize myself. The picture is so sexy.

ElizaBeth: Like I want to keep moving my hand down.

My breaths are already starting to feel uneven, my breasts moving up and down in heavy waves, and I'm waiting. Waiting to see what he says next.

And I swear, I hear the faintest "Fuck me" come through the wall behind me.

Holy hell. I don't know why it's so hot to think about him being right there, as close as he can possibly be without being in my bedroom. But it is. It's the most arousing thing I've felt in a long time. Maybe forever.

ThunderStruck: You're beautiful. Everything about

you is so fucking beautiful, and I've barely seen anything at all. Just thinking about what it would feel like to replace that hand of yours with mine has my cock so hard.

ElizaBeth: I want to see it. I need to see it.

A few moments later, a new picture appears in the chat. It's Beau's muscular body with a pair of black Calvin Klein boxer briefs still covering him. But it doesn't conceal his truth. He's hard. He's hard and he's big. Bigger than my brain had imagined he'd be.

Goodness.

I'm beyond aroused now, the throb between my legs becoming almost unbearable.

ElizaBeth: I don't... I don't know how much more of this I can take.

ThunderStruck: Slide your hand all the way down and touch yourself. Tell me if you're wet.

My fingers inch down, and it doesn't take long before they're coated with my arousal.

ElizaBeth: Embarrassingly wet.

ThunderStruck: Fuck. My hand is on my cock now. Slide your finger inside yourself. Tell me how you feel.

I do as I'm told, a compliant little minx ready to do whatever he asks.

ElizaBeth: Warm. Wet. Ready for you.

ThunderStruck: Put your finger on your clit and touch yourself until you can't hold back. Touch yourself until you come. But do it while you're imagining my cock inside you. Do it while you're thinking about my mouth on your pussy. Do it

***while you're picturing my lips, my tongue, my
fingers, my hard cock making you come.***

Oh my God. My hips jerk forward at his words, and I can't stop
from touching myself again. And again. And *again.* My index finger
circles and massages my clit until the waves of my pleasure build at
the base of my spine, Beau's face a repeat image in my mind.

I think about what it would be like to feel his mouth on mine.
His hands on my skin. And his cock inside me. I imagine how full I'd
feel when he's pushed all the way to the hilt. And I fantasize about
the way my breasts would move up and down as he fucks me.

I think about the way his eyes would look as he starts to go
over the edge and the way his moans would sound when they leave
his lungs.

And I don't stop touching myself or thinking about Beau until
my orgasm barrels through every cell in my body. I remember to
keep my moans to myself, but just barely. The feel of it all is so intense I have to drop my phone and shove my face into the pillow as
my climax rolls through me.

ThunderStruck: Fuck.

Only one crude word, but it says everything.

ElizaBeth: Yeah. Fuck.

**ThunderStruck: I fear I'm starting to get a little
too addicted to these chats.**

And I fear I've been addicted to Beau Banks for so long there's
no recovering from it. Especially not now. Not after this.

I entered this chat tonight thinking I was going to say goodbye,
but we've just crossed a plateau we can't come down from.

I need more, and I need it often. And one day, I'm going to
have to figure out how to work up the courage to do it in person.

Now that I know what that would be like…I can't go back.

Chapter 18

"**M**OM, NEXT TIME, CAN YOU LEAVE THE ONIONS OFF the steak?" Avery says, pointedly sliding the grilled onions off her filet with a look of disgust on her face. "Stank breath isn't something I want to be known for."

"Where do you have to go tonight anyway, princess?" Neil asks from the head of the table. "I thought you and June were choosing a quiet night in with us?"

"Neil," Avery says with a roll of her eyes. "You clearly don't understand the inner workings of Miami nightlife."

He flashes a smile at Diane before turning back to Avery. "Please enlighten me."

"First of all," Avery explains, "it's eight. Unless we want to grab an early-bird dinner at The Crazy Crab, shit doesn't start popping off until at *least* eleven."

Neil looks over at me, and I shrug. "Don't look at me. I don't make the plans. I just get forced to go along with them."

He chuckles, and Avery snaps her fingers at me aggressively. "Right. And don't even think of begging off tonight because I'm done with your shit. It's a Saturday. You don't have work tomorrow. You're coming."

"Avery," Diane chides, but my middle finger and stuck-out tongue are enough to keep the levity.

"So, what are you saying, Avery?" Neil teases. "Your quiet night in with your loving parents isn't really the main event? What's our cutoff time?"

"That's exactly what I'm saying," Avery replies, taking a sip of white wine. "But it's not anything you should concern your pretty little head with, Daddy. You'll already be in bed."

"Avery, honey, onions are good for your skin," Diane insists, pantomiming the nutrients by taking a bite herself.

Avery's face pinches in confusion at her mom's late reply, but Diane nods as though we weren't just having an entirely different conversation two seconds ago.

"They are. Fredrick told me they're high in antioxidants and vitamins that combat aging."

"Who is Fredrick?" Neil asks, and I smother a smile, knowing just how good this is going to get. Neil is the ultimate hype man for his wife, daughter, and me, but that's mostly because he's never seen the receipts. It's very military: don't ask, don't tell.

"Oh my God, Daddy!" Avery exclaims, laughing at him uproariously. "Mom's been getting facials from Fredrick for years."

"Oh, honey, not just facials. Fredrick does my Botox too," Diane adds, and Neil just sighs.

"Good grief," Neil mutters. "It's a wonder we have any money at all."

"You should be thanking her, Daddy," Avery counters. "I can guarantee Botox with Fredrick is cheaper than with Dr. Franks, which is who I go to."

"Well, thank everything for that," Neil says through an amused laugh. "Wouldn't want to get hosed on Botox for my daughter *and* my wife."

Avery and Diane dive into a conversation about some of the other services Fredrick's spa now offers, and I go back to eating my steak that Chef Stone cooked to perfection before leaving us to our dinner.

I'm not thrilled to be going out with Avery tonight, but I don't think it's a terrible idea either. Things with Beau and me really got out of hand a couple nights ago, and then it kind of—*definitely*—continued in that same dirty, orgasmic fashion ever since. If I sat at home tonight, there's no doubt I'd end back in the Midnight app at some point.

Don't get me wrong, I love the idea of that, but freaking hell, things are really starting to get complicated.

"Really, Avery," Diane comments around a bite of steak. "A weekly HydraFacial, I'm telling you, will revolutionize your life. You may not even need to keep up with the Botox for now and can just start back up in a couple of years."

I suck my lips into my mouth as steam builds in Neil's brain. His eyes ping-pong back and forth as Diane and Avery continue. My phone vibrates in my pocket just as I'm about to get dragged into their planning, so I pull it out and focus on it in my lap.

Anything to save myself from a conversation about filler.

There's a text message from my mom about her next stop in Thailand, and then an extensive list of social media notifications, but at the bottom of them all, a Midnight chat notice taunts me.

Not only is Beau in the chat, but he just sent a message too, and I'm sitting at a table with his sister, mom, and dad, for Pete's sake. I can't open this right now, no matter how badly I want to.

Panic damn near seizes my throat, and a small piece of steak gets lodged. I have to cough my way through the trauma until it starts to slide down with hearty sips of water.

Neil and Diane both jump up to help, and Avery passes me her glass of water across the table. For as close to actually dying as I am, I still expend an awful lot of energy to make sure no one can see my phone from behind, flipping it over and tucking it under my leg on the chair.

I raise a hand over my shoulder to Neil as he rubs my upper back and nod at Diane as she hovers in front of my face.

"Eat much, June?" Avery teases, now that it seems like I'm going to survive.

"Just went down the wrong pipe." My voice is hoarse from

coughing, my eyes are wet with unshed tears, but I'll be damned if I end up with Neil trying to give me the Heimlich. "I'm fine."

They eye me closely for a long moment, but after another wave and a thumbs-up, the two of them slowly retake their seats.

I know I shouldn't. Goodness, I know I shouldn't. But I can't stop myself from taking a quick peek in the Midnight app.

> **ThunderStruck: Big Saturday night plans?**

A small smirk lifts just the corner of my lips as I think about the truth. Beau himself would be here with me if he hadn't gone out for his buddy Maverick's birthday, but because I'm still a secret, in his mind, I could be anywhere. I don't want to taunt him exactly, but I've never felt this powerful before—our dynamics haven't allowed it.

> **ElizaBeth: Oh, you know, just having a wild night on the town. What about you?**

> **ThunderStruck: I'm at a bar in South Beach. So...if you're out...maybe you should consider coming to say hi.**

Ah, how easy that would be if I weren't who I am. As it is, I have so many lies going, I'm considering changing my name to Charlotte and spinning a web.

> **ElizaBeth: I'd love to, but I can't get out of my current plans.**

You know, just having dinner with your freaking parents and sister. No big deal.

> **ThunderStruck: That sounds ominous. Is there a man involved in these plans?**

I look across the table at Neil. *Oh yeah—your dad, in fact.* I'd probably laugh if it didn't feel like such a clusterfuck waiting to explode all over the place.

ElizaBeth: And if there was a man...would you be jealous?

ThunderStruck: That depends.

ElizaBeth: On what?

ThunderStruck: On whether or not you talk to him like you talked to me last night.

My cheeks heat as memories assault me, and I glance up at my dinner companions. They're all occupied, thank God, but thinking of orgasming at Beau's figurative hand while they sit five feet away causes anxiety overload. I have to wonder if, at some point, Beau and I were real and not a secret, would I eventually get over how awkward it would feel for my second family to know that we did intimate things?

For my sanity, I don't let myself go there. I have a million hurdles to jump over before that's even a remotely viable possibility, and quite frankly, I don't know if I've got the vertical lift to handle it.

ElizaBeth: Definitely not.

ThunderStruck: Good.

ElizaBeth: And what about you?

ThunderStruck: What about me?

ElizaBeth: Are you talking to any girls in South Beach like you did me last night?

ThunderStruck: Fuck no.

Not just no, but *fuck no*. A surge of confidence washes over me, so much so, I consider getting flirty again.

ElizaBeth: Good. I want you to—

"Who are you texting?" Avery questions, snapping my attention up from my half-typed message.

"N-no one," I stutter, fumbling to close out of the Midnight app as I do.

"You sure?" She quirks a skeptical brow. "Because if you're, like, making plans to go out tonight with someone else, you best be explaining. Ain't no way I'm going to spend my entire Saturday night with Neil and Diane. I have my calendar blocked off for you."

"You do realize we're both sitting here, right?" Neil questions, and Avery just rolls her eyes.

"Of course I do, Daddy."

He laughs at that.

"I'm not making plans," I explain in a rush. "I was just texting my mom."

"Okay, well, when you're done with that," she says, taking another sip of wine, "figure out what club you want to go to. David has VIP at TauTau, but I can't stop thinking about Echo." She shrugs. "I'm sure we can get VIP there too, even if it's new."

"David?" I question. "What happened to Seb?"

"Ugh," she groans. "Don't even get me started on that guy."

"Who is Seb?" Neil asks, looking between the two of us.

"He's a guy Avery went on a date with last week," I state, more than happy to throw my best friend under the bus to keep the topic of conversation far away from the person I was messaging with just a minute ago.

"You went on a date, honey?" Diane questions, a hint of excitement in her eyes.

"That guy is so boring that I swear, it would've been more fun to eat my new pair of Louboutins than go out with him," Avery states, flashing a glare at me as she does. "So, how about we change the subject before I have to strangle Juniper for even bringing it up?" she says. "I just got these acrylics yesterday."

"One day, honey, I hope you find a man who actually keeps your interest," Diane says, and Neil's chuckles are so loud they basically come from his toes.

"Diane, I think we need to invest our hope in Avery finding a man who can put up with her, not the other way around."

"Daddy, you know I'm a total catch," Avery retorts.

"Of course I do, princess," Neil says, warmth in his voice. "Catch of the century. Just need a man with an AMEX Black Card and a trust fund to reel you in."

"See? You get me," she says to Neil, pointing an approving index finger at him. "I deserve only the best."

"Exactly, princess," Neil agrees. "Both you and Juniper deserve the best. Which is why if you ever bring some schmuck home who doesn't meet that, you can bet your ass I'll be showing him straight to the door."

"I can't wait for the day I get to see both of my girls get married," Diane muses, her voice all soft and dreamy as her eyes look far off in the distance. It's like she's imagining our actual weddings.

But I guarantee the man I picture waiting for me at the altar doesn't come close to what's in her vision. And I sure as hell know that man wouldn't be in Avery's mind either.

How could it be, though? I've kept my secret crush on Beau from everyone for years, thinking nothing would ever come of it.

And now look at me.

The time is nearing eleven, and Avery is upstairs in her bedroom getting ready to go out. Sure, she doesn't live here anymore, but she refused to pack when she moved out. She just bought dupes of everything for our condo so she could leave a full set of her belongings here. It only takes me half the time to prep and fluff, so to keep myself occupied instead of sitting around and checking for messages from ThunderStruck—of which there are none—I've decided to grab my paddleboard and oar from the Bankses' garage and head down the sand-covered path that leads to the beach.

After we finished dinner, Neil sat down in his favorite chair to read his newspaper, and both Avery and I cuddled up on the sectional in the living room to kill some time before, in her words, "things get going."

Diane hand-served us the strawberry cheesecake that Chef Stone made before leaving their house, and Avery ate it while she whined about how she'll probably have to spend all day tomorrow in the gym in our condo building to work it off. Unlike me, she actually does work out from time to time. Though, I don't how she fits it into her vigorous social schedule.

By episode three of *Emily in Paris*, Diane and Neil called it a night and went to bed, and Avery went up to start getting ready. I threw on an old swimsuit to come out here.

I put on my headlamp and grab my board from its spot in the sand and head straight for the water. Most people would hate the idea of getting in the water this late at night, but it's something I've done a thousand times over the years. Truthfully, it's something I started doing with Beau when I was sixteen and is a welcome distraction now from the incessant thoughts of what Beau is doing at whatever bars in South Beach he and his buddies are enjoying.

Maverick, whose birthday they're celebrating, is pretty wild. At one of a few college parties Avery and I attended as high school girls while Beau was at the University of Miami, I witnessed Maverick Catalano do five keg stands in a row before he ended the night by streaking through their apartment complex with his twig and berries clutched in one of his giant hands. His ass is the first male butt I saw live and in person.

Between Beau, Henry, Ronnie, and Maverick, at least one of them is always getting into something. Any time Avery and I have run into them at the clubs, they're always enjoying a VIP section with a buffet of pretty girls and booze surrounding them.

Beau always tended to be tamer than his buddies, but that was when he was with Bethany. Now, he's single and he can do anything he wants. Talk to any attractive girl he wants. Take any girl he wants home.

Ugh. Stop it.

I try to remind myself of the messages he sent me earlier this evening. Try to tell myself that he's more interested in talking to me on Midnight than some random girl he meets in a bar. But that thought isn't all that reassuring when I face the reality of it.

He doesn't know Mystery Woman is me, and so far, all I've really done is string him along.

The moon is bright in the sky, and only a few clouds float around it. All in all, it's a pretty clear night by Southern Florida standards, and the water is calm as I move deeper into it so I can hop on my board.

It's a little chilly, but more exhilarating than anything else. I let my headlamp guide me, ignoring the eerie feeling that always comes with being in the water at night.

Once I'm on my board, I slowly stroke my oar through the water, carefully keeping an eye on the current as I do. The last thing I need is to drift out to sea. Though, with the mindfuck of a situation I've found myself in because of Midnight and my never-ending, secret crush on Beau, I can't deny there's a part of me that wonders if it would be kind of nice to go MIA.

The water is fairly calm, only a few ripples of waves to be seen, and I find a good but easy rhythm as I move along the coast. I stay far enough away from the sandbar that my board doesn't hit the bottom and send me catapulting into the water, but close enough to the coast to feel safe for being out here by myself at night.

There is always something so serene about being in the ocean at night. There are no sounds of other people, only the white noise of the water filling my ears. It's calming. Relaxing.

And completely at odds with what's going on inside me.

"Hey!"

I furrow my brow, looking around for the faint voice I swore I just heard.

"Juniper June!"

A dark, shadowy figure stands at the Bankses' private beach

gate, one hand waving while the other holds a board much like my own. He looks like Beau and sounds like Beau, but the Beau I know is supposed to be in South Beach with his pals, boozing and batting away women.

Surely he's a mirage. Surely I've just been thinking of him so much— too much—that it's like my mind is starting to hallucinate him.

"Stay right there!" Beau calls toward me again through cupped hands. "I'm coming to you!"

I stare in disbelief as he jogs to the water in a pair of black swim trunks, the muscles of his bare chest glistening in the moonlight like that one scene in *Twilight* where Edward's in Italy in that stupid red robe.

I look down at my board when my equilibrium threatens to pitch me to the side and then back up to watch as Beau paddles out toward me at a seemingly freakish speed.

Holy shit, he's really here.

I shouldn't be nervous, but I am. Beau Banks isn't the same old Beau Banks anymore, and I have the memories of his risqué photos to prove it.

So much has happened between us in those Midnight chats, and while he doesn't have a freaking clue, I've already found the wrench in the library and am interrogating Colonel Mustard. I know everything he's said and all of the sexy pictures he's sent, and I know how much deeper my feelings have grown.

There's an irrational part of me that wants to paddle as hard and as fast as I can in the opposite direction of him, but the smitten part—the one I've been smothering with a pillow for years— would never allow it.

So, I stand here instead, using my oar to stay balanced on my board, waiting to either expire from an exploding heart or Beau, whichever gets here first.

"Nice night," he says when he closes the distance between us. "Though, I'm not that thrilled that you're out here by yourself."

"It's fine, Beau."

He frowns at me, pausing his board so we're nearly side by side. "Still stubborn as hell, huh, Juniper June?"

Juniper June. A nickname that makes me feel more child than adult, but one I love all the same. There's so much wrapped up in our history together, I don't know where to find the end of the string.

"Not stubborn," I retort easily, maneuvering forward slowly. "Just not a little teenage girl anymore and well-versed in the dangers of night paddling."

"I know you're not a kid anymore, Juni." Beau's lips quirk up into an unexpected smile. "Trust me, I know. Doesn't mean I can't worry about you." He jerks his chin toward my feet. "By the way, I can't believe you still have that board."

I smile. He gave me this board when I turned sixteen, and I've been using it ever since. It could be split in half, and I'd find a way to glue it back together.

"It's a good board."

"Oh, I know it is," Beau says through a laugh. "That's why I gave it to you."

And that's why I kept it.

"Avery didn't drag you out tonight?" he asks, and I laugh at that.

"Oh, we're going. I had to leave a blood deposit and a sworn oath and testament that I wouldn't back out. But things, evidently, don't *pop off* until around this time, so she's upstairs getting ready."

Beau's chocolate eyes are warm and gooey with amusement. "And you didn't need to get ready?"

"It won't take me long." I shrug. "I'm not really in the mood to get attention anyway."

He snorts. "Yeah, good luck with that."

"What?"

"You don't need makeup to be beautiful, Juni. You know that."

Beautiful? He thinks *I'm* beautiful? My heart pounds like it's auditioning for one of those Fast & Furious movies. There's *no way* I can acknowledge the compliment. Not now. I'll spill all my guts if I do.

"I…uh…" I pause and lick at my now-dry lips. "I thought you were going out for Mav's birthday tonight? What are you doing here?"

"Figured I'd grab some leftovers from dinner on my way home," he says, an adorable smile on his lips. "Mav wanted to take a detour from South Beach to some new club that opened up downtown. I wasn't really in the mood, so I called it an early night. When I found the house basically deserted, I decided to take a quick paddle."

"Let me guess…*Echo*," I say with a knowing smile. "It's all Avery's been talking about for the past two days."

"It's *very exclusive*, according to Henry, whatever that means." Beau shakes his head and runs a hand through his hair before meeting my eyes again. "I know Avery's going to be waiting on you soon, but do you want to go down the coast a little bit?"

"Sure." I let him guide us, giving him room to go in front of me, but the entire time, my eyes are locked on him. I watch the way his muscular arms move as they slice the oar through the water. I take in the way the soft light of the moon bounces off his hair and skin. I admire how good his broad shoulders look. And I definitely admire how firm his ass looks beneath his swim trunks.

Beau Banks, the man of my dreams.

At one point in my life, I thought I'd eventually get over him. But now, after everything that's gone down, my heart only feels more certain. More…in love.

Because that's the reality. This isn't just a crush anymore.

I'm in love with Beau Banks, and he doesn't have a fucking clue.

Chapter 19

The Past
Seven years ago

"HAPPY BIRTHDAY, JUNE!" DIANE CHEERS AS NEIL CARRIES a cake to the dining table.

It's a giant cake, three big layers, with fancy buttercream icing and pink flower accents and sixteen candles that blaze at the top. The words, *Happy Sweet 16, Juniper*, stand proud in yellow icing.

Avery claps excitedly as Neil sets the cake down in front of where I sit at the table, and Neil, Diane, and Beau start to sing "Happy Birthday" to me.

They're all smiles and excitement, but my whole world feels like it's crumbling down. Their love is so big and vibrant, and still, it can't fill the hole my parents continue to dig. I thought maybe they'd come home this year—sixteen is a milestone, after all—but I should have known better.

I should always know better.

"Make a wish!" Neil says, Diane and Beau grinning behind him while Avery bounces on the other side of the table.

They're all so good to me—even Avery's big brother, Beau. At twenty-one, I figured he'd want nothing to do with a sixteen-year-old girl's birthday celebration. But Diane told me earlier that he specifically canceled plans with Bethany and his friends just to be here.

I look up into his smile as I think about all the things I dream of. Of the life I want to have some day. I get lost in his deep brown eyes for more than a moment.

Gah. Why does he have to be so freaking hot?

It takes an insane effort to pull my eyes away, but I do, inhaling a large breath of air and blowing out my candles as I silently make the same wish I've made for the past five years. *Please, dear universe… make my parents notice me and Beau Banks eventually fall in love with me. I know I'm young, so the timing is flexible on the second one. Thanks.*

Smoke lingers, licking at my nostrils and giving me an excuse for the tears in my eyes. I dab at them softly and paste on a smile as they all shift into action.

Diane starts to cut the cake, putting large slices on her favorite bone-colored plates, and Avery hops up from her seat to grab a stack of gifts they had hidden somewhere in a closet. Beau snags some forks from the drawer, and Neil gets rid of the candles in the garbage.

"Open this one first!" Avery cheers as she shoves a pretty gift with a pink bow into my chest. "It's from me."

I grin at her, but I've just barely removed the wrapping paper when she adds, "Though, you're probably going to have let me borrow it because I'm starting to have FOMO that I bought it for you instead of me. It was the last one available, too, so if you don't love it, you can regift it to me, even."

"Avery," Diane chastises, but I laugh. Avery is as reliable as an old Buick with a much heftier price tag.

"What, Mom? It's a cute bag."

I open the white lid that has Chanel engraved in black on the top and uncinch the protective felt bag inside. I pull out a little Chanel clutch, holding it in the air as I take in the black leather and gold-chained handles. "Thanks, Avery. I love it."

She frowns at that, and I laugh again. "You can borrow it whenever."

"Yay!" she says with an adorable clap.

Avery hands me another gift, but this time, Neil's and Diane's names are signed in pretty handwriting on a little card attached to a navy-blue bow. Inside the orange box sits a beautiful silk scarf from Hermès and a pretty bangle bracelet that I know Diane caught me eyeing when Avery dragged us out for a girls' shopping trip last weekend. But also, beneath the scarf and bracelet sits a fresh copy of *Pride and Prejudice.*

A soft sheen of tears covers my eyes, and a dab of pink heats the center of both my cheeks. It's not the gift itself, but the thought behind it. It's the fact that Diane noticed. That Diane knows me this well.

"Thank you so much," I say, clearing the ball of emotion out of my throat. "I love them."

"I knew you would." Diane winks at me and reaches out to squeeze my shoulder. "A mother knows when her girl is eyeing something she loves. Plus, I thought maybe you'd want a new copy of your favorite book. The old one is looking well-loved but tired."

My old copy of *Pride and Prejudice,* the one I've had for years, is definitely showing more than a little wear and tear these days. Just last week, I had to Scotch tape the spine just to keep the binding from falling apart.

Avery sets two more gifts down in front of me. "These got delivered to the house this morning."

Both boxes are huge, and I hate myself for reading the cards with each of them, hoping for something new, but I can't help it.

Happy Birthday, Juniper.
Hope you have a great day!
Love,
Dad

Juniper,
Happy Birthday, darling.
Can't wait to take you out to celebrate when I get back from Antigua next month!
Love,
Mom

My heart plummets to my shoes as I pretend to enjoy opening the gifts and seeing what's inside them. Each item costs more than the next, and my head feels like it's going to spin off my neck by the time I'm done.

Thankfully, Avery's excitement over my dad gifting me the limited-edition Hermès Birkin bag overshadows the utter devastation I'm feeling on the inside. She means so much to me, has changed my life so much for the better, seeing her happy is almost as good as feeling it myself.

This is the third birthday in a row that neither of my parents has been home to celebrate with me. My dad is on a summer-long vacation in the South of France with some twenty-five-year-old supermodel named Callie whom he just started dating. And my mother is on an Ayahuasca retreat in Peru.

I guess I should be glad they at least remembered today was my birthday, but the fact that my dad's card is in the pretty handwriting of his assistant Shirlene tells me he's probably too busy with Callie to even know what today is.

It's all shit. Just utter and total shit. But it's the story of my life.

The closest thing I have to a family are the four people in this room. Hell, Diane and Neil are more like parents to me than my mother and father have ever been. And it's been that way for as long as I can remember.

Avery is still obsessing over the Birkin bag my dad got me, and I'm just about to dive headfirst into a piece of my birthday cake when "You have one more gift to open" is whispered into my ear.

Instantly, goose bumps roll up my arms, and I look over my shoulder to meet Beau's smiling eyes.

"But you're going to have to come outside for it," he adds, and my hands are just about shaking as I take the napkin off my lap and set it down beside my plate of uneaten cake.

Avery is too busy begging Neil and Diane for the latest Birkin bag to notice Beau's and my departure from the table, and for that,

I'm grateful. The level of tail-wagging I'm doing right now needs no more of an audience.

Beau innocently grabs my hand as we walk out the doors that lead to the terrace, and my heart jumps straight into my throat.

"Follow me."

Beau is holding my hand. Beau Banks is holding my hand!

On the inside, I'm a vibration plate, but on the outside, I'm somehow managing to play it cool. At least, I think I am. With the speed my spirit is exiting my body, I should have an overhead view soon.

He lets go of my hand to grab his paddleboard and oar that rest on the white-picket-fence gate at the entrance to the beach path, and I fend off disappointment with everything I have.

"Happy Birthday, Juni," he says, and I furrow my brow in confusion. I don't see anything to go with the sentiment, and the last thing I want to be is a ditz who can't figure out her gift, but even at the risk of crippling embarrassment, I have to ask.

"Thanks, Beau. Um…I don't want to be rude, but are you supposed to be holding a gift when you say that?"

He laughs, but it's not at me. My delicate, crush-ridden psyche is eternally grateful. "Yes, I should be. So, I understand why you're confused. But the gift is this… I'm going to make your paddleboarding dreams come true," he says and puts the board in my hands. "Consider today your first lesson, and this is now officially *your* board."

"What?" I question, my voice a little hoarse to my own ears. Beau's board is incredibly important to him, which makes this gift deeply personal. "Are you serious? You're giving me your board?"

He nods, and the upward bow of his lips can only be described as the most perfect smile I've ever seen in my whole life. Straight teeth, plush flesh, and a genuine almost-dimple deep in the tan of his cheek.

For the past few summers, whenever Beau is home from college, I've watched him and his buddies surf and paddleboard on the daily out of pure personal torture. The muscles, the laughter, the skill—his version of it is addictive. On the tenth day of avid attention from me, Beau asked if I wanted to learn. Without a reason to be watching otherwise, I told him yes to the paddleboarding but passed on the surfing.

At the time, it was an excuse, but the more I've watched him, the more I've actually wondered if it might be fun.

And he remembered.

I didn't think it was possible with the way I was feeling earlier, but this is officially the best birthday I've ever had.

All thanks to Beau Banks.

Chapter 20

"**J**UST MAKE SURE THAT NED IS THE ONE WHO GETS THESE edits, okay?" Denise requests as she sets a stack of thick cardboard slides that contain content tag lines for a popular soda company on my desk.

"Will do," I tell her, standing up and stretching my legs. I don't normally sit for more than five minutes at a time around here, but this morning has been an absolute email onslaught.

I smooth my hands down my wide-leg Prada gabardine pants, adjust the brown Hermès belt around my waist, and pick up the slides from my desk. They're bulky but thankfully not heavy, and I'm only slightly awkward on my walk to the elevators without being able to see my feet.

It's not like I normally stare at my shoes when I walk, but something about taking them out of sight completely makes me feel off-kilter.

Juggling slightly as I step on the elevator, I punch the button for the fifth floor until it lights up—it's finicky sometimes—and wait as the doors close in front of me. I adjust the cardboard where it digs into my ribs and dance from side to side to pass the time. Now that I'm up and moving, my bladder is awake and screaming for a potty break after I drop these off to Ned.

The ride is quick from the fifteenth to the fifth, but just as I'm stepping off the cart, my phone vibrates inside my pocket.

I want to check it now, but a whole slapstick comedy routine of me and the slides and a split the Dallas Cowboys cheerleaders would be jealous of plays in my mind at the thought of chancing maintaining my tenuous grip with one hand.

People smile at me as I power walk down the hall to Ned's office, dropping the slides on his empty desk and peering around to see if he's anywhere nearby. When I don't find him—or anyone else, for that matter—I pull out my phone and use the sanctuary of his office to read it with privacy.

It's a notification from Midnight, and since I have zero willpower, I open the app and go to the one and only chatbox I have attached to my profile.

But I'm completely unprepared for what's inside.

> **ThunderStruck: I'm sitting in an important meeting right now, but I can't stop thinking about what color your panties are today.**

I bobble my phone in my hands and let out a gasp, startling even further when Ned's polite voice greets me from the door.

"Oh hey, June. Didn't know you were down here."

I clear my throat twice before tucking my phone back into my pocket, even as it buzzes a second time, and dab at my now-fiery cheeks with cool hands. "Yeah. Yep. Just dropping off some slides from Denise. They're for..." I shake my head, desperately trying to remember the account name instead of my white panties. "SoPop." I snap my fingers, and Ned smiles.

"A long Monday already, huh?"

I chuckle, the sound a little brittle around the edges. "Yeah. I guess it's that time of year. Fourth quarter and all."

Ned nods. "Yep. Everything needs buttoning up. Did Denise say when she needs these back?"

"No." I frown over my lack of knowledge. "Do you want me to run up there and ask?"

He shakes his head. "That's all right. I'll call."

"Okay!" I rush through the door as he steps to the side, dismissing myself with a wave over my shoulder and bolting for the elevator. When the doors close me into solitude, I pull out my phone with shaky hands and read the remaining Midnight message.

> **ThunderStruck: I want to tease you. Make you feel what you're making me feel by making me want you so bad but not telling me who you are. I want to put my mouth right there, right on your perfect pussy, but I'd make you keep your panties on so all you can feel is the warmth of my breath. And I'd keep my mouth there until you are soaked all the way through.**

Holy hell, is it just me, or is it hot in here? Maintenance should look into this elevator being one million degrees.

I should be ashamed of myself for the faint throb that's made itself known between my legs, but I'm not. I've dreamed of Beau saying these things to me for much longer than I'd like to admit, and I deserve to revel in the excitement of it actually happening…right?

Maybe I should make that trip to the bathroom, but instead of dealing with my bladder, I should hide in the stall and take an actual picture of my pussy and send it to him.

I've never, in my life, sent a guy a picture of my pussy. Never even considered it.

But over the past few weeks, I've danced on the line. Hell, just yesterday morning, in the wee hours before sunrise, fresh on the booze of going out with Avery after paddleboarding, I sent **ThunderStruck** an up-close-and-personal view of my breasts, hard nipples and all.

It was wanton and uninhibited, and when he woke up to it, he left me a slew of messages that talked me right through yet another orgasm when I got up just after noon.

On shaky legs, I walk off the elevator on the fifteenth floor, go through the front door, pass my cubicle, and head down the hall, my sights set on the bathroom.

But as I pass by one of the large conference rooms and spot Beau sitting at the head of the table and several of the members of his Midnight campaign team around him, I get a different idea.

Impulsiveness—*and pent-up sexual frustration*—driving my decisions, I double-back to snag a Post-it note from my desk and book it down the hall to where Beau's empty office sits. I survey my surroundings, making sure no one is paying too much attention to me, and slip inside. I'm thankful the blinds are down, covering the see-through glass walls, and pull the pen from behind my ear to quickly write out a little note on the pink Post-it in my hands.

I stick it to the edge of his open laptop screen and turn for the door—just as Avery is coming through it.

Shiiiit.

I move away from the note and Beau's desk as subtly as I can as she dives right into conversation.

"Oh my God, June! You wouldn't believe what I just heard about Helen Fox. You know, the girl who got pregnant in eighth grade and left school to go to Germany?"

My head swims as I try to shift gears from one Banks to the other. "Vaguely, yes."

"Well, you know that Toby Vincent, who got her pregnant, was always a prick and got what he deserved when he got dishonorably discharged from the Navy a couple years ago. But Helen just got engaged to a billionaire—with a B—in Dubai, and I heard from Taryn, who heard from her mom, who heard from Toby's aunt, that he's positively upchucking over the news."

"Wow." It's all I can manage in the face of the salacious gossip, but evidently, it's enough, because Avery carries on.

"I know! Anyway, I'm really happy for her. I always love it when the fucked-over humps back, you know?"

I nod. If there's one thing about Avery, it's that she's for the girls. She may gossip, but it's never to bad-mouth anyone who doesn't deserve it.

"What are you doing in here anyway?" she questions, stepping around me and heading straight for his desk. She plops down into his desk chair, rooting around in his files on top, and I want to die a very slow death at how close she is to that damn Post-it note.

"I...uh...I had to drop something off to him." She quirks an eyebrow, and I force myself to pull it the fuck together. "What are *you* doing here?"

"Seeing if he has any money lying around. I forgot my wallet, and I'm dying for an iced mocha latte. And my credit card doesn't work. They sent me some email about being over my monthly limit. Like, those things have limits? Whatever."

"Oh," I say, making my voice sound as laid-back as I possibly can, even though my heart is beating so fast it feels like someone is actually chasing it inside my chest. Her eyes start to move toward the screen of Beau's laptop, and instant panic clutches my chest. "You want to go to lunch?" My voice is a startling blurt and far too loud for the occasion, but Avery is too focused on the lunch part to notice. *Thank goodness.*

"Finally, yes!" she says through a relieved sigh. "I was getting ready to put you in workaholic rehab. But..." She pauses and points an index finger at me. "I get to choose, and you have to pay. I forgot my wallet, remember?" She starts to search Beau's desk again, muttering about how she can't believe he doesn't have any cash lying around, and I jump into action.

"You got it," I agree, grabbing her elbow to drag her to the door.

"Geez, June," she complains, pulling out of my grip to smooth out her sailor-inspired Miu Miu navy wool dress. "What's your deal—*oh my God*. Look at this!" Her voice is equal parts disgusted and appalled as she snags the Post-it note from the screen of Beau's laptop and shoves it at me.

My hand shakes as I take it, and she stomps her heel in anticipation.

"Read it!"

Funny thing, friend, but I already read it because I wrote it.

I do everything I can to see it with fresh eyes, but as the author, I have no idea if I pass.

White lace panties.
Who's the tease now?
-M.W.

"It's pathetic, right?" Avery questions, finally putting me out of my misery and removing the note from my hand with a yank.

"So pathetic," I respond, feeling exactly that.

From Avery's perspective, it looks like some slutty chick in this office is trying to seduce her brother, which is pretty pitiful. But when you consider that the slutty chick is me, it gets even sadder.

"Damn, these hoes are desperate out in these streets," she says, looking down at the note again before looking back at me. "Good grief, he's like a modern-day Lothario, pulling thirsty chicks from every direction. It's so tiring. At least I never have to worry about you pulling this kind of shit with him." She laughs. "Like, could you imagine?" She laughs harder. "Maybe I could take up employment as his pimp?"

My smile is brittle, and the laugh I have to force from my lungs is the very definition of miserable.

"Who do you think M.W. is?" Avery questions, her thinking cap making her Botox-filled forehead try to move. "Because I am not above going through HR files to figure it out. It has to be initials, right?"

The very last thing I need right now is Avery going through files. Like, sure, there's no way to track me to M.W., but with hundreds of employees, at least ten innocent women are bound to get involved.

"I bet it's some inside joke or something," I try to excuse, hoping she'll take the bait.

"Oh, you're probably right!" she quietly exclaims, pointing a finger toward me. "Plus, it's not like I have time to go looking through

HR files. Like, I've got enough work to do, you know?" She rolls her eyes. "My brother can deal with the floozies himself."

I don't even tease her about the work comment, I'm so relieved.

"Anyway," Avery singsongs and crumples up the Post-it note in her hands before dropping it into the trash can next to Beau's desk. "Let's go to lunch."

Shit. That was a close call.

Frankly, it was so close that my whole body feels seconds away from imminent detonation.

If Avery would've stepped into Beau's office just a minute earlier, she would've seen me putting that on his laptop, and everything I've been hiding would be out in the open with a certifiable belly flop into the raging waters of my sins.

Avery rambles about the lunch place she's decided she wants to eat at, and even though I'm doing my best at making small talk, on the inside, I'm falling apart.

These anonymous chats with Beau are getting dangerous. Playing with fire, to be exact.

And today made something I've been ignoring painfully clear in a way I can't just shake off—I'm not the only one at risk of getting burned.

Chapter 21

B Y THE TIME I GET HOME FROM WORK, I FEEL LIKE A ROBOT. Lunch with Avery felt next to impossible. Between pretending to be engaged in whatever she was talking about and trying not to internally drown in the guilt, I was a walking live wire of nerves when I made it back to the office. Avery peaced-out for the rest of the day in the name of getting a Brazilian.

And what I came back to at the Banks & McKenzie Marketing building wasn't much better.

It's a wonder we didn't have to call the fire department or an ambulance with the way people were running around with their heads cut off, putting out fires. One campaign had issues with legal. Another campaign had last-minute edits on a commercial that is supposed to air during a celebrity awards show this weekend. And two other campaigns had other issues that I can't even remember at this point.

Simply put, it was a shitshow. A perfect match to how I'm feeling on the inside.

I never messaged Beau back, pussy picture or otherwise, and now that I've had time to come down from the high, I'm not sure I should.

It's one thing to be engaging in a harmless, flirty, anonymous conversation with a random man, but it's a whole other thing when that random man is your best friend's brother and no one but you knows what you're doing.

Not only have I consciously withheld the truth from Beau, knowingly letting him wander down this wild path of innocent messages turning into something that's laced with hot sexual tension and deep, meaningful conversations, but I've also lied to my best friend. Actively and repeatedly.

Keeping my crush to myself was fine, but now that I'm vigorously pursuing it? That's a whole other level of deceit.

Nothing good can come of this, I'm sure of it, and I've got the gut-wrenching intuition that if I don't end this now, I'll regret it.

I promised myself I'd only lie to Avery one more time so that I could tell her I have a migraine, and she'd go out to Echo without me. All in the name of getting on Midnight and telling **ThunderStruck** goodbye for good.

Obviously, that's what needs to happen here. I'll carry the guilt and shame of where I let these conversations go, but I'll carry them knowing I stopped it before anyone else but me gets hurt. That's my burden to bear, and I take full accountability for that.

When I log on to Midnight, the last two messages **ThunderStruck** sent me taunt and tantalize just like before. But I inhale a deep breath and make myself do the right thing.

It takes me a good ten minutes to find my words, but eventually, I do.

> **ElizaBeth: I've been thinking a lot about what you said. About how our chats are reckless for someone in your position in the company. And it made me realize that you're right, Beau. We shouldn't do this, you know? It's not good for either of us.**

> **ElizaBeth: Mixing business and personal lives generally doesn't end anywhere good. It's why most companies have an HR policy revolving around preventing employees from fraternizing. And even though Banks & McKenzie doesn't**

have that kind of policy, I think we need to end this, whatever this is, that's happening inside these chats. I'm sorry, but yeah, I think this needs to be goodbye.

When I hit send on my final message, I feel like a total asshole for feeling sad, but it is what it is. Not a single ounce of relief comes from sending him those words, even when I know in my conscience it should.

Get over it, I tell myself. It's the only option.

But because I'm a masochist, I look at the messages one more time, even scroll through all the previous messages before, reminiscing over all the things we've shared with each other. All the playful, flirty things that've been said.

My finger hovers over the big red X that sits in the upper right corner of the screen that'll end this chat for good. Just one tap of the screen and it will scrub the hours spent inside from my phone and my life forever.

But before I can muster the courage to do it, **ThunderStruck has reentered the chat** populates on the screen. I almost click out before he can say anything, but as it turns out, I'm not strong enough.

ThunderStruck: I think you're wrong.

I stare at his words for what feels like forever. The only thing that pulls me out of my daze is the message that appears below them.

ThunderStruck: The risk is worth the reward. I know how you make me feel. I know that when I wake up, you've become one of the first things I think about. And when I go to bed, you're one of my last thoughts, too. I spend an insane amount of my day excited to read a new message from you, and I've spent twenty-eight years without anything close to that. I refuse to say goodbye without giving this a fair shot. Why won't you?

Tears hit my eyes as I force my fingers over the keyboard.

> **ElizaBeth: I don't know. It's just more complicated than you can even imagine.**

> **ThunderStruck: Fuck complicated, ElizaBeth. I think we're playing with soul-deep.**

A *soul-deep connection.* Between me and Beau. The thing I've been dreaming about for over a decade. *Freaking hell, if that doesn't strike a nerve.*

> **ThunderStruck: But how can we know if we don't take the leap? I think we need to meet. I think you need to stop being scared and finally show me who you are. We need to give this thing a real shot.**

When I don't respond, he sends another message.

> **ThunderStruck: Please. I need to meet you. It feels like you could be the woman I'm supposed to fall for. There's something here. And I don't want to let it go.**

His words are everything I've ever hoped and wished and dreamed that I'd hear Beau Banks say. And they're my final undoing. They make it impossible for me to deny what I want the most in this world, consequences be damned. I have to let myself have this. If I don't, I'll spend the rest of my life wondering.

> **ElizaBeth: Okay. Let's meet. But it needs to be somewhere outside of the office, and I need to be sure no one else will be there.**

> **ThunderStruck: How about the gym in my building? Tomorrow. At midnight. Seems appropriate, doesn't it? And I'm pretty confident it'll be desolate, too. I can send you the address.**

Considering the gym in his building is also the gym in *my*

building, it doesn't feel as risky as a club or bar. It feels…about as safe as I can get. Well, as long as I can make sure Avery isn't there.

ElizaBeth: Okay.

This is really happening. My fairy-tale messages with Beau are coming to a close. But Cinderella has one up on me this time.

I have no idea if my ending will be happy or not.

Chapter 22

MUSIC POUNDS FROM THE SPEAKERS PLACED strategically around downtown Miami's newest club Echo, and I look past the red velvet ropes of the VIP section Avery convinced her current boy toy Ben to reserve for us tonight. She's currently on the dance floor, making out with some guy with long, dark hair that reminds me of that big, muscular dude from *Game of Thrones*.

I steal a glance behind me, where Ben sits cluelessly on one of the posh black sofas, chatting with a friend of his named Jackson whom I just met when we arrived. Ben has no idea that the girl he's after, the one who is utilizing his generosity and willingness to cover the very expensive tab, is currently on the dance floor sucking face with a guy she just met.

But none of this is my concern when I check the time on my phone and see it's thirty minutes till midnight.

I hate myself for what I strategically put into action tonight and for what I'm about to do, but I do it anyway. I had to be sure Avery would be out so I'd have the building to myself.

Uber app pulled up on my phone, I order a ride back to our condo and send Avery a text message I know she won't see because she's too busy sticking her tongue down Mr. *Game of Thrones*'s throat.

Me: Feel a little sick from dinner but don't want to ruin your fun. Grabbing an Uber and heading home.

I hit send as I'm grabbing my purse and tell Ben and Jackson goodbye. They try to convince me to stay, but it only takes an excuse of feeling like puking for them step clear of my path toward the door.

Once I'm outside the club, I only have to wait a few minutes before my Uber appears, Lance driving a Silver Expedition. I double-check his license plate with what's showcased in the app and after a short but friendly greeting hello, I climb into the back seat and put on my seat belt.

He heads toward my condo building, and I try to relax as he manages to hit the lights on green at every intersection.

When we're about ten minutes from home, I open Midnight and scroll through the last messages that led me here.

ThunderStruck: I'm so glad you agreed to meet. I live in the 72 Park Building. 580 72nd Street, Miami Beach. The gym is on the fifth floor.

ElizaBeth: Okay.

ThunderStruck: I'll see you at Midnight. Right?

ElizaBeth: I promise. I'll be there.

When Lance pulls his Expedition to a stop in front of the entrance to *our* building, I have to take several deep breaths just to be able to get out of the car. My whole body feels like a shell of itself.

My fingers tingle, and my legs are numb as I pass through the lobby to the bank of elevators at the back of the building. I have no idea what's going to happen or how Beau is going to react, and the mere thought of him being *angry* with me is enough for me to push a different button than I'm supposed to inside the cart. Instead of heading to the fifth floor, I head to the thirty-second, where our condo is located, and unlock and close the door behind me without taking a single full breath.

I walk straight into my bedroom and slide off my heels and little black dress and change into a pair of workout leggings and a sports bra.

I don't know why, but looking the part somehow feels better.

I grab my phone, AirPods, and water bottle and head back out of my condo without giving myself any time to second-guess.

The elevator is still waiting from my earlier arrival, so I step on and push the button for the fifth floor as fast as I can.

Somehow, I've managed to do all of this without running into Beau, and that, in and of itself, is a minor miracle, given our condos are on the same floor. I check the screen of my phone for the time. Five minutes until midnight.

Am I really going to follow through with this? Am I really going to walk into the gym and tell Beau that I'm the woman he's been talking to on Midnight this entire time?

It sure looks like it, but for the life of me, I still can't be sure.

The elevator dings its arrival, and I step off, my feet somehow managing to move straight for the gym's door. I walk inside. The door closes shut behind me.

It's empty, which is the point of the late hour, but still, it's *empty*. No Beau in sight. I fiddle there for a few long moments before walking over to a bench press machine and pulling blindly at the little pin that sets the weights.

I don't know what I'm doing, but at least I'm doing something. Time drags and silence rings in my ears, and growing more nervous by the minute, I sit down on the bench and wobble my knees back and forth.

I check the screen of my phone again, a compulsion I can't stop. Two minutes until midnight.

Maybe he's changed his mind. Maybe he's—

My thoughts come to a screeching halt when I hear the elevator ding and the gentle whir of the stainless-steel-fronted doors opening. A shock of adrenaline hits when I hear footsteps moving down the hallway.

Shit!

I panic, jumping up from my bench and rocking back and forth on my toes, my mind trying to figure out what I should do. Any second, Beau could walk in here. Any second, he could find out the truth.

In a rush, I jog over toward the racks of dumbbells that sit in front of a massive floor-to-ceiling mirror, and I snag one into my hand, not giving a shit how much weight it is. The door opens, and I shut my eyes for the longest moment before I can muster the strength to take a peek into the mirror.

Handsome as ever in his undeniable reflection, the man of my dreams is here.

I expect Beau to be searching, to be checking every crevice of the gym, but instead, his warm brown eyes are locked and loaded, right on me.

Oh my God.

Oh my God.

OH MY GOD.

I don't know what to do. I honestly have no idea what to do. My heart is pounding so hard inside my chest, and it's truly a miracle right now if I'm actually breathing.

Everything is frozen. My legs. My arms. My face.

Our eyes lock in the reflection in the mirror, and a petal of my rose-colored cheeks wilts as wrinkles form at the sides of his eyes.

I was hoping for love and affection, but I got her evil, ugly stepsister—confusion. It's a completely fair and valid reaction on his part, but still...it stings.

"June?"

"Uh...hey," I say, but I don't dare turn around. Instead, I stand there and pretend to do bicep curls with the one lone weight in my hand.

"W-what are you doing here?" he asks, and I can see the wheels of his mind spinning and spinning as he tries to understand if I'm here by coincidence or if I've ensnared him with the impossible.

Me? His Mystery Woman? It couldn't be.

I open and close my mouth, my brain completely incompetent in forming words. For as many times as I've thought out this possibility, I never managed to think through the part where I actually explain.

"Beau, I…I wish I knew what to say—"

Unexpectedly, the door swings open from behind him, the wood nearly smacking him in the back. Avery, still dressed in her clubbing attire, screeches to a stop at the sight of us.

"June? Beau?" Her head swivels between us, and I start curling my weight again in a panic. My muscle burns at the sudden overuse, but I don't care. I keep pumping anyway. "What the hell are you guys doing here?"

Beau looks between the two of us, and I know, even though I'm trying *so* hard, I'm doing a shit job of hiding the outright panic on my face.

His brown eyes narrow, locking completely with mine, and I have to reach out a hand toward the mirror to steady myself. I don't know what my other arm is doing with the stupid dumbbell. It's a miracle it's still in my hand.

"Uh, hello?" Avery questions. "June? Pretty sure you have some explaining to do." Her hand goes to her hip, and my eyes go back to Beau. He's watching me closely as Avery reads me the riot act. "I can't fucking believe you would dip on me like that!" She stomps over toward the row of ellipticals and treadmills, her mouth moving a mile a minute. "Do you have any idea how annoying it was when Ben tried to act all alpha when he saw me with another guy on the dance floor? It was a fucking mess, June. You left me high and dry!" She snags something from one of the machine's cupholders before spinning back around to meet me. "What the hell happened?"

"I had a migraine again…" I pause, lying straight to both Beau's and her faces. "And I just thought maybe…you know…maybe a workout would help it."

"God, Juni," Avery says through a sigh. "You need to get those looked at. This is, like, the third time this month one of your migraines has gotten in the way of our good time."

Hook, line, and sinker, my best friend clearly trusts me way too much. She believes the lie and starts rambling more about how Ben was annoyed she was dancing with that *Game of Thrones*-looking dude, and I die a little more inside.

How many Banks hearts do I have to break before I turn tail and run?

PART 4

Beau

Chapter 23

MY PULSE FEELS THREADED, A RACING FLUTTER IN MY throat that refuses to quit. June's blue eyes turn down at the corners, worry and embarrassment and uncertainty warring within them.

How can June be the one I've been messaging with all this time? How?

I swallow hard, thinking of all the things she's said to me. The things I've said to *her*. They're sexy things, personal things—the kinds of things you don't come back from.

I'm just finding this all out, but her? She's known it's me the *whole* time.

Avery chatters on, unfazed by the sudden stop of Earth's rotation, but the two of us? We're in the middle of a metal-crunching, tires-shrieking wreck.

"I was going to invite Nathan Turlington to come with me to the annual Banks Halloween bash on Friday, but he refuses to wear a Zorro costume. And if he won't do that, I'm not sure what the point of taking someone who looks like Antonio Banderas even is, you know? Like, know your niche. If he looked like Glen Powell, we'd go with a white T-shirt and jeans and a cowboy hat like he wears in *Twisters*, but he doesn't. Plus, he wants to go as the Hulk. The *Hulk*. He has to be kidding me with that shit."

"At least Hulk is shirtless," June offers, her eyes still on me. She doesn't look confused like me—she wouldn't be, of course, being that she left the note for the Midnight meetup in the first place—but her ears are red-hot, and her bottom lip shakes just slightly less than her hands. She's nervous. Maybe a little embarrassed. But she's here. Her intention to meet me, to come clean about her identity, to put it all out on the table, is undeniable.

My brain is sludge and my heart out of rhythm. It feels impossible to make sense of and a little like I'm doing something wrong. Growing up so closely together, I had assumptions about how I'd see Juniper Perry for the rest of my life.

But the girl I grew up treating as a sister suddenly isn't seeming so sisterly at all.

"Oh. Yeah. I guess that's true," Avery comments with a clueless smile and a wink directed at June. It's clear she hasn't sussed out the elephant-sized tension in this room, but that's probably because my sister has never been good at sensing other people's emotions. "See, June, that's why you're my best friend. You can see through my bullshit and call me on it. I guess I'll tell him Hulk is okay, even if he is green."

"I'm not sure how, but I think that might be racist," I manage to remark, trying out my normally brotherly role on my tongue. It feels foreign, especially knowing that I expected this meetup to go an entirely different direction, but evidently, it's passable.

Avery shoves me in the shoulder like always, and I lift the corner of my mouth in a smile as I stumble back playfully. June grabs her by the elbow and pulls her toward the exit.

I plead for answers silently, hoping she'll find a way to ditch Avery back in their condo and come find me. Hoping she'll meet me on Midnight to put this all to rest. I need an explanation. I need answers, and truthfully, I'm not even sure I know all the questions.

The June I've known for most of my life and the June of our chats are two entirely different people, and now that the secret is out, I don't know which one she'll be going forward. *How in the hell are we supposed to move forward?*

"Shut up, weirdo." For the first time tonight, Avery notices my attire and the bottle of water in my hand. "Who even works out at midnight? Don't you have work in the morning?"

"I think, out of the two of us, you're the one we should be asking that question. Where exactly are you on your way back from this late, and why are you in the gym? I thought you did your workouts during work hours as an exercise in *multitasking*," I mock.

"Late?" Avery's laughter rings out in peals. "Oh my God, you've really gotten old, haven't you? It's just after midnight, for Pete's sake. I was the first one to leave the club. If I didn't feel like all the sushi I ate a Hosu House fucked up my stomach, I'd still be out. As soon as you said you felt sick, I started feeling sick too," she says, turning to June. "And I left my AirPods down here earlier today and wanted them to help put me to sleep. Unlike my old-man brother, my body is liable to revolt at the early hour."

I roll my eyes. "Whatever. Just go get some sleep so you can actually be a productive member of the company tomorrow."

"Productive?" She frowns. "That doesn't sound fun at all."

"Avery, go to bed."

"Man, June, can you believe this loser? He sounds just like Dad." She lowers her voice to what she thinks sounds like a serious man and mocks, "Business, business, business. Deals, deals, deals. Blippity, bloppity, bloop."

June sucks her lips into her mouth, a blush stealing across her high cheeks, and I feel the unexpected visual of her doing that while she's on her knees looking up at me. It's surprising and unexpected and, honestly, a little bit unsettling.

This is June. Juniper. My little sister's best friend.

And yet, not anymore. Because, as of tonight, she's also my Mystery Woman.

Fuck.

Night after night, she's turned me on in ways I've never experienced before. We've explored each other both mentally and physically, and for my part, I've had nothing but a hazy picture of a sexy woman.

I rake my eyes across her beautiful jaw, along her collarbone, and to the soft swell of her chest. Her skin is supple and smooth, covered in the same freckles I've seen for years, and the Cupid's bow at the top of her lips is dotted with the shine of her lip gloss.

She is sexy. Almost unbearably so, if I really let myself look at her.

But this isn't the June I know.

This isn't the *relationship* with June I know. Not at all. And that's befuddling as fuck.

"Beau is a kind, successful guy," June comments, her voice soft and quiet. "If he sounds like your dad—which I'm not sure he does—that's hardly a bad thing."

"Pfft," Avery hums on a laugh. "Yeah. Okay."

"I'm serious," June says, but this time, she's not looking at Avery at all. She's looking directly at me, her eyes deconstructing me piece by piece until they pierce a tiny hole in my soul. "You're a good guy, Beau. The best. I've *always* thought so."

The words punch well above their fighting weight, and I have to hold myself steady from stumbling again even with no shove involved.

Avery shakes her head, annoyed with the stupid conversation, but I know with pointed clarity that it's not stupid at all. It's a declaration. It's a decision. It's an admission.

June knew what she was doing pursuing me, and she did it on purpose.

But to what end?

Is this idea of us, this different view of what we could be, one she's had for a while? And if that's the case, why didn't she say something sooner? Why did she choose to message me like this? And why does it have to feel so messy?

Avery loops her arm through June's and pulls her out of the gym, chattering about her night out while June tries to listen. She looks back, just once, but there's no changing the outcome of what'll never be the same.

Juniper Perry isn't who she used to be, and I don't feel the way I used to about her. She's not a kid, and the chatter on the other end of my Midnight messages isn't a mystery.

As of tonight, my Mystery Woman is gone, and in her place is a version of Juniper Perry I don't know at all.

Then again, I guess things turning out differently than I expected isn't that new at all.

Chapter 24

The Past
Five years ago

BLACK CAPS WITH ORANGE TASSELS RAIN DOWN AROUND me, and the sheer volume of my classmates' cheering mimics the football games that normally take place in the space around us.

But this isn't about a touchdown or scoring points on the field. This is about a transition to adulthood—a new phase of life—and I relish the exciting challenge ahead.

The professors and deans on stage clap for us—this year's official graduating class of the University of Miami—and families disperse from their spots in the stands as they take on our victory as one of their own.

It makes sense, of course. The support of my family is largely what got me here and what keeps me vigilant in the pursuit of success.

My dad Neil is my role model. Successful. Loving. Driven and compassionate. He's everything I want myself to be as I build my own life and family.

My girlfriend Bethany jumps and waves from the second to last row, and my best friend Seth plays the air guitar from somewhere in the middle, all of us having been separated by the alphabetical seating arrangement, and my mom, dad, sister, and her best friend

Juniper all cheer from their seats on the side of the football stadium. Mav, Henry, and Ronnie all chose majors that require a fifth year—at least, they do when you party more than study—so they won't graduate until next year.

People around me hunt for their caps on the ground, but having had the forethought to throw mine in a way I'd be able to catch it, I skirt through the tight row of folding chairs and out to the edge, bracing myself as Bethany runs directly into my arms and rains kisses on my cheeks. She's way more affectionate than she has been in a while, so I eat it up, hugging her back before ending our embrace with one final kiss to her lips.

I know she's been stressed with finals and trying to line up a job after graduation, but having her acting normal again is a breath of fresh air. Her dad has at least five interviews lined up for her with different news stations in Miami, and I'm sure she'll land one of them without much trouble. She's got *the look*.

Seth saunters to us lazily, his smile upturned even more than ours by the whiskey I can smell pouring off him.

"It's ten a.m.," I say with a laugh, waving a hand in front of my nose.

"It's graduation!" he protests with a scoff. "Everyone knows there aren't any rules at graduation."

"The university actually has a list of explicit rules they sent us for this specific occasion," I contest, and Seth laughs.

"Okay, well...I didn't read them."

"Shocker," Bethany comments as she pushes out of my hold, forcing my hand at her hip to fall back into my space.

"Don't be jealous that I'm having more fun than you." Seth grins at her. "Maybe you should learn to walk on the wild side more, Beth. I can speak from experience, it's *fucking awesome*."

They stare at each other, my girlfriend glaring and my best friend looking completely entertained.

For as long as I've been dating Bethany, she and Seth have

always had a bit of tension. He annoys her on purpose, and she takes the bait every time.

"How about you leave my girl alone?" I chime in, amusement in my voice, and Seth just chuckles and holds up two lazy hands in the air and flashes a wink at Beth.

"I promise to be on my best behavior."

"Whatever." Beth sighs and glances at me. "I saw my parents watching from section 119. I'm going to go find them."

I nod. "Okay, babe. Check in with you later."

She smiles softly before glancing over at Seth one last time and walking away. I spot my own family through the crowd, heading toward me, and I take off at a run with one last pat on the shoulder for Seth. Our dads are business partners and best friends, but that doesn't mean they're not different. Chris McKenzie is pretentious rich. *Conceited* rich. He's self-important and takes himself way too seriously. Because of all of those things, he's waiting in the stands for Seth to come to him.

But not my dad. He's leading the charge down from their seats and onto the field, ready to pull me into a bear hug as soon as he closes the distance.

I match his energy with a big hug that sends him backward, accidentally knocking into my sister and Juniper as a result.

"My God!" Avery shouts, tumbling back and just catching herself by knocking completely into best friend. Juniper's balance doesn't recover as well—probably because there's no one behind her—and she ends up on her ass in the grass. We all rush to help pick her up, but I'm the first to get there to officially offer a hand.

"I'm so sorry, June," I apologize, helping her to her feet and holding both her hands until I'm sure she's okay. It feels like she's been around forever at this point, a certified member of the family.

"I'm fine." Her smile is easy and her cheeks pink as she shakes her head. "I just hope I'm that excited when I graduate so I can get you back."

"You can knock me over right now." I grin at her. "I won't mind."

"I think you should let her punch you in the balls, Beau," Avery comments while she stares down mindlessly at her freshly painted nails. She shrugs one nonchalant shoulder. "Seems only fair."

Juniper snorts. "Yeah, that's okay. I'm good." Her long, wavy copper hair is down and around her face, and a single piece sticks to her shiny lip gloss from the fall. I reach out and pull it back, and her blue eyes widen as my thumb brushes the corner of her mouth.

My stomach pitches strangely. It's weird, seeing her like this, with makeup and heels and a dress that is shorter than my brain wishes it would be.

But Juniper is eighteen now.

Most of the time I've known her, she's been a sweet, awkward kid. Suddenly, she's looking a whole hell of a lot more like a woman because she *is* a woman. A full-fledged adult *woman* who is stunningly beautiful in ways I hope all men don't realize.

"Come on," my mom says, taking me by the elbow and turning me around to walk toward the exit of the stadium. "We have reservations at Pasitinos and then a celebration party at the house."

I clasp my hand over my mom's and smile.

I've got a great family, a great girlfriend, and the job of my dreams lined up with my dad in the fall. The whole world is in front of me, and I can't wait to get started living in it.

Chapter 25

TODAY'S BEEN A BUSY DAY IN EXACTLY ZERO OF THE WAYS I intended, and my brain is on the fritz, trying to hold it all together.

After what went down in our condo's gym last night, I've messaged June a bunch of times on Midnight, but she's yet to respond. And when I got to work this morning, my first priority was finding her and guiding her toward a quiet spot in our office to hash everything out—to try to understand why she did what she did, to try to understand what it all means—but everything went to hell, and I've spent hour after hour putting out fires on multiple accounts.

Social media disasters, missed commercial spots, unreliable vendors—you name it, and it's come up since I arrived at the office early this morning.

This was supposed to be an easy day. I should've been able to coast right through to the weekend until my parents' big Halloween party tomorrow night, but my phone's Teams' notifications, paired with our Asana workflow, have sounded like a fucking swarm of noisy birds. One more chirp from the damn thing and I'm going to lose my cool. Or, you know, just fucking deal with it and try to keep my head from exploding.

Chirp, my phone announces right on cue, and a heavy sigh leaves my lungs as I look down at the screen.

Harry: The Gerry Meats contract is stalled in legal review. They've had it for three months, and we already have one hundred hours on this thing because of the drop date. Any cues on direction?

Me: I'll escalate the issue to Neil and Chris. Stay on task until I get another edict.

Harry: Understood.

Huffing out a breath, I round the reception desk, offering a friendly nod to Marlene, and head through the glass doors that lead to the cubicles in the center of the floor plan.

June's desk is empty—as is Avery's—but the deeper I get into the junior marketers' desks, the more flames surround me. I don't know what it is about holidays and their supposed "easy" status, but in my work world, statistically, they're the leading time for anything that can shit the bed to shit the bed.

I pocket my phone and pray, dead set on making it to my office before someone else can stop me or finding June and confronting her—at this point, either option will do.

Laura tries to meet my eyes, and Eddie waits outside my door, but I'm about as prepared to be a boss today as I was to find out June was my Mystery Woman last night.

Fucking not at all.

I finally spot June alone in the break room and take off toward her on a mission. She looks amazing in a crisp white blouse and black pencil skirt, and her bright copper hair is curled in a way that seems to glitter under the fluorescent lights.

Her feet are just barely crossed, one kicked back in a sexy lean as she waits at the Keurig for her coffee to finish brewing. I watch her movements closely, imagining all the erotic things she said to me in our chats coming to life with her face and body. The Mystery Woman's been nothing more than a hazy blur in my mind for so long, it's almost counterintuitive to allow myself anything else.

But fuck, she looks good. Beautiful. *Downright stunning.*

Though, it doesn't change the tornado of thoughts that have been swirling through my brain since I walked into our condo's gym last night and saw her standing there.

June is my Mystery Woman, and I still don't know how I should feel about it. There's a part of me that thinks I should be angry, but that anger has yet to come. There's another part of me that thinks I should feel completely violated by how things went down—by the very intimate direction our Midnight messages went—without me knowing it was her the whole time.

It was dishonest, to say the least, but if she'd never done it, if she'd never initiated our Midnight chats, where would that leave me?

The answer to that question makes my chest ache with the kind of discomfort that has me lifting my hand to rub at my sternum as I close the distance toward the break room, my eyes fixated on June the whole time.

I'm focused so intently on her, it's a surprise when I run into someone, nearly knocking them on their ass. A female voice shrieks and I stumble, and when I steady her on her feet, I realize who it is—Bethany.

What seems like a million fucking people in this office today, and it had to be her. I swear, today is a dumpster fire.

"Geez, Beau," she complains, smoothing her silk dress back down her legs and adjusting her purse onto her shoulder. "Pay attention much?"

"Sorry, Beth. Got a lot going on today."

"Obviously. Seth told me how busy you all are."

I nod. "Yeah, we thought it would be low-key since it's the Friday of Halloween weekend, but no luck."

Bethany studies me closely, and I lean to the side a little, trying to get a look over her shoulder. My stomach sinks when I see that June's no longer standing in front of the Keurig. In fact, I don't see her in the break room at all.

Bethany looks behind herself, my distraction obvious, and her mouth turns down in a frown. "I guess I'll let you get back to it, then.

Seth and I were supposed to go to lunch, but he ordered food to his office instead because of everything that's going on."

"Probably smart," I agree, looking down the hall to see if I can spot June making her normal rounds. Around this time in the afternoon, she checks in with all the execs first, then the team leaders, and then finally each member of the projects team to make sure they don't have any pickups or sendouts she needs to do or if there's any way to make their lives a little easier.

I don't envy her position in the company right now—it's the most overworked and underpaid of them all. And with Avery as her coworking-counterpart, it's even more burdensome. I don't know what happened with my sister, but her work ethic is lower than one of those underwater caves that leads to the center of the earth.

"Are you okay? You're acting really weird today," Bethany remarks, snapping my attention back to her. I'd almost forgotten she was still here. As for why she is, I'm not sure.

"I'm fine. Just busy. I'm pretty sure Seth's in his office," I say in dismissal. Her eyes narrow just slightly, and if I hadn't dated her for as long as I did, I might not have even noticed. But I did, and I do. Despite being engaged to Seth McKenzie, she's annoyed that she's not the center of my attention. Because that's Bethany's MO. She wants to be at the center of everyone and everything, no matter the consequences.

Unfortunately for me, it took far too long to see that superficial side of her. A harsh breakup because she was sleeping with my best friend, to be exact.

But now? She's not my fucking problem. *Thank God.*

I smile and step around her, giving nothing more than a little wave as I head down the hall toward my office, where Eddie waits. I have plenty of work to keep me busy—too much to torture myself with useless small talk with the Bethanys of the world.

June, though... I would welcome one-on-one time with her with open arms.

My phone goes off with a text, and even though it's a challenge,

I manage to take it out and read the message rather than shooting it like a basketball for a three-point shot into the water cooler trash can.

> **Henry:** Are we doing theme costumes for tomorrow?
>
> **Mav:** Theme costumes?
>
> **Henry:** Yeah. Like where we go as something matching.
>
> **Ronnie:** Fuck no.
>
> **Mav:** You're thinking of couple's costumes, Hen, and last I checked, you still refuse to suck my dick. So, no, I will not be matching you tomorrow.

More annoyed than amused by my friends' nonsense for the first time in a long time, I tuck the phone back into my pocket and keep walking without responding.

And I'm almost stepping into my office when I catch sight of June inside Chris's office. On impulse, I backtrack, heading straight in her direction, and just as she's stepping out of his door, I'm right there, ready to pounce on the first opportunity I've had to talk to her all day.

I don't offer a greeting, I don't ask questions, and I don't say a single fucking thing. I herd her directly into the supply closet across the hall and close the door behind us without so much as pausing. Eddie's eyes widen slightly before the door shuts, but he doesn't call any further attention to the weird behavior before averting his gaze to the floor.

I don't care, though. I'll make up something to explain it away to him later.

As for June, her eyes are startled and wide, and her mouth is worried. She backs up against the closed door, searching the small closet for another way out. "What are you doing, Beau? Have you lost your mind?"

"Just finishing what you started," I assert. "What the hell is going on, June?" It's a sharp lash, one I don't entirely intend, and she shrinks back into herself. I try to calm my voice, but the adrenaline of finally getting a chance to question her on everything that's happened between us maintains an edge. "Why did you start that message with me on Midnight?"

She shakes her head. "I really don't think now is the time to talk about this."

"Why not?" I scoff. If you ask me, the time to talk about it was yesterday. Or fuck, before the messages even started in the first place.

The position she's put us in…it's tenuous. We're in a dark room with no windows, fire licking at our heels, and I don't know if there's a way out. *I don't know if there's a way back.*

"Because we're at work. Because people are going to notice we're missing soon," she fires back. "Because Avery likes to hang out in *this* closet so your dad can't find her and assign her anything."

"Sounds like a list of cheap excuses just so you can avoid—"

As if on prompt, June is launched forward by the door swinging open, and I have to catch her by the biceps to keep both of us from crashing into the shelf behind me. Even this simple touch feels different now, my palms burning at the feel of her soft skin.

My sister scoots inside, her eyebrows drawing together at the sight of us.

"What in the hell are you guys doing? Are you having some kind of work-nerd meeting in here? Because I claimed this spot a long time ago. June agreed to the verbal contract."

June's eyes widen in terror for a long moment as she tries to come up with an answer, her lashes skirting the bottom of her eyebrows. My jaw grinds slightly with annoyance at my involuntary position in this mess of secrets, but I step in for her anyway, throwing out the first thing I think of.

"Avoiding Bethany. She's here for lunch with Seth."

I hate that it makes me sound like I give a single fucking shit about the two of them, but after running into her earlier, it's the first thing that came to mind.

Avery snorts. "Okayyy. Probably don't need to be in this closet anymore, then. I just came by his office, and they were in there with the door closed, if you know what I mean."

I roll my eyes. "We know what you mean."

Avery laughs, raising two well-manicured hands in front of herself. "Right. Well, sorry. Don't mean to be insensitive, but she whines like an alley cat when she's trying to be quiet and come at the same time." She waves in front of her face. "Oh, well. I guess you know that."

I glance at June to see her tucking her hair behind her ears nervously. I don't want her to get the idea that I'm still hung up on Bethany because I don't give a fuck about Bethany. But if she wants this to be a secret from Avery, I'm not sure what else to do.

I'm not going to get any answers like this—not with Avery here—and ending June's misery seems like the only considerate thing to do.

Being patient seems impossible, but eventually, she's going to *have* to talk to me. With how intertwined our lives already are, it's a physical certainty.

"I better get back to work," I say, excusing myself and stepping toward the door.

Avery nods. "Yeah, you'd better. There's only room for one Banks in this closet, and I called dibs a long time ago."

I don't want to leave it like this with June, but I have no choice. We'll finish this later.

But later had better be soon.

Chapter 26

PRIDE AND *P*REJUDICE HAS ALWAYS BEEN ONE OF JUNE'S favorite books. When I was a teenager and she was a kid, she used to carry a worn copy around with her to read every chance she got. Something about the enigmatic Elizabeth Bennet resonated with her, and now, I imagine that's why she chose **ElizaBeth** as her username on Midnight.

Maybe it was the confidence she wished she had, or maybe it was feeling like the black sheep of her family. I don't know.

But I know tonight, as I step out of my Escalade in my parents' packed driveway, that the Mr. Darcy costume I've chosen to wear isn't a coincidence.

It's a decision.

One I've been mulling over for the past forty-eight hours. Juniper Perry is my Mystery Woman, and every time I've pondered that reality, only one thing has been clear—*I can't stop thinking about her.*

I've pictured a million different scenarios of how this could go down, and every damn time, I've ended up back in the same place.

Yes, June is my little sister's best friend, and I've spent most of my life seeing her as just that. Yes, I should probably be mad at her for violating my trust, for initiating our Midnight messages and hiding her true identity.

But things are different now.

She's different now. And I can't find a single scenario in which walking away from her makes me feel good. Truth be told, the connection we built through our messages wasn't superficial. It was deep and intense, and I can't let everything we've spent the last two months building go to waste. I don't want to go back to the way things were before.

I want to explore what we could be, and I want June to have no doubt.

"Holy shit, dude. Bankses' Halloween means business this year," Henry comments from my passenger seat, pulling his Zorro mask down over his eyes before climbing out his side.

His observation is spot-on. The driveway is filled with cars, and we even passed a valet station at the gate. Music pounds from inside the house, and the outside looks like one of those pop-up Halloween stores threw up on it.

I retuck my white shirt into my high-waisted gray pants and pull my blue overcoat out of the back seat, swinging it on while he keeps chattering. It's an unbearably hot outfit for a party on the beach in Miami, but I don't care. When it comes to June, I need to make a statement tonight. And deep down, I know if I don't say something now, I don't think I'll get the chance to say something at all.

And then what? We just pretend it never happened? That doesn't sit right with me. Frankly, the mere idea of pretending everything that's transpired with June while she was my Mystery Woman doesn't exist feels unbearable.

It feels…*impossible.*

"You think Mav and Ronnie are already in there?" Henry asks, and I survey the cars around us for Mav's Jeep or Ronnie's Corvette, but when another five cars fill in, the task becomes too overwhelming to care.

I'm not myself right now, and I have a feeling I won't be until I finally get the chance to talk to Juniper.

"I don't know." I shrug one shoulder while my eyes are already looking toward the front door of my parents' house. "I guess we'll find out when we get inside."

Henry pulls his fake sword out from his side and swipes it through the air in a giant Z swath like a big kid. You can always count on a Halloween costume to bring out the inner child in everyone—though, it's less of a surprise for a guy like Henry, who's in the business of creating some of the most technologically advanced equipment for high-octane, dangerous sports. His company, Adrenaline Junkie, is a one-stop shop for people who like to jump out of planes and bungee-jump off bridges for fun.

He practically swings swords for a living.

Slamming the door and bleeping the locks, I follow Henry toward the house and stride through the wide-open front door. Bodies are everywhere, all in various forms of ridiculous dress, and I scan the faces that are unmasked, looking for Juniper.

Henry doesn't miss his usual beat and occupies himself with a group of women in various skimpy attire. A sexy kitten, an almost-naked witch, and I think—if I'm reading the costume correctly—a dominatrix Spider-Man?

I don't know. And I don't care. I use the opportunity for what it's worth and separate myself from my friend.

My mom and dad are in the kitchen when I make my way through there, dressed as a plug and a socket—*dear God*—and I pointedly avoid making eye contact as I scoot by.

For now, the more anonymity I keep at this party, the better. My bold choice to come as Mr. Darcy will fly right over most everyone's heads, but I'm not so sure about my mom's. She knows June as well as anyone can know someone and loves her like she's her own daughter. And a lot of times, love is in the details.

I spot Avery in the corner of the living room with Hulk, making out like eating face is the only way to save the world, and head out the back door to the pool deck. There's a crowd of people, of course, but none are the one and only person I'm looking for.

Nightfall is making it harder and harder to distinguish faces in costumes, and I start to get discouraged, but when a thought takes shape and I look out toward the beach, I find her sitting in a place I've found her many times before.

When her parents missed her dance recital in third grade. When she failed her algebra test in seventh grade because her parents told her about their divorce the night before. When her dad didn't show up to back-to-school night for her freshman year of high school but sent a Cartier bracelet instead. And when Avery had her first kiss at their first real party, this is where I found her.

We've had what feels like a million and one conversations on this beach throughout the years, and still, the one we're about to have feels entirely different.

My heart rate kicks up to the kind of speed I only get when Henry and I are hauling ass on our runs, and I swallow against the uncertainty that sits heavy in my gut.

I don't know how this is going to go, but I know we aren't kids anymore and, to me, she's not anything at all like a sister. She's not the awkward girl with the unfortunate name always tagging along. She's the woman I can't get out of my mind even if I try.

Quietly, I pad through the sand toward her, watching her back as she focuses on the reflection of the moonlight on the gently lapping water.

Her red hair trails down her back, and from this angle, it looks completely bare. Her eyes jump to me as I sit down beside her, leaning back into the sand on my hands like I've done so many times before.

"Hi, Juni."

Her voice is soft. "Hi, Beau."

I chuckle a little, opening my coat and smirking. "Actually, it's Mr. Darcy to you."

Surprised eyes jump to mine once again, and I nod. *I remember, June. Apparently, I remember everything when it comes to you.*

She glances down at herself. "Avery talked me into being Ariel."

I scan her shell bra and bare stomach, looking down to the

glitter of her green mermaid-tail skirt, and smile. "Far be it for me to agree with my sister on something, but she got this one right. You look incredible."

"Really?" she asks, and the only instinct I have right now is to kiss the self-doubt right off her face.

"Really," I confirm with emphasis. "I'm having the hardest time keeping my hands off you."

She startles into a laugh, and my eyebrows draw together, but she waves a hand in front of my face and grabs my elbow to keep me from disengaging at all. I don't know what to make of it, but when she finally speaks, I understand.

"I'm sorry, really," she says, her voice just barely over a whisper. "But you just have *no* idea how many times I've dreamed of you saying that to me, like, out loud." She pauses and looks over at me, her eyes scanning my face with hesitancy. "If you haven't caught on," she says, and her voice drops even lower. "I've, uh... I've had a bit of a crush on you for a while now. Years, even."

My smile is lazy and comfortable. For as awkward as I thought this would be, it's not.

It's us, just better.

"I imagine Elizabeth had to wait a while for Mr. Darcy, too."

The cutest fucking giggle escapes her lungs. "Yeah. You're right... Beau—"

"June—"

We both grin, and she hurries to usher me on. "You go ahead."

I sit up and drape my arms over my knees, turning my neck to look her directly in her pretty blue eyes.

"Why did you ask me to meet you on Midnight initially? Was it about Seth? Or was it because you wanted a way to talk to me?"

She shrugs gently, her bare shoulders nearly touching her ears, and admits, "Both, I guess. I wanted to help you, but mostly...I'm sorry for how things went, so damn sorry. And I know I've put you in a really bad situation, but I did it because..." She pauses and swallows hard. "I just wanted you."

Her words are a fucking dart that hits the bull's-eye of my chest. "June."

"I don't know how to go back to the way things were." Her voice shakes as she looks away from me to stare at the ocean. I know it's because she's scared—because the conclusion of this conversation could change our lives forever. I've been scared too.

But sitting here with her, finally talking to her about everything, I find myself looking at June in a way I think I've subconsciously avoided for a while. And being worried isn't in the equation at all.

"We don't," I say my truth. "We don't go back, June."

"Beau—"

"No, June. You can't start something like this—this big, this *great*, this deep—without finishing it."

"But..." She shakes her head and furrows her brow. "But Avery—"

"I don't give a shit about my sister," I chime in, not even letting her finish the thought. "I haven't thought about her at all, honestly. But I've damn sure thought about you. Every day, every night since you started this."

June's mouth curves down into a little frown. "Beau, she's my best friend."

"And you're my obsession," I admit, throwing all caution to the wind and leaning close enough that our warm breath mingles in the cool breeze of night. "I want you, June."

She sways forward, and I take it as a sign, pushing my lips to hers and drinking in her gasp as I do. She tastes like cherries and sunshine, and I linger in the feeling of her lips under mine as a tingle spreads down my spine and settles in my dick. She tastes so good, I could swallow her fucking whole.

I push her back into the sand and hover my body over hers, confident enough in the cloak of darkness and the sounds of the party that we won't be discovered. She moans, her legs falling open enough for my hips to find their way between them, and I shove up the mermaid-tail skirt to touch the skin of her thigh.

She kisses me back, opening her mouth and letting in my tongue, and I explore her further. It's magic in a bottle and better than I ever would have dreamed.

I'm desperate for more, but I don't want to scare her off either. I needed this moment—this ambush—to sort out how I feel.

But now that I know…I've got an imagination full of better places to take things to the next level.

Places where our family isn't. Places where June can completely let go.

Places I'm dying to explore with her.

"Meet me at Midnight," I tell her, repeating her first note to me right against her lips. She sucks in a breath as I pull away and climb to my feet, dusting off the sand and readjusting my now-hard cock in my pants. "This isn't over, June. It's just getting started."

Chapter 27

ThunderStruck: Meet me out in the hall.

I wait anxiously as the message shows as read, and then I watch as the wheel spins while she types a response.

For the past two nights since my parents' Halloween party, I've been trying to stage every rendezvous I can. So far, we've kissed in the downstairs gym locker room, had a hot and heavy make-out session in the elevator, and messaged back and forth—of the deliciously dirty variety—through our bedroom walls.

I'm chomping at the bit for more, but so far, this is all we've been able to manage. Strangely enough, I almost sent my contractor a thank-you email when he told me my move-in date for my house had been pushed back again. Something about June's and my bedrooms being a wall apart feels too good to give up.

ElizaBeth: Avery is still awake. What am I supposed to tell her?

ThunderStruck: Take out the garbage again.

ElizaBeth: Okay. I'll be out in five minutes.

I jump up from my bed as I hear motion on the other side of the wall that I know houses June's bedroom. To think we spent all these nights talking and flirting and sexting with nothing more than a wall between us is nearly enough to drive me crazy.

I jog to my front door and step out into the hall, propping the door open behind me and leaning against the wall.

I listen closely to the muffled voices inside June and my sister's condo and wait not-so-patiently for their door to open.

When June appears two minutes later holding a half-full bag of trash, I laugh out loud, and she jumps forward to cover my mouth.

With her in close proximity now, I grab her by the hips and back up into my apartment, pulling her with me until the door falls closed behind us. I don't pause before pushing her against the wall and moving my body to hers, sealing our lips together in a hot and burning clash of tongues.

She gets up on her toes, and I reach down to pull the trash bag from her hand, tossing it down on the floor. With her hands free, she sinks them into the hair on the sides of my head, and I wrap my arms around her waist and pull her in tight.

Damn, she feels like heaven.

We're out of breath when we finally pull back, and her blue eyes dance like the shallow waters of the Atlantic Ocean out my balcony window. "We're doing this," I tell her in no uncertain terms.

She snorts and then worries her bottom lip with her teeth. "I want to," she whispers then, her voice a little shaky. "Obviously, I want to, Beau. But how? I don't have that much of a social life to use as an excuse at the moment—at least, not one that doesn't include Avery—and there's only so much trash I can produce per day."

"Let me worry about that part."

"Beau—"

"Say yes, June," I tell her, desperate to get the answer I want. I can't go back to the way things were. I know too much. I've seen too much. We *come* together too much.

"All right," she agrees hesitantly. "We can try. But I'd better go take this trash to the chute and get back in there before Avery notices something weird is up."

I shake my head. "No."

"Beau!" she snaps on a laugh. "I've already been gone for, like, five minutes. She's going to think I fell down the chute."

I press my lips to hers, and she gives up the fight immediately, melting into me and kissing me back all over again. She tastes so fucking good it hurts. When I finally pull away again, we're both pretty much panting.

"Go ahead," I allow, smirking as she rolls her eyes. "You can go now."

"I have to run this trash down. I don't think it'll really sell the story if I go back in with it."

"I'll take it," I offer, placing a peck to her lips again, unable to get enough. "But only if you promise to meet me out on the balcony later. I'll message you."

She shakes her head on a laugh. "You're insatiable."

"Oh, you have no idea, Juni. You think you know, but you're going to learn some things about me that'll shock you."

"Oh yeah?" Emboldened, she winks. "Well, maybe I've got some things to teach you about me too."

"I have no fucking doubt." I grip her hips and press one more long, lingering, deep kiss to her lips. "And I can't wait."

Chapter 28

THUNDER RUMBLES FROM THE OCEAN OUTSIDE, AND I PULL my laptop higher on my lap in bed. My proposal for Midnight is coming along, thanks to the hard work of my team, but it's undeniably missing the kind of personal touch I normally put into my pitches.

I haven't been much into the game of meeting strangers for the last year or so, after my split with Bethany, and as a result, I'm a little out of the game.

But this thing with Juniper is starting to change that, and I find myself clicking out of the Midnight proposal I've been scanning through in my email, setting my computer to the side to grab my phone, and jumping into my ongoing Midnight chat with her just as the clock hits 12:00 a.m.

I haven't heard much through June's wall in a while, so I have a feeling she might be asleep, but that doesn't stop me from trying anyway.

> **ThunderStruck: Are you up?**
>
> **ElizaBeth: You think I can sleep when it's storming like this? No way. And don't even think about asking me to meet you on the balcony again tonight. I have enough nightmares of myself as a lightning rod as it is.**

I smile. When June first started sleeping at our house during her parents' divorce, she was terrified of the weather, and one particularly turbulent night when storms raged around us, I found her in my room, huddled under my comforter.

It was innocent—my room was on the lowest level of the house—but I still remember the pallet I made for her on the floor and that she slept there next to my bed all night.

> **ThunderStruck: Come over here and I'll keep you safe.**

> **ElizaBeth: I think you might be more dangerous than the lightning and thunder. I mean, the dirty things you made me do on the balcony the other night prove that...**

I chuckle. *The dirty things I made her do* is a bit of an exaggeration. She's the one who leaned over the small separation banister between our balconies and started kissing me. She's also the one who thought it was a good idea to play a little game of show-and-tell. And by that, I mean June *showed* me what she had underneath her little sleep nightgown—not a damn thing—and I haven't stopped thinking about how pink and perfect her pussy looked or how perky and soft her breasts appeared beneath the glow of the moon.

> **ThunderStruck: Only one way to find out. I'll meet you at my door.**

It takes a minute, but eventually, I hear the sound of her bed creaking as she climbs off it and makes her way out of her bedroom. I do the same, waiting at my front door just like all the other times I've asked her to sneak by in the last couple days, and look out the peephole until I see her.

She tiptoes like a cartoon cat burglar, and I laugh to myself before pulling the door open and ushering her inside.

"You, of all people, know Avery sleeps like a log, and yet, you're walking around like you've just helped a coyote carry a burlap bag with a dollar sign on it out of a bank."

"Hey, I'm new at this, okay?" She shoves a playful hand into my chest. "My teen years weren't very eventful."

I chuckle and shake my head. "I don't know. That's not quite how I remember it."

"I didn't start any of that," she refutes. "I was an innocent by-stander in all of Avery's schemes."

"That, I believe. But that doesn't mean you didn't find your share of trouble."

Her forehead wrinkles in an adorable frown. "I thought you were going to comfort me from these storms or something? Or did I read that whole chat wrong?"

"You read it right," I whisper, pulling her deeper into my apartment with my hands at her hips. I've been dreaming about seeing her laid out on my bed since I talked her into pretending to take the trash out for the first time a few days ago, and I desperately want to make it a reality now that she's here and we don't have to rush.

Fingers fucking crossed I can convince her to stay the whole night.

"Come on," I say, grinning down at her. "It's safer in my bed-room, under the covers."

She shakes her head on a laugh. "You're crazy."

"What?" I wink and playfully squeeze her hips. "That's where you always used to hide."

"You're right," she agrees, but her smile turns teasing. "But I have a feeling this suggestion isn't completely magnanimous on your part."

"Oh, but, June, you're so wrong. The things I want to do with you are one hundred percent with your pleasure in mind."

"And your pleasure?" she asks, but her cheeks turn the most adorable shade of pink.

"When it comes to anything revolving around you? My plea-sure is an unavoidable side effect."

We walk into my bedroom together then, hand in hand, looking at each other the whole way. We've spent most of our lives around each other, but I swear, it's like I'm *really* seeing her for the first time. Without this app, and our anonymous messages, I don't know that I ever would have let myself.

Not because she's not beautiful. Not because she's not undeniably interesting. But she was off-limits in ways I never would have challenged. She was pigeonholed in my mind.

Our Midnight chats changed that.

Classical music plays softly from my phone dock on my nightstand, and our eyes hold as I pull her toward the bed and push her down on the comforter. Her red hair stands out on the dark green fabric, and I urge her back with a gentle shove, desperate to see it fanned out there.

She smiles up at me, and I lean down to kiss the apex of her collarbone. Her exhale is soft but meaningful, and suddenly, I need to taste even more skin.

One inch at a time, I work my way along her neck and back, moving down to her chest and up to her cheeks one at a time. Her hands explore my back, and my hands run the line of her sides. It's a soft exploration of a place you've been before but have never taken the time to truly see.

It's a visit to the Statue of Liberty for the first time after living your whole life in New York. It's a swim in the ocean after staring at it from our view. It's a hike in the Grand Canyon after only seeing it from above.

And I don't ever want it to end.

She moans as my teeth tease at the neckline of her tank top, and I pull it down just enough to expose the lace of her bra. "Hear that thunder?"

"Hear what?" she asks, breathless.

Fucking perfect. I must be doing a good job, then.

In a quick move, I grab her hips and twist her as I fall to the bed myself, pulling her on top of me in a straddle. Her cheeks are flushed, and her eyes are wide, but her mouth is pulled up in an undeniable smile.

She leans down to kiss me, her whole body pressing into mine like it can forge us together, and I pull her hips forward as the thunder rumbles outside my sliding glass doors. If we don't stop soon, I'm going to take it all the way.

"I want you, June," I whisper against her perfect mouth. "I want to feel all of you."

"I want that too," she answers, her lips kissing mine greedily.

"Are you sure?" I question, pulling back to meet her eyes.

"Beau, I've been waiting since the moment Avery first brought me to your parents' house," she says with an adorable giggle. "I'm pretty sure."

"Yeah," I say with a smile. "I'm pretty sure too. Though, for clarification purposes, I have not been waiting that long. You were… very young."

Juniper laughs and I shake my head. She grabs both sides of my face and sinks her hands into my hair, putting her lips just barely against mine. "I'm not young now," she whispers there, earning a smile from me that disappears straight into a kiss.

It's hot and heavy and deep, and I grab her hips and rock her forward, making sure she feels how hard I am for her.

She moans in my mouth, and I roll us back over, putting her back on the bed and taking over again. Fingers curled around her waistband, I pull her pajama shorts down the length of her legs and off over her pretty feet, kissing her pink-painted toes as I do.

She giggles, and I relish the sound, inching my lips back up the inside of her leg, one kiss at a time.

Her breathing is erratic and heavy by the time I make it to her thigh, her sheer pink panties staring me right in the face when I get there. I push her legs open wider with gentle hands, sealing my mouth over the top of the thin fabric and inhaling every bit of her delicious warmth. Her back arches, and she moans, fisting chunks of my comforter in her small hands.

"God, Juni. I can't fucking wait to taste you."

"Beau."

"You want that, don't you? My mouth on your pussy?"

She digs her teeth into her bottom lip as her hips jolt up toward me. "So bad."

Slow and steady, I grab the thin sides of her panties and pull them down her body, tossing them to the floor with her shorts and resuming my position between her legs. Her thighs quake lightly as I put my mouth right to the top of her pussy and blow.

"Oh my God," she says softly, her voice way more ragged than smooth.

I lick around her clit just once before sealing my mouth over her pussy and drinking in the smell and taste of her with greed.

She arches again, putting her heels on my shoulders to find purchase and rocking her hips into my mouth. It's anything but shy and the complete opposite of what I expected.

I fucking love it.

I lick and taste and tease until she's wet in my mouth, and then I climb up her body and fall between her hips. Her eyes are shuttered and hazy, and I swear if I didn't need to be inside her so fucking badly, I'd eat her for the rest of the night.

"I need my cock inside you," I tell her, kissing her chest and pulling her top down to take a pert nipple in my mouth. She gasps as I suck hard, and she grabs my head to pull me up and press her lips to mine.

I kiss her hard and deep, but she's quick to steal control, sinking her hands into my hair and skirting my tongue with her own. When she pulls away, she's nearly breathless. "Beau, I want you. I *need* to have you."

I nod feverishly, reaching with one hand to shove my shorts and boxer briefs down and free myself. I stand up in front of her and stroke myself for a long moment, my hand firm and slow, my eyes completely fixated on how fucking incredible she looks sprawled out on my bed.

A goddess, that's what she is. *A fucking goddess.*

She watches avidly, pushing up on her hand in the bed, the skin of her chest, thighs, and face all mottled in glorious shades of pinks and reds.

"I just have to grab a condom," I say, rounding the bed to my nightstand, my hand still on my cock while she watches. I swear, I've never had a woman watch me the way June is—looking at me like I'm the best thing she's ever fucking seen, tasted, touched.

It's powerful and addictive, and even in the throes of exploring each other, I'm desperate for more of it.

Snagging the condom from my nightstand drawer, I rip it open with my teeth and roll it on before joining June again, my hips between hers and our chests fused together.

Her blue eyes shine and glitter as they bore into mine.

"God, June. You are so beautiful."

"You don't have to say that," she whispers, uncertainty worming its way into the downturned corner of her mouth.

"What do you mean, I don't have to say it?" I question without hesitation, my eyebrows drawn together as I run a hand through her perfect red hair. "June, I'm not just saying anything. You're beautiful. Always have been."

"Beau, please."

I shake my head. "Oh no, baby. Now, I have to go slow." I push inside her gently, my stroke so labored, I'm barely moving. "Now, I have to fuck you until you believe me, no matter how long it takes."

June's head drops back as I fully seat myself inside her, but I pull her head forward again, my hands at the sides of her face, forcing her to look at me.

She feels so good, I'd sell my soul to stay here for the rest of my life.

"June," I whisper.

"Beau."

"ThunderStruck has entered the chat."

She bursts out laughing, and so do I, our bodies meshed

together in harmonic vibration. I stroke slow and deep, grabbing her hips and rocking us together in a sweet symphony of the greatest pleasure I've ever felt.

This sex is different. This sex is new.

This sex is what happens when it starts soul-deep.

PART 5

Juniper

Chapter 29

FOR THE PAST TWO NIGHTS, I'VE SNUCK OUT OF MY CONDO in the name of having hot and wild sex with Beau. In *his* bed. The guilt is consuming, but so is the sex. It's what I'd tell my therapist if I had one, but instead, it's a feeling I carry with me every waking second of my new, secret life.

Beau Banks is everything I thought he'd be and more. I can't get enough of our secret romance, but every time I lie to Avery, I feel like my nose and my guilt grow seven times as big.

I run across the street carefully, making sure to watch for the crazy Miami traffic as my heels avoid puddles from the afternoon rain shower and pausing when a cab beeps its horn in the lane just in front of me. It's a common thing here, getting rain nearly every day, and I've learned to navigate water like a pro, but in these six-inch heels, I still need to be on my game.

Beau stands on the sidewalk of the restaurant, his smart suit from work still in place, and I move toward him at a run, a full smile taking over my mouth. He's so handsome it's disarming, and I completely let go of my inhibition as he pulls me in for a five-alarm kiss right there on the sidewalk.

"Hi, beautiful."

On the inside, teenage me squeals her giddy delight at the sound of his greeting, and I allow a smile that reaches all the way to the corners of my eyes from the version of me now.

I'm feeling more and more confident in the viability of us as a match by the day, and tonight, two weeks into agreeing to give this thing a real shot, going to this special dinner together feels like a long time coming.

Avery is out with some of her friends from hot yoga, and I begged off with excuses of a cold starting to settle in.

I know I'm going to have to tell her the truth about Beau and me at some point, but this is all so new. I just want a little more time to ourselves before I do. I've waited what feels like my whole dang life for this fantasy to become a reality, and I'm in no rush to change that.

For now, I *need* to keep my perfect Beau and June bubble intact.

Beau leads me inside with a pull of my hand, notifying the hostess of our arrival and getting us escorted to a table in no time at all. Cardone is one of the hottest restaurants in the city, so I'm surprised he was able to get a reservation at all, but he makes it seem like it's no big thing.

In this case, I guess our wealth and connections really do make all the difference.

The back room is dark, lit only with candles, and French glass doors separate it from the rest of the restaurant. Blood-red pillows are on high-backed black velvet chairs, and a waiter with a white linen draped over his arm waits at the side of the table.

Beau holds out the chair on the far side of the room for me to take a seat first, and I awkwardly curtsy before sitting down. His smile is warm and wide.

"What was that little thing you just did?" he asks, his smile equal parts sexy and amused. "Did you just *curtsy*?"

"I don't know." I widen my eyes as I look around the room. "I figured you must be royalty with this fancy setup."

He chortles. "I figured you'd want privacy just in case we ran into anyone we know."

"Oh. Yeah," I agree. "That's probably a good idea." I focus on putting my napkin in my lap and taking a sip of water as he takes the chair across from me. My cheeks are aflame—I can feel them—but I'm not entirely sure why.

"*I'm* not trying to keep us a secret," he hedges carefully. I guess he knows me well enough to know I'm having a minor internal crisis. "But I know that's what you want."

"It's just so much easier for now, don't you think?" I question, but an uncertain grimace shows my shaky truth. "Until we establish some footing? I mean, what happens if you decide to move on in a month? Suddenly, I'm not allowed at Banks' family dinners and have to settle for my parents' empty house instead?" I cringe and shake my head. "Sounds terrible."

"That would never happen," Beau assures. "If it doesn't work out between us for some reason, everything with the family will be fine."

"Are you sure?" I push, knowing Beau's tendency to promise the impossible. He's well-meaning, always, and so ambitious it's admirable, but this world we live in is hardly as perfect as we want it to be. Sometimes things don't work out. Sometimes things go wrong. Sometimes, even, everything falls apart.

He pauses, but he makes a point to lock his steady gaze with mine. "I'll make sure of it, okay?"

I shrug, playing off the ocean of anxiety that churns inside me now. The Bankses are the only real family I've ever known. I can't imagine what I'd do without them. "I just don't know how Avery is going to react either way."

"Why wouldn't she want her best friend to be with her brother?"

Beau's thinking is simple, how I imagine most men's is. But in the female mind, I know it's more complicated than that. It would be for me, and all I have to go on is my imagination. My parents thought having one child to ignore was more than enough.

I shake my head instead of answering. I don't know how to explain it.

"All right. Enough Avery for tonight. Let's focus on us."

"Okay," I agree.

He's right. I didn't get trussed up in a lace bra, thong, and a dress I can't breathe in for nothing. This is Beau we're talking about, and I'm on a *date* with him. Younger me would be absolutely apoplectic. *Why on earth am I wasting it talking about his sister?*

"You look really handsome tonight," I say, allowing myself the unexpected privilege of appreciating his hotness out loud.

"Oh yeah?"

"Definitely. Hard-cut jaw, just the right amount of scruff, and a well-fitted suit atop your muscles?" I close my eyes dramatically, push a hand to my chest, and then open them again. "It's your best look."

He laughs. "What's my worst?"

I shrug. "Probably the Tyvek suits you and Neil wore two years ago when your mom got a wild hair to paint the pool house door on Labor Day weekend."

He groans. "It might be a slight disadvantage that you know so much information. I'm used to being able to show a highlight reel for at least the first three weeks of dating."

"You?" I guffaw. "Are you kidding? I don't usually show guys pictures of me during that braces with a short, layered bob phase from eighth grade, and you saw it live and in full Technicolor."

"You were still cute." His smile is delectable enough to eat, but his words annoy a glower out of me.

"You're kidding me, right?" I question on a scoff.

"You were!" he insists. "In, like, a young Justin Bieber kind of way."

"Good grief," I groan, dropping my face into my hands. The waiter sets a plate on the spot directly in front of me, and my eyebrows draw together in confusion. I wait for him to step away and then lean in toward Beau to whisper. "Um...I don't remember ordering."

Beau smiles. "I preplanned everything when I made the special request for the room. I hope you don't mind. I made sure not to include any avocado or shellfish."

"Thanks." My mouth curls up at the corners. "I mean, the shell-fish thing could kill me, so that was definitely a good move, but the avocado is just slimy."

"Yeah." Beau's eyes dance with amusement. "I remember."

"You really know a lot about me already, huh?"

"I do." Beau leans forward to grasp my hands. "But I want to know more."

Me too, Beau. Me too.

Chapter 30

AVERY AND I DANCE AND SING TO EACH OTHER AS A GROUP of our friends from U of M dance around us on the boat they rented for the day. The speakers pump music throughout the entire bay, and people on their patios wave as we drive by.

This is the most I've let loose since this summer, and I have to admit, even if I normally fight it, it feels good.

Another week has passed by, and my secret romance with Beau is still aflame.

I'm talking hot, scalding, third-degree burns if it touches your skin kind of blazing chemistry. We message on Midnight *a lot*. I sneak into his condo, after Avery falls asleep, *a lot*. And when we're at work, he finds the most surprising ways to steal a kiss or a secret touch.

But sneaking around with him isn't easy, and with work getting busier and busier, Avery and I hardly have any time to hang out together. So, tonight, this outing together was much needed. Pretty much mandatory, even.

The last thing I want to do is give Avery the shaft because I'm too busy sneaking around with her brother. Hell, the fact that I'm even hiding anything from her at all is a tough pill to swallow.

Some days, I can put it out of my head and focus on why I'm doing it in the first place. But other days, it's hard keeping something as big as this from my best friend, the girl who is a sister to me in all the ways besides blood.

Kristin, one of Avery's sorority sisters and good friends, grabs her hand to drag her to the onboard bar, and Avery looks back at me. "Come on, June!" she yells. "Do a shot with us!"

I follow dutifully, figuring *why the hell not*, and buck up to the bar right beside them. Avery excitedly wraps an arm around my elbow, and the movement makes me wobble a little on my heels.

"Gahhh, Junebug!" Avery exclaims—right in my face. "It is sooo good to see you letting loose. I swear you went and became a whole-ass adult on me for some reason."

I roll my eyes on a laugh. "Probably because we *are* adults."

"Pshhht," Avery replies. "I refuse to believe that."

"Yeah." A very unladylike snort escapes my nose. "We can tell."

She waggles her eyebrows as the bartender hands over our shots of vodka, and I toss it back with a cringe. It burns as it runs down my throat, but by and large, it actually tastes good. I kind of forgot how good I was at this in college.

"Hell yes!" Avery cheers, clinking her empty glass with mine before grabbing them and setting them back on the bar. She drags me back to the makeshift dance floor up on the bow, and we dance so much my head swims.

Repeating the routine, we take two more shots before I need to sit down to take a breather. Avery laughs at me and calls me a lightweight before disappearing back into the crowd with Kristin, and I take out my phone, a small curve of my mouth loosening my expression along with my inhibitions.

I pull up my Midnight chat with Beau and start typing.

> **ElizaBeth: What happs, Mr. Man? You missin me or whats?.**

I see the spinning wheel indicate he's typing and wait for his message. It comes quickly, and I can practically see his serious face on the other side all the way from here.

ThunderStruck: Where are you? Are you drinking?

ElizaBeth: I think I'M drunnk on a boatt. HAHA Member that song???

ThunderStruck: You're not close to the sides of this boat, are you?

I laugh. Gosh, he's funny. And sexy. And perfect. And his cock is big, but, like, the perfect kind of big, you know? Not scary-big where you're afraid the tip is going to touch your tonsils. But where you feel so, so full in the best way.

ElizaBeth: Nope. Seated sitting right on my ass right now. No danger in sight.

ThunderStruck: That's good. I'm suddenly wishing I were on this boat with you.

ElizaBeth: Oh boy, Mr. Banks has FOOMA. HAHA You're funny

ThunderStruck: I don't have FOMO. But I do have some drunk June memories...

ElizaBeth: I only pukled on your shoes that one time a couple years agoo, and it wsnt even my fault

ThunderStruck: Where are you?

ElizaBeth: On. A BOAT. DIDn't we already estabish that???

ThunderStruck: I meant, where is the boat?

I giggle. What a silly question.

ElizaBeth: Um, in the water?

ThunderStruck: Forget it. I have Avery on Life360.

ElizaBeth: Wait, what'r you gonna do with that?

ElizaBeth: Beauuu, hellooo?

ElizaBeth: Did you fall overbord??/

ElizaBeth: Oh. Wait I'm on the boot. HAHAHAH

"Oh well," I mutter to myself, standing up and making my way down below to pee. It's a quick trip, and when I come back up, Avery and Kristin are taking another shot, so I join them.

A couple of guys cheer us on, and Avery pulls me over to flirt with them.

"June, this is Garrett. Garrett, this is my bestie, June."

Garrett has blond hair and a lazy smile, and I don't feel even a smidge of attraction. I picture him trying to be as cool as Beau, and it makes me laugh out loud. Garrett's eyebrows draw together, and Avery laughs, chiding, "Whew, girl, you're gone. You'd better get yourself together quick because we're going to Luau Room after this."

I give her the thumbs-up, and she shakes her head, explaining to Garrett, "She doesn't get out much anymore. She's a highly motivated individual, you know? Super smart, bound for success, and all that."

He smiles and shrugs. "She's hot too."

"Smokin'," I correct, and that makes him laugh.

"Love the confidence, babe."

I nod. It's not me normally, but right now with this many shots in my system, and while I'm on Midnight talking to Beau, I'm ready to take on the whole wide world. Probably Mars, even.

A boat horn blows, making me nearly jump out of my skin, and Avery turns both of us around to look. I lean on her heavily.

"Oh my God!" she shrieks. "What the hell is Beau *doing*?"

"Beau?" I question. Shock urges a bucket of adrenaline to dump into my veins. Hell, I'm probably one more boat-horn-blow away from being scared into sobriety.

"Yes!" she screams. "He's on that boat over there! See him?"

Black shorts, a white shirt, dark hair, chiseled face, and a bright smile, he stands out like the sun in the middle of a group of clouds. *Oh, I see him, all right. I see him and then some. If I could hop on his boat right now and fuck him, I'd do it in a nanosecond.*

Avery pulls me toward the side of the boat where he's pulling up, and I do my best not to fall down while I'm keeping up. When she gets within talking distance, she starts shouting across the space between us. "What are you doing here?"

"I was out and then saw you were close on Life 360."

It's a hollow excuse at best, but she doesn't question it at all. Part of me can't believe it, but I guess she has no reason to suspect her brother and best friend are sneaking around behind her back either.

"Are you headed back in now?" she asks, pulling me forward and making me trip over myself. "Because this one could really stand to end her partying a little early."

"I can see that." Beau smiles at me, and the wild urge to fuck him on a boat grows tenfold. "Take her to the back of the boat, and we'll get her switched over."

"Great!" Avery agrees, completely unaware that she's leaned right into what I suspect was Beau's plan all along. I might be a little boozed-up, but I know mischief and ulterior motives when I see them.

I teeter to the back of boat and down onto the stern deck, and Beau places a walking pick between the two boats for me to cross.

I look down toward my feet and back up at Beau.

"C'mon, Juni," he says, and when I look at the water beneath the walking pick, I can feel my eyeballs get *real* big.

There's not a chance in hell I'm going to risk falling overboard, so I drop to my knees and start crawling across the damn thing.

"Oh my God, June," Avery mutters behind me. "What are you doing?"

"Worry about yourself!" I shout back to her, and I'm graced with one million laughs from her big fat mouth.

By the time I reach Beau's boat, his smile is beaming, and he helps me to my feet with a gentle but strong hand.

"Get some rest and hydrate!" Avery waves an excited good-bye, and I give her a thumbs-up as the boat she's on starts to move away from us.

By the time Beau gets the walking pick back on deck, guides me toward the front of his boat, and we sit down on the bow cushions, Avery's party boat is too far away to even see her.

And the only thing I feel right now is relaxed. Relieved, even.

Beau wraps an arm around my shoulders and pulls me close, shoving a bottle of water in my face without delay.

"Where'd you get that thang?" I ask, a laugh making my last word sound weird. "Are you a magician?"

Beau smirks. "I have a slight advantage at the moment for the element of a surprise. You're not exactly completely aware of your surroundings."

"True," I agree, tipping the bottle to my lips and drinking the clear liquid greedily.

"How are you feeling, really?" Beau asks, concern softening his voice. "Do you think you're going to get sick?"

I smile, leaning into his hard chest and taking a whiff of his unbelievable scent. "Uh-uh. I feel so good. So, so good now that I'm with you."

He laughs. "I'm feeling better now that you're with me too, Juni."

"Did you ever know I liked you?" I ask, the alcohol in my system destroying any hesitation I'd usually have in telling him all the down and dirty details of my forever-long crush on him. "Like, back in the day, when you were still in high school, I was crushing on you so hard." I laugh at the irony of it all. "Guess things haven't changed much, huh?"

"I'm crushing on you pretty damn hard too, Juni." Beau pulls me closer to his chest. "And, no, I didn't know you liked me back in the day." He gently runs his fingers through my hair. "But I'll be honest, I think I never even let myself consider it because you were so off-limits. I noticed you at my graduation, though. And after. I've always thought you were beautiful, but if you hadn't messaged me on Midnight, I don't think I ever would have let myself go there."

"I figured I'd get over it at some point." I snort. "I thought it'd be on your wedding day to Bethany, but I thought I'd get over it."

His mouth is a bowed line, and he sinks his hand deeper into my loose hair at the side of my head. My stomach flips on itself, butterflies awakening. "This is a much better option," he whispers, so close I can feel his breath on my face.

"Yeah," I whisper back.

This *is* a much, much better option. I don't know what I'd do if we ever went back to the way things were.

Chapter 31

THERE'S SOMETHING SEXY AND DANGEROUS AND exhilarating being out on Beau's boat—just the two of us—with only the night's sky hovering above us. After I managed to chug two bottles of water and neutralize the booze in my body, we've been sitting here, at the bow, for the past two hours.

Maybe longer. I can't be sure. All I know is that kissing Beau is an aphrodisiac that has my nipples hard, and a deep, Beau-craving ache makes itself at home between the apex of my thighs.

I've always enjoyed kissing, but I've never *felt* kissing like this. Never been so entranced by kissing a man that I find myself completely unaware of time, my surroundings, pretty much everything but him. Frankly, the only reason I still know we're on his boat is the gentle rocking motion that occurs each time a wave laps against the sides.

Beau sits with his back against the boat, and I straddle his hips. My mouth tastes and teases and kisses his, and his big, strong hands touch my thighs and my hips and my hair and pretty much every part of my body as we just kiss each other.

He deepens the kiss as his fingers skim the skin at my hip. His lips move from my mouth to my collarbone, skirting along the delicate spot with the kind of softness that urges goose bumps to appear on my skin.

I sink my hands into his hair and moan at the feel of him on me. I've fantasized and dreamed and envisioned for years and years, and still, the real thing is ten times better. I'm still not used to the satisfaction of truly feeling him, and I'm starting to wonder if I ever will.

I could have Beau for breakfast, lunch, dinner, three snacks, and a midnight fourth meal, and I'd still be hungry for more.

Right now, he's gentle and connected, his every move, every touch, every kiss, intentional in a way that sends energy all the way to my toes. His touch is commanding, and yet, I feel at the helm at the same time. My responses are a road map as he learns my body and all the simple touches that make me tick.

I sure wish he'd been with me all this time, but I have to appreciate the benefits of him being a man with experience.

"God, Beau," I whisper, gasping lightly as he nips at the lace of my bra.

The breeze of the water blows through my hair as his boat travels at a mild clip, heading slowly through completely open waters, but it's no match for the raging fire inside my body.

His hands on my skin, his mouth on my skin, *it's everything.*

"Feel good?" he asks. I answer with a swift intake of breath as he pulls my nipple into his mouth and sucks.

"Incredible." A moan escapes my throat when he shifts me on his hips a little, and I can feel how hard he is beneath his clothes. "I want you so bad," I manage through ragged desperation.

He kisses the skin of my chest, up along my neck, and ends with his lips at my ear. "Right here?"

"Yes," I agree readily. "Right here. Right *now.*"

"Out in the open like this?"

"I don't care." Truth is, it almost sounds exciting that someone might see. I don't know what woman is having these thoughts because she sure as hell doesn't sound like me, but I don't question her. I want Beau, and I want him now.

Beau finishes pulling my dress down from where it rests at the bottom of my breasts, and I lift my hips to help him get it off. My nipples stand at attention in the cool wind, and my core absolutely rages in contrast, but when he covers me with his body and presses his lips to mine, all that leaves my mind completely.

His fingers find the line of my panties and slide underneath, sinking into the wetness at my center and swirling.

"Fuck," I curse on an exhale, digging my hands into his shoulders and arching my back.

His touch is gentle as he explores, dancing around my clit until I can't stand the feeling anymore.

I writhe under him, and he smirks down at me, his brown eyes positively twinkling. "Feel good?"

"More," I shamelessly beg. "Please."

He moves his finger again, sinking it inside all the way to the knuckle. "Is that enough?"

I shake my head. "More. I need more."

Moving another finger in to join the first, he rubs at my G-spot with expert strokes. My head falls back on a moan, and I paw at his chest, willing him to be even closer.

The material of his white shirt is nice and all, but I want skin.

"I want your shirt off," I command, tugging at it from the bottom hem to exaggerate my point.

He hinges at the hips, sitting up without taking his fingers out of me and pulls his shirt over his head with his free hand. I take in his tanned chest and tattoos, licking my lips.

He pulls his fingers out slowly, to toss his shirt to the deck of the boat, and my body shakes at the loss.

I'm shocked when he lifts them to his mouth and sucks them clean.

That might be the hottest thing I've ever seen in my life.

"Beau."

"I had to taste you."

He pulls a condom from his pocket and unbuckles his belt,

sliding his shorts down just enough to free his hard cock. I stare at it hungrily, watching avidly as he strokes the condom down its length and secures it at the base.

I'm a horny mess, wanting so badly to suck him into my mouth but also wanting to feel him inside. Since the condom is already on, though, I settle for the latter.

I pull him down on top of me and between my legs, and he tugs the lace of my thong to the side and fills me with his cock, his stroke smooth and slow.

I groan at the feel of him, my head falling back and my eyes closing.

He grabs at my chin and pulls it back forward, and I open my eyes to look at him. "Look at me," he whispers. "Other people might be watching us, but while I'm inside you, you look at me."

I nod. His command isn't a hardship. After coming from crushing on him for what feels like my whole life to here, I'll look at him all fucking day long.

We're panting softly, our breathing mingles, and our eyes hold as he moves in and out of me, his cadence a perfect, steady beat. It's not too fast and not too slow, and if I weren't already so close to coming, I swear I'd let him keep doing it forever.

His teeth nip at my bottom lip just once before he reengages eye contact, and I wrap my legs around his hips to clasp them at the heels. Pleasure seeps into every fiber of my body, working so deep, I swear it's in my bones.

"Beau, you feel so good."

He nods, his brown eyes soft as he sinks a hand into the hair at the side of my face. "Keep talking like that and you're going to make me come."

I smile, and he shakes his head.

"Holy fuck, you're sexy."

"Beau," I moan, my climax rolling in so fast I almost don't expect it. My eyes flutter and my head lolls, and time as I know it ceases to exist.

He puts his lips to mine, breaking the seam of their seal with his tongue, and I gasp as he picks up his pace, his strokes hitting even deeper. He's chasing his own pleasure now, and it's the hottest fucking thing I've ever been a part of.

We're not just as good as I always thought we'd be—we're better.

Chapter 32

"**D**UDE, I SWEAR YOU WERE GREEN BY THE TIME MY brother showed up on his boat last night!" Avery says through a laugh, her ass on my desk atop the pile of papers I very much need. "You've got to do some reps, come out with me a little more, get your game back. I can't be taking a lightweight everywhere I go!" She snorts. "What if Beau hadn't shown up?"

"Yeah," I muse vaguely. If he hadn't shown up, then I definitely wouldn't have ended up having sex with him. On his boat. On the open water for anyone to see.

"Did you actually yak? Or did you just feel sick? Because you actually look a little skinnier."

"Ave." I eye her shiftily. "I'm fine."

"Yeah, *now* you are!" she bursts with a laugh. "But I mean yesterday."

Technically speaking, I didn't feel good. I felt *consumed*. By Beau. So, kind of the same difference, right?

Right.

"Yeah, I definitely didn't feel good," I lie, raging guilt niggling at my every nerve.

"Well, you look better today. Really good, actually." She swings her legs back and forth on my desk. "Have you made some changes to your skin care?"

It's your brother.

"Avery, I need to get back to work," I say instead of answering, a dismissive laugh making the words raspy. "I'm supposed to take those campaign projections down to Accounting right now, and I can't do that if you're sitting on them."

She rolls her eyes, hopping off my desk with a thud. "You know, I really hope you get some sort of award at the end of the year for all this hustling you're doing. Like a trophy. Or an Emmy!"

I laugh. "You could do some work too, you know? Then I wouldn't have to hustle so much."

She wrinkles her nose, her whole face disgusted. "Yuck. That sounds terrible." Her face morphs into a smile, and she snaps her fingers in front of my face as an idea hits her. "You know what, though? I will go down to the break room and get a snack, so I'm out of your hair if that helps."

"Oh yeah. It's like I barely have anything to do now."

"Great!" she replies cheekily. "I'll see you later, then. But seriously, try not to concentrate so hard." She gestures a hand in front of her eyebrows. "It's bad for your elevens."

I snag the file folder from where she was sitting, power walking to the accounting office at the far end of the floor. Brad, one of the numbers guys with a big brain, takes the folder gratefully but doesn't say much else, not that that's a surprise. He's not a very social person.

I check in with Chris and Neil, running some documents down to HR for them on the third floor, and then get back to my rounds of checking in on everyone on the team. I'd be lying if I didn't say that stopping in Beau's office first isn't strategic *and* selfish.

Unfortunately for everyone else these days, seeing him is a little—okay, *a lot*—more fun than seeing them.

Plus, after making excuses with Avery, I'm feeling an extra need to talk to him. This whole game of secrets and sneaking around and lying to my best friend is becoming an albatross around my neck.

Brow furrowed, he's typing on his computer when I knock on the jamb of his office door, but when he looks up and spots me, his whole demeanor changes.

Serious is a memory; concentration is gone. *Hello, handsome-as-hell smile that reaches his eyes.*

Instantly, I'm warm all over, like having his attention directed at me is the equivalent of being wrapped up in a cozy, already toasty flannel blanket on a chilly winter day. I only ever *dreamed* that he would look at me this way.

"Hey there," he says, his voice is all raspy from concentration, and my mind drifts back to my conversation with Avery as I round his desk and come to a stop beside his black leather chair.

He spins around to face me, full-blown smile still engaged, but I don't quite return it. It's hard to feel happy right now when I feel like I'm constantly lying to someone I love like a sister.

Of course he notices. "Wow. Don't look so happy to see me."

"Get real, Beau. I'm always happy to see you." I laugh, smiling in apology. "I'm just… I don't know how much longer I can do this…"

His eyes widen, his hands come up, and his fingertips dig into my hips as he stands. "Do what?"

"The secret-keeping," I answer, my voice just barely over a whisper. "I know it was my idea not to say anything and all, but I don't think I can lie to Avery much longer. It's killing me."

"Let's tell her, then," he says straightaway, and panic locks up my chest.

"Now?!" I feel like a psychopath, given the fact that I'm the one who just said we shouldn't keep it a secret, but I'm scared. *Terrified*, actually.

How will Avery even react? Will she be mad? Furious? *Hate me?*

He reads me correctly, and his face gentles as he suggests, "How about next week? We'll get through Thanksgiving first, and then we'll tell the whole family. That way, you don't have to stress about the holiday being awkward."

"Okay." I let out an exhale of air on a whooshing rush. A grateful smile follows. "Yeah. That's a good plan." I stare up into his gorgeous, entrancing eyes, and it's almost pathetic how quickly my mind shifts. "Though, I'm not entirely excited about not being able to touch or hug or kiss you."

He smirks, squeezing my hips gently. "We'll find our moments."

"When?" I whisper.

"Every chance we get." And he punctuates that statement by flashing a secret but sexy wink at me.

His hand finds mine, our fingertips dusting together lightly. It feels forbidden and top secret, and I'm ravenous to cross all the boundaries I should keep firmly in place.

I want his lips on mine and our bodies pushed close together. I want to feel his heartbeat in my chest and have him touch the wetness between my legs.

It's a dangerous urge, one I can tell he's considering giving in to just as much I am by the swipe of his tongue across his teeth.

I tingle as we move a little closer, the hum of our bodies vibrating nearly audible between us. I smile and he winks again. Temptation taunts us both.

"Hey!" Seth's voice snaps unexpectedly into the space. I jump, but Beau manages to stay still. I turn around woodenly, hoping all the dirty things in my mind don't show on my face. "Juniper, I've been looking for you. I need you to go down to the graphics department and pick up my prototypes."

I nod quickly, springing into action. I don't look back at Beau as I scoot past Seth at the door and hurry down the hall, and I don't hear what they say after I'm gone. But it's not because I don't want to.

Longing to do just that burns at my skin as I force myself away, knowing I have to act as casually as possible in front of everyone in this office. Especially Seth. He'd be the worst person of all to find out what's going on between us. He'd love more than anything to find controversy where Beau is concerned. Which, considering the mess he and Bethany created a year ago, is the most ironic form of irony possible.

But Seth and his shenanigans aren't my focus for long.

Beau's words repeat in my mind. *We'll get through Thanksgiving first, and then we'll tell the whole family.*

Soon, we're going to tell Avery, and then Neil and Diane. The people who are my found family, and the ones I care more about than almost anything in this world.

We just have to get through Thanksgiving first.

Chapter 33

GLITTER-FESTOONED STALKS OF CORN CRISSCROSS UNDER the sconces at the sides of the Bankses' arched front door as Avery pulls to a stop in front of her parents' house. And as I hop out of the passenger's side door, the gift I found in our building's mailroom when we were leaving burns a hole from its spot inside my purse.

I want to open it, *am damn near desperate to see what's inside*, but I'm also fearful over the hope that's been blooming in my chest ever since I pulled it out of our mailbox.

It's officially Thanksgiving, and from the décor that greets us on the outside of the Bankses' house, I know Diane has ensured this year's day of thanks is a true celebration. *Just like she always does.*

Avery runs ahead of me, chattering on the phone to one of her many suitors, and shoves through the front door without knocking. My entrance is much more mindful as I follow her at a walk, closing the door behind us.

The Bankses' housekeeper Linda waits just inside the door, accepting Avery's Prada leather jacket and matching handbag as she hands them to her and waits patiently for mine. But I clutch my purse to my hip with a smile.

"That's okay, Linda. I'm going to hold on to mine."

"Very well."

Avery heads straight for the kitchen and I follow dutifully, but after she crosses the threshold to the entrance, a hand shoots out from the hall and yanks me to the side. I almost scream, but Beau covers my mouth and drags me to the first open door.

He shuts it behind us, and I back up against the sink of the half bath, breathing hard.

"Sorry," he apologizes quickly, his voice a rushed whisper. "I didn't mean to scare you, but I wanted to kiss you hello."

My body melts as he presses himself to me, forging our lips in a delicate battle for supremacy. He tastes delicious as usual, and already, he's got me feeling better.

The holidays always hit hard with absent parents, and my mood hasn't been the best. But there's a reason I love the Bankses as a whole, and there's a reason I've loved Beau for as long as I have— they're the best kind of people and all the family I never had but always wanted.

"Meet you out there," Beau whispers against my lips, pulling me to him and giving my ass one final squeeze before hurrying out the door. He closes it behind himself, and I take a moment to get myself together, washing the smudged lipstick off my face and fluffing at my hair.

When I'm satisfied my appearance passes for normal, I exit the bathroom and head down to the kitchen.

Diane and Neil stand by the fridge filling cups with their special Thanksgiving punch, and a catering staff works to finalize the touches on the spread of the meal. Beau and Avery are both sitting on the living room couch with their feet up, bickering about what to put on the TV.

I opt for stopping to see my pseudo-parents first. Neil smiles as soon as he sees me approaching, putting down the pitcher of punch and opening his arms for me to walk inside. I savor the feel of his warm hug, and I imagine, just for a moment, what it must be like to be born with parents like them.

"Happy Thanksgiving, sweetie," he says, kissing the top of my head right in the center of my hair.

"Happy Thanksgiving," I reply, squeezing him extra tight before pulling away. Diane is waiting for her turn too, and I scoot into her arms as she wraps them around me. She smells of Gardenia by Chanel, but not the one you can purchase in stores. It's their Parfum Grand Extrait version, a highly coveted scent I know goes for almost twenty thousand dollars.

My parents got me my first bottle of it when I was five years old, and if I'd known I was going to associate it with the woman who's been more of a mother to me than anyone else in my life, I probably would have kept it around. At the time, it was just more *stuff*.

"Dinner should be ready soon, Junebug. Are you hungry?" Diane asks as we pull away from our hug.

"Enough to consider cannibalism."

Both she and Neil laugh, and Avery shouts from the living room, "Eat Beau first!"

I can barely keep myself from turning the color of a tomato when Beau replies, "Fine by me," and tosses a look of pure debauchery toward me over his shoulder.

I hold my breath, waiting for anyone to question Beau's devious words, but everyone just brushes it off as normal. Probably because there're only two people in this house who are aware of the secret relationship Beau and I have been engaging in for the past month.

Everyone else is still clueless. *But that's not by their choice. It's by yours.*

Guilt and shame and a whole bunch of other emotions I don't want to feel right now stab at my gut, but I swallow hard against them and force a smile to my lips when Diane starts laughing over the squabbling about what to watch on the television that comes from Beau and Avery in the living room.

"These kids, June," she says with an amused shake of her head. "I don't know what I'm going to do with them if they can't stop bickering before we sit down to eat."

"I'll go sort them out."

She leans forward and kisses me on the cheek. "Thanks, hun."

I cross the open space to the living room and plop down on one of the chairs that's perpendicular to the couch, avoiding Beau's eyes. I know if I meet them, they'll be filled with sex and scandal and all sorts of trouble.

"What the hell took you so long to get in here?" Avery asks, wrestling for the remote with one hand while Beau holds it with one of his.

"I had to pee," I lie easily, internally sighing at how naturally being deceitful has started to become. I'm starting to fear that if I don't set myself free with the truth soon, I'm not going to know who I am anymore.

"Again? You just went before we left the condo. Do you have a UTI?" She glances back to her parents, quieting her voice just slightly. "You know if you're having sex with someone, you should always pee right after you're done, right?"

"I don't have a UTI, Avery." I sigh, but I don't mention that I pee right after every time her brother and I bang.

"Irritable bowel?" she questions, and Beau laughs out loud.

I don't hesitate to snag a pillow from the chair beside mine and lodge it at his head.

He returns the favor, and before we know it, the three of us are in a full-blown pillow fight. Which, if you've seen the Bankses' big-ass, cozy sectional, you'd know there's a hell of a lot of pillow ammunition.

"I thought you were going to calm things down, June!" Diane shouts from the kitchen. I blow my hair out of my face, breathing hard, and Beau pulls me into a headlock while Avery wrestles to free me.

It's just like old times—except, it isn't.

"Come on, you hooligans!" Neil calls. "Come eat before you destroy my house."

Beau holds on to me but loosens his arm on my neck, pulling my back to his front instead. Avery tosses her pillow down and heads for the dining room table, and I work to even my breathing as Beau whispers directly into the shell of my ear.

"I can't fucking wait to wrestle you later. Though, I'm going to make damn sure we're wearing a lot fewer clothes."

"Beau," I breathe back, my chest tightening around how long we're taking to join everyone.

But he's cool, calm, and collected, offering a little smirk in my direction and a secret squeeze of my ass with his hand. "Sit beside me, Juni."

He lets go of me, and I rush to the dining room, taking a seat on the side of the table with two empty chairs. Avery laughs at me as I sit down across from her, eating a piece of asparagus like it's a French fry.

"Your hair's a mess."

I try to brush it out of my face, but before Beau sits down, he reaches in from behind me and pulls the full length of it behind my back. My eyes cut up to him quickly and then to Diane, Avery, and Neil, but they're all preoccupied by their own thing. He winks.

One of the catering staff puts a plate full of food in front of me, and I smile up gratefully as Beau takes the seat beside mine, immediately reaching out and touching my thigh under the tablecloth.

My nerves stand on end, sizzling with the mix of guilt and excitement. I never thought I'd be the type of woman to enjoy clandestine sneaking and hidden touches. And I definitely don't know what it says about me or how to make sense of why it feels so damn electrifying.

But it wouldn't take a genius to deduce why it's got me all flustered. I've been into Beau since the moment I was old enough to notice boys in the first place. This isn't some extramarital affair— this is my ultimate fantasy come to life.

"How's your presentation for Midnight coming, Beau?" Neil asks, cutting a piece of turkey with his gold-bladed knife and sticking it in his mouth.

Beau clears his throat, his voice changing noticeably from the playful boy in the pillow fight to a businessman with his sights set on success. "It's going well. We've had some holdups on the branding, but Laura told me they'll have a finalized concept for the logo next week and three potential styles for the app design the week after that."

"And your pitch? What about that? I assume you're going for—"

"Neil," Diane says on a groan, cutting her asparagus and shaking a piece of it toward him on the tip of her fork. "Do you think we could save this absolutely riveting shoptalk for another time?"

"Yeah," Avery complains. "I'm not supposed to fall into a turkey coma until *after* the meal."

"Sorry," Neil apologizes on a chuckle. "Beau and I can talk later."

Diane nods, turning to me. "Where are your mom and dad these days, June?" Her voice is soft, compassion for what she already knows the answer will be in her tone.

I shrug. "Last I heard from her, she was headed to Bali. Something about the spiritually healing power of the Sacred Monkey Forest Sanctuary and a hike on a volcano. Nothing like some monkeys and lava to help you find God, amirite?"

Beau snorts, but I don't dare glance toward him. I feel too raw to do it without exposing everything I'm feeling for him and then some.

"And my dad and Lola are in Paris, I guess. At least, that's what the postmark said on his latest gift."

His latest gift that still sits in my purse.

"Is that why you've been clutching your purse like it's got the jaguar's eye from Jumanji in it?" Avery asks, her tone unnecessarily judgmental.

I don't have anything to say to that; the sting of her words and the sad reality they're referring to are too much for my pathetic heart. I look down at my small clutch, still slung over my shoulder, and drop it to the floor.

Avery, in a rare moment of self-awareness, apologizes. "Sorry, June. I didn't mean to upset you."

I shake my head, and Beau's hand reaches out to my leg again under the table, squeezing my thigh gently.

I feel itchy all over and like I'm going to come out of my skin. I take two deep breaths, but when they don't do anything, I shove my chair back and stand, grabbing my purse from the floor once again. "Excuse me."

Walking quickly, I make my way back to the half bathroom again, shutting the door behind me and leaning into the sink. I set my purse on the marble surface and stare at it for a long moment before prying it open. My heart beats fast beneath my ribs as I rip off the packaging and tear into it, uncovering a Rolex box with a small note card on top.

I close my eyes briefly and turn over the card in my hand.

"One, two, three," I whisper before opening my eyes to read it.

The scribbles are an immediate disappointment, my dad's assistant's handwriting so recognizable at this point, I know it almost better than my own.

I don't know why I got my hopes up—what possessed me to think that this time might be different. I don't know why I even fucking care. Like, it's pretty damn clear my parents don't give a shit about me. And even though things like Thanksgiving and Christmas and my birthday might be important to me, I'm not important to them.

I have to stop expecting them to change. I'm twenty-three years old, for fuck's sake. How long am I going to keep hoping that one day they'll both wake up and realize they actually love me and want to be a part of my life?

A single tear runs down my cheek, and I wipe at it furiously, pulling at the now-mottled red skin of my face. The door cracks open gently, and I swallow as another wave of emotion hits me square in the chest.

I'm expecting Avery or Diane. The sight of Beau, though—it breaks me.

"Shh," he comforts as wetness coats my cheeks and my

breathing stutters. He pulls me into a hug and kisses the top of my head in the same way he's done more than once over the years.

"I just don't understand," I murmur into his chest, the feel of his racing heart beating against my eardrum. "Why did they have me if they don't want anything to do with me? It's not like they needed the tax deduction."

"I don't know, June. I don't know at all. But I know you don't deserve this."

The door cracks open again, and this time, Avery pokes her head in. I cry harder, knowing how messed up everything is these days, and Beau shifts me into her arms and steps away.

Guilt eats at me for wanting to be back in his embrace, for wishing Avery wouldn't have come in here, and for hiding all this shit in the first place.

I wonder what things would be like if I'd ever bothered to share with Avery just how much I've always liked her brother from the start. Would she have encouraged it? Or would what's happening now be even worse and tangled up in more webs of lies?

I hug Avery tighter and hope. Hope for a smooth resolution. Hope for our friendship and a relationship with Beau all at once.

Hope I haven't ruined the only real family I've ever known for good.

Chapter 34

GOLD HANDLE IN HAND, I SWING OPEN THE HEAVY DOOR to our office building, show my badge to the security guard Steve in the lobby, and head toward the elevator, contracts for the Higgins Chocolate company clutched to my chest. I'm on my way back from picking them up at the lawyer's office and absolutely freaking starving for lunch.

I didn't get a chance to stop today, and unfortunately for me, I probably won't before it's time to go home. I'm way too busy to do anything but try to get through the massive amount of work on my plate even though last week's Thanksgiving meal has more than worn off.

I push the button to call the elevator and wait for the doors to open, my hair whooshing away from my shoulders when the cart stops at this floor and air is pushed toward me.

When the doors open, I step inside and push the button for the fifteenth floor, watching as the doors close in front of me. They're almost shut when a well-manicured hand shoots inside, Avery's voice yelling from the other side.

When they don't immediately bounce back, I panic, jumping forward to hit the door-open button while she shrieks. The contracts fall from my hands and scatter everywhere, but I get the door open just in time to stop the elevator from starting to go up with Avery's arm caught inside.

"Oh my God, I almost died!" she says dramatically, one hand to her chest and the other clutched around a fresh cup of Starbucks coffee. I squat and pick up the papers from the floor, piling them haphazardly until I can sort them out at my desk. "Clearly," Avery tsks. "This is yet another reason to tell Neil that me having a job isn't a good idea."

"Are you *just* getting here?" I ask suspiciously. I haven't exactly been in the office all day, but she wasn't here this morning, and her *morning* coffee order in hand makes me question it. Avery's morning Starbucks is always of the hot variety. Her afternoon order comes with ice.

"Technically, yes. But I was working remotely. I mean, it *is* the week after Thanksgiving, you know. There's just a lot of shit going on."

"Working remotely?" I laugh. "Doing what exactly?"

"The same thing I do at the office."

"So...nothing."

She smiles, unashamed. "Exactly." She digs in her purse for her lip gloss and smooths some on her lips while she chatters. "But you know how it is. I was out at Novu until three last night, and then that guy from Hermès, Fester..." She laughs, and I scrunch up my nose. "Yeah, the name's not the best, but he's hot, okay? Anyway, he wanted to go get tacos from that little truck after, and I told him I would as long as he ate my taco too."

A shocked giggle escapes my throat. "*Avery.*"

"What?" She waves a careless hand in the air and flips her hair over her shoulder. "He's a little weird, but he has unbelievable tongue control."

"So, I guess that's why you didn't come home last night?"

She nods. "Yeah, he's got a place downtown, so it was easy."

I can't deny that Avery not coming home last night was not an issue for me. It gave me the glorious opportunity to sleep in Beau's bed. All night long. Though, we only slept part of the time. The other part, he spent fucking me so good I can still feel a delicious throb between my legs.

The elevator dings, and the two of us step out, headed for my desk. Avery doesn't even bother with stopping at her own before sitting on the surface of mine. "Anyhoo, I'm going out with some of the guys I met while I was with Fester last night. We made plans for this Saturday, and you should really come. It's not, like, a work night or anything, so your shawl can survive the night at home without you."

"I don't know," I say on a shrug.

"Come on!" she insists. "You haven't been out with me since you got drunk on the boat. That was weeks ago. Plus, we're going to the new club that's opening this weekend." She waggles her brows like that means something. "It's called Sage."

My desk phone rings, and I lean forward to pick it up, but Avery slams a hand down on top of it. "I'll let you answer if you say yes."

"Avery, I bet that phone call is important."

She smiles. "Say yessss, Juuuune."

"Fine!" I agree on an annoyed snap. "I'll go, I'll go. Just let me answer the phone."

Satisfied, she moves her hand and jumps off my desk with a wink and a wave, off to God knows where. I put the phone to my ear quickly, before I miss whoever is on the other end.

"Juniper Perry," I greet, picking up my notepad and a pen just in case.

"Come by my office," Seth McKenzie says on the other end. "I have something you need to drop off with the courier."

"Sure," I agree easily, listening as he hangs up the call without anything else. I toss down my pad and pen and hustle down the hall to his office, knocking on the doorframe as I lean in.

He waves me in from his spot behind his large desk, talking on the phone at the same time. He holds up a finger to me as he unearths a large manila envelope from beside his laptop and hands it to me, tucking the phone underneath his chin to whisper sternly, "It needs to get there by five today."

I nod in understanding, even though I'm mentally thinking about how he's a bit of a dick, and just like that, he's back to his business again and ignoring my presence entirely. *Yeah, he's definitely a dick.* I scoot back into the hall with the envelope, curiosity getting the better of me. It's not sealed yet, an oversight on his part, so I pry it open *just* enough to peek.

A Midnight campaign slogan, *No Curfew, No Rules,* is the first thing that stands out, and my feet come to a skidding stop in the middle of the hallway as my head turns into an out-of-control Ferris wheel.

I know this slogan. I've seen this slogan because it's the foundation of *Beau's* campaign. And I know it's Beau's campaign because, well, I spend a hell of a lot of nights at his place these days.

Seth, the sneaky fucking snake, was actually successful in his endeavor to steal Beau's pitch?

I dart my eyes around the room, thankful that no one has noticed that I'm currently standing here with my jaw sitting on the damn floor and slam the envelope shut before running to the bathroom with it to take a closer look.

Once I'm inside, I lock myself in a stall and pull the paper out of the envelope with shaking fingers.

It's a single document, outlining the breakdown of what seems to be Beau's entire campaign with specifications for the printer. Seth is expecting me to send this out today, for print next Tuesday, an entire week before Beau's print deadline of mid-December. He's stealing Beau's shit and trying to finish it first so he can claim himself as the victim if he needs to. *Gah, this fucker will do anything to keep Beau from being able to beat him in this little competition.*

My hands shake as I leave the bathroom and speed walk down the hall to Beau's office. He's, of course, nowhere to be found, and the panic I feel is overwhelming.

What in the hell am I supposed to do? What in the helllll am I going to do?

I listen intently for the sound of Beau coming home for the evening through our walls, the envelope sitting on the edge of my bed. I didn't take it to the courier like I was supposed to, and I'm not exactly sure what that'll mean for me in the morning.

When I'm certain he's in his bedroom, I get on Midnight and send him a message.

> *ElizaBeth: Thank God you're finally home! I've been waiting all afternoon.*

His response is immediate and cheeky.

> *ThunderStruck: I like the sound of that. Eager to see me, huh? Don't worry, I can be hard by the time you get over here.*

I huff out a breath. *This isn't the time to be flirty and dirty, Beau.* Nearly hysterical at this point, I cut to the chase.

> *ElizaBeth: No, no. This isn't about that. You can keep THAT in your pants for now. This is about a situation at work you need to be aware of.*

> *ThunderStruck: Oh, boo. That's no fun.*

How can he be so freaking nonchalant right now? This is a five-alarm emergency we're dealing with here!

> *ElizaBeth: Beau, I'm serious. You need to know what Seth is doing.*

> *ThunderStruck: No, Juni, I don't. I don't want to know, remember?*

> *ElizaBeth: This is different.*

> *ThunderStruck: It's not. I appreciate what you're trying to do here, but I'm a big boy, okay? Seth*

> *can do whatever hc needs to do, and I'll be able
> to handle it. You don't need to protect me, I
> promise. Whatever it is, just let it go on however
> it's supposed to.*

Just let it go on? Is he serious? I suck in a breath and dig my teeth into my bottom lip.

> *ElizaBeth: I don't know if I can do that.*

> *ThunderStruck: You can, and you will. I know
> you just as well as you know me, and I know
> you'll do the right thing. I'll be fine, whatever
> it is, I promise.*

Dear God almighty, I sure hope so.

Beau may be confident, but I have a bad feeling that *everything* is just moments away from going up in smoke.

> *ThunderStruck: But you know what won't make
> me fine?*

Hope blooms in my chest, my mind utterly desperate for him to let me tell him what Seth is up to.

> *ElizaBeth: What?*

> *ThunderStruck: If I don't get to lick your pussy
> tonight and fall asleep with you in my arms.*

My body perks up, awakening from her slumber with hard nipples and a smile. And my heart has momentarily forgotten the whole Seth debacle, grabbing her pillow and pjs and sorting out the quickest way to make a night in Beau's arms happen.

This man. *I swear.* He sure knows how to make me forget all the bad things.

Chapter 35

THE *WE'LL TELL EVERYONE THE WEEK AFTER THANKSGIVING*
deadline has officially left the building, and guilt over not
telling Avery about Beau and me is starting to eat a hole in
my stomach. I'm either going to have to stock up on Pepcid and
Tums or find a way to bite the I'm-with-your-brother bullet and
tell her the truth soon, but facing the reality of how long I've been
carrying this lie is easier said than done.

Tonight, I've gone with being medicated.

Avery slams down into the seat next to mine, a huge smile on
her face as she leans into hug me. "I'm so glad you're out with me
tonight, Juni. I feel like I've barely seen you lately!"

I laugh. "Avery, we live and work together."

"No, no, I know, but I mean *quality* time."

Green velvet covering the walls, strobe lights, and go-go danc-
ers in cages wafting sage into the air as they shake their asses for
everyone in the club on a Saturday night isn't generally my idea of
quality time, but for Avery, having me out for a booze-filled party
with her is the pinnacle. She's always down for a mani-pedi too, but
seeing as she usually goes for those during work hours, coming to
Sage was the only option.

I can't help but laugh again as she screams over the obnox-
ious level of noise around us, lights strobing across our faces as the
DJ builds a beat. "Oh yeah. The quality of this time is unmatched."

When she gives me a thumbs-up and stands up to dance, her drink in hand, I know she didn't even hear me.

I sip on the signature green-colored cocktail that I've been nursing for the past hour and pull my phone out of my purse when it buzzes. A Midnight notification on the screen makes me smile, and I open the chat to a message from Beau.

ThunderStruck: How's the club?

I look up to see that Avery is currently busy grinding on that guy Fester and type out a response.

ElizaBeth: Pretty much as expected, I'd say. But Avery sure is enjoying herself.

ThunderStruck: I bet. What did you say the name of it is again?

ElizaBeth: Sage. It's got a whole witchcraft vibe going.

ThunderStruck: Lol. Appropriate, I suppose, for feeling like you're being burned at the stake.

ElizaBeth: It's not that bad. Just not my vibe, you know. It'd be better if you were here.

I smile to myself as I picture him getting all flirty back but startle when Avery snatches my phone out of my hand and hides it behind her back.

My heart thrums, hoping she won't decide to look at the screen. Flirting with Beau in secret was a good time—but the good time is gone. And in its place, *pure panic.*

"Juniper freaking Perry, put your phone away this instant! I need a partner in crime."

Using the path of least resistance, I agree, grabbing the phone back from her and tucking it in my purse before she can decide to take a look at it. She smiles and drags me onto the dance floor, and the two of us flail around like a couple of happy wackos.

It is fun, I'll admit, especially since none of Avery's male suitors are with us at the moment. I sing along to the song and bounce up and down, my hair springing as I bob my head back and forth. The lights go into an intense show as the DJ kicks the song up a notch, and everyone on the dance floor jumps up and down, shouting at the top of their lungs.

I join in until my lungs feel sore and my feet start to ache.

I point to the VIP booth and Avery nods, and the two of us hold hands as we make our way off the dance floor and fall onto the green velvet bench seat. Sweat sticks to my chest, and I blot at it with a napkin while Avery downs another glass of vodka cran.

I want to pull out my phone and check it, but I know it'll end in disaster if Avery gets a hold of it again. Instead, I survey the writhing room of bodies, my ears perking up when I notice Seth and Bethany about ten feet away.

I elbow Avery to draw her attention to them, and I instantly regret it when she starts waving her arms wildly to get their attention.

Shit.

Bethany's wearing a skintight blue dress, and Seth trails behind her like a puppy as they make their way over to us.

Seth's expression is stalwart, and I know it's because he's still a little mad at me for failing to get his envelope to the courier by five on Tuesday. I played it off innocently enough, but I wouldn't be surprised if he's holding a grudge. Which, whatever, because *fuck that guy.*

"Hey, girls," Bethany greets, a smile as fake as her tits on her face. "Having a fun night out?"

"Just getting started," Avery tells her on a hoot that makes me roll my eyes.

"Speak for yourself."

Bethany's expression is cunning as she smiles directly at me. "I know this isn't quite your scene, huh, Juniper?" She laughs out loud and *at* me. "Oh my God, you were so awkward as a teenager! All arms and legs and unsure of yourself." Her nose wrinkles up before she leans in close to make sure both Avery and I can hear her. "Did you ever get over your crush on Beau? You used to be so obsessed with him."

My ears run hot and my lips dry as I try not to freak out right then and there. I knew she was around a lot, but I had no freaking clue she had any idea I was mooning over her boyfriend. Her sharing it with the room is a real asshole move.

"What?" Avery explodes, laughing so hard I have to suck my lips into my mouth. "Juniper did not like my brother!"

I swallow hard, trying my best to smile like I agree with the joke.

"That's the most ridiculous thing I've ever heard." Avery shakes her head at Bethany. "Next time Seth's done banging you, close your legs before the air gets to your brain."

Bethany's eyes narrow in anger, and an even more dangerous tone settles over our powwow than before. I don't know exactly what this bitch would like to do, but it's a good time to shut it all down before she has a chance.

"It was nice seeing you, Bethany, but Avery and I have more dancing to do," I say in dismissal, adding a little wave to make it as friendly-chic as possible. When she backs out of our immediate space, I stand up and grab Avery's hand, dragging her back to the dance floor without looking back at Bethany or Seth. We find a hole in the center and start our head-rolling moves yet again, but Avery isn't quite on the same *let's not talk about this page* as me.

"I swear she's still in love with Beau even though she's the one who broke that shit up. She's one of those have your cake and eat it too twats, and it shows."

I shake my head. "It doesn't matter."

"It matters if she's going to spew blatant lies about you for no reason!"

I keep my mouth shut and dance, startling only when a large set of hands settles on my hips from behind. They leave just as quick as they arrive, but when Avery shouts her brother's name in my face, I understand why.

I turn around and come face-to-face with Beau's gorgeous eyes and perfect smile directed at me.

I'm so glad he's here, but the timing is *not* impeccable. If Bethany sees us together, we're cooked for real. It already seemed like she was on quite the warpath—with me being the target. My mind can't fathom what else she'd say in front of Avery if given the motivation and chance.

"Oh my God, I can't believe you dragged your ass out of your hole too!" Avery exclaims, slapping a hand down onto Beau's chest. "Both of you in one night! Is it the apocalypse?"

Beau keeps smiling, and I have to look away to keep myself from staring. "Just thought it'd been a while since I'd done a night out with you guys."

"I'm glad you're here, actually," Avery says, her energy still way up from the bitchy-ex encounter. "We just ran into Seth and Bethany, and she was…" She pauses to regain her composure as she laughs. "She was trying to start shit, talking about June having some crush on you when we were younger like it isn't the most ridiculous thing in the world!" She shakes her head, yelling directly at him over the music. "I swear, you could have her back if you really wanted her. She's so preoccupied with you, still."

Beau glances to me before shaking his head. "I'd rather eat fuck-ing nails than go down that road again. Time for new paths."

"Yay!" Avery claps her hands excitedly. "Oooh, maybe I should find someone to hook you up with tonight."

My eyes widen, ready to snap in panic, but Beau is much more composed than me. "Thanks for the offer, but that won't be neces-sary. I can find my own pussy."

Avery cackles, but I can't find a single ounce of energy to pre-tend to enjoy the path of this conversation.

Overwhelmed, I beg off, citing, "I need to go sit down for a minute, you guys. I'll meet you at the booth."

I can feel Beau searching my face, but Avery just nods and holds him captive, starting a conversation about some old high school buddy of his she saw on the dance floor.

As quick as I can, I walk away from them, fishing my way through the crowd to make it back to our spot in VIP. I'm almost there when the stress and embarrassment and anxiety of it all feels like maybe I need to splash a little water on my face.

Rerouting, I head for the bathroom and duck inside, taking solace in the immediate change in noise and atmosphere. There are several women in here, cycling in and out of the stalls, so I make my way to the sink and wash my hands, splashing just a tiny drop of water on my cheeks in an attempt to calm myself down without ruining my makeup.

I lean into the porcelain and take a long, hard look at myself, wondering how much longer I can keep this shit up.

Not only is Bethany far more observant than I thought she was, she's also just catty enough to use it. With the amount of time she spends in the office feeling up Seth, and with her still out there somewhere, lurking in the club, how in the hell am I supposed to know for sure she's not watching me?

Am I being paranoid? I don't know. But my intuition tells me I'm treading shark-infested waters the longer I stay at this club now that Beau has arrived.

What if Beau and I get lost in the moment, *like we always tend to do*, and Avery manages to notice? What if Bethany or Seth witness something that they would gladly use against us?

Suddenly, it feels like I'm being tracked by the damn FBI. Maybe I'm better off just going home. Getting out of here and climbing into bed to smother myself in a pint of ice cream sure feels a hell of a lot safer than this clusterfuck of a situation.

The bathroom door shoves open, and through the reflection in the mirror, one of the last people I want to see steps inside. *Son of a bitch.* I stand up to my full height, trying to act as nonchalant as possible, while my gaze discreetly tracks Bethany through the mirror. She notices me right away, of course, and saunters over in my direction with a smile on her face as I start the process of washing my hands again.

It's the easiest mode of distraction as she comes to a stop beside me and starts to talk. "Your secret is safe with me, you know?" she says, making me lick my lips.

I turn to look at her, doing my damnedest to steel my features against anything that'll give me away. "My secret?"

"Yeah. About your crush on Beau." She narrows her eyes, and her mouth quirks up into a sneaky smile. "I wouldn't have brought it up if I'd known you didn't want Avery to know. Honestly, I thought she knew." She laughs and waves a dramatic hand in the air. "I mean, God, it was so painfully obvious with the way you were always staring at him."

"What can I say?" I play off her words by smiling, even as I feel my stomach churn. "He was cute."

Bethany's returning smile is big and confident, her victory of getting me to admit the truth clearly making her happy. "He was. Still is, really." She sighs and shakes her head. "Anyway, have fun out there."

"Yeah." I lift my cheeks, my smile the equivalent of peanut brittle. "Yeah. You too."

She pops into a stall, and I don't waste any time leaving the bathroom. I don't know how much longer I can keep this shit up, but how in the hell am I supposed to tell Avery now?

Beau and me. *The most ridiculous thing in the world,* my best friend said.

The insecure girl inside me rears her evil head.

Maybe, just maybe, Avery's right.

Chapter 36

THE RIDE UP IN THE ELEVATOR IS QUIET. WELL, BESIDES Avery's gabbing, that is.

I don't know what she's talking about, my brain too focused on not looking at Beau as we ascend toward our floor to be able to process the words racing out of her mouth like a sprinter out of the gate.

Tonight at the club was…strange. Confusing and anxiety-inducing, all thanks to that witch Bethany and my best friend's current obliviousness to Beau's and my relationship. *And clearly, the latter is all your fault.*

An odd mix of exasperation and guilt settles into my lungs and wants to escape in the form of a sigh, but I swallow it down. I can feel Beau's eyes on me. It's something you simply know is happening when you've spent half your life in love with a guy.

I steal a glance; I can't help it, and the secret smile he flashes at me makes my heart pound against my ribs.

From the pit of low to the soaring high I go, and it's safe to say things are becoming more and more complicated.

The elevator dings its arrival, and all three of us step off the cart. Beau, always the gentleman, making a gesture to go first.

"So Beau, what do you think?" Avery asks, and Beau just chuckles.

"I'll be honest, Ave, I didn't hear a fucking word you just said."

"Excuse me?" she asks, and when she glances at me, my body tenses up. Lord knows I haven't heard a word she said either.

"Good night, ladies," Beau says, pulling Avery's attention back to him—*thank goodness*—as he steps up to his door and pulls out his keys.

"That's it?" Avery questions. "What if what I was saying was really important?"

"Was it?" Beau questions with a challenging tilt of his head.

"I guess you'll never know," Avery sing-songs and Beau just shrugs.

"Okay." He unlocks the door to his apartment. "Good night, ladies."

"God, you're such an old man!" Avery groans, but Beau just flashes a grin and walks inside his condo and shuts the door.

I unlock the door to our condo, stepping inside, and Avery follows. She heads straight for the kitchen and tosses her purse onto the marble island.

"Gahh, tonight was the best, wasn't it?" she questions and plops down onto one of the stools. "I swear DJ Andre is so good, he has to be a part of the illuminati."

"What?" I ask on a shocked laugh.

"You know... sold his soul to the devil for fame and stuff."

I shake my head as she heads to the fridge and grabs a bottle of Fiji water. She won't drink any lesser brand, and even at that, she turns up her nose at the cheapness of the bottle. "Ugh. I just don't understand why they wouldn't use all glass bottles."

I shrug. "Probably because of cost."

"What a stupid reason," she scoffs, but she takes a drink anyway.

"Avery, *honey*," I say through a soft laugh. "You've never had to worry about money when it comes to groceries, but other people do."

"Not you," she challenges.

"No, not me. My parents have gifted me with all the things money can buy and, still, look at me. Certified proof that money doesn't buy happiness *or* love."

"Screw them," Avery says to that, setting her bottle on the counter and walking toward me. "Use what they gave you and forget the rest." She pulls me in for a hug that doesn't quite make sense when combined with her words. "You are in a position of privilege. You can do what you want with it."

"Yeah." I shrug again. "I guess you're right."

Seriousness sufficiently spent, she chucks me on the shoulder before picking her bottle back up and heading for her bedroom. "Okay, then. I'm gonna go diddle my doodle to fall asleep. Toodle-oo until tomorrow!"

Goodness, she's crazy.

I watch her retreat all the way down the hallway, and I don't stop looking in that direction until I hear her door fall closed. Instantly, as if it's a premeditated routine—*probably because it freaking is*—I pull my phone out of my purse and open my Midnight chat with Beau. I hate that we didn't get to kiss goodbye, but messaging is at least something.

> **ElizaBeth: Are you still awake over there?**

Not even ten seconds later, my phone vibrates in my hands.

> **ThunderStruck: We just got home. Of course I'm still awake.**

> **ElizaBeth: I hate that we didn't get to have a real goodbye.**

Trust me, I know there's a host of other things I should be thinking about right now, very serious things I should be focused on—like how I'm going to tell Avery the truth about Beau and me—but my Beau-craving body has something else in mind.

> **ThunderStruck: Oh yeah? What would you have done if Avery hadn't been with us?**

My answer is immediate.

ElizaBeth: Kissed you.

ThunderStruck: And then?

ElizaBeth: I'm not sure I would have been in charge.

ThunderStruck: Why not? You in charge sounds sexy. In fact, maybe you should be in charge right now. Go into your bedroom and get on your bed, and we can put each other to sleep with a little sexy messaging.

Oh boy. I'm already walking to my bedroom and shutting the door behind me.

ElizaBeth: It's a damn shame you can't undress me right now.

ThunderStruck: Fuck. What's your underwear look like?

ElizaBeth: What underwear?

ThunderStruck: Fuuuck, June. You know what? I think we should scrap the message idea and you come over here instead.

ElizaBeth: No way. I'm already excited about touching myself while you tell me what to do.

ThunderStruck: You're a danger to society saying shit like that. Fuck. I might burn this building down just so you have to go outside.

I giggle. But my body also burns with anticipation as I take off my clothes and slide under the covers of my bed.

ElizaBeth: Tell me what to do, Beau.

ThunderStruck: You're naked?

ElizaBeth: Yes.

ThunderStruck: Wait, give me a minute to join you.

I listen to him moving on the other side of my wall until the noise stops, and I know he's there, on his bed. My mind instantly envisions him with his hard dick in his hand and, at the visual, a deliciously deep throb pulses between my thighs.

ElizaBeth: Are you hard?

ThunderStruck: It should be illegal to be this hard.

My cheeks heat and my body hums, and I fist my comforter with my left hand while I send him another message with my right.

ElizaBeth: Tell me where to touch myself.

ThunderStruck: Start with your thighs. Just barely touch yourself, enough to tickle, sliding your fingertips up until you get to the center. Don't touch too much, though. Just a tease.

I do as he says, my head falling back with a thud against the wall I know he has to hear.

ThunderStruck: Are you wet, baby?

I touch myself, right there, just barely, my index finger sliding lightly through my arousal.

ElizaBeth: Yes.

ThunderStruck: Good. Add a little pressure, then rub your clit in a slow circle. Let me hear you.

I do as he says, moaning when the pleasure from the touch to my clit runs up my spine and down to my toes.

ElizaBeth: It feels too good.

ThunderStruck: My cock is so fucking hard for you.

As if that message wasn't enough to push me closer to the edge, the second one seals the deal.

> **ThunderStruck: Put your phone down and stick two fingers in your wet pussy. And rub yourself faster while you use your fingers as a replacement for my cock. I'll stroke and listen, I promise.**

Exhaling a deep breath, I set the phone down like he says and concentrate on touching myself. Two fingers of my right hand inside, I stroke at the inner wall while circling my clit with the fingers of my left. I thought it'd be a cheap excuse for Beau's real touch, *for Beau's perfect cock*, but I'm so fucking turned on, it doesn't even matter.

I groan as my pleasure builds, and I hear Beau curse on the other side of the wall. I imagine his strokes moving faster up and down the hard length of his cock, and I have to lick my lips to keep my eyes from rolling back in my head.

"Beau," I moan softly, keeping my voice at a level that I know Avery won't hear from her bedroom, and the sound of him groaning spurs me further.

Faster and faster, I spin my fingers around my clit and stroke myself inside, my head rocking against the wall as I climb toward my climax. It feels almost impossibly good.

I come with a small shout, and he follows shortly after, the sound of his muffled, "Fuck," vibrating all the way through my chest. I lie there for a long moment catching my breath, and from the lack of movement on the other side of the wall, I suspect he's doing the same.

I pick up my phone and type out a message.

> **ElizaBeth: Holy hell.**

> **ThunderStruck: Yeah. Tomorrow night, I'm going to need the real thing.**

> **ElizaBeth: Me too.**

I know we're headed for a train wreck, but there's no stopping this now.

PART 6

Beau

Chapter 37

ANOTHER TWO WEEKS OF BEING LOCKED TIGHT IN THE sexy embrace of a secret rendezvous with June, and I don't see any way for me to stop. I don't see any way out of this at all. *Because you're falling for her.*

Yeah. I am.

I don't want this thing between us to be a secret anymore, was more than ready to announce the good news to my family right after Thanksgiving, but my gorgeous June is dragging her feet a bit.

I've made a point not to read into it, knowing her hesitancy stems from not knowing what Avery's reaction will be, and instead of pushing her, I've set my sights on enjoying every little moment I can steal.

Take now, for example. She stopped in my office to drop off some files for the Dalencia Fashion campaign, and while I did need the shit inside said files, I need her more.

"Bye, Beau," June says, a little smile on her lips, and I grab her hip, tugging her back toward my desk.

"No," I whisper. "Don't go." It's a whine and I know it, and she laughs at me before pulling her hand away and pointing at the door.

"I know it's getting stressful, but you need to focus, okay? The pitch for your campaign is in less than two weeks, and as I've said previously, Seth is up to *something*."

I frown. "I'd rather flirt with you."

"Beau."

"Come on, June," I beg because I'm not above begging when it comes to her. "Help me procrastinate."

She shakes her head cutely, her red hair dusting at the tops of her breasts. I try not to imagine the feel of them as I groan again.

"If you'd let me tell you what he's doing, maybe you'd have time left over to—"

I shove back in my chair and sigh. "No. I don't want to know."

"Okay, then. That's what I thought. And you know what? I even respect it. But yeah, I can't distract you. I'm sorry."

"Fine." I roll my eyes dramatically. "Go work, then."

She snorts. "I'm going. But you have to let go of my leg."

"I'm not holding your leg," I lie. I'm most definitely holding on to her leg, and now I'm running my fingers up her thigh. But just when I start to slide under her skirt, she pulls away on a giggle.

"You're insane," she says, still giggling as she waves a hand softly before spinning toward the door. She's almost out of it when Avery appears, shoving her back in and closing both her and June in my office.

I settle back into my chair. If my sister's history is anything to go by, I can expect this to be good. "You need something?" I ask.

"Christmas Eve," Avery says, and I steeple my arms on the edges of my chair and rest my chin on top of my hands.

"Generally speaking, Christmas Eve is a great day to spend time with family…"

"Shut up, Beau," Avery says as her eyes roll heavenward. "We need to talk about the specifics of *our* Christmas Eve."

"Oh God," June says with a moan, and I stifle the urge to laugh.

"Don't *Oh God* me, Juniper Perry." Avery glares at her. "Last year was a disaster, and you know it. I want to set ground rules for this year."

"Or you could just be an adult and take Christmas as it comes," I offer, and she shakes her head.

"No. No way. That's the last damn thing I'm going to do."

"Fine." I laugh. "What are your Christmas rules?"

"No, and I mean absolutely *no* gifts of white gold or silver," Avery announces like it's of the utmost importance. "Clearly, I'm a yellow gold girlie, and any failure to realize that on your part is willful ignorance at this point. Weaponized incompetence, even."

June chews on her bottom lip, her mouth curving up intently. It's one of her prettiest looks, and suddenly, letting Avery spin her wheels with ridiculous guidelines doesn't seem like such a bad idea.

"All right. Yellow gold." I sigh. "What else?"

"I'll also only accept the watching of *The Santa Clause*, *The Holiday*, and *A Christmas Story*, in that order. None of that *White Christmas* 1950's bullshit you tried to pull last time."

"Of course," I agree, watching June just as closely as before. Her blue eyes sparkle.

"Diane's already got her shit lined up for the food, but I won't be tolerating anything other than chocolate chip cookies left out for Santa either." Avery points a serious finger at me and then June. "No healthy options, no crap about him not being real. You'll leave them, and you'll like it."

"Is that all? Or is there something else?"

"I will also be the first to open gifts," my sister states, and since it's all about Avery and Avery getting gifts, I know she's finally getting to the nuts and bolts of the matter. "And I reserve the right to return anything I see fit. Don't even try to guilt-trip me into keeping something I don't like."

I shake my head on an amused sigh. "Fine."

"June?" she questions. "Are we on the same page here?"

"Oh. Yeah. Sounds good to me," she agrees easily, rolling her eyes at me and making Avery shove her.

"Glad we understand each other," Avery says, turning on her heels and offering a little wave over her shoulder.

Whipping open my office door, she's gone as quick as she came, leaving June and me alone once again. June turns to leave, but I whisper a "Pssst" before she gets out the door.

When she turns back toward me, her eyebrows are raised in question.

"Just so you know, I have a list of Christmas Eve requirements too."

She quirks an adorable brow and crosses her arms over her chest. "Oh really?"

I nod. "Yeah."

"And what are they?"

"Well, for starters…" I tap my chin thoughtfully and make a show of glancing down at her skirt, my mind very much busy with what's beneath it. "Absolutely no underwear allowed."

She snorts. "Pretty sure Neil's going to avoid going commando under his suit."

"Ah-ah." I waggle a finger at her. "These rules are just for you."

"Right." She nods, but her cheeks flush pink as thoughts I know are one hundred percent dirty start to fill her pretty little head. "And what are the other rules?"

"You think about me eating your pussy at least ninety percent of the day," I say and lock my gaze with hers as my lips twitch into a smile. "If my math is correct, which, yeah, I think we can both agree it is, you'll need to think about it for *The Santa Clause, The Holiday,* and at least half of *A Christmas Story.*"

"Beau…" She pauses, but I don't miss the way her chest moves up and down with a shaky exhale of air.

"Yeah, June?"

She swallows, looks toward the windows of my office for a brief moment, and then her blue eyes are back on mine. "How about get back to work, Mr. Banks?" she chastises with a tsk. "Pretty sure you have much more important things to be worrying about than my panties."

"Oh, I don't know, June. Your panties—or lack thereof—are pretty fucking important."

She laughs, shakes her head, and heads straight for my door. "Get back to work, Beau."

I smile and waggle my eyebrows as she leaves the office, and even though there are a hundred dirty ideas rolling through my head, I drop it for now.

June is right. Today's the last day before the office's Christmas break, and I need to spend all the time working I can.

With the way I'm starting to feel about June, the rest of my time is likely to be filled by her.

Chapter 38

I MOVE MY ESCALADE THROUGH THE GATE IN FRONT OF MY parents' house and pull into the driveway, the bright lights of Christmas nearly blinding me. Clearly, my mother and her go-to Christmas décor company went a little overboard this year trying to beat out Martha May Whovier.

I pull to a stop in front of a large inflatable snowman, and Avery and June climb out the passenger's side while I cut the engine and hop out. The sounds of actual Christmas carols coming from discreet outdoor speakers placed around the yard fill my ears, and I don't know whether to be amused or horrified that the entire neighborhood has had to listen to "Jingle Bells" on a continuous loop since the day after Thanksgiving.

My grandfather Phil's Mercedes is already parked in the front of the house, the hood cold to the touch as I walk by, and I glance back one more time to make sure I've parked in a way that puts my car in no danger when he goes to leave later.

He's fine on the road, but for some reason, any situation involving parking causes a real complication for him.

Since moving into Coral Village last year, a senior living neighborhood for the uberwealthy, both sets of our grandparents have taken to carpooling everywhere they go. To the doctor, to the movies, or here for the holidays—it's all scheduled to be a group activity.

And because they're all completely unhinged, despite his finicky record, my grandpa Phil is the best driver out of the bunch.

And when I say they do everything together, I mean it. We never see them on Thanksgiving because, for the past decade, they've been taking the same monthlong cruise on the same cruise line across the Mediterranean. Last Christmas, my grandpa Bill got his knee replacement surgery the same day they docked—which was the day before our Christmas Eve dinner—and they didn't even think to consider other dates.

Grandpa Bill spent the whole damn night with his leg propped up on pillows and his face pinched in a grimace, pain pills stunting his appetite for dinner.

Avery and June are already inside by the time I make it in the door, and Linda takes my sport coat to hang it up for me before I join the rest of them in the kitchen. The inside of the house matches the outside, and I have to maneuver past what feels like a forest of Christmas trees before I can find everyone.

My mom is dressed to the nines in a red sequined dress, and my dad wears one of his black velvet suits to match the occasion. Both my grandfathers—Bill and Phil—wear bow ties, and my grandmothers—Bev and Judy—showcase ballgown-style dresses. The moment all four of them see what Avery, June, and I are wearing, the looks of disgust are palpable.

"I swear, kids are caring less and less about the way they dress these days," my grandma Bev chides, whispering to my mom in an anything but quiet voice.

You'd think we're all schlepping it in sweatpants, but Avery is in designer jeans and some kind of complicated top she probably spent too fucking much money on, and June is wearing a cream-colored sweaterdress. I'm in jeans and a dress shirt, and while it's not black tie, I wouldn't say we look disheveled either.

Avery grabs a carrot from the vegetable tray and crunches on it as she jumps directly into the fray of Grandma Bev's dress code annoyance. "Maybe I'm just waiting for you to bestow me with a gift worthy of wearing, Grandma. Versace, Balenciaga, Gucci? What is it? Give it to me now, and I'll go change."

Grandma Bev shakes her head, but she also smiles. "Avery, honey, you really need to start sticking with the classics."

"I can't even imagine you'd want to wear Balenciaga after their horrid Paris show," Grandma Judy chimes in with a scoff.

The classics they speak of involve Chanel, Hermès, Ralph Lauren, and Yves Saint Laurent. I shouldn't know any of this shit, but when your little sister is Avery with a black AMEX, you find your brain being filled with things whether you like it or not.

If it isn't already clear, both sets of my grandparents come from money. Very old, very WASP-esque kind of money. Frankly, they're so set in their old-fashioned ways, there was a period of time they weren't thrilled about my dad's choice of starting a marketing firm back in the day. They thought it was too edgy, and his dad, my grandpa Phil, was horrified that his son wasn't going to continue the Banks name in the financial world.

Eventually, though, when they saw how well my dad was doing, they got over it.

My mom just laughs off my grandmothers' passive-aggressive chatter about proper Christmas Eve dinner attire, and my dad directs us all to the living room for premeal cocktails that are already arranged on a silver tray.

June loiters until I catch up to her, and the two of us walk in together, my hand gently touching the small of her back. It's not something I never would have done, but it's not exactly innocent anymore either.

I'm more than ready to have all of this in the open so I can love her out loud.

The thought stalls me for the briefest of seconds as I consider it. *Do I love June?*

It sure seems like it these days. Any time we're apart I spend wishing we were together, and I'm happiest when she's around. She's even come more into herself, and the new comfort we find together is something to be envied.

I grab a glass of champagne from my dad's tray and hand it to June before grabbing a glass of neat whiskey for myself. My fingers itch to pull her closer to me, to feel the warmth of her body pressed against mine, but I take a seat in one of the chairs beside the fireplace to keep myself from misbehaving. If I sit on the couch with June, I'll be running my hands all over her legs without even realizing it, trying to find the skin under her sexy, thigh-high boots.

Avery takes the seat next to June, and I focus on my dad as he stands in front of the mantel to make his traditional Christmas Eve toast. Our stockings hang behind him, the glow from the fireplace casting warm shadows over them, and I spot the one with *Juniper* written on it directly beside the one with *Beau*.

Internally, I smile, thinking back to the first Christmas my mom added a stocking for June. She was ten and I was fifteen, and the way her eyes brightened when she spotted her name on the mantel lit up the whole damn room.

My eyes move back to June, taking in the way her long red hair hangs down her shoulders and the way her mouth turns up into an adorable grin when Avery whispers something to her.

She looks happy and carefree, but I know today, just like every other holiday, is hard for her. Knowing her parents' house is just down the street from here, empty while her dad travels the world without her, wouldn't be easy on anyone.

"Welcome, everyone," my dad announces, his face curling up in a genuine smile. "Diane and I, as always, are so grateful to have all of you to call family and love spending this special day with you. Chef Stone has prepared a special Christmas Eve feast for us tonight," he says, extending a hand toward the kitchen and prompting all of us to turn in that direction and raise our glasses toward the chef, "and we can't wait to share it with you. You…all of you…make our lives so much better, and we don't know what we'd do without you." He lifts his glass, and we do the same, taking a drink before he turns to each of us individually. "Mom, Dad, I appreciate the sacrifices you made to put me in the position I am now." My grandma Bev and grandpa Phil smile, and he turns to my mom's parents then.

"Bill, Judy…I want to thank you for this amazing woman you raised. She's my better half in every way, and without her, I would be lost. She keeps our lives running and gave me two beautiful children. I love you, Diane, with my whole heart, whole soul, whole being."

My dad takes a moment to step over to my mom and press a little kiss to her lips. But their sweet moment is popped like a needle to a balloon when my sister chimes in.

"Ooh, do me now!" Avery demands, making us all laugh.

My dad's smile only grows as he walks back over to the mantel, his eyes on Avery now. "My dearest daughter…you're unequivocally you, and I pride myself on giving you the opportunity to be just that. I hope you don't change and that people will give you the chance to show your kind spirit and giving heart like you show to me. I'm also unbelievably grateful for the shy little girl you brought home with you from Hollis Academy on that first September day, and for the opportunity to love her now."

"Gosh, you guys are so lucky to have me," Avery says, lifting her glass in the air for herself. "Cheers to me!"

My dad just chuckles as he turns to June, and I can't help but turn to face her too, knowing this moment right here from my dad is all she's ever wanted in this world from her own mother and father. "June, our little angel. God sure did bless us by bringing you into our lives. I'm proud of your sweet nature and your giving soul and your undeniable work ethic you've shown since joining the firm this fall. I'm so proud of you, if I could, I'd call you my daughter too."

June licks her lips and nods, and I know when she looks down to her lap, she's crying real tears.

One day, she's going to have all the things she's ever dreamed of. I'm going to make sure of it.

He turns to me then, and I have to sit up straighter in my seat to refocus myself on him. These days, I swear, I feel like I'm particles of myself, constantly scattered throughout the room and always hoping to get closer to June.

"Beau. Son. I'm so proud of the man you're becoming and the care and attention you put into the business I built on my back," my dad says, his smile big. "I know you're dedicated to continuing the firm's legacy long after I'm retired and gone, and the thought makes me incredibly proud. But more than all those things, I'm proud of who you are as a person. The integrity. The honesty. The unwavering dedication to doing the right thing." My ears burn with a sudden wave of guilt over hiding what June and I are from not only my dad, but everyone in this room. My mom. My grandparents. Even my sister. She's a pain in the ass on even the best of days, but she'd do anything for me or June at the drop of a hat. I don't like that we're still lying to them—in this moment, I'm starting to hate it, actually—and I hope beyond hope we figure out a way to break the news soon. "Beau, I know it hasn't always been a smooth road for you, but you've risen above and come out on top."

When the speech finally breaks and everyone disperses toward the dining room table where Chef Stone is bringing out appetizers, I shake my dad's hand and give him a hug, and then promptly start searching for June.

She's nowhere to be found, and I have a feeling it's because she's feeling just as guilty as I am about the secret we're hiding. We've had what feels like a hundred conversations about this, and if my father's words tonight affected her in the same way they affected me, the shame of hiding our relationship from everyone is feeling like a path that's more than run its course.

I start at the half bath and then go out back to the pool and even down to look for her at our spot on the beach, but I come up empty-handed at all of them.

When I go back inside, I climb the steps to the second floor and start peeking inside bedrooms as I make my way down the hall.

Most are empty, with made beds and untouched knickknacks, including the one she used to sleep in every night she was here growing up, but when I get to mine at the end of the long second-floor hallway, she's lurking in front of my bookshelf.

"Hey," I say softly, hoping not to startle her as I step inside and shut the door behind me.

"Hi," she replies, her teeth worrying the skin of her bottom lip.

"What are you doing in here?"

She laughs, shrugging. "Hiding from my culpability, I guess."

"Yeah." I nod. "I'm feeling pretty guilty too."

"How are we going to tell everyone, Beau?" She sinks her face into her hands. "Listening to your dad down there, I felt so bad. I love your family so much. Just as much as I've always loved you. I just… I feel like we've backed ourselves into a corner. And trust me, I know this is more my doing than yours."

"Hey, don't do that. We're a team, okay?" Stepping forward and pulling her into my arms, I hug her tight. "And we'll figure out a way to tell them. Everything is going to be fine, I promise. They love both of us, right? Why wouldn't they want us to be happy and together?"

"Maybe they would have been okay a few months ago, but Beau, we've been *lying*," she whispers into my chest. "We're lying right now!"

I put my hands to the side of her face, lifting her gaze to mine and studying the cornflower blue of her irises. "I'm going to figure out how to fix it. I promise."

She nods, and I press my lips to hers. The kiss starts out soft and gentle, but it only takes a few beats before it turns altogether heated. Her hands pull at the back of my dress shirt, and I lift the hem of her cream dress. The skin of her thigh feels warm and inviting, and I move my tongue deeper into her mouth to get more.

God, she tastes so good. Feels so good. I'll never have enough. I could touch and kiss June every second of every hour of every day for the rest of forever and I don't think I'd ever have my fill.

A little moan escapes her throat, and I swallow it down as passion and heat and white-hot need release themselves inside our kiss.

"I've been looking all over for—*oh my God!*" Avery screams at the top of her lungs, and both June and I startle apart as the door to my bedroom swings open so hard it bangs against the wall.

Fuck.

I thought I locked it.

But I thought wrong.

"What in the holy hell is going on here?" Avery questions, her eyes wide as they dart back and forth between us.

"Avery, I can explain," June says immediately, stepping around me and all but pushing me out of the way.

"No need, June. I've got eyes," Avery snaps. "And my eyes just saw your tongue down my brother's throat! Why was your tongue down my brother's throat, June?" Her voice rises in irritation.

"Avery—" I start to interrupt, but she's on a warpath now.

"My God, are you two a thing?" Avery shouts. "Are you two, like, *together*?"

"We were going to tell you," June says, her voice shaky. "I just—"

"How long?" Avery cuts her off to ask. "How the hell long has this been going on?"

June's face is red with distress as she glances back at me. "A few months," I respond, knowing she needs me to say the words for her.

"Months? *Months?*" Avery screams. "You're telling me you've been lying to me for months?" she says directly to June, her voice trembling with hurt.

"I'm so sorry, Avery," June apologizes. "So, so sorry."

"Oh my god! All that shit with Bethany?" Avery questions, anger and pain lacing the edges of her voice. "She was right, wasn't she? It wasn't bullshit. All this time and you've had a thing for my brother?"

June stares down at her hands for a brief moment, her fingers fidgeting nervously, before she finds the strength to meet Avery's eyes. "Yes. I…I've always had a thing for Beau."

"And what was I?" Avery tosses both of her hands out in front of her. "Just a way to get to him?!"

"No!" June yells, upset, and tears now stream down her cheeks. "Of course not! I love you like a sister, you know that!"

"I don't know anything, Juniper. Not one single thing. Because ten minutes ago, I knew my best friend in the world would never, *ever* lie to my face or do something this big behind my back on purpose. I knew that with my heart and soul. And yet...look where I am now."

"Avery," I chide, my voice rough.

"No." She points an angry finger at me. "Don't even fucking bother, Beau." She snaps a glare at June. "Don't either of you bother."

Avery takes off at a run, and June chases after her.

And I, almost comically, run after both of them. It's a full-on *My Best Friend's Wedding* moment, and I'm playing the scumbag role of Julia Roberts.

I've hurt the two women I care about most in this world. The two women who are the reason I'm able to make this stupid movie reference at all, and I have to find a way to make it right.

Fuuuuuuck.

PART 7

Juniper

Chapter 39

I RAN AFTER AVERY, OUT OF HER PARENTS' HOUSE, DOWN THE street, and I didn't stop chasing after her until she miraculously hailed a cab. I tried to reach her before she sped off, but I was too late and had to call a freaking Uber because Miami isn't New York and cabs aren't exactly easy to come by.

The instant my driver pulled up to the front of our condo building, I saw Avery heading into the entrance doors on quick feet. Of course, she didn't hold the elevator for me, standing there, glaring at me as the doors closed in front of my face before I could get inside.

Two minutes felt like an eternity as I waited for another elevator to come back down to the lobby level.

The cart dings its arrival on our floor, and I trip on my way out as I run toward our condo door. My lungs are one wheeze short of seizing up, still out of breath from running what feels like all over the city after Avery.

I try the doorknob to no avail, and then I take out my keys to unlock it myself. The door gives five inches as I push it open but jerks to a stop, thanks to the door chain, after that.

"Avery!" I yell inside through the crack, shoving my face into the opening. "Please open the door so we can at least talk."

Mr. Pickles, our neighbor across the hall's Chinese Crested dog, yips from behind their door, but I ignore him and keep pleading. "I know I messed up. I know. I take full responsibility for the way I treated you, and I want to do whatever it is you need to make it up to you."

I wait in silence, hoping to hear movement on the other side, and finally, I hear a stomping walk that ends with the door being shoved directly into my face to close it again.

I wait for a moment, the rattle of the chain bolstering some hope, and rush forward as soon as she pulls the door back. She holds up a hand to stop me, and I screech to a stop, my body half-way inside.

"Accountability is only half of the equation this time, June. Apologies won't do me much good if I don't even know who the fuck you are." She shakes her head, and I suck my lips into my mouth, clasping pleading hands in front of my chest.

"Please, just let me come inside so we can talk. If you're still mad at me after that, I'll understand, and if you want me to go and give you space, I will."

Just then, the elevator doors open behind us, and Beau comes sliding out, his hurried appearance not far off from my own.

I know my hair's a mess and my chest is covered in a full-blown sweat, but looking good is hardly my biggest concern right now. I am wishing, however, I'd have been less concerned with Christmas theming and more concerned with the Miami heat when I picked this sweaterdress.

"Oh great," Avery remarks at the sight of her brother. "The gang's all here, I guess."

For the first time in forever, I find myself wishing Beau away. If it's going to drive apart the only family I've ever known, it's not worth it.

It doesn't matter how much I love him; I can't bear the responsibility of breaking apart the Banks family. Even if that means I have to sacrifice myself.

Avery starts to shut the door again, but I hold it open with a strong hand, turning back to Beau, my eyes pleading. "Beau, please. Give us time to talk. Your being here is only making it worse."

"I'm here because I'm part of it," he contests, and my chest twists.

"I know. But please, give us some space."

He studies me for a long, aching moment before walking to his condo and unlocking the door. When it shuts behind him, I feel the vibration crack against my heart. God, this is awful, and it's all my fault. Beau was ready to tell them the truth, but I kept delaying it. And now, he probably feels just as bad as I do right now. But I don't know how to carry on from here if Avery and I can't fix what I've broken.

I push through the door as soon as Avery shows signs of letting me and shut it behind us as she walks over to the couch, slumps down, and crosses her arms over her chest.

I start again with an apology, though, I know that in and of itself won't make this better.

"I'm sorry, Avery. I'm sorry for being the kind of person I wouldn't want as my own friend, let alone yours."

She chuffs. I keep going.

"I lied and I snuck around, and I did it knowing it would hurt you." I shake my head. "I've...I've always been into Beau. Even *way* before I had any business seeing him as anything of the sort, and all through his relationship with Bethany. But I didn't use you to get to him, and I would never dream of giving up what we have to have something with him."

"But that's exactly what you did, June," she says, narrowing her eyes. "You set me aside. Our time together, my feelings—all of it was disposable for a good time with my brother."

"It wasn't just a good time, Ave," I start to respond, but the way her face wrinkles up with disdain makes me shut my mouth. I look down at my lap, twisting my fingers together. There's not much you can say when you know you've wronged someone. There's not much you can say when you're facing the hurt you've caused on your best friend's face.

"Putting aside the fact that he's an old man and my brother...

it's the way you treated our friendship like it was some third-class *Titanic* ticket." She lets out a deep sigh. "Oh well, I guess it's going down with the ship, huh?"

She shakes her head and starts to get up, and I reach out for her hand with a plead. "What can I do to make it better? How can I make it up to you? Fix it? I don't want this to be the thing that drives us apart. We've been friends for way too long, and you mean way too much to me. I love you, Avery. I love you so much. What can I do?"

Avery's face is as serious as I've ever seen it. "I don't know if there is anything, June. I really don't know, but I think you need to leave. Just being in the same room with you is too much for me."

My heart breaks into a million tiny pieces, but I swallow down the urge to sob and head into my bedroom to pack a bag.

Avery wants me gone, and the last thing I'm going to do is cause her more pain than I already have.

PART 8

Bean

Chapter 40

PACE MY ROOM AS THE CLOCK TURNS OVER TO MIDNIGHT, MY message on the namesake app still unread.

> **ThunderStruck: June, are you okay? Where are you?**

I heard their apartment door slam several hours ago, right at the culmination of June's heated conversation with Avery that I couldn't quite make out through the wall, and I've been worrying about June ever since.

Her room is silent, and Avery plays loud, angry music meant, I know, to make a point to me.

Antsy, I send another message.

> **ThunderStruck: I'm worried about you. I know you're not home. Please, I need to know you're safe.**

When the wheel spins to indicate she's typing, I stand up straighter, my heart in my throat.

> **ElizaBeth: I'm safe. But please, I need you to leave me alone.**
>
> **ThunderStruck: I don't think I can do that.**
>
> **ElizaBeth: If you can't, I'm going to have to do**

*it for you. This isn't a good idea, and I'm sorry I
was the one who started it. I ruined everything.*

**ThunderStuck: Don't say that. Avery is going
to get over it.**

ElizaBeth Ended the Chat

My phone beeps, and everything we've ever said to each other
inside Midnight disappears. Months of conversations, gone in an
instant.

I swallow thickly and sit down on my bed, my phone in my
hands and my mind adrift.

Is there really a chance this is over? It can't be. I don't want it
to end.

But fuck, what if I don't get a choice?

My parents' driveway is empty as I pull into it and put my car in
park. Dark circles hollow the skin under my eyes, last night's lack
of sleep on full display.

Holiday décor and jingles greet me as I get out of the car, and
I groan, the spirit of Christmas Day not touching me in the ways it
normally would.

I still don't know where June is, and Avery won't open her door
to talk to me either. Normally, we'd all head to my parents' house
for Christmas brunch, but it's clear by the "**I'm not fucking going**"
message I got from Avery when I attempted to text her an olive
branch in the form of offering a ride to our parents' that nothing
about today is normal.

I know what June and I did wasn't right, and I know Avery has
every right to be pissed. And if there's anything I need right now
more than ever—*besides June, that is*—it's a voice of clarity to tell
me like it is.

Thankfully, my mom Diane is the unequivocal best at that task.

I push the doorbell at the side of the arched entryway, staring at my shoes while I wait for someone to come to the door. Linda is there pretty quickly, and upon seeing my face, she smiles sympathetically. She witnessed the whole sordid chase of June running after a screaming and crying Avery and me running after a distraught and crying June.

We created quite the scene, and I have a feeling the next time I see our grandparents, I'm going to get a passive-aggressive earful about proper etiquette and all that.

"Merry Christmas, Mr. Banks," Linda says. "Your parents are on the back patio."

I nod gratefully. "Thanks, Linda."

"Of course, hun."

The house is quiet, emptied of both last night's Christmas cheer and the unexpected drama that occurred before Chef Stone even served dinner. Just as Linda said, my parents are on the patio, holding hands while my dad reads the newspaper and my mom drinks from a coffee mug.

I hold my breath for a moment, offering up a silent prayer that my dad doesn't read me the riot act, and force myself to face them both head on.

"Hey, guys," I say simply, lifting both of their gazes. They exchange a look with each other, my dad's face pinched with disappointment, and my mom pats him on the arm.

"Why don't you go on in and make some more coffee, sweetie? I'll talk to Beau."

Neil nods and stands, walking past me without a clap to the shoulder or a massive hug like usual, and my confidence that everything about this is going to turn out okay crumbles even further.

I didn't want to hurt my family. I didn't want this. But I *do* want June.

"Come on, honey," my mom says, patting the gray-cushioned patio chair right beside her. "Come sit down."

I do as she says, taking my dad's spot and sinking my head into my hands. She reaches up and rubs my shoulder, and for the first time in a long time, I feel like a little kid.

"I don't know what to do now, Mom. I didn't mean for it to get so messed up."

She hums. "Why don't you start with the important parts?"

"The important parts?"

Her smile is soft but stern. "What is going on with you and June? Is it serious? Because if you willfully got involved with her knowing it wasn't going anywhere, I'm going to be disappointed."

"It's not nothing," I hedge immediately. "It's something. It's… Mom, I'm in love with her."

She smiles gently, a hint of something else settling into her knowledgeable green eyes. "Does she know that?"

I shake my head. "I haven't told her."

She sits back in her chair, a distant look of fond memories hazing the intensity of her gaze. "You know, I remember the first time Juniper Perry caught sight of you. Avery had just convinced her to come over after school, and you were on your way in from surfing out back. You smiled at her and said hello, always my polite, charming boy, and her whole world spun upside down."

"Wait… You knew all this time?" I question. "You knew June was into me?"

"Into you?" My mom laughs. "Oh, honey. She's been in love with you since that first moment she saw you. The only people who didn't know June was in love with you were you and Avery."

Memories of June and being with June and loving June fill my head, and the cold realization that there's a stark possibility I might never be able to hold her or touch her or kiss her again makes my face break into a clammy sweat.

"I don't know how to fix any of this," I say, my voice just barely above a whisper. "How to make any of it right."

"Is June okay?" my mom asks, and I look down at my hands, worry bowing my shoulders forward.

"I don't even know where she is."

"Oh, sweetie," my mom whispers, rubbing my shoulder. "She just needs time. And so does Avery. It sounds like the two of you love each other, and I can tell you from experience that love is a very powerful thing."

I glance inside at my dad as she does. "I want what you guys have. I want the family. The love. I want it with her."

My mom's gaze is steady and poignant. "Then you need to tell her."

"How do I tell her if she won't even talk to me?"

"Oh, Beau," she says, reaching out to pat my hand. "You'll find a way. I know you will. You always do."

I *have* to find a way. There's no other option for me but June.

PART 9

Juniper

Chapter 41

MY HANDS SHAKE AS I SET A CUP OF COFFEE IN FRONT OF Marcus Hughes at the conference table, the projection screen on the far end of the room lit up and waiting with Seth McKenzie's presentation.

Today is New Year's Eve, the day Beau and Seth are due to pitch their Midnight campaigns and showcase all the hard work—*or in Seth's case, hard-scheming*—their teams have put in over the past few months.

Honestly, knowing what I know, it feels like I'm waiting on disaster, and my nerves are raw with anticipation.

For the last week, I've been hiding out at my dad's empty house to give Avery some space. Beau tried to reach out to me several times through Midnight, but I just left the conversation because the mess I've created, the pain I've caused, feels too much to overcome. He then resorted to texts and calls, but I ignored those too. Not because I don't want to talk to him—of course I do—but because I refuse to be the reason I cause a rift in the best family I've ever known.

I'd be lying if I didn't admit that Christmas Day was quiet and lonely in my dad's big, empty house. There was staff, of course, but I spent most of the day locked away in my childhood bedroom, bawling my eyes out.

Thankfully, I've cried so much that my tear ducts have gone on strike, and I've somehow managed to pull myself together enough to show up at work this morning. Though, I guess that strength stems from the changes I've already put into action.

At the start of the year, I've agreed to start working for my dad, one simple text to him the other day putting it all into motion.

Of course, I'd never leave Banks & McKenzie hanging, knowing what's at stake with the Midnight account. So, I made the hard decision to email Mr. Banks my official resignation this morning, with a request for a meeting this afternoon after the Midnight pitch conference is over.

Then, this chapter of my life will officially be done, and I'll start the new year as the newest employee at Perry Enterprises. *Yay.*

I take a spot against the back wall as Seth starts his presentation, and Beau takes a seat at the table, his hands steepled in front of him as he looks on.

He's as handsome as ever, and a war rages inside me with the knowledge of what's to come. Seth is a snipe and a snake, and his campaign is built off the back of Beau's ideas. It doesn't matter, though, since he's going first.

He's going to end up getting all the credit, and Beau… Well, I don't know what Beau will do. All I can do is wait and see.

"Gentlemen, ladies, on behalf of Banks & McKenzie, we'd like to thank you for coming today," Seth announces to the room. "We're unbelievably excited to share our vision with you for what we think is going to be the next big app in the space. Buckle in, because we're going dark."

The lights dim and the screen flashes, and in the center of it all, the branding I know Beau envisioned from the start flashes on the screen. It's a black background with gold lettering, and the word midnight is in capitalized, simple text. Underneath is the slogan. **NO CURFEW. NO RULES.**

"Midnight is a lust-filled, uninhibited experience between consenting adults under the cover of darkness. It's sexy and shameless, and there are no rules when it comes to being yourself. Kinks? You can explore them. Fantasies? They're real now. Midnight is an immersive experience for meeting strangers and turning them into lovers, and it's an experience for the masses," Seth explains magnanimously.

"We know how important it is to you to reach the biggest audience the space has to offer, and this does that in spades. Being over eighteen is the only restriction, and the world is your oyster. You can chat anytime, anywhere, with just the device in your hand. The interface is simple, and all access is code-based, just as you suggested. One of the biggest problems in today's advertising space is overcomplication. We're giving complex connection, but we're not doing it at the expense of ease. I think you'll find that this, this vision, is exactly what the people are looking for."

Seth hands out booklets with some of the finer details of the campaign and logistical implementations, and the lights come up on the room as everyone claps. Neil and Chris share a look, and the execs from Midnight whisper to one another as I clear their coffee and help set up for Beau's presentation.

I avoid his eyes as I help his team prepare materials and reset the projection computer so he can load his own files, and then I check if I can get anyone anything before melding back into the wall at the rear of the room.

Avery steps inside just as he's about to start, a fresh Starbucks in hand, and my heart kicks up a notch with the need to say something to her.

I don't, though. Because I know giving them all the space to heal their family unit without me, the girl who messed it all up, is the best thing I can do.

Beau takes his position at the front of the room, his warm smile and captivating brown eyes just as mesmerizing as ever. He looks remarkably composed for someone who should have just watched his entire presentation get snatched right out from under his nose, and I hold my breath in anticipation as he starts talking.

"Ladies and gentlemen, again, thank you for your patience with us as we prepared these campaigns for you. I, like you, find Seth's vision compelling and undeniably interesting—and, dare I say, it's almost as though it's something I might have come up with myself."

His eyes glare daggers at Seth, but the rest of his expression is composed as he smiles at the clients. Seth looks away slightly, and out of the corner of my eye, I feel like Neil might actually notice. Still, it's short-lived before he focuses back on his son, and I do the same.

This might be one of the last times I see him up close, so I drink in his beauty in great detail.

"When my team and I were initially brainstorming for this unique app, we went much the same direction as Seth's team," Beau announces, continuing to work the room with confidence that out-right confuses me. "But upon some introspection, we found it lacking in personality and relatability. This is a social app. An app of connection and personal moments and real people looking for real things. Imagine this, if you would. What would you do if you were a woman with a crush on man?"

Everything inside me freezes, my heart stuttering through several pounding beats.

"A crush that you've had for years without the means to do something about it," Beau continues, and I almost can't hear him over the ringing in my ears. "Maybe you're a little shy, and maybe putting yourself out there for the chance at a relationship feels impossible. Impossible, until…you hear about a new app called Midnight."

He puts up an image on the screen of a dark background filled with stars and the moon and an unspoken hope I can't quite describe.

"This app allows for anonymous messages with a securely generated code, and because of the mysterious nature, you actually get up the nerve to share that code with your crush."

The screen flashes again, and the logo appears, a tagline under it I recognize all too well.

"Meet me at Midnight," Beau says, a smile growing on his face. "Such a simple conversation starter, and a simple premise for opening the lines of communication. You can get to know each other, you can flirt, and if you're really lucky, you can fall in love."

Avery glances at me, her eyes wide, and I swallow, forcing myself to look forward at Beau as he finishes his speech.

"You can fall in love," he repeats, his voice a raw whisper I feel all the way into my bones. "The ultimate human experience. The thing we're all after at the end of the day. To love and be loved by someone and to have the confidence to make it happen. Midnight isn't just a place for sexy hookups and depravity. It's the missing link in millions of lives all over the world. You don't have to be afraid. You don't have to say it aloud. All you have to say is…Meet me at Midnight."

He looks directly at me, his eyes imploring. "Meet me at Midnight. Meet me at Midnight tonight. Meet me at Midnight forever. Meet me at Midnight."

It's all…too much. His words, the way he's looking at me, the love for him that very much still sits inside my soul. My heart is racing, and my tears ducts have decided to start working again as I stand here, in the corner of this conference room, with Beau's eyes on me.

My legs start moving toward the door of their own accord, and before I know it, I'm hurrying out of the room—tears now streaming down my cheeks—down the hall, and straight out of the office.

I don't look back as I ride the elevator all the way to the bottom floor and out of the building just like stupid Cinderella.

Beau Banks loves me, and I love him too. But this isn't the kind of thing you fix with a glass slipper.

Truth be told, I don't know if it's the kind of thing you can fix at all.

PART 10

Bean

Chapter 42

THERE'S A ROUND OF APPLAUSE AS JUNE RUNS OUT OF THE room, and I follow her down the hall with my eyes until I can't see her anymore. I try to step around my dad, who's gotten up to give me a hug, but my team crowds me too, giving me handshakes on a job well done after months of work and a last-minute change-up. The last week has been filled with late-night meetings and overnight pizza, and I couldn't have pulled it off without any of them.

Still, the only person I want to see right now is June.

"We think both directions have potential, but yours felt truly personal, Beau," Marcus Hughes states with a small smile. "It's sex without overdoing it, and we think it's the perfect launch for Midnight. We're excited to be working with you and your impassioned team, and you can bet we'll be back with some of our other companies that need a rebranding."

I shake Marcus Hughes's hand, elated and deflated all at the same time. At the start of all this, I couldn't have named something that would mean more to me than winning this campaign. Today, I hardly care at all. "Thank you, sir. It was truly a firm effort to bring you the best options we could. I'm really looking forward to working more with you in the future."

He steps away and lassos a finger, rounding up the rest of his team as they pack up their stuff on the table, and my dad's assistant

Denise escorts them out of the office. My dad pulls me into another hug and shakes my hand. "I'm proud of you, son."

Chris shakes my hand too. "Good job, Beau. Interested to see where the next year takes us."

I nod as he and Seth leave the room together, Seth trailing behind, a little dejected. I'd love to feel worse for him, and maybe I would if he hadn't tried to rob my whole campaign right out from under my nose just like he did with my ex-girlfriend.

Ironically, I changed my team's campaign pitch because of June. But not because she told me more about Seth's scheming, but rather because my love for her is the ultimate inspiration.

Because I felt like this was the only way to reach her. Ever since Christmas Eve, she's refused any contact with me, and this pitch felt like the only way for me to tell her how I really feel about her. To tell her that I love her.

Quite a risk, given the importance of the pitch, but I guess when you find the one person you want to spend the rest of your life with, you're willing to put it all on the line.

Though, right now, after June disappeared from the room, I don't have a fucking clue where I stand with her. And that reality is the only thing my brain is fixated on, even as my dad continues to tell me congratulations and comment on how great he thought my pitch was.

"Hey," Avery says, shoving in where my dad and I stand at the front of the room. She's out of breath, and her normally carefully crafted appearance is frayed around the edges. "I tried to catch up with her, but Steve says she was already out of the building before I got downstairs."

Instantly, her words give me hope that my sister has finally come around to the idea of June and me together. Because if Avery is okay with us, then maybe, just maybe, I can get my June back.

"What?" my dad asks.

"June," Avery and I say at the same time, and once again, his eyebrows draw together.

"I'm confused. Are the two of you speaking again? Have you made up with June?"

Avery rolls her eyes. "Geez, Dad, didn't you hear Beau's presentation? Of course we're speaking."

My dad just stares at her. "Say it slow for me because I still don't understand."

Avery stomps a little foot, and I remember everything I've always loved about my sister. She may be flighty and work-averse, but she also believes in doing what's right for the people she loves. "Dad! Beau just professed his love for June, live and in color in front of all these people in here."

My dad's jaw gapes as he looks at me. "He did?"

"The whole campaign is their story!" Avery nearly shouts.

"So, we're good?" I ask.

Avery's smile is huge. "Are you kidding? My bestie for the restie is actually going to end up being my real sister one day. This is the best-case scenario times a million."

I shake my head. "Yeah, well, none of that is going to happen if I don't find a way to convince her."

"Wait, wait," my dad cuts in again. "You're in love with June?"

"Yes, Dad!" Avery and I both say at the same time.

"Well, then I should probably let you know she emailed me her resignation letter this morning," my dad updates, and my stomach plummets to my fucking shoes. "Starting in the new year, she plans to go work for her father."

"What?" Avery shouts. "No way! No way is that ho taking that job and leaving me behind to do actual work here!"

"Avery," our dad chides, and she holds up a playful hand in his face to talk directly to me.

"No, Beau. We're not letting that happen. Not on my watch." She pokes a stern index finger into my chest. "Beau, you just be at the company party at midnight tonight with a plan and a speech to win our girl over. I'll get her there, okay?"

"You know where to find her?" I ask, and her nod is solemn.

"I've got a pretty good idea."

"All right," I agree. "I'm counting on you."

"Save your counting for sheep, Beau Banks," Avery says, heading for the door. "I'll have Juniper Perry at that party tonight one way or another. That's a guarantee."

And all I can do is offer up a silent prayer that she manages to come through.

PART 11

Juniper

Chapter 43

A BANGING KNOCK SOUNDS ON THE FRONT DOOR OF MY parents' house, so much so that I wonder if it's the police. I don't think my dad is doing shady business shit, but how the hell do I know? I've seen too many news stories of wealthy people getting raided by the FBI for money laundering and other illegal shit.

I run from the living room to the front, trying to see through the glass sidelights but coming up empty. When there's another violent bang, I pull it open and hold my breath in hopes that I'm not going to be escorted into a police cruiser.

But all the air in my lungs comes out in a shocked whoosh when I see Avery standing in the doorway.

She's sweaty and out of breath, and her long brown hair sticks to the top of her forehead like it does when she does hot yoga.

I swear, I've never seen her sweat for anything other than a workout, and suddenly, the worst comes to mind. *What if something happened to Neil or Diane? Or Beau?*

Did Seth fight him or something after I left?

"What's going on?" I ask, panic in my voice now. "What are you doing here?"

Avery doesn't answer before shoving both herself and me through the door and back into the house. "Holy shit, June, do you know how many places I had to look for you before I found you here?" She drops her Hermès Birkin down onto the Italian marble table in the foyer with a quiet thud before turning to face me. "How many hotels? Why on earth wouldn't you be ordering room-service ice cream at the Ritz instead of holing up in this big, empty house your dad owns?"

Her rant only confuses me more. "Avery, is everything okay with your parents? Your…brother?"

Her eyebrows draw together. "Yes. They're fine. A little heart-broken, but fine."

I shake my head, silently trying to make sense of it all. "Then… what are you doing here?"

"I came to make sure you don't make some stupid fucking mis-take like martyring yourself." She throws her hands in the air. "I mean, my God, why does the woman always have to be the martyr?"

"Wait…" I pause, blinking several times over her words. "You're not mad at me anymore?"

She laughs. "You were in the room when my old-ass brother professed his love for you in front of the whole dang office and a bunch of money-hungry Hughes International execs, were you not?"

"Of course I was," I whisper.

"Well, then you should know that anybody willing to make *that* big of a fool of themselves for my best friend, of all people, wins a golden ticket to see Wonka and to get out of jail with Avery Banks. It's like a package deal."

"Avery," I say her name because I don't know what else to say. Everything she's telling me right now feels too good to be true. Just like being with Beau always did.

"June," she says seriously and puts two firm hands on my shoul-ders so I'm forced to meet her stern gaze. "Don't be an idiot. I was mad at you for all the right reasons, but you betrayed me for even better ones." She shakes her head. "You and my brother. In love." She smiles. "We're probably going to be sisters one day, you know?"

I scoff. "Yeah. If Beau even still wants to deal with me. I ran out of the office and—"

"Shut up," Avery cuts me off. "That's why I'm here. We have to get you ready."

"Ready for what?"

She hands me a folded note, a coy smile on her face.

In the center of it, in Beau's chicken scratch handwriting, one thing is clear.

Meet me at midnight.

PART 12

Beau

Chapter 44

I STARE DOWN AT THE CITY FROM UP ABOVE, THROUGH THE glass windows of the top floor of the Veneta, an oceanside venue on the south end of Miami and the usual location for Banks & McKenzie's New Year's Eve party.

I've been attending since I started working at my dad's company after graduation, but tonight has a completely different vibe.

The celebration over our new big account is in full swing with the team, and a bunch of department heads dance with their significant others as the countdown to midnight gets closer and closer.

It's reminiscent, in a way, of Prince Charming's ball where he met Cinderella, and my chest pangs thinking about that early conversation with June on the Midnight chat.

My dad and my mom make the rounds, greeting people from all departments and levels, and Seth stands in a corner with Bethany, sulking about his loss.

I don't want to be preoccupied with him or them, though. Because, for me, all that matters tonight is having June show up so I can tell her how much I love her.

I pace the carpeted floor so much I stand to wear a hole in it if I do it much longer.

Glancing back at the entrance of the room yet again as the DJ announces it's only ten minutes until midnight, I straighten my tie one last time.

"Come on, Avery," I mutter to myself, my stomach twisting as people chatter around me about the new year.

Harry, Eddie, Laura, Madeline, and Jay wave at me from the bar, but I can't even fathom carrying on a conversation with them right now. I barely know my own name.

Finally, I catch a peek of my sister's dark hair and a long green dress as she steps through the front door, looking for me. I wave from across the room, and she nods, a cocky smile spreading across her face.

Thank God.

My heart pounds and my palms sweat as I step forward, craning my neck around people to get a look at June as she steps through the door behind Avery.

Her long copper hair is swept to one side of her head, falling down in a line in front of her shoulder, and a long red, *unbelievable* dress hugs her body. Supple skin shows through cutouts in the side without her hair, and her strong shoulders sit high with a confidence I haven't seen in her in a long time. Her makeup is perfect and subtle, and *my God*, does she ever take my breath away.

I'm a fool for not seeing her earlier. I'm a fool for letting her go. I'm a fool if I don't hold on to her now and make her mine forever.

Her walk is sultry and slow as she comes toward me through the crowded room, and my chest thuds with the strength it takes to stand and wait. It's not a hardship to watch her, though. She's the most beautiful, interesting woman I've ever known in my entire life. It just took Midnight messages and a fresh perspective to see it.

"Hi, Beau," she says when she makes it to me, and my hands itch to reach out and touch her. I don't because I want to get out what I have to say first, but it's a full exercise in self-control.

"Hi, Juni."

Her smile is soft and exploratory. Mine leaves no questions.

"You look so fucking beautiful, but that isn't a surprise. You always look beautiful."

"Beau." She blushes and her eyes avert from mine.

"I don't need a shoe to know, June," I tell her, and she looks up at me again. "I don't need to scour the village. I don't need to scour anywhere. This connection is soul-deep, and I want to be better than Prince Charming."

A gasp escapes her lips and she reaches up to cover her mouth, but I steal her hand, taking it in mine instead.

"June, you and I are forever. I know it. And I hope you know it too."

She blinks a few times and shakes her head gently. "Just so you know, I can hardly believe the words you're saying right now are real. I've dreamed of hearing you saying these things for so long, it's pathetic."

I squeeze her hand in mine "I swear you won't have to dream anymore. I love you, and it's not just some crush. This is the real thing, and when the time is right, I'm going to make you a real part of the Banks family. You've been a part of it for nearly as long as I can remember, but I want you to be *my* part."

"My Prince?" she asks, and I nod.

"My Mystery Woman."

She shakes her head again, and I pull her in to push my mouth to hers.

"You're my forever, Juniper June," I whisper against her lips.

The countdown to midnight starts all around us, a growing chant of the numbers from the DJ echoing from his microphone.

"Ten, nine, eight, seven, six, five, four, three, two, one!"

"Midnight," she whispers, her gorgeous blue eyes staring up into mine.

"Forever," I reply and kiss the hell out of *my* June.

Epilogue

Two Years Later…

Juniper

THIS IS THE DAY I'VE DREAMED ABOUT SINCE I WAS THIRTEEN years old.

Not just in theory but in vivid detail, down to the color and arrangement of my flowers and the way I'd wear my hair. I imagined the cake and the tux for my groom, and I imagined all of it with Beau Banks.

And today, it's happening.

I smooth on another layer of lip gloss over the Chanel lipstick shade called Adrienne, my lips curving naturally into a smile. I don't feel nervous or unsure or preoccupied with what could go wrong. I'm ready to get married.

And I'm ready to do it with my soul mate.

Avery rushes into her childhood bedroom where we're getting ready for the most magical night of my life.

The Banks house has always been my shelter and my happiness, and the symbolism of marrying Beau here was always something I carried in my mind.

"Oh my God, June," she cries, sitting down on the settee beside me and twinkling her fingers together excitedly. "You're never going to believe the next-level, out-of-this-world, holy-shit-I'm-dying tea that's been spilling downstairs for the last half hour while we've been up here getting you ready for eternal happiness and all that stupid shit."

I shake my head on a laugh. "What happened?"

"Evidently, Seth and Bethany got into this big fight while they were taking their seats. Something about how he's fed up with how distant she's been, and he accused her of still being in love with Beau!"

My heart drops, but Avery waves her hands to keep me on track.

"Now, don't get too excited, but it went even crazier than you'd imagine after that. Not only is she not in love with Beau, but she told Seth in front of everyone—we're talking all of your guests and all the people we know from work—that she's been having an affair with *his father* for the last three years."

"Shut up."

Avery nods excitedly. She also keeps spilling. "Bethany and Chris have been doing it like bunnies since she broke it off with Beau! Literally, the entire duration of her relationship with Seth, she's been banging his daddy too!"

"No way!" I have to take a step back to wrap my mind around the news. "Nooooo!"

"Yes! I missed most of it, but Chris and Seth were shouting at each other, and Mrs. McKenzie slapped Bethany in the face before Chris said he wanted a divorce!"

"Holy shit!" I exclaim. "And then what happened?"

"Pretty much nothing. Mom kicked them all out and told them to take their bullshit somewhere else today because it's about you and Beau. And Henry, Mav, and Ronnie made sure they complied."

"Wow. Go Diane."

"I know," Avery agrees. "Also, go Henry. The man just about turned into the Hulk and ripped off his tux to kick out Seth and his dad." A little pout forms at the corners of her lips. "Not gonna lie, I was kind of hoping Henry and Seth would've had a good old-fashioned brawl in the front yard. Henry's shirt off, of course."

"You were *kind of* hoping?" I question, staring at her with a knowing look.

"Okay, fine." She shrugs. "I might've started yelling 'Fight!' and 'Take your shirt off!', but I can't be sure. It was all happening so fast."

I cackle. "I bet Beau just loved hearing you scream that."

"Beau has no room to talk." She rolls her eyes. "He's marrying *my* best friend."

"That's true." I nod, and a snort escapes my nose. "Boy, that'd be the ultimate revenge. You marrying Henry, *your brother's* best friend."

"Get real, Juni." It's Avery's turn to cackle. "Henry is the last man on earth I'd marry. He's as clichéd as you can get when it comes to the bad-boy player type. Like, c'mon, you know? We get it, you're hot. You're charming. You're smooth. But how about you stop trying to ram your cock through the whole female dating pool?"

"You're still pissed that he said you're not his style," I tease, but also, say what I know to be true out loud. For years, Beau's friend Henry has caught Avery's eye. And for years, it's always seemed like she's attempted to flirt him into bed. But somehow, from what I know, nothing has happened besides one single kiss when they were at a Miami club together years ago. Back when Beau and I were engaging in our secret affair.

She glares at me. "Juniper, are you trying to start shit with your maid of honor on her big day?"

"Pretty sure you mean *my* big day."

"It's not always about you, June." She scoffs. "Anyway, back to the important shit—aka Bethany banging Seth's dad." She laughs, but then her eyes turn very serious. "I don't know if you can come up with something wild to do in the next five minutes so your whole thing isn't boringgg in comparison, but we're going to have start brainstorming now if we want to figure it out before you walk down that aisle."

"We're good, Ave." I grin. "Truth be told, I think coming to terms with the fact that I'm actually marrying your brother is wild enough."

Avery nods, her eyes narrowing. "Are you sure you wanna go through with it? He's so...Beau. I can totally call for a getaway car and have us out of here in no time."

I grab her hand in mine, smiling. "I'm sure. In fact, him being 'so Beau' is my favorite part."

She wrinkles up her nose and shoots to standing. "Suit yourself."

Her black dress fits her body perfectly, and she looks as beautiful as ever as she hands me my bouquet before picking up her own.

"Avery."

"Yeah?"

"I'm also really excited that you're going to be my sister."

She winks. "Yeah, obviously. That's the best part. Now, let's do it before another brawl breaks out."

I nod, and she grabs the back of my train to help me down the stairs. Neil waits at the bottom, ready to escort me, even though my dad is here in the crowd with Lola, and my mother is also sitting somewhere with her latest boy toy she apparently met in Antigua. I'm glad they made the effort, my dad arriving earlier on the beach in his helicopter and my mother showing up via her guy driving them in a neon-green Lambo, but Neil Banks is the man who should walk me down the aisle. I'm certain of it.

"Oh, Junebug," Neil says softly at the sight of me. "You look so beautiful."

Avery clears her throat, and Neil smiles. "You look beautiful too, Avery, of course. I was just complimenting the bride specifically."

Avery snorts. "Like there's some law that you can only compliment the one in white? Get real, Neil."

"I love you guys so much," I cut in to say. As weird as it sounds, this is exactly how I pictured this part too. Avery and Neil and Diane and Beau—they're my family. After today, that'll be official.

Avery hugs me quick before sniping, "You bitch. You made me cry."

I smile. "It's worth it this time."

Avery shoos me away with her hand. "Okay. Shut up. Time for me to do my thing down the aisle so you can follow." She turns to Neil and points a finger in his face. "She'd better not fall, Daddy. It's your job to make sure of it."

He gives her a thumbs-up. "You got it, honey."

"And don't do that," Avery says, nodding toward Neil's offending thumb. "Ever again." She turns on her heels and steps up to the back patio door as soft violin music starts to play.

She walks on her cue, and I wait inside, my arm clutched in Neil's and my breath shaking. I can't see Beau yet, not with the way the back is set up. We put plexiglass over the pool and a white runner and flowers down the aisle, and all the guests sit on each side in white-bow-festooned chairs.

The altar is at the front, with the beach in the back, and even though I can't see him, Beau is waiting up there too. For me.

He's waiting for me.

Neil pats at my hand. "Love you, Juni. I'm a proud man today and a proud man every day. Thank you for blessing us with your gifts. Beau couldn't have picked anyone better."

A tear pricks my eye, and my nose stings with the fight to stave it off. I can't believe in just a few short minutes, Banks is going to be my last name.

The music shifts to the "Wedding March," and Neil goes through the door first, holding a hand back for me to take next. I step through and arrange my dress, and after one more deep breath, we walk to the edge of the patio and out into the sun, where everyone can see us.

The guests are on their feet, and Beau stands at the altar, his friends beside him in a row. Avery stands on the other side, waiting for me, her face a natural smile of pure happiness at the sight of me.

She may joke like it's otherwise, but Avery is quite possibly the biggest believer in love of all of us.

Beau's smile is wide, his happiness undeniable as he takes me in. Neil starts to walk, holding tightly to my arm, and I tread carefully down the professionally constructed aisle.

When we get to the front, the minister is waiting, and Beau steps forward to take me from his dad. He must be a little too excited, though, because he doesn't wait to be asked to do it, instead grabbing me and pulling to him.

Everyone laughs as the minister puts a hand to his chest and tsks.

"Whoa there, cowboy. I know you're ready, but we're not quite there yet."

Beau laughs, and his friend Henry drags him back to his spot.

The minister pretends to double-check over his shoulder for movement a few times before continuing, and everyone laughs again.

"All right, then," the minister says. "Who gives this woman to be married?"

Neil's voice is rougher than normal as he answers, "I do."

"Perfect," the minister remarks, turning back to Beau then. "Okay, dude, you can come get your bride now."

Beau steps forward and shakes his dad's hand before taking mine and helping me step carefully up onto the altar that's raised slightly above the rest of everything.

Avery straightens the small train of my dress and takes my bouquet, and when I turn back around, my favorite warm brown eyes are waiting.

I smile and take Beau's hands in mine, squeezing tightly with the need to be his forever already.

"Welcome, everyone," the minister addresses the crowd. "We're here today to join Juniper and Beau in a legal union of love. We want to thank you for being here to join in their moment of happiness, but mostly, we want to thank Juniper and Beau for falling in love."

Beau smiles at me, his whole body vibrating with excitement.

"Juniper, do you take Beau to be your lawfully wedded husband, in sickness and in health, in wealth and in poverty, in good times and in bad?"

I nod. "Yes. I do."

Beau's smile is the one he always gives me right before kissing me, and I know with my whole heart he's wishing he could get to that part already.

"Great. Now, Beau. Do you take Juniper to be your lawfully wedded wife, in sickness and in health, in wealth and in poverty, in good times and in bad?"

"I take June in every circumstance. Yes. I do."

"Love the enthusiasm." The minister chuckles. "That seems to be a theme, and let me tell you, folks, that's a good thing during a wedding."

More laughter comes from the crowd, and I fall deeper into Beau's smile as it grows even more.

"Now, for the rings."

Beau turns back to Henry for my ring, and I turn to Avery for his. When we turn back around, I hold out my left hand, ready to seal our commitment to each other with my finger.

"Beau, you've made these promises today in front of your family, friends, God," the minister states, looking at Beau. "Repeat after me. With this ring, I thee wed."

Beau obeys immediately. "With this ring, I thee wed."

"Perfect. And now you, Juniper." The minister's attention is on me now. "With this ring, I thee wed."

I repeat the vow and slide Beau's ring onto his finger just like he did with mine. His hand looks even sexier, and trust me, after the things I've felt them do, I didn't think that was possible.

"Congratulations. I now pronounce you husband and wife, and you may kiss the bride!"

Beau leans in and plants one on me, and I give it back as good as I get it. It may not be demure or appropriate for mixed company, but it is love. And I wouldn't have it any other way.

We're officially married!

Beau

June and I dance close, our faces pressed together in the center of the pool dance floor. Everything from the ceremony has been cleared out of the way, and an intimate, candlelit dinner setup replaces it. We have a sweetheart table at the front of it all, but by and large, we've spent our time like this, plastered together and swaying to the music.

Stars dance in the sky above us, and a full moon hangs low on the horizon. The sound of ocean waves isn't audible with the music, but memory tells me it's there in sharp detail.

I desperately want a moment alone with my new wife, and an idea hits me as if by kismet.

"Come on," I whisper, taking her hand and dragging her off the floor slowly. Her eyebrows draw together as she looks back at all the other guests, including Avery and our parents, but I put a finger to my lips as a cue and whisper, "Shh."

Smiling, she nods, and we trot off together, bound for the beach. When we get to the end of my parents' bush-lined path, we pause briefly so she can take off her heels, and I help her lift the train of her dress so we can run through the sand together. It's dark back here, with only the moonlight to light our way, and we don't stop, her giggles echoing around us, until we make it to the spot.

Our spot.

The place we always came together as kids.

I pull her close and kiss her deeply, tasting her tongue and mine together a million little times. Her hands pull at my hips under my jacket, and I sink mine into the pretty red hair at the sides of her head.

We breathe each other in, the lapping ocean telling its story behind us.

"I love you, Beau."

"I love you, Juni. At midnight and ten a.m. and every other minute of the day until the end of time."

"You know, it's getting close to midnight right now, actually," she whispers, and I tilt my head to the side.

"Is it?"

"Mm-hmm," she says with a nod, her forehead moving against mine as I refuse to back up more than an inch.

I kiss her again, lingering this time and nipping at the flesh of her bottom lip with my teeth.

"And what are you going to do with this midnight that you haven't done with the others? You've landed me, enthralled me, married me... What exactly are you going to do now, Mrs. Banks?"

She smiles, just a hint of excitement I can't place behind her eyes, and then kisses me again. When I feel her rustling something out of the top of her dress, I pull back to find her holding a photo between us. She lifts it up to show me, and instantly, I realize what it is—*a sonogram picture.*

"Is that... Are you...? You can't be serious." My eyes bounce back and forth between June's beautiful face, her belly, and the picture. "June...are you going to have my baby?"

"We're having a baby, Beau." Tears kiss her eyes as she nods, and I scream my excitement into the silence of the night, lifting her off her feet and swinging her around. She laughs, but me...I cry.

The two of us, we're getting everything we've ever dreamed of.

June…June is getting the thing she always wanted most in the whole entire world. A family.

And I get to be a part of it.

"I love you so much, Juniper."

"Not as much as I love you."

"Maybe when you were thirteen that was sort of true…" I pause to kiss her again. "But not now, baby. I love you just as much as you love me. I love you more than anything."

Three Years Later…

Juniper

Avery lifts the teacup to her lips, sipping on the imaginary tea her niece made for her. I look on from my spot in Neil and Diane's kitchen, and Beau, Neil, and Diane work on hanging the final stocking on the mantel.

Christmas is coming up, and just like always, we're celebrating at the Bankses' house. Beau and I live in the house he built while we were falling in love, and our two-year-old daughter Addy is already a little beach bug. We take her paddleboarding on the weekends when she isn't having tea parties with Aunt Avery, and by and large, all of my dreams have just about come true.

My parents still aren't around often, but after a conversation with Beau last year, my dad is making more of an effort. For me and for Addy. We know what it's like to have a loving support system, and we want the same for her—as many people as we can get. My mom is still too preoccupied with her search for…something, but she did visit for Addy's birth and her first and second birthdays. She even called me on my last birthday. Not a text message, but an actual phone call that lasted for over an hour and included her taking genuine interest in my life. It's still not a lot, but it's more than she's ever given me in years.

"How's that look, Addy?" Beau asks, pointing to the stocking they've just hung for her soon-to-be-announced little brother.

Everyone else thinks they're hanging it for Addy's imaginary friend, but the truth is, in five months, he won't be so imaginary.

I smile to myself as Beau waves me over, and I wipe my hands on the towel beside the sink to dry them before heading toward him.

Addy gives the thumbs-up while everyone chatters, and I take my spot under Beau's strong arm as he clears his throat.

Diane and Neil look in his direction first and then Avery, and I don't even bother to hide my smile as Beau starts to talk. "Well, now that we've got the stocking hung, we've got a little bit to be thankful for today. For family and love and midnights."

"Oh yeah." I nod. "Have to be thankful for midnights, especially now that we're looking at even more midnight feedings."

Avery narrows her eyes. "More midnight feedings? What are you guys talking about?"

"Well," Beau says. "We know we told you this stocking is for an imaginary member of the Banks family, but next year, he'll be pretty real."

"What?" Diane whispers, tears hitting her eyes. "You're… Junebug, you're going to have another baby? And he'll…? It's a boy?"

Instantly, I'm crying too. "Yep. Due in May."

"Congratulations! I can't believe I'm going to be a grandpa again!" Neil exclaims, damn near jumping up and down on his feet.

"Ahh!" Avery shrieks, jumping up from her spot at the coffee table and wrapping me in the tightest hug. "Yay! Oh my God, a little surfer boy. I can see it now."

"Someone else to fall in love with." I smile through my tears, and Beau presses a kiss to my forehead.

"Another piece of you and me, here forever."

"I'm so happy for you!" Diane yells, racing over to wrap me in a hug. I squeeze her tightly and soak it all in.

This is the dream. This is the fantasy.

Who'd have thought? It all started with a single crush on Beau Banks by a young girl with stars in her eyes.

Maybe Cinderella had it right after all. There's magic at midnight.

"Am I interrupting?" The deep male voice comes from behind us, and when everyone turns around to find Henry standing in the Bankses' living room, his face morphs into concern. "Wait…what'd I miss? Is everything okay?"

"Beau knocked June up again," Avery answers. "But why in the hell are you here?"

"Relax, Ave. I invited him," Beau responds through a soft laugh as he heads over to Henry to give him a man-bro-hug thing. You know, the one where they hug but, like, keep their muscles flexed at the same time, while simultaneously clapping each other hard on the back.

Yeah, that.

"But why is he here?" Avery questions, Beau's answer clearly not enough of an explanation.

"None of your business," Beau responds, but Henry just shrugs.

"Beau here, took pity on me and invited me to attend your Christmas festivities in the name of making sure I don't end up with my head face first in a bottle of whiskey." He looks over at Diane and Neil. "I hope you don't mind."

"Of course not," Diane responds and walks over to him to give him a hug. "It's so good to see you, Henry. Everything going okay with you?"

"I'm okay," Henry says, a little sadder smile in place than normal. "Things are just a little different this year." Henry's dad passed away after a battle with cancer a few months ago, and I can only imagine the change is startling. His father raised him alone, and for all intents and purposes, he was the only family Henry had. Because of the cancer's progression, they've both had a year to prepare for this inevitable moment, but that doesn't make being without your loved one any easier.

Thankfully, as I know better than anyone, the Bankses are about as good as a substitute gets.

"Well son," Neil says, shaking Henry's hand. "It's always good to see you. And you know I always love to hear some updates about the adrenaline-junkie business."

Henry smiles. "And you know I always enjoy giving them to you."

"Dada!" Addy exclaims as she barrels over to Beau and wraps her arms around his legs. When she looks up and sees Henry standing there, her eyes light up with excitement. "Henny!" she squeals and switches legs altogether. And from Beau to Henry she goes.

He doesn't hesitate to pick her up and swing her around. "Hi, Addy."

"Hi, Henny." Addy smiles at him and places her two chubby hands on his face. "Play tea party with me now."

"Addy," I say on a sigh. "You need to ask nicely, not bossy."

"Play tea party with me now?" she asks, basically using the same tone with the same words and just lifting her voice a little at the end in question.

"I'd love to," Henry says through a chuckle and sets Addy back on her feet. She takes his hand, clearly giving him no other option, and drags him over to the table she was playing with her aunt Avery earlier.

I head into the kitchen to help Diane set out drinks, but as I'm standing behind the kitchen island, I don't miss the fact that Avery has migrated over to the tea party.

I also don't miss the way she puts her hand on Henry's shoulder and whispers something in his ear. He looks up at her, from the tiny kiddie chair his over-six-foot frame is currently sitting in, and his face flashes with a tenderness I rarely see from Henry. "Thanks. That means a lot."

Avery turns on her heels, but just before she makes the full one-eighty, she spins back around to face him again. "Oh, and just so you know, I have a boyfriend."

My head jerks back. *Avery has a boyfriend?* Unless it's some kind of secret boyfriend she hasn't told me about and that she never spends any time with, I call bullshit.

Henry laughs. "Got it."

"So, no flirty stuff, yeah?"

"Heard you loud and clear, Avery."

"Good."

"Good," Henry responds. "Glad we got that settled."

Avery walks—more like, sashays—away, and I don't miss the way Henry's eyes follow her the whole way. I also don't miss the fact that when she comes to help Diane and me in the kitchen, her eyes find their way back into the living room where Addy is bossily telling Henry, "Drink yous tea, Henny. Alls of it."

Is it just me or does it feel like there's *way* more to this story?

I look out toward the patio, where Beau stands talking to his dad, and when he glances over his shoulder to meet my eyes, I smile and blow him a little kiss.

He pretends to snag it from the air, and when Avery catches on to the whole cheesy scene, she pretends to gag.

"Gross."

"You know, Ave, one day, when you're blowing kisses to your future husband, I'm going to remind you of this moment."

She just rolls her eyes, but I swear, as they make the circuit from the ceiling and back to the floor, they stop on Henry for a hot second.

Is my best friend secretly in love with her brother's best friend?

Boy, wouldn't that be something.

THE END

Preorder *Leave Before I Love You* (Avery's book) today!

Need more Max Monroe right now?
What about "he's her billionaire boss" + "they don't like each other" + "they're forced to work VERY closely together on an important project" + "he's also her new neighbor"?
Start reading The Billionaire Boss Next Door now.
This book is a hilarious, laugh-out-loud, rockin' good time.

Sign up for our newsletter, and we'll keep you up-to-date on all the book news AND a lot of times we share fun teasers and excerpts!
Plus, our newsletter is hilarious! Laughs guaranteed. If you're already signed up, consider sending us a message to tell us how much you love us. We really like that. ;)
www.authormaxmonroe.com/newsletter

Need EVEN MORE Max Monroe before our next release?
Never fear, we have a list of nearly FIFTY other titles to keep you busy for as long as your little reading heart desires!
Check out our Suggested Reading Order on our website!
www.authormaxmonroe.com/max-monroe-suggested-reading-order

Follow us online here:

Facebook: www.facebook.com/authormaxmonroe

Reader Group: www.facebook.com/groups/1561640154166388

Twitter: www.twitter.com/authormaxmonroe

Instagram: www.instagram.com/authormaxmonroe

TikTok: vm.tiktok.com/ZMe1jv5kQ

Goodreads: https://goo.gl/8VUIz2

Acknowledgments

Usually, we write a very lengthy section here where we thank all of the most important people in our lives.

But we've been doing this so long, you know who you are.

We love you.

We couldn't do this without you.

How do you feel? Acknowledged? ;) ;)

To all of our reader friends, THANK YOU, THANK YOU, THANK YOU for reading.

XOXO,
Max & Monroe

Made in the USA
Coppell, TX
14 December 2024

42476868R00208